SPUTNIK'S CHILD

Fred Ledley

To my parents, Robert and Terry Ledley,
who taught me to look toward the stars,
and to my wife, Tamara Ledley,
who helped me reach for them

 *Sputnik's Child* is a Certified Imagination Product™. This designation identifies entertainment products that inspire new generations to take an active interest in space.

 Proceeds from sales of this book are donated to the Space Foundation.
www.spacefoundation.org

Follow *Sputniks Child* on Facebook or at www.sputnikschild.com

Sputnik's Child

Prologue: The Poster Child

December 2000

1

Book One: The Age of Aquarius

September 1969

7

Book Two: The "Me Generation"

June 1970

93

Book Three: Irrational Exuberance

January 1985

179

Notes

323

Prologue: The Poster Child
December 2000

K atie was admitted to the Children's Hospital several days after Christ-mas and taken immediately to the intensive care unit. She had tried to ride her scooter down the rocky hill behind her house, and had almost made it, when the scooter landed on a boulder and she was thrown headfirst to the ground.

Not even the helmet she was wearing was sufficient to prevent the veins around her brain from breaking and the surrounding space from filling with blood. She cried out for an instant as she hit the ground. Her body convulsed once. Then she was still.

How could this happen? How could I let this happen? Jackie thought, as she sat beside her daughter's hospital bed, watching her struggle for life. Jackie was at once angry with her daughter, angry with herself, and bleeding inside with her daughter's pain. *What was she thinking? She should have known there could be rocks. Did she think she could fly?*

Again and again, Jackie came back to the questions: *How could this happen? How could I let this happen?* But she had no answer; no idea what else she could have done.

Katie had been in the intensive care unit once before. She had been play-ing soccer, when she hit her head and suffered a seizure. That was when her bleeding disorder was first diagnosed.

1

Then, Jackie had believed that medicine could work miracles, that doctors could cure disease, and that the manifest power of the insights and instruments in the vast, windowless world of the ICU would bring Katie through. Every light on the computer monitors over her bed had presaged her recovery; every injection of medicine had promised life. Jackie never doubted that diagnostic tests would reveal the cause of Katie's disease and that drugs would provide a cure; all she had to do was have faith. Katie would live.

This time, as Jackie watched the doctors and nurses hovering over Katie's limp and unresponsive body, it was different. This time, the bright, artificial light was blinding, the din in the air was deafening, and the orderly progression of Katie's care seemed ominous. This time, experience with impotence tempered the appearance of power. This time, nothing was certain; not life or death, not day or night, not the light of the Sun or its reflection from the Moon; not her faith that Katie would live.

How could this happen? How could I let this happen?

It was past midnight when the doctors and nurses who were caring for Katie took Jackie and Steve into a cluttered conference room to talk about their daughter's condition. The doctors reported that they had been able to stop the bleeding around Katie's brain, though she was still unconscious. It would be several days before they could determine how much damage she had sustained. The nurses said they were hopeful. Several said they would pray for her.

Steve peppered the team with questions about Katie's care, their plan, and her prognosis. Jackie sat through the meeting motionless and mute, hardly aware of anything but the dissonance of her thoughts: *How could this happen? How could I let this happen?*

When the meeting ended and the doctors returned to Katie's care, the nurses suggested that Jackie and Steve try to get some sleep. Steve decided to stay at the hospital. He found the hospital's chapel and spent some time in silent prayer before returning to the ICU. Jackie drove home so she would be there in the morning when Katie's siblings awoke and asked about their sister.

Jackie did not sleep that night; she did not even try. Instead, she spent the last hours of darkness roaming restlessly through the house. She wandered through the living room, where the abandoned Christmas tree still stood, with ornaments precisely positioned on its branches; through the playroom, where the twisted metal of Katie's scooter lay on the floor; through the kitchen, where a seeming lifetime of unwashed dishes waited in the sink; to Katie's room, where a jigsaw puzzle lay unfinished on a table. Then, guided by force of habit, she turned purposefully toward the dining room.

For the past year, the dining room had been the headquarters of the Living Genome Foundation, which Jackie had formed to find a cure for Katie's disease. During that time, the once-elegant room had been carelessly reconfigured as an office. The room was crowded with metal folding chairs. Computers and printers covered the ornate mahogany table. The walls, once decorated with modern art, were papered with posters from the Foundation's marketing campaign.

Each of the Foundation's posters featured a larger-than-life image of Katie's face. There were posters showing Katie at home, at school, and at play; posters of her being treated by doctors and visiting with scientists; and posters of her accepting donations from philanthropists and the well wishes of celebrities and politicians.

Katie's face was everywhere, and the lights from the screen savers on a dozen dormant computers almost made her seem alive. Ceaseless spirals of shape and shadow shimmered across the walls, creating the illusion of motion and emotion on Katie's face. Her hair seemed to flutter. Her lips seemed to quiver. Shifting sequences of blue, green, yellow, and red projected impressions of sadness, anger, fear, and joy in her eyes.

Jackie yearned to feel the emotions streaming across her daughter's face. She wanted to hold her and consoler her, to kiss away the restless and relentless patterns and the pain, but there were too many emotions and they were moving too fast. Her breath trembled. Blood rushed to her face. Her pulse exploded in her ears. Her head began to spin. She struggled for breath as the heat and oxygen seemed to ebb from the room. The sweat from her brow and tears from her eyes blurred her vision, until Katie's face began to float off the walls and fade away into darkness.

Jackie tried to reach for Katie; to call her, to catch her, to bring her back before she disappeared; but she was paralyzed and mute. She saw herself in a nightmare that had recurred since childhood; a dream in which she would be soaring blissfully through space, when there would be an explosion around her, windows and walls would shatter, vehicles and buildings would crash to the ground, and the people she loved would disappear into a space beyond her reach.

This time, however, Jackie knew she was not dreaming. She frantically groped the wall for the light switch that would bring Katie back from the abyss. Her nails grated against the coarse sheetrock again and again until her fingers finally landed on the smooth plastic of the switch. Instantly, brilliant white light burst from a dozen bare bulbs in the chandelier, blinding her and blanching the colors that animated the room.

Katie's face was still on the wall.

In the light, Jackie walked slowly into the room and along the walls, tracing the contours of Katie's face on the posters, touching her lips with her fingers, caressing her cheeks with the palm of her hand. Jackie knew the angles of her forehead, the long blonde hair draped behind her shoulders, the freckles on her nose, the reluctant smile; yet there was also something she could not touch: the eyes.

In life, Katie's eyes expressed life itself. They could turn on her mother's tears and dry them with joy; they could communicate the most intimate and intricate emotions between mother and daughter. Now, Jackie searched the digitized eyes, fractal lines, and airbrushed brows of a dozen iterations of Katie's face and felt nothing.

They were not Katie's eyes; they never had been. They were the eyes of a poster child. They expressed an idea: the innocent confidence that, in an age of technology, when men could land on the Moon, see inside a living body, and sequence the genome, there would be a solution to her suffering; but they could not respond to her mother's terror or her tears.

* * *

Jackie was born on October 4, 1957, the day that *Sputnik I* became the first human object to escape the gravity of Earth. She was *Sputnik*'s child, the product of an age of technology given life by the pulse of a human star in the heavens.

Jackie was eleven years old on Christmas Eve in 1968 when men first reached the Moon and looked back at Earth. She was not yet twelve in August of 1969 when black-and-white images of Armstrong stepping onto the lunar surface flickered across her TV screen. Her generation was indelibly shaped by the promise of technologies that could project men into the heavens and provide a perspective of Earth as it appeared to God.

Hers was a generation that bore witness to the miracles of technology. It was a generation that saw the power of computers increase more than ten million fold and the Internet connect the corners of the globe; one that experienced the eradication of smallpox from the planet, the invention of machines capable of seeing inside the living human body, and the engineering of new forms of life. They came to believe that infant mortality, cancer, malnutrition, and poverty could be eradicated in their lifetime, and they experienced an age of unprecedented, exuberant prosperity and unparalleled social progress that seemed to portend an end to the traumas of history.

Never in her adult life had Jackie doubted the power, the probity, and the promise of technology. She had believed with perfect faith that science would provide a cure for Katie's disease, that she could fly past the boulders and land safely on a sea of tranquility, that she could survive explosions in space and parachute gently back to Earth.

Now the bubble had burst. Katie lay in a coma. Jackie was terrified.

How could this happen? How could I have let this happen? Jackie perseverated inconsolably. *What was I thinking? How could I not have known there could be rocks in the way? Did I think I could fly? How did this happen?*

Book One: The Age of Aquarius
September 1969

When the Moon is in the Seventh House, and Jupiter aligns with Mars
Then peace will guide the planets, and love will steer the stars
This is the dawning of the Age of Aquarius

Top song of 1969: "Aquarius/Let the Sun Shine In," recorded by The Fifth Dimension

1

Jackie Cone started sixth grade at Spring Elementary School in the fall of 1969. The first day of school in Connecticut was scheduled for Tuesday after Labor Day, but it had to be postponed for a week due to the riots in nearby Hartford.

Jackie had spent the Friday before the Labor Day weekend with her father, Bert, at the family's general store on the north side of the city. The store occupied the ground floor of a once-elegant brick building built a half-century before, during the heyday of Hartford's reign as an industrial and financial center. The outside of the store was old and in disrepair, like the neighborhood around it. The merchandise inside was generally of poor quality, intended for customers who lived from month to month on inflated credit and welfare checks.

To Jackie, however, the store was a paradise, filled with furnishings, appliances, toys, clothes, and jewelry that provided ideal props for an active child's imagination and play. Many of her earliest memories were about playing at the store while her father waited on customers, stocked the shelves, or worked on the books in his back office.

Jackie had been three months old when her mother died in a car accident. In the years before her father remarried, she had spent many of her days at the family store. After he had married Mary, she'd rarely had the opportunity to spend time at the store with her father.

Her father's marriage had occurred suddenly, weeks before Jackie's sixth birthday. Bert had been introduced to Mary, a distant cousin, at a family event, and they were married three months later.

Jackie had been excited about the wedding. She loved dressing up in a white dress and spreading flowers on the aisle in front of the bridal party, and she was thrilled when her father decided to move from their cramped apartment over the store to a house with a yard, where she could play outdoors. Mary warmly adopted and cared for Jackie as her own daughter, but they grew apart over the ensuing years as Mary gave birth to two boys and two girls. Jackie had little affection for the annoying and smelly infants who increasingly dominated the household and competed for her father's attention.

It had become an annual ritual for Jackie to go to work with her father on the last day of summer to get the things she needed for school from the store. For weeks, she pestered him to make sure he remembered their date, made lists of all the school supplies needed for sixth grade, and talked excitedly with her friends about getting new clothes.

Jackie spent the morning at the store, happily collecting school supplies from the stockroom and trying on blouses and skirts, until she found several that her father would let her keep. By late morning, she was playfully modeling the faux jewelry displayed in the glass case near the cash register, exploring the shelves filled with toys, and inventing games to play with various household goods and furnishings. The store was unusually quiet, and after much pestering, Jackie convinced her father to join her for tea in a make-believe world of stuffed animals, where she was the omnipotent queen.

At noon, Jackie joined her father for lunch at the diner across the street. She ordered her favorite foods; macaroni and cheese, Coca-Cola, and a chocolate ice-cream sundae, and smiled politely as her father's friends and neighbors commented on how grown up she had become. She did not pay much attention to the adults' conversation, which quickly turned to the rising racial tensions in the surrounding community.

For several weeks, there had been rumors that an elderly Puerto Rican man had been assaulted and beaten by a white motorcycle gang. Since then, there had been a number of rock-throwing skirmishes between gangs of white, black, and Hispanic youth. Several of these clashes led to confrontations with Hartford's largely white police force, whose aggressive response provoked claims of police brutality and institutional racism.

Returning to the store after lunch, Jackie occupied herself in playfully decorating her book covers and notebooks with stickers and pictures drawn in brightly colored Magic Markers. Then, she started decorating signs and price tags around the store, until her father put her to work placing the new stocks of winter clothes on the shelves. Jackie rapidly became bored arranging clothes on the shelves according to size, the way her father had instructed, and decided instead to organize the clothes by the colors of the rainbow, with violets and indigos on top and oranges and reds on the bottom.

It was late afternoon when the sound of an explosion and breaking glass shattered Jackie's bliss. Bert was in the stockroom at the back of the store when he heard the report and Jackie's scream. He rushed out onto the floor, where he saw a gaping hole in one of the plate glass windows, a fist-sized rock and shattered glass on the floor, and Jackie standing transfixed near the door.

Jackie was unhurt but paralyzed with fear and confusion. She was unaware of anything that was happening as her father pulled her away from the front of the store and pushed her into the windowless stockroom at the back.

Gradually, a crescendo of sirens outside the store drowned out the silence and brought her back to perception. A solitary police car raced past the windows on the now-deserted street, its flashing lights casting the appearance of protection. Jackie watched furtively from the stockroom as her father quickly locked the front doors, pulled down the metal shades that shielded the windows, and emptied the contents of the cash register into the safe in the concrete wall.

"Let's go, Jackie," Bert said as he returned to the stockroom, struggling to keep his voice calm. "Give me your things."

"What happened, Daddy?" Jackie asked, as he threw her school supplies and drawings into an empty box.

"We have to go."

"What's going on?"

Bert deflected her question. "Everything will be all right. Let's go."

Bert picked up the box with Jackie's things, grasped her elbow awkwardly, and pulled her toward the door at the back of the store. Her arm hurt in his grasp. He cautiously opened the door, paused to be sure no one was lurking in the alley, then led Jackie across the refuse-strewn pavement to the station wagon parked several yards away.

The heavy metal door slammed behind them. The noise echoed through the deserted alley.

Bert peered through the car's windows before opening the driver's-side door and pushing Jackie inside. As she clambered across to the passenger's side, he shoved the box with her things into the backseat, climbed in beside her, and immediately locked the doors. He took a deep breath and grasped the steering wheel to stop his hands from shaking. Then, he started the car and drove cautiously to the end of the deserted alley and onto the main street that passed in front of the store.

Jackie's heart was racing. She sat forward on her knees, her elbows braced on the dashboard, straining to see out the windows. She was torn between alarm and adventure, fear and fascination. Her eyes darted from side to side. Her body contorted as she tried to see in every direction at once.

Hours before, when they had walked across the main street for lunch, there had been cars and life on the thoroughfare. Now it was empty. The storefronts were shuttered and dark. The restaurant where they had eaten lunch had a large sign in the window that said, "CLOSED."

At the end of the street, she saw a squad of police officers holding shields and batons gathered around a bus. For an instant, Jackie thought it was a school bus. Then, she saw that it had metal bars on the windows and grown men inside.

Bert picked up speed as he approached the end of the street and turned onto the entrance ramp of the elevated highway that would let them fly over the troubled streets of Hartford to their home in Spring seven miles away. The acceleration pushed Jackie down into her seat. She craned her neck backward and watched as the store faded away into the distance.

2

The Cones lived in a small, blue cape, distinguishable from the neighboring houses only by the color of the paint on the siding, the small gable over the front door, and the collection of children's toys scattered around the yard. The town of Spring had been a small farming community until the baby boom of the 1950s and the spread of interstate highways triggered the movement of middle-class families out of the city and into the suburbs. By 1969, fields that, for centuries, had held dairy farms and orchards, had been bulldozed to create neighborhoods of winding streets and frame houses, as well as the schools, stores, and offices of a rapidly growing population.

Part of the old town of Spring remained; the town hall, the Common with its memorial to citizens who had died in centuries of war, a handful of aging Victorian mansions, and the colonial steeples of the Episcopal, Congregational, and Unitarian churches. Almost everything else was new; a Catholic church, a synagogue, a Howard Johnson's, supermarkets, strip malls, and a modern, suburban lifestyle, which was only loosely anchored to traditions of the old town or the once-great city nearby.

When they arrived home, Jackie gave Mary a breathless recitation of everything that had happened during the day. She told Mary how she had chosen new clothes and collected supplies for school, what she had ordered for lunch, how she had organized the clothes on the shelves by the colors of the rainbow, and how they had left quickly when the front window had exploded around her.

"Daddy wouldn't tell me what happened," she concluded, her excited prattle suddenly sounding cautious, "but it sounded like someone shot a gun! Daddy was very brave!"

Jackie turned and buried her head in Bert's ample stomach, and he folded his arm gently around her. Suddenly, she did not know whether to cry or to be courageous, to be scared or secure that her father would keep her safe, to stay swathed in his arms or stand on her own. She wished her father would tell her what had happened at the store, but she was also not sure she wanted to know.

Bert did not say anything in front of Jackie, but Mary saw that he was shaken. "Why don't you get ready for dinner?" Mary interrupted, gently separating Jackie from her father. "You must be very hungry after such a busy day."

Jackie held her father even tighter for an instant. "Go ahead, Jackie," Bert concurred, releasing himself from her grasp. "See if you can get your brothers and sisters ready for dinner. I need to talk to your mother." Jackie reluctantly let go of her father and walked away.

* * *

Violence consumed the streets of Hartford shortly after sunset that night and continued for an entire week. A racist remark attributed to a white firefighter ignited the pent-up anger of the Puerto Rican and black communities. Within hours, rioting broke out on the city's north side. When a white police officer shot and killed a black teenager, thousands of people took to the streets in rage.

A massive police response and an around-the-clock curfew did nothing to stem the fury of the black and Puerto Rican communities against the white establishment and their police. Through the holiday weekend and the week of chaos that followed, more than fifty fires were set, many buildings were burned to the ground, hundreds of stores were looted, sniper shots were fired at police and firefighters, and more than five hundred rioters were arrested. When it was over, forty square blocks of Hartford had been virtually destroyed.

Bert and Mary tried to shield Jackie from news of the chaos in Hartford, surreptitiously listening to the radio and television when she was playing, and then retreating to their bedroom to talk alone. Jackie knew that something was wrong the next morning when her father did not go to work. Nevertheless, she was happy he was home, and spent the morning trying to engage him in a long list of projects and games.

Bert tried to be attentive to Jackie, but took every opportunity to slip away and listen to the latest news on the radio. After several attempts to keep her father's attention, Jackie angrily announced that if he would not play with her, she would walk to her friend Karen's house to play.

"I don't want you walking to Karen's today," Bert answered.

"Why not?" Jackie asked petulantly.

"It's too far."

"I walk there all the time," she insisted. "I go through the woods. It's like five minutes."

"I don't want you out by yourself today, sweetie."

"Why not?"

"I can't explain it to you now."

"Will you drive me?"

"Not today. We have other things to do."

"Like what? What's going on anyway?" Jackie demanded, irritated by her father's inattention. "Why didn't you go to work today? What's going on? Everything is so weird. Why won't you tell me anything?"

"It's nothing you have to be concerned about, sweetie."

"Why won't you tell me?"

"You're too young to understand."

"I am not. I'm eleven!"

"Yes, you are, sweetie." Bert reached out to stroke her hair, but she pulled away defiantly. "I'll explain everything when you're older. Now, why don't you go play?"

"There's nothing to do," Jackie pouted.

"Then go help your mother. I'm sure she could use some help looking after your brothers and sisters."

"Ick!" Jackie contorted her face to express her displeasure and walked away unhappily.

Sunday was more of the same. The family went to church together in the morning, but when services were over, Bert stayed to talk with Father O'Brien, rather than coming directly home where he could play with her. Unable to keep her father's attention, forbidden to leave the house to visit her friends, and uninterested in helping her mother change diapers and clean up after her siblings, Jackie sulked in her room the rest of the day.

That evening, Jackie saw pictures of the riots on television for the first time. She saw buildings and barricades on fire, people bleeding and bound, and police officers confronting angry crowds behind shields and batons. She heard the voices of fear and frustration, anger and authority, racism and resistance, prayer and persuasion. It seemed distant. It didn't make any sense. She had a million questions, but her father refused to tell her anything and her mother was busy taking care of the babies.

Jackie was disappointed when the first day of school was postponed because of the continuing violence and curfew. Bert tried to play with her that morning, but he was soon called away by a telephone call. He spent the rest of the day in long telephone conversations followed by hushed conferences with his wife behind their closed bedroom door.

On Wednesday, a police officer came to the house and spent several hours talking with Bert, alone, in the kitchen. When the officer left, Jackie saw that her father's face was red and his hands were shaking.

As the week went on and Jackie saw her father become increasingly anxious and afraid, she began to feel fearful herself. She started to lock her bedroom door and latch the shutters on her windows at night. Before leaving the house, she would look up and down the street to be sure no one was there. When she overheard a reporter on the radio talking about racial problems spreading to suburban towns like Spring, she hid her toys and stuffed animals in a box in her closet.

Jackie's most precious possessions were the two pictures of her mother that sat on the night table beside her bed. One was a formal picture of her parents, taken at her mother's high school prom, the night her father had proposed marriage. The second was a faded snapshot of Jackie in swaddling clothes, sleeping in her mother's arms in front of an elaborately decorated Christmas tree. They were the only pictures Jackie had of her mother, and the little Jackie knew about her came from hours of gazing at the face in the pictures and imagining what she might have been like.

At first, Jackie buried the pictures carefully under the stuffed animals in her closet. Later, she took them out of the closet and hid them under her bed. That night, when she went to sleep, she took them out again and placed them in her pillowcase, where she could hold them securely in her arms.

It was not until the following Sunday, nine days after the riots began, that the fires in downtown Hartford were finally extinguished. The family went to church that morning and walked home together when services ended.

When they arrived home, a police officer was waiting for them in front of the house. Bert and Mary talked to the officer for several minutes, out of earshot of the children. Then, Bert climbed into the police car with the officer and drove away.

Mary prepared Sunday dinner, as she did every week, setting the table with a linen tablecloth and the family's best china. By late afternoon, when Bert had not yet returned, she put the prepared food and unused china away, made peanut butter-and-jelly sandwiches for the children, and sent them outside to play.

It was after eight o'clock that evening when the police brought Bert home. Jackie knew that there was something wrong from the look on his face as he said good night to the officer, shook his hand, and came into the house. She ran toward him and buried her face in his belly.

14

"So?" Mary asked hesitantly. "Did you go to the store? How is it?"

"It's gone," Bert answered, his voice shaking.

"It's gone?" Mary echoed. "Oh my God!"

"The windows were shattered. Everything's gone. It's like it all just blew away."

"You were afraid of something like this."

"You could feel that there was an explosion coming."

"What are we going to do?"

At that moment, Bert lost control of his tears. Jackie stepped back, alarmed. She had never seen her father cry.

Bert turned away from Jackie and picked up a dishtowel to wipe his face. Mary put her arms tightly around him and pulled his head down onto her shoulder.

"What are we going to do?" Mary repeated to herself as well as to Bert.

"I have no idea," Bert answered.

He looked down at Jackie, who was staring at him with fear etched on her face. "Isn't it past their bedtimes?"

"I'll put them to bed," Mary answered, releasing Bert from her grasp. "I made dinner. There is food in the refrigerator if you're hungry now, or I can put out something nice for you after I put the children to sleep. We'll talk."

"I'll wait. We'll talk."

Mary put the children to bed quickly, skipping the usual bedtime rituals of lullabies and stories, but Jackie could not sleep. She lay awake for hours, eavesdropping on her parents as they talked in the kitchen about things she did not understand; insurance, leases, loans, liens, relief, rebuilding, relocation. Nothing made any sense. What did her father mean when he said the store was gone? What had happened to the stuffed animals that had been her kingdom, the toys, the jewelry, and the clothes that she had arranged so beautifully by the colors of the rainbow?

When Jackie finally fell asleep, she saw herself playing on the street in front of her father's store in a picture-perfect world of stuffed animals, jewelry, and toys. Suddenly, there was an explosion. The glass in the windows and picture frames shattered. Everything around her disappeared into thin air; her world, her father, her stuffed animals, and the mother she knew only as a face in photographs. She tried to call out to them, to reach out to hold it all together, to keep it all from disappearing, but everything faded into the distance and was gone before she could move or make a sound.

3

The curfew was lifted the next morning so that school could begin. Mary did not want Jackie walking to school alone, so Bert drove her the half-mile from their house to Spring Elementary.

Spring Elementary was a long, one-story building built in the early 1960s to accommodate children of the baby boom. It was built in the International Style, with a flat roof and an unornamented façade of concrete, metal, and glass that contrasted harshly with the red brick, gabled roof, and neo-classical columns of the old high school across the street.

"Are you going to be okay walking home alone, sweetie?" Bert asked, as Jackie opened the car door.

"I'll be fine, Daddy," Jackie said impatiently, seeing her friends waiting for her on the curb.

"Try to walk home with some of your friends if you can. Your mother will feel better."

"Bye, Daddy. You can go now."

"I love you, sweetie."

"I love you too!" Jackie answered quickly, ducking her father's kiss and climbing out of the car. She was immediately greeted by Karen Altman and several other girl friends from her sixth-grade class. It took only seconds for Jackie to forget about the riots and her nightmare as she joined her friends in animated banter about their summer experiences, their camps and vacations, and the new clothes they had bought for school. The only serious topic of conversation concerned their sixth-grade teacher, Mrs. Leslie.

Mrs. Leslie was an institution at Spring Elementary School. She was the teacher every parent wanted for their kids, and the one teacher all the kids feared the most. Older children in the community told stories about Mrs. Leslie giving hours of homework and enforcing the dress code, which required girls to wear hemlines below their knees and boys to wear button-down shirts tucked in at the waist and hair cut above the collar. Throughout the summer, Jackie's friends had talked in hushed tones about their teacher assignments for the fall. Most hoped they would be assigned to anyone except Mrs. Leslie.

"I guess we better get to class," Jackie suggested, after several minutes of conversation at the curb.

"I'm not ready!" several others complained.

"Let's go," Jackie said, ignoring them and turning to walk into the building. "Come on."

Jackie's friends followed her, until she reached the door to Mrs. Leslie's room. There, the others hesitated, unwilling to be the first to enter. Jackie did not pause but opened the door, pushed into the room, and placed her books on her accustomed seat in the first row.

Seeing that Mrs. Leslie was not yet there, Karen followed Jackie into the room. "You don't want to sit in the first row this year," Karen whispered, just as Jackie was about to sit down. "Sit in the back with us."

"I'm okay," Jackie said without turning around.

"But it's Mrs. Leslie," Karen warned. "Sit with us!"

"I'm okay." Jackie brushed her off more emphatically.

"You're making a big mistake," Karen said ominously, as she retreated to a seat in the last row.

Jackie always sat in the first row. She had started sitting in front during first grade so she could see the blackboard more clearly. It was not until the second grade that her teachers realized she needed glasses, and her father took her to an optometrist for a prescription. Since then, her oversized pink-framed glasses had been a constant feature on her round, freckled face, not only helping her see more clearly, but also keeping her long, honey-brown hair out of her eyes. While she no longer had trouble seeing the board, she was used to being at the front of the class and at the center of attention.

Her classmates liked having her sit in front. Jackie was always the first to raise her hand when the teacher asked a question and generally had something to contribute to every class discussion. As long as Jackie was in front raising her hand to answer every question, teachers rarely had to coax answers out of those who preferred to sit silently in the back. There was a calculated comfort in letting Jackie take the risk of answering first, knowing that if her answer were incorrect, the teacher would often rephrase the question and they would have a better chance of answering correctly.

There was also an ineffable quality about Jackie, which made it seem natural for her to be in front. She was talkative, energetic, and fun; imaginative and mischievous; always active and at the center of a crowd of friends.

Jackie was not, however, a good student. She was fidgety in class, found it hard to concentrate, and habitually neglected to turn in her homework assignments or study for tests. Only when she spent afternoons with Danny Cohn did she do any significant work outside of school.

Jackie and Danny had been in the same class every year since kindergarten. With the last names Cone and Cohn, they were frequently assigned to adjacent seats and, over the years had become inseparable friends.

Once they had even tried to convince a substitute teacher that they were twins. The teacher had contrasted Danny's dark Semitic complexion, black curly hair, and angular facial features with Jackie's round forehead, freckles, and fine, sun-touched hair and concluded that they came from very different backgrounds. Danny had maintained a straight face while arguing emphatically that his name was misspelled in the roll book and that Jackie was really his twin sister. When the teacher asked Jackie whether Danny was really her twin brother, she managed to maintain a straight face while answering, "Yes, ma'am." Then, as the giggles of her classmates reached a crescendo, she had burst into loud laughter and blown their cover.

That was the only time Jackie had ever received detention. It was not the first time for Danny, who was often truculent in class and was sometimes given detention by his teachers just to remind him of their authority.

Danny's punishment was never severe. He was always the best student in the class, turned in exemplary homework, and had the highest grade on every test. When he was given detention, he generally spent his time helping tutor students in the lower grades.

Most of Danny's classmates, put off by his perfect grades and his occasionally contemptuous manner, tended to avoid him. Jackie was his one friend. They often walked home from school together and stopped at Jackie's house to have a snack, talk, and do homework. Jackie's infectious zest for life complemented Danny's intense and introspective nature. His careful attention to schoolwork was the reason she turned in any homework at all. They kept each other true and on course.

Danny was the one person who would listen to her chatter and treat her as if she were smart. She was the one person who could see through his opaque moods and occasional temper and make him feel at ease. They knew almost instinctively when to listen to each other, when to laugh and tease each other, and when they each needed to be left alone.

Despite their friendship, they found it awkward to be seen together at school. Behind her back, Jackie's friends gossiped about why she spent time with someone as uncool as Danny. Over time, such mutterings had made Jackie and Danny self-conscious about displaying their friendship in front of their classmates.

Jackie was happy as she unpacked her pencils and papers and arranged them carefully in her desk. She was glad to be back at school with her friends and away from her annoying brothers and sisters at home. She had no particular interest, however, in what she might learn in sixth grade.

The problem with school, Jackie thought, as she looked around at the empty blackboards, American and Connecticut flags standing in the corners, geopolitical maps on the walls, and colorful illustrations of arithmetic and grammar, was that the teachers never taught her anything interesting. So many things in the world were fascinating, but arithmetic and grammar were not.

It had been only six weeks since the astronauts of *Apollo 11* had walked on the Moon for the first time and less than a month since Thor Heyerdahl had tried to sail a reed ship, the *Ra*, from Egypt to South America, only to abandon his voyage in the face of an approaching hurricane. Jackie regularly watched *The Undersea World of Jacques Cousteau* on television and marveled that people could live underwater and build colonies on the sea floor. She loved the *National Geographic Specials* about Jane Goodall, who was living with the chimpanzees in Africa and getting to know them as friends.

Jackie wanted to know what scientists would find when they studied the rocks the astronauts brought back from the Moon, how long it would take to start a lunar colony, and when she would be able to visit. She wanted to know what language the Egyptians had used to talk to the Indians when their reed ship landed in America, and what language astronauts would use to talk to the Martians when they landed on Mars. She wanted to know what it was like to live in the forest with chimpanzees and in the oceans with the whales, and what it was like to soar through space and swim beneath the waves. Jackie could not wait until she was old enough to join the astronauts who had traveled to the Moon and the divers who swam to the ocean floor.

Jackie was not alone in her enchantment with the exploration of Earth and space. Scientific adventure and discovery were a familiar part of a child's experience in 1969. There were stories about space exploration on the evening news almost every night. The movie *2001: A Space Odyssey* had been a blockbuster the previous summer, and the recently cancelled television show *Star Trek* had spawned a cult phenomenon among young people. Jackie could reasonably dream of diving to cities on the ocean floor or climbing onto a *Saturn V* rocket that would take her to the Moon. Her generation had never known it any other way.

She was growing up in a world profoundly shaped by the launch of *Sputnik I* in October 1957. People around the world had listened to the radio transmissions from *Sputnik* and searched the night sky to observe the transit of the first man-made star. Politicians had also paid attention, recognizing that, by launching the first satellite, the Soviet Union had won a major victory in the global contest with the United States for world supremacy.

For a decade after World War II, the United States had been the unchallenged world leader in science and technology, building the atomic bombs that had won the war against Japan, the hydrogen bomb, and fleets of advanced jet fighters, bombers, and nuclear-powered ships. America's cold war strategy relied on its technological prowess to project its prestige and power around the world, against the much larger armies of the communist nations. With the launch of *Sputnik* in the fall of 1957, however, the Soviet Union had not only matched the United States in developing nuclear weapons, but had become the first to reach into space.

Within months, Congress responded to the Soviet's accomplishment by passing legislation that would shape a generation. The Advanced Research Projects Administration (ARPA) and the National Aeronautics and Space Administration (NASA) were inaugurated to coordinate massive new initiatives in advanced technology, computing, and the push into space. Billions of dollars were invested through these agencies to build great research centers that brought together military, industrial, and academic interests in the fight against communism. The results were dramatic. In a little more than a decade, America would launch hundreds of satellites and win a tightly contested race with the Soviet Union to land men on the Moon. Within this decade, too, America's universities, defense establishments, and commercial enterprises would invent microchips, computer networks, and new understandings of biology that would be the seeds for an age of technology.

Congress also responded by passing the National Defense Education Act (NDEA) of 1958, which allowed the federal government to invest billions of dollars in public education and, in the process, revolutionize the nature of education itself. Traditional education, based on the "three R's" and rote recitations of facts, was abandoned. The "new math" became the exemplar of a radical new approach to education that emphasized abstract concepts and inquiry over memorization and pedantic problem solving.

Jackie was a child of this age. She was schooled in the new math. She was exposed to pictures of the world brought into her living room via communication satellites and was inspired by the race to the Moon. Nothing else was nearly as exciting.

4

Mrs. Leslie came into the classroom and sat down at her desk just as the bell rang to begin the school day. She was a tall, thin woman with prematurely gray hair, cropped just above her shoulders. She wore an unadorned, dark-blue suit with a collared white blouse, a single strand of pearls that hung just below the collar, clip-on pearl earrings, and sheer nylon stockings with short-heel shoes. Her only accommodation to fashion was her pale-pink lipstick, which failed to add any elegance to her face but, instead, seemed to emphasize her disproportionately small mouth and nose. In any case, her lipstick was generally no longer visible by midmorning, when she would tire of adjusting her uncomfortable earrings and would drop them, along with her lipstick, into her desk and close the drawer for the day.

Mrs. Leslie opened her roll book and looked out over the class. "Good morning, class."

"Good morning," the class murmured the conditioned response.

She stood and walked over to the blackboard. "I'm Mrs. Leslie. Well, had an extra week of summer we didn't expect. Is everyone ready for school to begin?"

There was no response.

"Welcome to sixth grade. This is your last year at Spring Elementary School. How many of you have been here since first grade?"

About half the class raised their hands.

"I see that most of you like to sit in back." Everyone looked down uncomfortably. "I would like to seat the class in alphabetical order, at least until we all know each other better."

"Oh no," more than one student sighed.

"I will read through the class roll. When I call your name, take your things and move to the seat I assign you." Mrs. Leslie walked back to her desk and picked up her roll book. "Karen Altman. Miss Altman, please sit here."

Mrs. Leslie indicated the first seat in the first row. Karen looked crestfallen but dutifully collected her things and sat in the desk next to Jackie in the first row.

"It's not fair," Karen whispered to Jackie as she slid into her new seat. "Just because my name begins with *A*, I always have to sit in front. I should change my name."

Mrs. Leslie continued. "Daniel Cohn, please sit behind Miss Altman. Jacqueline Cone, please sit behind Mr. Cohn."

"Mrs. Leslie," Jackie interrupted with her hand raised.

"Yes?" Mrs. Leslie replied.

"I wear glasses so I can see the board. Can I stay in this seat?"

"Do you have your glasses?"

"Yes," Jackie replied nervously.

"Can you see the blackboard with your glasses?"

"Yes, but I'd rather sit in front anyway, you know, just in case."

Mrs. Leslie contemplated Jackie for a moment, and then made a notation in her book. "Okay, you can stay where you are."

Mrs. Leslie paused imperceptibly before reading the next name. "Ted Davis, please sit in the next seat." One of the two black students in the class stood and began to collect his things. The other students stared at him uneasily. It was the first year that Spring was participating in a controversial desegregation plan, termed Project Concern, which involved busing students from the inner city to suburban schools. Many of Hartford's suburbs had adamantly opposed the project. Thousands of residents had signed petitions against the project, and there were many inflammatory headlines in local newspapers and heated exchanges at Town Hall before Spring's participation in the project was approved. Jackie looked cautiously at the new student, wondering if he had anything to do with the riots and why her father's store was gone.

"Mr. Davis, welcome to our school. I hope everyone here will make you feel welcome." One of the boys in the back of the class audibly snickered, which elicited an angry stare from Mrs. Leslie. "I *expect* everyone here to make you feel welcome," she restated with emphasis before resuming the roll call.

It took five minutes for Mrs. Leslie to read the twenty-two names in the class. When she finished, she sat down at her desk without a word. There was considerable commotion as the students relocated their belongings to their newly assigned places. Books and pencils clattered into the desks. Chairs scraped across the floor. Conversations, left in the hallway only moments before, resumed as if there had been no interruption.

Mrs. Leslie sat silently at her desk, focusing on her roll book, until the students became aware of her conspicuous silence and settled down. When the class was quiet, Mrs. Leslie stood and walked back to the front of the class.

"Since this is your sixth year of school, I am sure you already know what the first day of school is like. We have a lot of things to do today. Does anyone have any questions before we start?"

There were none.

"Sixth grade is a very important year. This is your last year of elementary school."

A few boys cheered. Mrs. Leslie almost smiled.

"You are the top class in the school. I'm sure you know there are special privileges associated with being in sixth grade—your own place to sit in the cafeteria, special field trips, finishing school a week before the others." Again, there was a faint cheer.

Mrs. Leslie waited until the class was quiet before continuing. "As the oldest students in the school, your most important responsibility is being a role model for the other grades. The younger students will look up to you. They will notice how you behave, how you act, what you say, how you treat one another, how you treat our building, and how you dress."

Mrs. Leslie looked around the room. "I am sure you all know that Spring Elementary School has a dress code, and I expect everyone in this class to adhere to it. There will be no jeans, T-shirts, or short skirts. Shirts will remain tucked in at all times. There will be no torn clothes. I expect each of you to have an appropriate haircut. If you have any questions about the dress code—"

"Why do we need a dress code?" a voice interrupted her from the side of the classroom.

A silent panic swept through the room. How could anyone dare challenge Mrs. Leslie?

Mrs. Leslie walked back to her desk and looked in her roll book. "Mr. Cohn." She walked to the far side of the room, away from where he sat. "In the future, please raise your hand if you have something to say."

"Yes, ma'am." Danny Cohn smothered his reply.

"Now, please repeat what you said so we can all hear it."

Danny looked up in surprise and cleared his throat. "I don't think we should have a dress code. It isn't fair."

"It isn't fair," Mrs. Leslie repeated, looking around the room at the two dozen faces frozen with fear. "Does anyone else in the class share Mr. Cohn's opinion of the dress code, that it isn't fair?" Surely, Mrs. Leslie knew that everyone hated the dress code. This had to be a trap.

A girl spoke up from the middle of the room. "I don't see anything wrong with the dress code."

"I do," Danny blurted out. "You can't tell me how to dress. I should be able to wear anything I want. This is a free country!"

Mrs. Leslie stopped him with a penetrating look. "Again, Mr. Cohn, please raise your hand when you have something to say." There was a pause. "Mr. Cohn, are you concerned about the dress code because it isn't fair or because you think you should have the freedom to wear whatever you want?"

Danny was startled that Mrs. Leslie had taken his comments literally. "Both—I think," he stammered.

Mrs. Leslie turned her attention back to the whole class. "Does anyone know why we have a dress code?"

Jackie raised her hand and said hesitantly, "So we all look nice?"

Danny spoke up again with growing boldness in his voice. "My brother is in high school. He says the dress code is a form of mind control, a way of making us act and think like everyone else."

Mrs. Leslie turned to him. "Mr. Cohn, in *this* class we *will* listen to everyone's opinion," she said abruptly. "You will *not*, however, speak without raising your hand and being recognized. Do you understand?"

Danny slouched back in his chair.

Mrs. Leslie walked slowly to the back of the class. The students kept their eyes forward. No one dared to turn in their seats. Danny was taking a huge risk by confronting Mrs. Leslie.

"Who agrees with Mr. Cohn that we should not have a dress code?"

Two or three boys mustered the courage to raise their hands halfway.

"Does that mean you think we should be able to wear anything we want?"

"It shouldn't matter what we wear if we do our work and get good grades," one student offered.

"I learn better when I'm comfortable," said another.

"Does anyone think we *should* have a dress code?" Mrs. Leslie asked. A half-dozen students raised their hands. "What about the rest of you?"

"I don't know why we need a dress code, but I don't see anything wrong with it," one student spoke up.

"I think B.O. should be against the dress code!" a boy jeered from the back of the class. "Some people stink!"

Several students laughed nervously. Mrs. Leslie ignored them.

"I don't want to look the same as everyone else. I want to look like me."

"I don't want to dress like you, either," one of the black students said with an edge in his voice. "We don't dress like you in the hood."

"I don't see anything wrong with dressing nice," a girl stated. "My father is a police officer. He wears a uniform to work every day, and he thinks we should—"

"I don't care what your father wears or what you wear," Danny interrupted. "This is a free country. We should be able to wear whatever we want." Danny's voice became defiant. "My brother said that no one in the high school is going to obey the dress code this year. If the principal wants a dress code, my brother said all the students are going to boycott. You can't tell us what to wear. What are you going to do, call the police?"

"That's enough," Mrs. Leslie cut him off abruptly.

Danny had crossed the line and would get them all in trouble. Every eye in the room turned away. This was not a good way to start the year. Mrs. Leslie walked slowly past Danny's seat, deliberately drumming her fingers on his desk as she passed. Danny was afraid to move. The silence was intimidating.

Most of the students in the class knew Danny's brother, Ruben, who was a senior at Spring High School. Ruben was a talented musician, who played bass guitar in a popular rock band at many school dances and town events, as well as bass in the school orchestra and sousaphone in the marching band.

Everything about Ruben embodied the image of a radical and an artist. He wore his long, black hair down below his shoulders in the fashion of the Beatles, carefully combed his emerging facial hair into straggly sideburns and a beard, and routinely wore torn T-shirts and jeans to school. Even when he wore the uniform of the marching band or the black suit and starched white shirt that were required for performances of the school orchestra, his bearing, posture, and gait conveyed an unmistakable aura of artistry and rebellion.

25

Mrs. Leslie returned to the front of the room and faced the class. "This is a good discussion. Many of you have interesting ideas about the dress code—ideas that go beyond simply what clothes we wear."

Danny looked up, surprised. This was not what he expected to hear from Mrs. Leslie. Her reputation suggested that she would send him to the principal's office.

"What is fair? What is freedom? What are our rights? When should we conform to others? When should we be different? These are important ideas," Mrs. Leslie continued. "Maybe we will talk more about these ideas another time. Let me be clear, however. There *is* a dress code in my classroom, and I expect each of you to adhere to it. Perhaps the reasons for the dress code are not apparent to all of us. For *now*," she said with emphasis, "the dress code is the school's policy, and I will enforce it." She paused to look at the clock over the door.

"I think we should move on. We have a lot to do today before we can get on with our lessons."

Jackie and Danny exchanged quick glances. She was glad Mrs. Leslie had not sent him to the principal's office.

5

Mrs. Leslie sat down at her desk and proceeded with the required recitation of school policies that Jackie had heard every year since first grade. No one was allowed in the hallways during the day without a hall pass. The doors to the building would be closed after the first bell and had alarms that would sound if they were opened. No one would be admitted to school late or excused early without a parent's note, and the principal would call parents if their children were absent from school, unless they brought a note to the office in advance.

Mrs. Leslie described the emergency procedures to follow in case of fire, the location of the nearest exit, and how to escape from the building. Then she described the procedures to follow in case of a nuclear attack. She reminded the class that if the civil defense sirens sounded an "alert" signal, a steady blast lasting three to five minutes, it indicated that an attack could come soon. When this happened, Mrs. Leslie would lead her class to the basement of the high school across the street, which was equipped as a local fallout shelter that had stocks of canned food, powdered milk, a Geiger counter, and supplies for decontamination after the attack was over. She also reminded the class that the "take cover" signal, a wailing tone or series of short blasts, indicated that an attack was imminent and that there was no time to go to the fallout shelter. If they heard this signal, they should "duck and cover" by crouching under their desks and covering their heads with their arms to protect against injury.

Mrs. Leslie read the rite in an efficient, brusque manner, without elaboration or emotion. Jackie tried to tune it out and busied herself by drawing pictures on the covers of her notebooks and the corners of her desk. She drew the Sun in the sky and spaceships soaring among the stars, planets populated by tribbles and other fanciful creatures, and cities crowned with otherworldly dwellings. She could not, however, ignore it completely. When Mrs. Leslie talked about being sick or hurt, Jackie drew little pink Band-Aids on her multicolored creatures. When Mrs. Leslie talked about fire, Jackie drew bright red flames coming from their dwellings. When Mrs. Leslie talked about preparing for a nuclear attack, Jackie obliterated her drawings under clouds of black ink, the force of her strokes flattening the tip of her Magic Marker and tearing through the page to the desk underneath.

"Okay," Mrs. Leslie concluded, as she reached the end of her monologue and paused to look around the class. "Let's move on," she began with more energy in her voice. "I want to tell you about something new. One of the things we are going to do this year is spend some time every day talking about current events. There are many things going on in the world right now that must be confusing, even frightening."

The classroom became unusually quiet. Jackie looked up from her doodling and squirmed uncomfortably in her seat. She thought she heard a police siren in the distance and listened carefully to be sure it was not a warning of a nuclear attack.

World events had not seemed terribly relevant to Jackie when she was nine or ten. Now that she was almost twelve, they were becoming harder to ignore. The riots in Hartford and the loss of the family store had brought the social upheavals of the 1960s abruptly into her life. So did the presence of black students in her class for the first time.

The war in Vietnam had also begun to intrude on her childhood. On Memorial Day, there had been a rally on the Common for a townsman who had been missing in action in Vietnam since the Tet offensive the year before. The missing soldier had been one of Jackie's favorite babysitters before being drafted into the army. She had many happy memories of evenings spent playing, reading books, and singing silly songs together while waiting for her father to come home.

Jackie and Bert had attended the rally and watched as a military honor guard marched down Main Street to the Commons and fired their guns in a grave salute. They listened as a colonel in the Connecticut National Guard gave a speech about her babysitter's patriotism and his bravery fighting against communists who wanted to destroy America and the American way of life.

The following week, there had been an antiwar protest in Spring led by the Students for a Democratic Society, which had tried to organize a rally at the high school across the street. Jackie and her classmates had watched out the window as the protesters marched noisily down the street, shouting antiwar slogans. Before the protesters could reach the school, a phalanx of parents had confronted them, blocking the road and refusing to let them pass. For an hour, Jackie had heard protesters, parents, and police hurl unintelligible insults and invectives back and forth. Ultimately, the protesters had retreated, and more than two hundred students walked out of the high school to attend a noisy antiwar meeting at the Congregational church around the corner.

It was not just the riots in Hartford, the integration of her school, a babysitter who was missing in action, or antiwar protests that had encroached on the sanctity of her space and her childhood. It was also television, which brought terrible images into her living room each night, with graphic depictions of riots and wars and ghastly details of death and destruction. Hers was the first generation that had to synthesize the information of live television and instantaneous, worldwide communications into a coherent worldview, a generation brought up with the fear of Mutually Assured Destruction and the threat of international terrorism. As Jackie approached adolescence, she was increasingly afraid that the world around seemed to be exploding.

Many adults found it difficult to respond rationally to the dissonance of world events in 1969. It was even harder for children, who could not place world events in a historical context. War and social conflict seem more apocalyptic when a child is unaware that wars and conflicts historically end. The ascent of evil is more frightening when a child is unaware that evil can be successfully confronted and defeated.

Few children could conceive that national boundaries change, that governments could be overthrown, or that the historical record evolved to reflect the sensitivities of the society in which it was taught. Few were able to delineate world events that were likely to be of lasting importance from those that would soon be forgotten. Few were able to distinguish fact and fiction amidst the inflamed political rhetoric of the times.

Jackie tried to ignore the troubles of the world and focus her attention on other things, like school and space. Now, Mrs. Leslie was going to bring world events into the classroom. She shifted nervously in her seat and started to doodle a picture of a rocket escaping from Earth toward the heavens.

"Who can tell the class about some of the news events over the summer?"

Jackie raised her hand immediately. "Astronauts walked on the Moon."

"Good. Someone else?" Mrs. Leslie prompted.

"There were the riots," another student started, before glancing sideways at the new black students from the city. "I guess everyone knows that." He stopped abruptly.

"There is a lot of fighting in Vietnam."

"Everyone is protesting to end the war."

"There is, like, a war between Israel and Egypt."

"The British army attacked Ireland."

"An American plane was hijacked and blown up by Arabs."

"Half a million people went to Woodstock for peace and love and music."

"A river caught fire somewhere—I think it was Cleveland."

"A bunch of hippies murdered someone—some actress, Sharon Tate."

"Paul McCartney is dead." There was an instant buzz of conversation. The infamous story had not yet reached the proportions that it would within several months. Mrs. Leslie paused until the room was quiet again.

"Anything else?"

"There is a war in Biafra. Everyone is starving."

"Russia and China are fighting a war."

"Two countries in Central America are fighting a war because of a soccer game or something."

As the litany of wars and tragedy continued, Jackie grasped her pen so hard her knuckles turned white. She tried to turn the conversation to something less threatening. "There's like this new airplane. I think it is called the 747, and it has two floors with, like, a piano and a staircase in the middle."

One of the black students from Hartford spoke up for the first time. "Some brothers were killed by the pigs because they belonged to the Black Panthers."

"We do not refer to police as *pigs* here," Mrs. Leslie interjected sternly.

"We call them *fuzz*," a white student said from the back of the room, eliciting laughter from some of his classmates.

"Same thing," the black student muttered.

"Don't call my father names!" a girl spoke up in protest.

"Does he shoot people?"

"No!" she answered indignantly.

"Okay, that's enough." Mrs. Leslie stepped in to restore order. "This is not appropriate for our classroom."

Jackie exhaled deeply and loosened her grip slightly on her pen.

"Here is what we are going to do," Mrs. Leslie started again. "Your assignment is to watch the evening news or look at the newspaper every day. At the beginning of each day, I will ask two students to give the class a report on something in the news, a current event that is interesting to you. You can talk about anything you want. Everyone will be assigned a turn, and we keep going around the class.

"You should talk for ten minutes about your current event and be prepared to answer questions from your classmates. When you give your reports, tell us not only what happened, but also try to tell us why it happened, how it relates to things in our classroom, and how it relates to our ideas about things." Mrs. Leslie paused for breath. Jackie raised her hand immediately. "Yes, Miss Cone?"

"Do you mean, like, if I give a report about landing on the Moon, I should talk about how the astronauts saw Earth from space—you know, how it looked like the map on the wall?"

"Yes, thank you," Mrs. Leslie answered. "I especially want you to think about how the event affects your ideas about things. Miss Cone just mentioned, for example, that from space, the Earth looked like a map. Did it look exactly like the map on the wall over there? Do you think the astronauts saw roads and cities? Do you think they saw boundaries between different countries? Does it give you any ideas about the world?"

Jackie started to answer, but Mrs. Leslie continued. "Let me give you another example. When we were talking about the dress code, Mr. Cohn brought up the ideas of fairness and freedom. What do we know about the idea of fairness? What do we know about the idea of freedom?"

Mrs. Leslie glanced around the class. Most of the students looked confused.

"Can someone tell me what an *idea* is?" she asked, changing directions to keep the class's attention.

Jackie raised her hand. "An idea is when you think of something, like, when there are words in your head."

"It is like a thought," someone else added.

"It is like when you have a thought or a picture in your head, you might say, 'Hey, I have an idea!' or something like that," another girl stated.

One of the boys in the class then grabbed his head and shouted, "Oh no! There's an idea in her head! There's an idea in her head! Get it out! Get it out!" to a chorus of derisive laughter from his friends.

Mrs. Leslie ignored the interruption but paused until the class was quiet. "Good, so you can have an idea, a thought in your mind," she continued. "Can anyone tell me something else about an idea?"

Jackie raised her hand again. "An idea doesn't have to be inside your head. I could, you know, tell my idea to someone."

"You can write it down," someone else offered.

"An idea can make you do something," a boy said uncertainly.

"Can you give us an example?" asked Mrs. Leslie.

"Well, I could have an idea, like, how to build a doghouse, and I could, you know, build it."

"Very good," Mrs. Leslie answered.

A boy raised his hand. "If I have an idea for, like, a better way of doing something, I could tell it to other people, and they could do it, like, the way I said."

"So you can teach people your idea?" Mrs. Leslie reformulated the comment.

"Yeah, that's what I meant," he replied sheepishly.

Another student spoke up. "Ideas can make people do things together."

"What do you mean by that?" Mrs. Leslie prompted.

"If a lot of people have the same idea—or if I have an idea and I tell a lot of people about it—they might, like, get together and do it."

"Do you think some of the current events we hear about might have begun with an idea?" she asked.

"I guess so."

"You can believe in an idea," Karen offered.

"Can you explain?" Mrs. Leslie encouraged.

Karen looked flustered. "Well, you know, you can have an idea that you believe is right."

"Can you give us an example?"

"I don't know." Karen was stumped.

"Can anyone help her?" Mrs. Leslie asked the class. Jackie started to raise her hand and hesitated.

"Can any of you think of an idea that you believe in?" Mrs. Leslie rephrased the question.

The question hung unanswered in the air for several moments. A boy raised his hand, and Mrs. Leslie called on him. "This might not be what you're asking, but you might, like, believe in an idea if it was a good idea and, like, not believe in it if it was a bad idea."

"Good." Mrs. Leslie turned toward the class. "Do you think there are good ideas and bad ideas?"

Several students nodded their heads.

"Can someone tell me the difference between a good idea and a bad idea?"

Jackie raised her hand. "If I have an idea that leads to bad things, that would be a bad idea."

"If an idea is wrong, then that would be a bad idea," someone else answered immediately.

A boy raised his hand. "I could have an idea that gets me suspended from school—that would be a really bad idea." This brought laughter from his friends.

"I could have an idea for something that doesn't work," another boy said. "Like, if I built a doghouse, and the roof fell down, like when the dog was in it, and the dog got hurt. That would be a bad idea."

"What about good ideas? Can anyone tell me what a good idea is?" Mrs. Leslie asked.

Jackie again was the first to raise her hand. "A good idea is something that is really smart."

"A good idea makes good things happen," a girl added.

"A good idea gets you things you want."

"A good idea is one everybody believes," said another girl.

Mrs. Leslie turned to her. "Does everyone have to believe in an idea for it to be good?"

The girl appeared flustered. "Well, if it is a good idea, then everyone should believe in it," she answered softly.

"If you have an idea and no one agrees with it," another student continued the thought, "then it probably isn't a good idea."

Danny had been quiet throughout the discussion, but now he spoke up. "It doesn't matter whether other people agree with your ideas. If the ideas are right, they are good ideas, whether or not people agree."

"So you can have a good idea even if no one else agrees that it is a good idea?" Mrs. Leslie asked.

"Sure," Danny said.

"How about a bad idea? If you have an idea and a lot of people agree with it, can it still be a bad idea?"

"Sure," Danny said again.

"So, then how do you know if an idea is good or bad?" Mrs. Leslie asked.

"I ask my parents," one girl said meekly.

"If it is against the law, then it is a bad idea," proposed another.

Mrs. Leslie pushed the thought. "If something is legal, does that mean it is a good idea?"

"Yes," several students answered in unison.

"No," Danny answered at the same time. "There can be bad laws."

"Can you give me an example?"

One of the inner-city students spoke up before Danny could answer. "Laws that don't treat blacks like people are bad laws!"

"Or laws that tell you what to think," Danny spoke up again," laws that say you can't protest, laws that—"

Mrs. Leslie realized the discussion had gone off course and interrupted Danny, just as he was warming up. "Good. Let's change the topic slightly. Does anyone know what an *ideal* is?"

Jackie raised her hand. "An ideal is like an idea that—" She had not thought out the rest of the sentence, and she let it drop. No one else in the class picked up her thought.

"Anyone?"

There was no answer.

Mrs. Leslie looked around the room. "Okay, that's enough for now. I know you all need a break. Before we do, however, I want to give you your first vocabulary words. As I write the words on the blackboard, please copy them into your notebook. Your homework is to look in a dictionary, learn how to spell these words for a spelling test on Friday, and write a definition for each word, which you will also turn in on Friday."

Some of the students looked around the room in disbelief. "Homework already, on the first day of school," one student complained.

Mrs. Leslie ignored the murmur. She picked up a piece of white chalk and wrote on the blackboard as she talked. "The vocabulary words for tonight are *idea, ideal, idealism, idealist, idealistic, idealize, ideally.*" Mrs. Leslie stopped and walked back to her desk.

"I know it has been a long morning already, and I can see some of you are having trouble sitting still." She stopped until everyone was paying attention again. "I want to say one more thing about what I hope we can accomplish this year. Sixth grade is mostly about growing up. This is your last year of elementary school, the last year when you will have the same class every day, with the same teacher, and the same friends all learning the same thing. Next year, you will be in junior high school. You will have more choices. Then you will go to high school, then college, then—" She let her words trail off, knowing that sixth-graders have little notion of anything beyond grade school.

"What I want to do this year is teach you how to think," she continued.

Jackie looked up, startled by this unexpected comment.

"I want to teach you how to think," Mrs. Leslie repeated. "We are going to talk a lot about ideas this year. We will learn how to think about ideas, how to listen considerately to everyone's ideas, how to decide whether we agree with them, and how to disagree respectfully. We will talk about how to decide whether an idea makes sense, whether it seems right or wrong, good or bad.

"Most importantly, we are going to talk about finding your own ideas. You are going to encounter many different ideas as you grow up—" she continued, "some really good ones and some really bad ones. You will have to learn how to think for yourself—how to decide for yourself what you believe. Part of growing up is learning how to think—how to find your own ideas."

Mrs. Leslie stopped and looked around at the class. The students' glazed looks told her she had strayed beyond their awareness and attention span.

"That's enough for this morning. Any questions?" There was no response. They were all eager to get out of their chairs. "All right. Take a break. Please be back in your seats in fifteen minutes."

6

Jackie had come to school that morning happy to be back in the routine of friends and activity, relieved to put the nightmare of the past week behind her. Now she was afraid that this year school would be different.

"I want to teach you how to think." Mrs. Leslie's phrase kept running through her mind. Why did she have to think about riots and wars and things that were frightening? It was easier not to.

"Mrs. Leslie is weird," Jackie's classmates complained to each other as they congregated in front of the water fountain and restrooms.

"I have no idea what she's talking about," said another.

"Who gives homework and vocabulary words on the first day of school? Give me a break!"

"I wish I had gotten another teacher."

Jackie walked toward the water fountain and pushed into line behind Danny. "What do you think of Mrs. Leslie?" she asked.

"I don't know," he replied. "Ruben had her for sixth grade. He didn't like her."

"I didn't understand what she was talking about this morning. Did you?"

"No," Danny responded, lost in his own introspection. He, too, was troubled by the way the school year had started, but for different reasons than Jackie. The discussion about the dress code bothered him. Mrs. Leslie had encouraged him to say things he had not planned, and he wished he had been able to express his ideas more clearly.

"What do you think she was talking about?" Jackie pressed her question, hoping Danny could help calm her anxiety.

"I don't know."

"The stuff on current events could be interesting."

"Maybe."

"What are you going to talk about?"

"I haven't thought about it. How about you?"

"Maybe Mrs. Leslie will let me talk about the Moon landing."

A smile briefly crossed Danny's face. "I figured that's what you would want to talk about."

"So, tell me, what you are going to do your report on?" she asked again.

"I really don't know. It's been a strange summer. There's a lot of stuff I need to think about."

"Do you want to talk about it?"

"Not now."

Danny had spent much of the summer of 1969 hanging out with his brother, Ruben, and the members of Ruben's band. They had spent many hours rehearsing in the garage and sitting by the community pool talking about girls, music, and politics.

Danny idolized his brother, who tolerated his presence as long as he was quiet and willing to run errands. While Danny did not share the older boys' preoccupation with girls, he was quite happy to be on the sidelines and listen to their music and conversation.

When Ruben's friends left at the end of each day, Danny and Ruben would sit together and talk. Ruben was proud to convey the wisdom of his eighteen years to his admiring younger brother. These conversations made Danny feel grown up and gave him a repertoire of information, ideas, and language that made him sound precocious.

At the beginning of the summer, Ruben and his friends had been preoccupied with John Lennon and the Beatles. They spent weeks learning every song from the Beatles' recent *White* and *Yellow Submarine* albums. They discussed every detail of the Beatles' experience in transcendental meditation with Maharishi Mahesh Yogi, John Lennon's marriage to Yoko Ono, their bed-in to promote world peace, and their evolving New Age ideas and music. They talked earnestly about how love, peace, and spiritual harmony could combine to create a consciousness that could conquer the world.

By mid-July, their attention turned to Woodstock. Anyone who was with it was going to be there. On the first day of the festival, Ruben and the other band members crowded into a friend's car and drove eighty miles to Yasgur's farm. They were among more than four hundred thousand people who made the pilgrimage to celebrate three days of peace and music that became the icon for the Age of Aquarius.

Danny had begged his parents to let him go to Woodstock with Ruben. They said no; Woodstock was no place for a kid.

They were right.

Ruben returned from the concert four days later covered in torn clothes and foul-smelling mud. He had an insensible look in his eyes and told incomprehensible stories about the things he had seen and heard. His speech was pressured as he talked about the music and the mobs, the songs and the spirit, and the visions he had seen in the Sun. After talking almost nonstop for hours and eating virtually everything in the refrigerator, he fell asleep and slept for most of the next two days. Danny was secretly glad his parents had not let him go.

Woodstock was a seminal event for Ruben and his friends. They spent the last weeks of summer reliving their experiences at Woodstock, rehearsing the songs the bands had performed, repeating every remark that had been made from the platform, and recalling the spirit of rebellion that had been in the air. Idle conversations about girls and music were supplanted by expressions of frustration with society and fear about the future. Songs about teen affections were replaced by summer hits like *Bad Moon Rising* and *Ghetto*. As their music became harder, their opinions became less compromising, their attitudes more strident, and their behavior more unpredictable. Days dedicated to the ideals of love and peace had galvanized their resolve to be part of a radical new age.

Danny struggled to understand his brother as he changed. Ruben and his friends wanted to promote peace, but they were willing to condone violence to achieve it. They demanded democracy, but denounced its decisions. They insisted on their right to freedom of action, speech, and thought, but seemed intolerant of others' actions, speech, and thoughts. They were prepared to wage a war within America to protect their rights, but they saw no virtue in fighting wars abroad to protect the rights of others. They talked about spirituality, but rejected religion. Danny did not understand how a bed-in, a concert dedicated to peace and love, or music that challenged the senses and sensibilities of the audience could change anything. He had no knowledge of how drugs had begun to shape Ruben's ideas.

Danny knew that he was not like Ruben. Sometimes he was jealous of his brother's intuitive ability to express his most profound ideas and emotions through music. Danny had to take more time. He had to listen closely, collect information, and construct his sentences carefully before he could express his ideas correctly.

Talking with Jackie was one of the things that usually helped. He could tell her things he was afraid to tell anyone else and usually felt better when he did. At that moment, Danny wanted to talk to Jackie as much as she wanted to talk to him, but he wasn't ready. There was too much on his mind. He needed time to collect his thoughts.

The line for the water fountain moved ahead slowly. When it was Danny's turn, he took a long drink and turned back toward the classroom. Jackie took a quick sip and followed him.

37

"I'm surprised you didn't get sent to the principal's office for that stuff about the dress code," she said, when she caught up with him.

"So what?" he replied dismissively.

"I thought you might get suspended," Jackie said with genuine concern.

"Mrs. Leslie wouldn't do that."

"She said the dress code was important."

"She has to say those things—she's a teacher."

"Are you going to get a haircut?"

"My parents will probably make me," Danny replied. He did not seem upset.

"What did Mrs. Leslie mean when she said she wanted to teach us how to think?"

"I don't know."

Jackie was getting impatient with Danny's short answers. "Is she going to try to brainwash us?" She knew this would provoke him.

"I'm not going to be brainwashed!" he replied, finally engaged. "Look, I don't know what she means. Ruben said that Mrs. Leslie is always difficult and confusing. Maybe it's just something she says. It may not mean anything. I could ask Ruben, but it's kind of hard to talk to him right now."

Danny saw the insistent look in Jackie's eyes and felt bad. He just wasn't in the mood to talk. "Look, Jackie, I'm sorry. Everything is weird right now. I don't know what else to say. I'm sorry."

"We better go back to class," she said uneasily. Danny had been no help.

Once everyone was back in the classroom, Mrs. Leslie began the routine of elementary education, reviewing math concepts they had learned in fifth grade and introducing the topics they would cover in sixth. The students found it hard to sit still after a summer of freedom. Their discomfort mounted as the temperature outside soared to over ninety degrees. By the time the bell finally rang at three o'clock, everyone was thankful the day was over.

"Before class is dismissed—" Mrs. Leslie raised her hand as the class began to bolt for the door. "—I would like two volunteers to make the first current events presentations on Friday."

Jackie's hand went up automatically.

"Thank you, Miss Cone. Anyone else?"

Danny raised his hand halfway.

"Thank you, Mr. Cohn." She looked down at her roll book to be sure she had their names right. "You two certainly do not look related." She laughed to herself. "Okay, we will begin with Miss Cone and Mr. Cohn on Friday morning. I will post a schedule for the rest of the class. Class dismissed."

The students gathered their books and headed out the front doors toward Main Street. Danny left the room ahead of Jackie, who ran to catch up with him as he was walking up the street.

"I was surprised you volunteered to give a report on Friday. You don't usually volunteer for anything," Jackie said.

"I wasn't going to make you get up there alone."

"Do you want to work together?" she asked. "I'm going shopping with my mom for clothes today, but maybe you can come over after school tomorrow?"

"I can't come over tomorrow," Danny said. "I have my first Bar Mitzvah lesson."

"Well, maybe Wednesday or Thursday."

At that moment, Karen caught up with them and immediately began talking to Jackie without acknowledging Danny's presence. Danny started to walk away. "See you tomorrow," he said, as he retreated awkwardly down Main Street.

Jackie was already engaged in a new conversation with Karen and did not answer.

7

The television in the living room was always tuned to the *CBS Evening News with Walter Cronkite* a half-hour before dinner. Walter Cronkite's fatherly manner, black-framed reading glasses, melodious voice, and careful commentaries on world events made him an American icon and "the most trusted man in America." His presence guided the nation through political conventions, elections, and assassinations, the civil rights movement, the Vietnam War, and antiwar protests. Above all, his was the voice of the space program. He told the world about the successes of *Mercury* and *Gemini*, the tragedy of *Apollo 1*, when astronauts Guss Grissom, Ed White, and Roger Chaffee died in a fire on the launch pad, the triumph of landing on the Moon, and the boundless potential of the future.

Bert always arrived home from work minutes before the evening news began. He would take a beer from the refrigerator and sit at the dining room table, sorting through the day's mail, with his chair angled so he could see the television out of the corner of his eye. Mary would prepare dinner in the adjacent kitchen, occasionally calling out, "What did he say, Bert?" when the noise of the sink drowned out the television. Jackie would sit on the couch with her homework, while her brothers and sisters, ranging in age from one to five, would congregate in the living room with their toys. Eventually, Jackie would complain that they were too noisy, and Bert would tell them to go play somewhere else.

Jackie generally did not pay much attention to the news, except for stories about the space program, Earth exploration, or stories featuring cute animals. She sat in the living room mostly to be around her father. The world news was simply white noise in the background.

For the week of September 8, 1969, the *CBS Evening News* was a snapshot of a world in turmoil. There was a relative lull in the Vietnam War, when the North Vietnamese called a cease-fire to mourn the death of their leader, Ho Chi Minh. The South Vietnamese government refused to accept the cease-fire and, despite the American government's entreaties, continued to fight. Three Americans died on Monday. By the end of the week, the war had escalated again.

In Europe, the Israeli embassies in West Germany, Belgium, and the Netherlands were bombed by a nascent terrorist group, the Palestine Liberation Front, which had been responsible for a series of dramatic aircraft hijackings over the summer. In the Middle East, Egypt's war of attrition with Israel continued with the sinking of several Egyptian boats in the Suez Canal and the deaths of hundreds of soldiers. In Belfast, Northern Ireland, the killing of a Protestant by Catholics led to a violent protest that was broken up by British army troops using tear gas. The British army announced that it was going to build a "peace wall" that would keep Protestants and Catholics apart. In the United States, there were angry confrontations in Georgia, Alabama, and Mississippi, as black children headed to formerly all-white schools under court desegregation orders. Experts predicted there could be a wave of unrest in junior and senior high schools across the country. In Alaska, the federal government began selling leases for oil exploration on the shores of the Arctic Sea, and the USS *Manhattan*, an oil tanker outfitted as an icebreaker, became stuck in the polar ice. In Washington, a joint session of Congress was scheduled to honor the *Apollo 11* astronauts. At Cape Kennedy, the *Saturn V* rocket that would take *Apollo 12* to the Moon was moved to the launch pad in anticipation of a November flight.

Jackie found it hard to pay attention to the news as Mrs. Leslie had directed. She shuddered at the sounds of explosions and the images of bombs destroying buildings on the ground and jets exploding in the sky. She started to cry at the sight of coffins. She sat through much of the evening news, clutching her favorite stuffed dog tightly to her stomach and sometimes holding it over her eyes and ears when the images became too much.

"You don't have to watch," Bert said, watching her struggling in front of the television.

"But Mrs. Leslie said—"

"I can talk to your teacher."

Bert listened to the news of the world with detached emotion. "There isn't anything I can do," he told people when conversations turned to the social revolutions occurring around them. "I pray every Sunday. That's what I do!"

His demeanor was very different, however, when the news stories were about the "troubles" in Northern Ireland. In mid-August that year, years of simmering conflict between Protestants and Catholics had exploded into street warfare. Thousands of British army troops had been called in to Northern Ireland to restore order but had been unable to stop the violence. Instead, the presence of Protestant soldiers in Catholic communities made the situation worse. A paramilitary group, the Irish Republican Army, emerged for the first time, unleashing a series of lethal attacks against Protestant civilians and the largely Protestant police force.

Whenever there was news about Northern Ireland, Bert would silence everyone with a loud "Shhh!" and begin to pace the room. He often added his own commentary, cursing, "Damn British!" under his breath, when there was a shooting in a Catholic neighborhood, "Tell the truth, you bastard!" when Protestant politicians or British army officers were interviewed, or "We're with you, lad!" when a Catholic leader spoke. As he fumed, he became flushed and his voice changed. Jackie thought he began to sound like the distant relative who had visited from Ireland the year before and spoke with an accent that didn't even sound like English.

Jackie did not understand why her father got so upset. She knew that her grandparents had come to America from Ireland to escape a famine. She had heard people talk about how the neighborhood around her father's store had once been Irish, and how it had changed. Jackie's only exposure to Ireland was through their church, Saint Patrick's Parish. At St. Patrick's, Jackie not only learned catechism, but also Irish history, culture, and folklore, and she danced in an Irish folk dance group that performed at Christmas pageants and St. Patrick's Day celebrations around town.

One evening that week, there was a story on the *CBS Evening News* about Bernadette Devlin, a fiery Catholic member of the British Parliament and champion of Irish independence, who was touring the United States. When the story was introduced, her father began to pace the room, cheering, "Way to go, lass!" and "You tell them, lassie!" When the report was over, he turned back to the newspaper and the mail.

"Daddy," Jackie called.

"Yes, sweetie."

"Why do you care so much about Ireland?"

Her father stopped what he was doing and came over to sit next to her on the couch. "Why do we care about Ireland? Well, we're Irish," he answered directly.

"I thought we are American."

"We are American, but we're also Irish."

"Do you wish we lived in Ireland?"

"Of course not."

"Do you want go to Ireland?"

"I would like to visit someday, but I don't want to live there."

"So why do you care about Ireland?"

"We care because, even though we are Americans, Ireland is where we're from. It's who we are. It's how we think. It's our history, our tradition, our church. We don't want the British to take that away."

"Are the British going to take our church away?" Jackie interrupted with concern, wondering again for an instant what had happened to her father's store.

"No, of course not. But, if the British can take away part of our land and our people, they are taking away something we care about very much. We can't let that happen."

"But why?"

"Because that is who we are."

Jackie didn't understand what her father was talking about, but one of his comments stuck in her mind—"It's how we think." Mrs. Leslie had said something similar at school.

42

"Daddy, do Irish people think differently from other people?" she asked tentatively.

"What do you mean, sweetie?"

"You said that being Irish is how we think. Do Irish people think differently?"

"Well, in a way we do. There are things in our Irish experience—hardship, religion, tradition—that make our ideas different from other people's."

Again, Jackie thought her father sounded like Mrs. Leslie.

"Because we are Irish," her father continued, "we know what it is like to be oppressed by the British. We know what it is like to starve. We know what it takes to preserve our hope, our families, and our faith. All of this has made us strong, given us strong ideas, confidence, and pride. It has made us value our ideas and our identity. It makes us become missionaries for our ideas, for who we are, for what we believe."

There was much more that Bert wanted to teach Jackie about Ireland. He wanted her to know that she was a part of a people who had once transformed a small, cold island in the North Atlantic into a center of Western culture, part of a people who had defended civilization and Christianity through the Dark Ages in Europe. He wanted to teach her about the Irish writers who had translated Irish myth and conscience into great works of literature and art. He wanted to teach her about the Irish scholars who had nurtured the Christian faith and about the Irish missionaries who had traveled the world to bring the knowledge of heaven to all humanity.

Jackie's eyes told her father that she was not listening. "I want to teach you how to think," Mrs. Leslie had said. Her father said that there was an Irish way of thinking and a set of Irish ideas. Is this what Mrs. Leslie was talking about? Did Mrs. Leslie want to teach her how to think like the Irish?

"Daddy, do you think Mrs. Leslie is Irish?"

"I don't know, sweetie. Why do you ask?"

"Never mind."

After talking with her father, Jackie considered doing her current events report on the troubles in Northern Ireland. For several nights, she paid close attention to the news about Ireland and pestered her father with dozens of questions.

Bert did his best to explain. He told her about how the Catholic Church had come to Ireland in the early centuries of the Christian era, about the apostasy of the English who had rejected the Church, and about the resolve of the Irish to preserve the faith. He told her about centuries of warfare between Catholics and Protestants, about the bloody English victory in the Battle of Boyne and the loss of Irish freedom. He told her about the Protestants killing the Irish Catholics, the insurrections that had led to the secession from Britain and partition of the island, and the troubles that the Protestants had provoked that summer.

Jackie listened attentively, but his stories about Ireland sounded as horrible as the pictures on the evening news. One night, she had a nightmare in which she was on the battlefield of Boyne with her father, when there was a gunshot and he disappeared. A moment later, she was standing with him on a street in Belfast in front of the family store and their church when, suddenly, everything around her exploded in flames and disappeared. She awoke with an anguished cry that brought both Bert and Mary out of their room to be sure she was okay.

Bert sat on the side of her bed for several minutes, stroking her hair, until her breathing became steady and her eyelids began to close. Then he kissed her on the forehead and turned to leave. Jackie watched as he disappeared down the darkened hallway; then she reached for the pictures of her mother inside her pillowcase and, cradling them tightly in her arms, quickly fell asleep.

8

Jackie was not able to speak to Danny alone until Thursday. As they walked home from school together, she chattered aimlessly about the stories she had heard on the news, how her father had reacted to news regarding Ireland, and all the things her father had told her about being Irish.

"Even though my dad thinks that being Irish is important, I would rather go to the Moon than to Ireland," she concluded cheerfully.

Danny, as usual, let Jackie talk without interrupting. Her chatter helped clear his head and compose his thoughts.

"It's the same with my parents," Danny interjected, when Jackie paused for an instant. "Not about Ireland, I mean. My parents get upset when there's fighting in Israel. The fighting with Egypt and the bombings of Israel's embassies—they've been upset a lot lately. They are very involved in supporting Israel, planting trees, and things like that."

"I don't see how it's the same," Jackie challenged him. "My family is from Ireland. My father says we're, like, Irish. Your family isn't from Israel."

"We are, sort of. My name, Cohn—" He struggled for a way to explain. "My Sunday school teacher says that, in the Bible, the Kohen were the priests in the temple in Jerusalem, you know, after the exodus and all that stuff. The names *Kohen* and *Cohn*—" he emphasized the pronunciation of the words, "—are, like, the same word. So, my family did live in Israel, you know, in bible times."

"Wow! That was a long time ago," Jackie said incredulously.

"I know."

"Is that why your parents care about Israel, because of the Bible?" Jackie asked.

"I don't think so—we're not very religious. I don't know if my parents really believe in God or anything. Ruben doesn't believe in God, and I know I don't," he added quickly.

"Then why do they care?"

"I think they're scared."

"Scared of what?"

"They say they're scared of the Holocaust, scared it could happen again, scared it could happen here."

For an instant, Jackie thought about Anne Frank, the teenager whose diary she had read the summer before. "That could never happen here," she answered reflexively.

"My parents say it *could* happen here," Danny countered. "A man who lived through the Holocaust came to talk to my Sunday school class last year. He lived in Poland, and he said his parents didn't think anything could happen to them. Then, one day, the Nazis came to their house and took him and his family to a place called Babi Yar, then shot them. He told us how he saw everyone in his family—his mother, father, sister—shot right in front of him and pushed into a hole. Somehow he got away."

Jackie knew Anne Frank and her mother had died in the Holocaust, but she had never pictured how it might have happened. Suddenly, she felt goose bumps on her arms and struggled not to shiver.

"So, why do your parents plant trees in Israel?" She tried to change the subject, hoping to dispel the images of Babi Yar and Anne Frank from her mind.

"It's just something people do. When you have a birthday or a celebration or something, your relatives will plant a tree instead of giving you a gift. No one actually goes there and plants trees or anything. It's like—" he paused, struggling for words, "—like you're supposed to make the world a better place by planting a tree."

Danny knew there was much more to the idea of planting trees. He knew that Israel was a desert and that planting trees could help reclaim the land. His rabbi had taught him that planting trees was a way of staking a claim to a promised land and a way of helping God complete creation. Yet he felt completely incapable of expressing these ideas to Jackie.

"That's a nice idea," Jackie responded offhandedly, still struggling with images of the Holocaust.

"Do you worry about something like that happening here?" she asked cautiously.

"Like what?"

"Like what happened to the man who talked to your class."

"I have nightmares a lot." His voice wavered. He began speaking very softly, his eyes lowered to the ground. Jackie could hardly hear him. "I have this nightmare where I'm with my family, and I see them being shot."

"I have bad dreams too," Jackie answered quietly, and then stopped abruptly as Danny's nightmare materialized vividly in her mind. Only now, the scene looked less like Babi Yar and more like the streets of Hartford, Belfast, and the battle-field of Boyne. She saw her mother, father, and Danny lying among the victims.

"Sometimes I'm really scared," Danny continued, scuffing his feet nervously on the ground. "Sometimes it seems so real that I'm afraid it's actually happening."

Jackie had a sudden impulse to take Danny's hand, to put her arms around him, the way her father held her when she had a bad dream. She reached out until her hand brushed his elbow. His arm recoiled imperceptibly. His eyes turned up toward hers and made contact. They froze, staring intensely into each other's eyes.

Jackie withdrew her hand and dropped her eyes to the ground. A long, awkward silence replaced the easy confidence of their previous conversation.

"It's just a nightmare," Jackie offered, breaking the intense silence. "Just a bad dream."

"Yeah," he answered bleakly.

"It is," Jackie insisted, desperately wanting to comfort Danny but also wary of reawakening her own nightmares.

"We should head home," Danny said, to change the subject.

"Yeah, we should," Jackie agreed uncertainly.

Danny was still disconcerted by his Holocaust nightmare and his inability to explain his thoughts to Jackie. He was too young to understand the ideas of a people who believed God had chosen them to bring order to creation, or the impact of a two-thousand-year Diaspora, during which his ancestors had been subjected to murderous crusades, inquisitions, expulsions, and pogroms. He was, however, becoming aware that his parents and Sunday school teachers shared a characteristic way of thinking that combined idealism with an insidious fear of anti-Semitism. As he struggled to make sense of these ideas, it occurred to him that perhaps this was what Mrs. Leslie meant when she said she wanted to teach him how to think.

They resumed walking in silence, shuffling their shoes along the sidewalk, as if feeling their way over unsure ground. Gradually, their pace quickened, and the cadence of their steps became more certain.

"Do you want to come in?" Jackie asked, as she stopped at the bottom of the sidewalk that led to her front door.

"No, I better go home," Danny answered, without looking up from the ground. "I have things to do."

"Are you okay?"

"Yeah. I have to prepare my current events report."

"So do I," Jackie answered.

"It's your fault, you know!" he teased gently, looking up at her.

"What's my fault?"

"That we have to give reports tomorrow."

"Why is it my fault?"

"Because you can't learn to keep your hand down in class, and you always volunteer for everything without ever thinking. You know that Mrs. Leslie is going to kill you tomorrow, just to set an example for the rest of the class!" He continued making fun of her.

"It's *my* fault?" she repeated with exaggerated indignation.

"You know, someday I'm going to do you a favor and glue your hand to your desk and tape your mouth shut so you won't keep getting yourself into trouble all the time."

"And exactly how did raising *my* hand force *you* to do a report tomorrow?"

"I wasn't going to make you do your report all alone in front of Mrs. Leslie." His voice betrayed genuine concern.

"You're protecting me?" She pretended to be offended. "You think I'm scared of Mrs. Leslie?"

"No."

"You think I'll mess it up!"

"I know you'll do a good job," he said, offering an awkward apology.

"And you, Mr. I-Don't-Think-There-Should-Be-a-Dress-Code, Mr. What-Are-They-Going-to-Do-Call-the-Police, *you* are the one who really needs to have your mouth taped closed! Maybe I should do it right now!"

With an impetuous laugh, she lunged at Danny, pushing her hand across his mouth, knocking his books out from under his arms, and shoving him onto the grass. She sprawled on top of him, trying to pin his shoulders to the ground and cover his mouth at the same time. She succeeded in holding him to the ground for several seconds before he scrambled free, grabbed her arm, and twisted it behind her back.

"I got you now, Jackie Cone! You're never going to raise your hand in class again. Say it!" Danny taunted, holding her arm behind her back. "Say it! Say you'll never raise your hand in class again."

"No way! No way!" She giggled, struggling to get away.

"Say it!"

"Never!"

A second later, he released her arm. They fell happily onto the lawn side by side, their shoulders touching and their hands inches apart.

Danny looked over at Jackie. Her face was turned toward the Sun, her eyes were closed, and her mouth rested in a peaceful smile. Strands of her hair radiated across the grass and blew across his face and into his eyes. He made no effort to brush them away.

9

Jackie spent the evening sitting on her bed, preparing her report for the next day. The walls around her were decorated with posters of Paul McCartney, Ringo Starr, John Glenn, and Neil Armstrong. The ceiling was adorned with stars cut from sparkling silver wrapping paper, a Moon crafted from aluminum foil with mountains and craters in Magic Marker, and a mobile of the solar system made from white tennis balls colored with finger paint. A variety of stuffed animals, dolls, and model spacecraft were scattered across her bed and her small student desk. Among the colorful dresses and sweaters in the closet was a spacesuit she had made for Halloween the year before, constructed of aluminum foil, hangers, and duct tape.

Most nights, after Mary put her to sleep, Jackie would lie in bed staring at the Moon and stars on the ceiling and dreaming about space. Sometimes she would arrange pillows around her face and pretend she was an astronaut looking out through the windows of the *Apollo* spacecraft as it approached the Moon. She would imagine that she was the first girl to ride a *Saturn V* rocket into space and that her stuffed animals and dolls were friendly aliens she had met on distant planets while traveling with the crew of the *Starship Enterprise*.

Once, when she was sick with the flu and had a temperature of 104°F, she had experienced a feverish sense of soaring, weightless, vertiginous motion that made her believe that she was actually flying through space. She had felt the pressure on her head like the g-forces of a rocket at liftoff, and had felt the release as she entered the disembodied weightlessness of space. The Moon had appeared to move across the ceiling, and stars had sailed past her eyes, as if she were watching through the window of a spaceship moving at warp speed across the universe. The sensation had been thrilling. Jackie secretly hoped she would get sick again so she could relive the experience of flying through space.

Sometimes, she tried to re-create the feeling by breathing heavily with her head buried beneath her covers. On occasion, she would feel herself soaring dizzily among the stars on the ceiling and see her bed and Earth floating in the distance. Usually, it just helped her fall asleep.

On Christmas Eve in 1968, Jackie had shared the drama of humanity's first voyage to the Moon. The *Apollo 8* mission had launched from the Kennedy Space Center four days before Christmas and entered lunar orbit early on Christmas Eve. That night, there had been a live television broadcast from the Moon.

All that day, Jackie had been restless with anticipation of the broadcast and had been annoyed that her parents insisted on first going to an early Christmas Eve Mass. They promised that Mass would be over in time to see the broadcast from space.

There was always a lot of energy in the congregation attending Christmas Eve Mass, but that year there was an unusual sense of awe. Conversations rapidly turned from routine holiday greetings, to talk about the astronauts in orbit around the Moon. Jackie chattered breathlessly about the flight with anyone who paused to listen, until her parents reprimanded her and sent her to watch over her siblings.

When the service began, Jackie took a seat next to her father and, as she always did, passed the time playing with his hands and fingers, toying with his tie and cuff links, and exploring his pockets for trinkets and treasures. She was always fidgety in church, but that night she was more active than usual. Mary warned her repeatedly to sit still or she would send her straight to bed when they got home.

Father O'Brien began his homily by saying, "I want to talk with you about what is happening in heaven tonight." Jackie looked up expectantly. "Maybe he will talk about *Apollo*," she thought, crossing her fingers. "Maybe he wants to get home in time to see the broadcast, too. I hope he won't talk as long as last year!"

"As I was leaving home this evening," Father O'Brien continued gravely, "I heard something very disturbing. I heard a television commentator say that the astronauts were exploring heaven. The commentator was wrong." Father O'Brien paused and looked around the silent congregation. "No matter how far men fly into space, they will never explore heaven. Heaven can only be explored through faith in the heavenly Father; his son Jesus Christ, who was graciously given to us on this Christmas Day; and the Holy Spirit—the one God."

Father O'Brien returned to this theme throughout his homily. "It is not the men who are orbiting the Moon tonight who have found their place in heaven—it is those who are here in the circle of Christ. Heaven cannot be seen through telescopes—only through the teachings of His church. Heaven cannot be reached with rockets, propellants, and guidance systems—only through the grace of God."

Father O'Brien's focus on heaven caught Jackie's attention for a while. As a young child, when Jackie would ask her father why she did not have a mother, he would say that her mother had gone to heaven and was with Christ. That was what had first drawn her attention to the night skies, the stars, and the Moon. Lying in bed at night, she would often stare out her window toward heaven, wondering whether her mother was really there and whether a spaceship might someday bring her home.

Jackie often tried to imagine her mother in heaven. She pictured her face in the stained-glass windows over the dais at St Patrick's, sitting with Christ on a celestial throne, surrounded by the apostles and angels. She sometimes wondered whether the astronauts would see the same thing when they passed through heaven on their way to the Moon and whether they would see her mother.

As Jackie grew older, she came to understand that her mother had died, and concluded that she did not believe in heaven. If her mother were truly out there somewhere, she surely would have come back already.

Jackie also concluded she did not believe in God. Walter Cronkite had told her everything the astronauts would encounter on their voyage to the Moon. He had not mentioned that they would see Christ, the apostles, or angels.

As Father O'Brien's homily continued, Jackie's eyes closed, and she drifted through her own ethereal space. She circled the Moon in the *Apollo* command module, flew on the *Starship Enterprise* to explore distant planets and civilizations, and had conversations with the beings who built monoliths on the Moon and canals on Mars. She was far away when Father O'Brien approached the end of his homily, and the crescendo of his voice brought her back to Earth.

"Those who think they are wise men because they have found a stairway to the Moon and to the heavens, and those who think they have seen the birth of a new age on this day are not wise men. The men who followed a star to a manger in Bethlehem—the men who knew that the Lord our savior Jesus Christ had been born on that day—they were wise men. Those who think they are wise because men walk on the Moon, and those who think they can find truth about heaven through scientific experiment and measurement are not wise men. The wise men are those who walk with Christ, those who know they can find the truth in His words and in the teachings of His church on Earth."

Jackie didn't understand what he was talking about. She didn't care. She was afraid he would never stop talking and that she would miss the broadcast from the Moon.

Mass ended shortly after nine o'clock. She did her best to exit the church with decorum, pausing briefly at the door to touch Father O'Brien's hand, then leaping down the stairs and running home ahead of her family to turn on the television.

The broadcast from the Moon began at 9:35. Jackie and a half billion people around the world sat mesmerized by the grainy black and white images of the Moon's stark, cratered surface. "The vast loneliness is awe inspiring," Lovell said. "It makes you realize just what you have back there on Earth."

Jackie thought it was heavenly.

At 9:58, Anders spoke. "We are now approaching lunar sunrise, and for all the people on Earth, the crew of *Apollo 8* has a message we would like to send you." He began reading from Genesis: "'In the beginning, God created the heaven and the Earth. And the Earth was without form, and void; and darkness was upon the face of the deep. And the Spirit of God moved upon the face of the waters. And God said, Let there be light: and there was light. And God saw the light, that it was good: and God divided the light from the darkness.'"

Then Lovell said, "And God called the light Day, and the darkness he called Night. And the evening and the morning were the first day. And God said, Let there be a firmament in the midst of the waters, and let it divide the waters from the waters. And God made the firmament, and divided the waters which were under the firmament from the waters which were above the firmament: and it was so. And God called the firmament Heaven. And the evening and the morning were the second day.'"

Borman continued the reading: "'And God said, Let the waters under the heavens be gathered together unto one place, and let the dry land appear: and it was so. And God called the dry land Earth; and the gathering together of the waters called the Seas: and God saw that it was good.'"

Borman then brought the broadcast to an end: "And from the crew of *Apollo 8*, we close with good night, good luck, a Merry Christmas, and God bless all of you—all of you on the good Earth."

The voices from the Moon faded into static. The images reverted to pictures of Mission Control in Houston. Walter Cronkite resumed his commentary.

Jackie continued to stare at the screen in a blissful trance. The vision of the Moon, with Earth in the distance, burned into her eyes. She saw heaven, the awe-inspiring landscape of the Moon, the pinnacle from which God and men could both look down on Earth and see it was good. She heard voices from heaven, and they were the voices of men.

Later, after Mary had put Jackie to bed, Lovell relayed another message from heaven. "Please be informed," he reported, "that there is a Santa Claus." Jackie was already with him, flying around Earth in a spaceship drawn by reindeer.

10

Jackie was supremely prepared to give her current events report on Friday morning. Her father drove her to school so she could carry all the things she wanted to show the class: her models of the *Saturn V* and the *Apollo* spacecraft, a picture showing the astronauts' flight path, and an official patch of the mission.

Mrs. Leslie came in promptly at nine o'clock and took the class methodically through the morning exercises. Jackie found it hard to pay attention to the announcements, the pledge of allegiance, and attendance.

As Mrs. Leslie began to collect the assigned homework, Jackie raised her hand. "Mrs. Leslie, I don't have my homework."

"How come?"

"I was, you know, working on my report."

"Well," Mrs. Leslie replied, making a note in her book, "I'll let you turn in your homework Monday, but if it is not turned in first thing Monday morning, I'll give you a zero."

"Yes, Mrs. Leslie," Jackie answered without concern.

After she collected all the homework, Mrs. Leslie stood behind her desk. "Two people volunteered to give current events presentations today. Miss Cone and Mr. Cohn, which one of you would like to go first?"

Jackie turned and gave Danny a desperate look while silently mouthing, "Please?" She couldn't wait any longer. She had to go first! Danny smiled.

"I can wait," he said.

Jackie turned back to face Mrs. Leslie. "I'll go first."

"Thank you. Since this is our first current events presentation of the year, let me remind you of the assignment. You should talk for ten minutes about your subject. Then, I would like the class to have a chance to ask questions. I will give you a grade for your presentation, and I will also be grading class participation. I want everyone in the class to be respectful, pay attention, and contribute to the discussion. Are there any questions?"

There were none. "Good. Miss Cone, you can proceed. What are you going to talk about today?"

"Well, it isn't really, like, a current event. I mean, it didn't happen this week. I am going to talk about the landing on the Moon."

"Very good. You may begin whenever you are ready."

Jackie stood up and moved her props to the front of the class where everyone could see them. Mrs. Leslie sat down at Jackie's desk to listen.

That summer, Jackie had followed every step of the *Apollo 11* mission to the Moon. She had listened to Walter Cronkite detail the plans for the mission, followed each phase of their journey, and watched every moment of their historic walk on the Moon. It had been thrilling. Now she had a chance to share her excitement with her friends.

Jackie began by showing the class her models of the *Saturn V* and the *Apollo* spacecraft, demonstrating how the three stages of the rocket separated during launch and how the lunar module, which landed on the Moon, separated from the service and command modules. She told the class that the lunar module was named the *Eagle* and the command module was named *Columbia*.

Jackie described the launch of *Apollo 11* from Cape Kennedy, how the spacecraft had orbited Earth before heading to the Moon and entering lunar orbit, and how Astronauts Armstrong and Aldrin had descended to the Sea of Tranquility in the *Eagle,* leaving Astronaut Collins behind in the *Columbia*.

"The really scary part," Jackie explained with excitement in her voice, "is that there were rocks on the ground where they were supposed to land. They would have, you know, crashed if they had landed there—so the astronauts had to fly the space ship to a different place where there were no rocks, and they barely had enough fuel to get there and almost crashed. Anyway, they did land safely and, when they did, they named the landing site Tranquility Base."

Jackie then described the Moon walk, during which Armstrong had climbed out of the *Eagle* and onto the Moon's surface for the first time.

"Everybody thinks Armstrong said, 'That's one small step for man, one giant leap for mankind.'" she told the class, "but he really said, 'That's one small step for *a* man, one giant leap for mankind.' There are going to be girl astronauts, too, you know! I'm going to go to the Moon someday!" Jackie interjected spiritedly.

She continued describing about how the astronauts had worked on the Moon's surface, raising an American flag, unveiling a plaque with a picture of Earth and the phrase "We came in peace for all mankind," doing scientific experiments, and collecting Moon rocks to bring back to Earth. Jackie was splendid.

With the confident cadence of her voice, her carefree gestures, and her casual flipping of her hair to keep it out of her face, Jackie commanded the classroom like a virtuoso. She loved to be the center of attention and she loved to talk, especially about space.

More than twenty minutes passed before she told the class how the astronauts had returned to Earth, splashed down into the Pacific Ocean, and entered a quarantine chamber to protect the Earth against contaminants they might have acquired on the Moon. Without pausing to catch her breath, she started talking about the experiments that would be performed on the Moon rocks.

Mrs. Leslie looked at her watch and interrupted her gently. "Miss Cone, thank you for an excellent presentation. I think we should let the class ask questions now."

"Yes, Mrs. Leslie." Jackie glanced at the clock on the wall and realized for the first time how long she had talked. "I think I talked too long. I'm sorry. Does anyone have any questions?"

One person asked how the astronauts talked to each other on the Moon, since they were wearing space suits and helmets over their ears. Another asked whether there was life on the Moon, even though the astronauts had not seen any plants or animals at the landing site. A third asked why it looked like the American flag was flying in the wind if there was no air. Jackie had no trouble answering these questions.

A girl in the class said, "You know a lot about the Moon. In the song 'Aquarius,' I was wondering if you know what it means when they say, 'When the Moon is in the seventh house'?"

Jackie was stumped.

Danny came to her rescue. "That's astrology, not astronomy. Some people believe that the planets and stars and Moon determine what happens to people. Astrology isn't science. It's nonsense."

Jackie looked gratefully at Danny.

Another student spoke up. "It is not nonsense. The seventh house is the part of the sky that makes people come together and cooperate to, you know, make the world a better place. When the planets come together in the seventh house, all the people of Earth will come together, too—just like at Wood-stock—and there will be peace. It's not nonsense."

"That's stupid!" Danny retorted.

"It's not stupid. I read my horoscope every day, and it's usually right!"

"Then you're stupid!" Danny muttered under his breath.

"Mr. Cohn," Mrs. Leslie stepped in, "that is not proper language for a classroom."

"But everyone knows astrology in nonsense," Danny persisted. "It *is* stupid."

"Mr. Cohn, you may not believe in astrology, but you will speak respectfully to others in the classroom. It is never appropriate to call people names," Mrs. Leslie concluded with emphasis.

"I'm sorry," Danny said sheepishly, wishing he had found a much more insulting word to express his disdain.

"Now, does anyone else have any other questions for Miss Cone?" Mrs. Leslie looked around the room and then turned to Jackie. "I have a question. Do you know why President Kennedy decided that America should send astronauts to the Moon?"

The question startled Jackie, and she fumbled for an answer. "Well, President Kennedy gave a speech, and he said that we should go to the Moon and—"

"That's not what I asked," Mrs. Leslie corrected. "Do you know *why* President Kennedy thought it was important for America to send men to the Moon? What was the idea behind sending men there?"

"Do you mean, why did we want to go to the Moon?" Jackie repeated, trying to think of an answer.

"Yes, why?"

"Maybe because no one had ever been there before, because we wanted to explore space," she answered uncertainly.

"So, the reason for going to the Moon was to explore?"

"Yes."

"Is that the only reason?"

"Well, we need to have a colony on the Moon so the rockets can stop there for supplies on the way to Mars—you know, because there is less gravity on the Moon—" Jackie answered, gathering momentum.

"Thank you. Can anyone else think of other reasons for going to the Moon?"

"To win the space race," another student offered.

"Oh yeah." Jackie jumped back into the conversation. This was her report, and she wanted to stay in front. "I forgot to say there was a race to see who could reach the Moon first. America won!"

"Why was it important to win the race to the Moon?" Mrs. Leslie asked, turning toward the class.

"Because Russia is our enemy," answered one student.

"Because communists want to take over the universe," said another.

"So that the Moon belongs to America and we can, like, start colonies."

Danny raised his hand. "We wanted to show the world that America is better than communism. We want people around the world to believe that our way is better."

"Very good," Mrs. Leslie responded. "How many of you have heard of *Sputnik*?"

"I have," Jackie said, trying to reassert her position in the discussion. "*Sputnik* was the first satellite. It was Russian."

"That's right. And does anyone know why it was important?"

"It happened the day I was born!" Jackie quipped, with childish pride at having been born on a significant day.

"It was the beginning of the space age," someone answered.

"It let the Russians spy on us."

"It was because the Russians did it first," Danny answered. "They were the first to send a satellite into space. It made people think that Russia was better, that communism was better, that they had better rockets, that their people were smarter. We want people to believe that America is better. That's why going to the Moon first is important."

"That's a very good answer. Thank you," Mrs. Leslie said, returning to the front of the room. "I want to thank Miss Cone for her report and everyone in the class for their participation. You can sit down now."

Mrs. Leslie waited while Jackie stashed her props in the corner and returned to her desk. "One of the reasons we are spending time on current events is to learn how to think carefully about events. Where did the idea of going to the Moon come from? Why was this idea so important?" she asked rhetorically.

Jackie was suddenly worried. Was Mrs. Leslie saying she had not thought carefully about the landing on the Moon?

"Miss Cone, I have another assignment for you. If I give you a copy of President Kennedy's speech in which he proposed that America send a man to the Moon, could you read it—"

"I've heard it," Jackie interrupted, defensively, uncertain where Mrs. Leslie was heading.

"—and give us a report next week about why he wanted to send men to the Moon? What the idea was?"

"Yes, Mrs. Leslie." Tears began welling up in her eyes. Mrs. Leslie thought she had done a bad report. She had to do it over and was crestfallen.

"Would Monday be okay?"

"Yes, Mrs. Leslie," Jackie mumbled, looking down at her desk so no one would see she was starting to cry.

"Good." Mrs. Leslie looked at the clock. "It's late. We have spent much more time on current events this morning than I had planned. Mr. Cohn, would you mind if we waited to hear your presentation on Monday?"

"That's fine," Danny said, relieved.

"Good, and please try to keep your presentation to ten minutes."

"Yes, Mrs. Leslie."

Mrs. Leslie looked at the clock again. "Let's take a short break—then we will begin math. Please come back promptly in five minutes. Class dismissed."

All the students, except Jackie, jumped out of their seats and headed for the hallway. Mrs. Leslie left the room and went to the teacher's lounge.

Jackie stayed in her seat, afraid that if she had to talk to anyone, she might cry. Mrs. Leslie didn't think she had thought carefully. She had talked too long. Mrs. Leslie was making her do it over on Monday.

"Nice job, Jackie!" Karen said, as she walked past her toward the hallway.

"Cool stuff!" a boy said on his way out.

"Yeah, really neat!"

"You're some space cadet!" another student teased.

Danny came up to her. "Are you okay?"

"Yes," Jackie lied.

"You look like you're going to cry."

"Mrs. Leslie hated my report. She's really mean, just like everyone said."

"That was a great report, Jackie."

"She hated it."

"She didn't hate it."

"I talked too long. She said I have to do it over!"

"That's not what she said."

"She's going to give me an F!"

"Come on, Jackie. She's not going to give you an F. You know that! You gave a great report. No one knows more about space than you do." Danny tried to cheer her up. "Anyway, you were the first one—you had no way of knowing what she wanted. If you're worried about your grade, you should talk to her."

"What should I talk to her about?"

"Ask Mrs. Leslie what grade she gave you on your report. That's what I would do."

Jackie was scared, but underneath her disappointment, she recognized that Danny was probably right. She knew a lot about space, and she *had* done a good report.

"Why don't we talk to her at recess?" Danny suggested.

"We?"

"I'll go with you. I have to give my report on Monday. I don't want to get a failing grade too!" he teased.

"Danny! Stop it!"

"Look, Jackie, you didn't fail. I promise. Let's talk to her." Jackie didn't answer. "Okay?" He shoved her on the shoulder.

"Okay," she agreed without conviction.

At that moment, several students came back into the classroom. Danny felt self-conscious standing next to Jackie and retreated to his desk.

Jackie tried to pay attention to the morning lessons, but instead spent the time covering pieces of paper with pencil drawings of stars and planets. She was proud of how much she knew about the space program and had worked hard getting ready for her report. She thought she had done a good job, but Mrs. Leslie wanted her to do it over.

Tears began to overflow her eyes, and she wiped them quickly on her shirtsleeve. Danny was right; she needed to talk to Mrs. Leslie.

At lunch, Jackie sat with her girlfriends but had trouble engaging in their banter. When the bell rang for recess, she started leading her friends out to the playground, as she always did, but Danny was waiting for her in the hall. When she stopped to talk to him, her friends continued without her.

"Let's go talk to Mrs. Leslie," he said.

"I don't want to."

"Come on." He pushed her toward Mrs. Leslie's room with his hand at the small of her back. Jackie halfheartedly followed his direction.

11

Mrs. Leslie was sitting at her desk eating her lunch when Jackie and Danny came to the doorway. She looked up, surprised.

"Aren't you two supposed to be at recess?"

"Yes, ma'am," Danny answered. He looked quickly at Jackie. He had assumed she would do the talking, but she didn't look like she was prepared to say anything. "Jackie wanted to talk with you about something," he said.

Jackie shot Danny an angry look.

Mrs. Leslie noticed Jackie's discomfort and put down her lunch. "Come in. What is it?"

Jackie hesitated. Mrs. Leslie was very scary.

"Go ahead, Jackie," Danny urged gently.

"I wanted to know—" she began hesitantly. "I wanted to know my grade. I mean, I wanted to know what grade I got on my report." Jackie was trembling and could barely speak audibly. She wanted to run away.

"You got an A, of course," Mrs. Leslie answered, surprised. "You gave an excellent report."

Jackie was stunned. Danny broke into a broad smile. "I knew it!" he whispered.

"I got an A? I thought you didn't like it. I talked too long. You said I had to do it over."

"I asked if you would continue your report on Monday," Mrs. Leslie corrected gently. "You gave a fine report. You clearly know a lot about the space program. I asked if you would do more on Monday because I thought the class might want to hear more about the idea behind the space program. I thought you might want to—" She paused, still unsure why Jackie and Danny had come to see her. "If you don't want to do the additional report Monday, you don't have to," she concluded.

"No. I'll do the report," Jackie said quickly.

"Good. I look forward to hearing more from you on Monday. Mr. Cohn, did you have a question also?"

"No," he started, but immediately felt awkward. "I mean, yes. I wanted to ask what I should talk about on Monday, you know, when I give my report."

"You can talk about anything you want. What would you have talked about this morning, if I had called on you?" Mrs. Leslie was perplexed.

"I was going to talk about Woodstock, but I could talk about something else—like civil rights, if that would be better."

"Either topic would be fine."

Mrs. Leslie sized up the two students fidgeting in front of her. Danny and Jackie were affectionately referred to as the "terrible twins" among the teachers, recalling their now-infamous twin scam of the year before. Jackie was a favorite student because of her outgoing nature and enthusiastic class participation. Teachers were more ambivalent about Danny, who consistently had outstanding grades but could be challenging in the classroom. Together, they were notorious for ganging up on teachers or other students in spirited arguments. More than one teacher commented that Spring High School would have a great debate team when those two were older. She surmised that Danny and Jackie had not skipped recess simply to ask about Jackie's grade and for assurance that Danny had chosen an acceptable presentation topic.

"Would you two like to talk more about what I expect from your presentations?" Mrs. Leslie asked.

"Yes, ma'am," Danny replied for both of them.

"Sit down." She gestured to several chairs at a small round table and took a chair across from them. "I want you to learn to think carefully about current events—why they happen, what they mean, why it matters."

Jackie began squirming uncomfortably in her seat, more uncertain than ever about what Mrs. Leslie was trying to say. She looked over at Danny, whose eyes were focused intently on her face, carefully studying her words.

Mrs. Leslie sensed Jackie's confusion and turned to her. "Your report on the lunar landing was excellent, but there is much more to the Moon landing, isn't there?"

"I guess so," Jackie murmured without conviction.

"There are many interesting questions you can ask about the lunar landing. For example, is there any similarity between our country sending astronauts to explore the Moon and Lewis and Clark being sent to explore the American West? Do we really think people will live on the Moon?"

"Of course people will live on the Moon," Jackie interjected, anxious to answer every question as soon as it was asked. Mrs. Leslie raised her hand to Jackie, signaling that she wasn't finished.

"Would we have sent men to the Moon if the Soviets had not launched *Sputnik* or if there was no space race?"

"Sure." Jackie tried unsuccessfully to interrupt again.

"Did landing on the Moon really convince people that capitalism is better than communism or that the United States is better than the Soviet Union? Does it change the way we think about America, about people, about the Earth, about the future?"

"It *does* change the way we think about things," Jackie interrupted emphatically, unable to restrain herself any longer.

"How so?" Mrs. Leslie asked.

Now Jackie fumbled for words, her eagerness to answer Mrs. Leslie's questions having run ahead of her thoughts. "It shows that people can live on the Moon, that we can build rockets and spacecraft and spacesuits to, like, go to Mars, that we can—"

Danny recognized that Jackie had missed the point and stepped in to help her. "What Jackie is trying to say is, if men can walk on the Moon, it makes us think we can do almost anything."

"Many people have that idea about the space program," Mrs. Leslie agreed with him.

Jackie did not want to cede the conversation to Danny and quickly blurted out the first idea that came to mind. "When the astronauts fly around the Moon, they see Earth the same way God sees it—you know, from heaven."

Mrs. Leslie was startled at this unexpected comment coming from an eleven-year-old. However, she had also watched the Christmas Eve broadcast from the Moon and knew where Jackie's idea had originated.

"Does it give us the idea that we are a little bit like God?" she asked cautiously.

Jackie's initial impulse was to say "yes," but she recoiled in panic without saying anything. Father O'Brien would be angry! "N-n-no," she stammered. "That's not what I meant. I'm sorry," she apologized quickly, lowering her eyes and hoping Mrs. Leslie would drop the subject.

But Jackie had meant exactly what she said. The pictures the astronauts had broadcast from space were very much on her mind as she sat in church on Sunday mornings. Sometimes, she would imagine that the Holy Trinity pictured in the stained-glass windows over the altar were three *Apollo* astronauts looking down on Earth, that the white spheres around their heads were space helmets and the ethereal stars and colors around them were suns and galaxies in space. Sometimes, she amused herself by pretending the window was the giant display on the wall of Mission Control and that the celebrants on the dais and the congregation in the pews were Mission Control officers communicating with the messengers in space.

Mrs. Leslie sensed Jackie's angst. "That's okay. You didn't say anything wrong," she said in a calming voice. "In fact, you may have discovered something important—that events have shaped your ideas—ideas about what people can do on Earth, perhaps even your ideas about God."

"But Father O'Brien," Jackie started defensively, still worried about heresy. "Father O'Brien says—" She stopped, uncomfortable with continuing her thought.

Mrs. Leslie interrupted before Jackie could go any further. "I don't want to disagree with anything Father O'Brien teaches you."

Jackie still looked distressed. Mrs. Leslie turned quickly to Danny to change the subject. "Mr. Cohn, you said you might report on Woodstock. You should ask yourself the same kinds of questions. What were the ideas that led to Woodstock? What ideas came out of Woodstock? Do you think these ideas are right?"

Danny looked at her with interest. These were exactly the questions he had struggled with ever since Ruben had returned from the festival. He had no idea what the answers might be.

"But how do we know if an idea is right?" Jackie interrupted, asking the question that was on Danny's mind as well. "How do we know if—" She paused, wanting to ask whether Father O'Brien's idea of heaven was right or whether her own ideas were right, but not daring or knowing how to put such questions into words.

"—if there are different ideas about something, how do we know which one is right?" Danny finished her sentence.

Danny and Jackie were too young to understand that their youthful diffidence had led them to ask one of the fundamental questions of philosophy: How do you know if an idea is true? Not until college would Jackie and Danny realize that the nature of truth had been the subject of conjecture and controversy for centuries. Only then would they be introduced to the great philosophers who sought truth in revelation or reason, logos or logic, intuition or inference, as well as those who questioned the very concept of truth itself.

"How do you know if an idea is right? How do you know if something is true?" Mrs. Leslie repeated Danny's question. She looked across the small table into the eyes of two preteens who were staring at her, hoping she would give them a simple answer.

Every year, Mrs. Leslie faced a new class of children who were on the verge of adolescence and were beginning the struggle to find their own truths, their own dogma, their own doctrine, and their own direction. Every year she had to tell them she did not have the answers they were looking for.

Mrs. Leslie was part of the "over thirty" generation that the youth culture of the 1960s mocked. Her generation had grown up with different fears, and found direction in different ideas.

She had been eleven years old and in sixth grade in the fall of 1941 when the Japanese attacked Pearl Harbor. She had lived through rationing and blackouts, the tangible fear that family or friends would be killed in Europe or the Pacific, and the anxiety that the Axis could actually win the war.

Great leaders like Roosevelt and Churchill had used their formidable rhetorical skills to convince people there was only one path forward from fear. Her generation had been indoctrinated with their ideas and ideals; the importance of unity, structure, and order, unambiguous definitions of right and wrong, the inevitable triumph of good over evil, and the imperative of personal sacrifice. When Mrs. Leslie graduated from college in 1952 and began teaching, these were the lessons that she was prepared to teach her classes.

Teaching changed radically after *Sputnik*, however. Standardized, structured curricula gave way to educational philosophies that emphasized personal expression and exploration. Self-discovery supplanted discipline. Individualism superseded community. A generation of baby boomers moved through school empowered by an emphasis on intellectual freedom, but also imperiled by the elimination of the instruction, institutions, and ideas that had provided their parents with a well-formed worldview.

Many teachers continued teaching the same ideas they had learned growing up, and found themselves angrily rejected by the rising generation. Others indiscriminately discarded the received view, leaving students to fend for themselves and, in the process, losing their respect.

Mrs. Leslie knew there were no simple answers to the questions that adolescents asked. All she could do was try teaching her students how to think for themselves and help them find their own answers.

"One way to think about an idea," Mrs. Leslie began, "is to ask yourself whether the idea makes sense in different situations. For example, Mr. Cohn, you were quite rude this morning when someone asked a question about astrology."

"Astrology is nonsense," Danny answered defensively.

"Why do you think it's nonsense? Have you ever checked your horoscope?"

"I read my horoscope sometimes," Jackie confessed sheepishly.

"And does it ever tell you what is going to happen to you that day?" Mrs. Leslie asked.

"Sometimes it's right. Usually it's silly."

Danny spoke up again. "It has to be nonsense. Just because two people are born the same day—just because the stars and the planets are the same, doesn't mean that everyone born that day has the same experiences all their lives. It doesn't make sense."

"Good. So, even if a horoscope might be right once in a while, you think astrology is nonsense because it can't be generally true. Is that what you're saying?"

Danny nodded.

"Good. Miss Cone, we talked earlier about how going to the Moon made people think that it would be possible to solve problems on Earth. Do you think that's true?"

"Sure," Jackie answered, sounding surprised that someone would even ask the question.

"Can you give me some examples?"

"Well, like, the computers that were used to figure out how to reach the Moon could be used to figure out solutions to problems on Earth. Also, if there is not enough water, like in a desert, the ways the astronauts save water could help. If there is not enough food, you might be able to grow food the same way the astronauts will grow crops on the Moon when there is a Moon colony. There are lots of things—"

"So you think this idea generally makes sense?"

Jackie could think of a hundred more examples and started to describe them. "Sure. It could also—"

Mrs. Leslie cut her off. "And, Mr. Cohn, you said you might consider doing a current events report on civil rights. Does it make sense that everyone should have civil rights?"

"Yes," he answered.

"How about people who live in different countries, people from different cultures, people who don't have any education?"

"Everyone has the same rights," Danny insisted forcefully.

"So, one way to think about whether an idea is right is to ask whether the idea makes sense in different kinds of situations."

"I don't understand." Jackie was still struggling to see Mrs. Leslie's concept.

"Use your imagination. Try to apply the idea to every situation you can think of—real situations, imaginary situations, and impossible situations. Think about all the ways an idea can be applied, then ask whether the idea still makes sense. If it does, then it is probably a good idea. If not, it probably isn't."

"What she means, Jackie," Danny started to explain a bit condescendingly, "is that, since someone could be born on a spaceship or in another galaxy and wouldn't be born under the same stars or have a horoscope, horoscopes can't be that important. That's something you should understand!"

"So, what about the Martians who live on Mars?" Jackie immediately challenged him. "You probably think they should be treated like people, too? Do you think they have civil rights?"

Danny started thinking about an answer before realizing she was laughing at him.

"Good examples, actually," Mrs. Leslie interrupted. "I think you both understand."

"But what if the idea doesn't always make sense?" Jackie asked cautiously.

"No idea is going to make sense *all* the time. Even good ideas sometimes just don't fit—that's okay. Look for the best idea—ideas that work the most."

"You're going to be exposed to many different ideas as you grow up," Mrs. Leslie continued. "and many people will try to convince you that their ideas are right. Your friends will tell you their ideas and will want you to agree with them. Your parents will want you to accept their ideas. Your priest or your rabbi will teach you ideas about God and religion. Every book you read, every movie you see, every song or piece of art expresses the ideas of the artist. Commercials and advertisements try to make you believe something you might not normally accept. Some ideas will come with rewards like money, prizes, or honors. Some ideas will come with risks. There may be ideas that you really want to be true, even if you have doubts."

"Over time, you will find that there are a small number of ideas that make sense to you, ideas that come up repeatedly, ideas you find are useful. As you grow up, one or two ideas may become particularly important, that you find you believe in and can rely on. These ideas will define who you are, what you believe, how you think."

Mrs. Leslie stopped as other students began drifting into the room from recess. "I need to get ready for our classes this afternoon. Are you both okay?"

They nodded.

"Miss Cone, are you okay with continuing your report on Monday?"

"Yes, ma'am," Jackie answered, more certain about what Mrs. Leslie was asking, but no more certain that she knew the answer she was looking for.

"And, Mr. Cohn, you will also give your report on Monday?"

Danny nodded.

* * *

Monday morning, Jackie finished her report on the lunar landing. She read parts of the speech President Kennedy had given before Congress in May 1960, in which he proposed the goal of sending men to the Moon. She described how the lunar program was intended to demonstrate the superiority of freedom to the world. Her report was short and delivered largely without enthusiasm. She hated the idea that the flight to the Moon might have been simply a victory in a battle against communism.

Danny did not report on Woodstock; he did not know how to answer the questions that Mrs. Leslie might ask. Instead, he described the arrest of several members of the Ku Klux Klan, who had plotted to kill Charles Evers, a civil rights leader and the mayor of Fayette, Mississippi. Charles Evers was the younger brother of Medgar Evers, a civil rights activist, who was murdered in 1963. Danny described how Charles Evers had taken up his brother's work and that his motto was "Have no fear." This motto had helped him become the first black person in almost a century to be elected mayor of a racially mixed town in the South.

Danny briefly described how blacks had been subject to discrimination by laws that denied them the right to vote and enforced the segregation of buses, schools, and lunch counters. He described lynchings, firebombings, and killings of civil rights activists that went unpunished. He compared these experiences to those of the Jews in Russia, the Ibo in Nigeria, blacks in South Africa, and Buddhists in Tibet. He talked about how nonviolent protests had brought changes to the South and how similar protests could work in other places as well.

His report was concise and complete, and his manner was impassioned and intense. He wished he had been old enough to have marched with Medgar Evers and Martin Luther King, Jr.

That afternoon there was an air-raid drill. Civil defense sirens around the town sounded a wailing tone. Jackie and her classmates practiced how to duck and cover.

* * *

Mrs. Leslie wanted to teach her students how to think. With Jackie and Danny, she had succeeded. As the school year progressed, neither of them could sit through class or listen to current event presentations without searching for the underlying ideas and testing whether those ideas made sense in all sorts of possible and impossible situations. Over time, other students in the class learned Mrs. Leslie's lesson. As they did, the class discussions became more vigorous, the questions more pointed, and the answers better prepared. Those who came to understand Mrs. Leslie no longer found her threatening. Those who did not perpetuated the legend that Mrs. Leslie was a difficult and confusing teacher.

12

By October, the school year had slipped into a routine. Danny, as usual, had the highest grades in the class. Jackie became increasingly distracted by her extracurricular interests, rarely turned in any homework, and barely maintained a B average.

Throughout the fall, the stories on the evening news became more and more troubling. In Vietnam, the Vietcong launched major new offensives targeting American troops. President Nixon declared that he would not be the first president to preside over an American defeat and began to escalate the war with more troops and bombings. The seemingly endless peace talks in Paris floundered, causing the frustrated American ambassador to resign in protest. There were reports of American soldiers committing atrocities against Vietnamese civilians in the hamlet of My Lai, and criminal charges were brought against the soldiers who were responsible for the killing. There was also growing concern about thousands of American soldiers who were missing in action. Many were held in North Vietnamese prisons under brutal and inhumane conditions; many more were unaccounted for, and the communist government refused to confirm whether they were dead or alive. Wives of the missing soldiers made high-profile, heartrending trips to Paris and Vietnam, begging officials for information about whether their husbands were alive, or whether they were widows.

In Jerusalem, a Christian religious fanatic attempted to set fire to the Al Aksa Mosque, hoping to instigate the war of Armageddon. Lebanon became a battleground between the Christian government and Palestinian refugees. In Northern Ireland, battles between Protestants and Catholics escalated to the point that the British considered asking for NATO troops to help in the fighting. In Nigeria, a brutal civil war raged over the secession of the Ibo province of Biafra.

Wars also seemed to be breaking out on the streets of America. Bombs exploded in the skyscraper headquarters of General Motors, Chase Manhattan Bank, and RCA in Manhattan. Several government buildings and university research buildings were bombed. There were gun battles between the police and members of the Black Panthers in Chicago and San Francisco.

It was hard to find any voices of reason. Jackie's friends were playing Beatles records backward, searching for subliminal messages that might tell them whether Paul McCartney was really dead. Then, the Fabulous Four announced they could not get along with one another and, at the height of their fame and influence, announced they were disbanding forever.

Even the hopeful signs were ambiguous. The United States and Soviet Union signed a treaty banning nuclear weapons from the sea floor and agreed to negotiate limits on nuclear arms. The treaties did not, however, reduce nuclear weapons; they only slowed the growth of arsenals that could already destroy Jackie's world many times over.

The United States and the Soviet Union also agreed to negotiate a treaty that would ban missile defenses. Jackie did not understand what was wrong with trying to shoot down missiles before they could kill her. It made more sense than trying to survive a nuclear attack by duck and cover.

Many of Jackie's classmates gave current events reports on the Moratorium movement, which had begun to galvanize public opposition to the Vietnam War. They described the massive demonstrations that had taken place across the country in October and plans for an even larger Moratorium in Washington in November.

One student reported on a speech by Senator Gaylord Nelson, in which he proposed an annual Earth Day to raise public awareness about the deteriorating state of the environment. Earth Day would be a day of grass-roots demonstrations and teach-ins, modeled after the methods of the civil rights and antiwar movements, to protest environmental degradation and push for public action remediation. The first Earth Day would take place in April.

Another student reported that the Mets had won the World Series. Maybe anything was possible after all!

Karen did her first current events report on three American scientists who won the Nobel Prize in Medicine for their work on the genetics of viruses.

Karen had no interest in science, but her father was a physician who wanted his daughter to follow in his footsteps, and he pressured her into reporting on a subject related to medicine.

Karen and Jackie were friends, but they were very different. Puberty had begun early for Karen. At age eleven, she already had a developed figure and was well into her adolescent growth spurt. Her size and physical maturity were complemented by the precocious social sophistication that came from being an only child and spending most of her time talking to adults. Jackie, in contrast, was very slight and would not achieve similar levels of physical or social maturity until high school.

Karen was also very close to her mother, who taught her how to cook, sew, dress, wear makeup, and maintain the home. While her father told people that Karen would go to medical school, Karen told people she wanted to get married and be a homemaker like her mother.

Jackie was thankful that Mary never tried teaching her how to be a home-maker. Jackie wanted to be an astronaut and go into space.

What Karen and Jackie shared was a love of dancing. At the first signs of puberty, Karen's mother decided it was important for her daughter to know how to dance and enrolled her in a ballroom dancing class. Mary was happy to find an outlet for Jackie's abundant energy and enrolled her in the class as well.

While Jackie found the protocol of ballroom dancing and the presence of boys to be barely tolerable, she liked the movement, the motion, and the music. After taking ballroom dancing for several semesters, Karen and Jackie found that they preferred jazz, and they continued taking dance classes together for years.

The two girls danced, played, and went to movies and parties together. Jackie did not talk to Karen about serious things the way she talked to Danny. Instead, they gossiped about friends, personal things, girl things, and things their mothers were too embarrassed to discuss with them.

Karen hated her father's insistence that she show interest in medicine, and it led to a seemingly endless series of conflicts. When her father demanded that she sit down with him so he could help her prepare a report on the Nobel Prize–winning experiments, she purposely invited Jackie over to play at the time her father chose, hoping that Jackie's presence would dissuade her father from insisting that he help her with the report.

Instead, Dr. Altman suggested that Jackie join them. He brought out several of his medical books and began teaching the girls about the prize-winning research. He had them trace diagrams from his books showing that when a virus infected a cell, it caused the infected to cell to produce thousands of new viruses that would circulate around the body and infect other cells. He described the Nobel Prize–winning experiments on DNA. He described how scientists had been able to purify the DNA found within a virus, and then inject this DNA into a cell with a needle. When they did, the cell began to make a new virus, just as if it had been infected normally. He explained how the experiment proved everything necessary to make a virus was contained in its DNA.

Karen was petulant and angry about capitulating to her father's demands and did her best to be disruptive. Jackie was always curious about how things worked and found the lesson interesting. While she did not understand much of what Dr. Altman said, she reasoned that a virus was like a rocket that could carry people to Mars, and DNA was like the plans for building more rockets that would take them to planets that were even more distant.

Dr. Altman worked with Karen and Jackie for almost an hour. Jackie and Karen then made visual aids for the report, practiced the presentation, and conspired to have Jackie ask a question that Karen would know how to answer.

Karen delivered her presentation the next morning without enthusiasm. When she finished, Mrs. Leslie was not surprised that Jackie's hand was the first one raised with a question.

"Yes, Miss Cone, your question."

"Karen, really good report!" Jackie began earnestly, barely concealing a conspiratorial smile. "Can you tell me why these scientists won the Nobel Prize in medicine, rather than in some other field like chemistry?"

"These discoveries could help doctors learn how to treat infections, like colds or the flu, that are caused by viruses," Karen recited her prepared answer.

Mrs. Leslie recognized that Jackie's question had been planted, so she pursued it further. "So, Miss Altman, do you think that knowing about DNA teaches us anything about people?"

Karen was stumped but had to say something. "Well, you know, genes are made of DNA, and people think that our genes are involved in lots of different things. I guess knowing more about DNA could, like, help us understand lots of things better."

"Do you know what these things might be?" Mrs. Leslie ignored her evident discomfiture at the question.

"No, ma'am," Karen answered, looking down at the floor.

"Does anyone have any idea how knowing more about DNA can teach us about ourselves?"

There was no answer.

Jackie had no way of knowing that the experiments Karen described that morning would someday have a profound impact on her life. Over the next decades, scientists would learn how to manipulate DNA in the laboratory and how to engineer entirely novel DNA molecules. They would realize that the human genome carried all the information necessary for human development and reproduction and that it had a major role in determining health and disease. These discoveries would lead to a new science called "genomics" and a Human Genome Project to determine the complete sequence of human DNA, a project that would be comparable in size, scope, and significance to the space program that landed men on the Moon.

Jackie gave her second current events report at the end of October. She talked about the launch of three Soyuz spacecraft designed to dock together and form a permanent space station in Earth's orbit. It was the first step in an ambitious plan to build a "stairway to the stars" with space platforms that would reach the Moon and beyond. However, when the docking mechanisms failed, the spacecraft and cosmonauts returned to Earth without accomplishing their goals.

Jackie also told the class about the world tour of the *Apollo 11* astronauts, who were being acclaimed in parades and celebrations around the world for their giant leap onto the surface of the Moon. She described how Soviet cosmonauts had visited the Houston Space Center and how the United States and the Soviet Union were talking about cooperation in space.

"It would be really great," said Jackie, "if instead of a space race, the United States and Russia could work together on space exploration. Maybe people would stop fighting."

Jackie did not tell the class, however, about the launch of another Soviet satellite, *Cosmos 248*. News reports said that *Cosmos 248* was an anti-satellite weapon, designed to intercept and destroy craft in space, and described how it had successfully located and destroyed a target satellite in space by flying alongside the target and blowing itself up. Even the American government was unaware, at the time, that *Cosmos 248* was only one of a series of sophisticated anti-satellite weapons that were deployed by the Soviet Union during the Cold War.

Jackie could not accept that space, too, could become a place of death. Instead, she finished her report by saying that the next flight to the Moon, *Apollo 12*, was scheduled for November.

* * *

Throughout the fall, world events seemed to spin increasingly out of control, and Jackie found it more and more difficult to watch the *CBS Evening News*. Many nights she would sit in front of the television, grinding her teeth until she had a headache. Some nights she was so upset that she became nauseous and lost her appetite for dinner. Occasionally, she would lash out angrily at her younger brothers or sisters, who strayed into her path. Bert frequently had to intervene by turning off the television and sending Jackie to her room until she calmed down.

Jackie was relieved when Walter Cronkite turned from the seemingly endless stories about death and destruction to the plans for *Apollo 12*. Amidst chaos on Earth, humankind was moving on. The Moon and the planets were within reach. There was hope.

Jackie was convinced that Walter Cronkite shared her sense of respite. When he stopped talking about the war and turned to stories about space, she heard a different tone in his voice, saw him look at her with more intensity, and felt more energy in his eyes.

Apollo 12 blasted off from Cape Kennedy just before noon on November 14, 1969. Danny was not in school that day. It was the second day of the Moratorium protest against the war, and he had gone with his parents and Ruben to Washington to join in the demonstration. They were among the more than 250,000 people who came from all over the country to participate in the largest demonstration ever held in the nation's capital.

Astronauts Charles Conrad, Jr., Richard Gordon, Jr., and Alan Bean flew uneventfully to the Moon and entered lunar orbit. Conrad remained in orbit while Gordon and Bean landed on the Ocean of Storms, less than two hundred yards away from the unmanned *Surveyor III*, which had landed on the Moon two years before. Astronauts Gordon and Bean spent thirty-one hours on the Moon's surface. They walked more than a quarter mile from the landing site, collecting rocks and setting up scientific experiments. They visited the dormant *Surveyor III* spacecraft and removed one of its cameras to bring back to

Earth; then they left the Moon and landed back on Earth ten days after they had left. It was a flawless mission.

The reaction on Earth was subdued. The extraordinary interest and enthusiasm that had accompanied the flights of *Apollo 8* and *Apollo 11* was absent. *Apollo 12* was nothing new. When the video camera designed to provide live, color television pictures from the Moon burned out after being accidentally pointed at the Sun, there was not much to see on television.

Jackie and Walter Cronkite were the only ones who seemed to care.

13

In the months following the flight of *Apollo 12*, Jackie did not pay much attention to news reports regarding the resignations of many senior officials at NASA. First, the head of geological research resigned, arguing that the space program was not sufficiently dedicated to science. Soon thereafter, the director of the Houston Moon Lab resigned to protest the appointment of engineers rather than scientists to key positions. Then George Mueller, the head of the manned space program, credited with guiding the program to its successful climax, also resigned.

The resignations reflected an unresolved conflict at the core of the space program. The primary purpose of landing men on the Moon, as President Kennedy had stated from the beginning, was to demonstrate the promise and power of America and impress the world with the inevitable triumph of capitalism and democracy. It was also expected to provide tangible benefits through the development of communications and weather satellites and ballistic missiles. Very little of the NASA budget went for science or deep space exploration, and politicians never seriously considered establishing colonies on the Moon or sending a mission to Mars.

The public, on the other hand, was sold on the adventure of space exploration, the heroism of the astronauts, and the potential for traveling beyond the Moon to establishing colonies on planets throughout the solar system. These stories appealed to America's pioneering tradition and sense of manifest destiny. This was the idea that had captured Jackie's, and her generation's, interest in space; that human progress was inevitable and invaluable, and that the exploration of the Moon and planets was a certain step toward the future.

There was always an inherent conflict in public support for science and discovery. Scientists and adventurers wanted to push back the frontiers of knowledge and human experience. Taxpayers expected practical returns. When Thomas Jefferson sent Lewis and Clark with the Corps of Discovery to explore the western half of the American continent, he described different purposes of the mission to different audiences. In a secret missive to Congress requesting funds for the Corps of Discovery, Jefferson described a mission intended "for the purpose of extending the external commerce of the United States" and, not incidentally, preventing the Russians from extending their territorial claims south from Alaska. He also noted that, if "it should incidentally advance the geographical knowledge of our own continent, [it] cannot be but an additional gratification." To the Spanish, who were threatened by the prospect of westward American expansion, he described a mission of scientific discovery, telling them, "In reality it would have no other view than the advancement of the geography."

In fact, the Corps of Discovery's real goal was to plant the American flag at the frontier of the known world and establish the power and manifest destiny of a free people. So too, the manned space flight program was designed to plant the American flag at the frontier of the universe.

By the end of 1969, the space program's political goals had been achieved, and the interests of space scientists, politicians, and the public began to diverge. The divide was exacerbated by the strain on the nation's economy caused by the escalating war in Vietnam. Drastic cuts were being made in many government programs, including education and medical research. Only programs that were essential to the national interest would survive. The government continued to build ballistic missiles and send spy and communications satellites into space, but there was little public or political support for spending money on space science or exploration.

For Jackie, the space program had become a vital exemplar of hope for a world that seemed to be exploding around her. Despite the discord on Earth, or, ironically, because of it, men had successfully ventured into space. She had come to believe that if men could land on the Moon, anything could be accomplished. If Russians and Americans could talk about launching joint missions into space, they could learn to get along on Earth. If it were possible to create ecosystems on the Moon or on Mars, it would be possible to preserve Earth's environment. Space had become a diversion, a distraction, a refuge distant from the tribulations of a troubled Earth.

It was an idea that made sense in all sorts of real, imaginary, and impossible situations. Already, the world was experiencing a "green revolution" brought about by new strains of crops and new approaches to farming. The World Health Organization was close to eradicating smallpox, a disease that only decades before had killed more than ten million people per year. Congress was laying the groundwork for legislation that would make the conquest of cancer a national priority through an ambitious "War on Cancer." Walt Disney was building the Experimental Prototype Community of Tomorrow (EPCOT), a high-technology utopia for Earth, and had worked with Dr. Wernher von Braun to imagine space stations and colonies on the Moon.

Jackie could not wait until she was old enough to go to the Moon, to hold a Moon rock in her hand, and to look back at the Earth spinning in the heavens. She had no doubt it would happen.

14

When school resumed in January, environmentalism was suddenly at the top of the public agenda. Senator Gaylord Nelson's call for an International Earth Day had galvanized media interest and public concern about the environment. For several months at the beginning of 1970, the environmental movement provided the public with a much-needed relief from world conflict. The *New York Times* reported: "Rising concern about the environmental crisis is sweeping the nation's campuses with an intensity that may be on its way to eclipsing student discontent over the war in Vietnam."

President Nixon, recognizing an opportunity to deflect public attention from adverse world and domestic news, issued a proclamation dedicating the 1970s to rescuing the environment. Educators around the country turned their attention to teaching about the environment in preparation for Earth Day. Momentum grew rapidly. On the first Earth Day, April 22, 1970, more than twenty million people joined in demonstrations, teach-ins, protests, and festivities around the world to support environmental action.

Mrs. Leslie restructured the sixth-grade curriculum to coordinate with Earth Day. In geography, the class learned about the major waterways of the world and identified the great cities that were polluting them. They read about different nations, studied their populations, resources, and economies, and learned where the environment was in greatest jeopardy. In English, the class learned how to compose letters by writing to their senators and congressional representatives, asking them to pass laws to protect the environment. In arithmetic, the class learned to graph using numbers that showed population growth and the amount of farmland, forest, and desert. In science, they planted seeds, and when the plants were large enough, transplanted them outside to help rejuvenate the Earth.

For the first time in her life, Jackie was energized by school. She learned about generating energy from the wind, the Sun, and the tides, about recycling waste into useful resources, and about ways to produce food without destroying the forests or extending the deserts. She gave a report on the remote sensing experiments performed by astronauts in Earth orbit. Then, she described NASA's plans for a series of Earth Resources Technology satellites, later renamed *Landsat*, which would permanently orbit Earth to visualize where crops could be grown, where forests were being lost, and where the desert was growing. In Jackie's letter to her representative, she wrote that one way to prevent pollution would be to put all the toxic chemicals in big rockets and shoot them into the Sun.

* * *

In March of 1970, the East Coast of the United States witnessed a total eclipse of the Sun. Mrs. Leslie took the occasion to teach the class about the orbits of Earth around the Sun and the Moon around Earth. She showed the class how the Moon passed directly between Earth and the Sun, creating a shadow on the surface of Earth. She cautioned the students never to look directly at the Sun, or they could burn their eyes and become permanently blind.

The eclipse occurred on a Saturday morning. Mrs. Leslie arranged for students and their families to watch from the playground behind the school. She borrowed welder's helmets from a local mechanic and arranged for several pinhole projectors and telescopes with solar filters so that everyone could safely watch the Sun disappear and then return.

Jackie and Danny watched the solar eclipse together, sitting on a blanket several yards away from the others. Jackie was in awe as the Moon gradually moved in front of the Sun and the daylight dimmed. The Moon encroached on the sphere of the Sun until all that was visible was the black circle of the Moon, the brilliant corona of the Sun, and scattered stars. She felt the cold wind that followed in the shadow of the Sun and felt the temperature drop as if it were night.

"It does look like an eye—like the eye of God," Jackie commented, repeating something she had heard on television. She would always associate the Moon with the accomplishments of men; now she watched in wonder as it blocked out the light of the Sun.

* * *

With the coming of spring, the war in Vietnam began to dominate the news again. Communist armies launched coordinated attacks against the governments of Laos and Cambodia, and America found itself engaged in a war that suddenly seemed to engulf all of Southeast Asia.

Jackie tried to ignore news about the war, by focusing on the upcoming flight of *Apollo 13*. She gave a current events report about the flight that would take astronauts to the hilly lunar highlands in a command and service module named *Odyssey* and a lunar module named *Aquarius*.

Apollo 13 was launched on Saturday, April 11. Danny and Jackie watched the blastoff together in the living room of the Cone's house. Danny sat on the couch, while Jackie crouched in front of the television giving her own breathless commentary on everything that was happening. She was always one step ahead of Walter Cronkite and his team of reporters. Whenever they described something first, she would look chagrined, and after blurting out, "I should have told you that," and would continue talking even faster than before.

Jackie had insisted that Danny watch the launch with her. He generally avoided watching rocket launches. The explosive force of the *Saturn V* made him think about rockets raining fire across Vietnam and the nuclear missiles waiting in their silos, and he found it hard not to associate the Navy and Air Force officers who flew the *Apollo* spacecraft with the pilots who spewed death from the skies over Southeast Asia. Even Jackie's animated narration was an inadequate diversion from these ominous images.

When the launch broadcast ended, Jackie continued her excited prattle outside on the lawn. Danny lay back on the grass in thought, with his eyes half closed, while Jackie alternately sat beside him and turned cartwheels. "I'm so excited!" she exclaimed. "I can't wait to watch the Moon walk. It's going to be so cool! Aren't you excited?"

"Not really."

"Why?"

"Ruben says that the rockets are really being built for nuclear war, and that sending soldiers to the Moon is like an invasion of another planet."

"You don't believe that?" Jackie scolded him.

"Maybe I do. I don't know. It bothers me."

"How can you not be excited?" Jackie was irritated at Danny's lack of enthusiasm. "Can you imagine what it would be like to walk on the Moon. It would be, like, being in heaven—but a real heaven where you could run around and jump into craters and pick up Moon rocks and things. You could even throw them at people!" she concluded playfully, picking up a handful of gravel and sand from the driveway and throwing it at Danny.

"Stop that."

"No." she teased, picking up another handful and flinging them again.

"Stop that," he laughed. "Stop throwing things at me."

"Make me," she taunted him, retreating from his reach.

"I'm going to get you!" he warned, engaging in her game. Thoughts of warfare and conflict faded from his mind. Her enthusiasm was irresistible. As she danced away from him, Danny was also acutely aware of how cute she was.

Jackie grabbed several more handfuls of dirt and threw them mischievously at Danny. "If we were on the Moon, you couldn't catch me, you know," she taunted. "I would be able to jump out of the way." She skipped away in giant strides the way the astronauts walked on the Moon, then turned back toward Danny. "But we're not on the Moon," he replied, jumping up to tackle her playfully by the legs, then spinning her around and around until they were both light-headed and wobbly and collapsed onto the grass.

* * *

The next day, the astronauts fired the rockets on the *Odyssey* command module and started on a trajectory toward the Moon. The following evening at 9:30, there was a live television broadcast from space. Jackie watched with her parents from their living room as the astronauts talked about their mission, demonstrated the mystery of weightlessness, and showed how they would sleep and eat during their stay on the Moon.

It was several hours past her bedtime when the broadcast ended. Bert immediately turned the television off and sent Jackie to bed. Then, he turned his attention to completing his income taxes, which were due the following day.

Minutes later, oxygen tank number 2 on the command module exploded, and the astronauts transmitted a succinct alarm back to Earth: "Houston, we have a problem."

Jackie was unaware of the crisis that unfolded in space while she slept. She did not witness the frantic attempts by the three astronauts and thousands of experts on the ground to determine what had happened, limit the extent of the damage, and devise a way to bring the astronauts back to Earth alive. With oxygen stores depleted and fuel cells failing, the *Odyssey* was unusable. The crew transferred to the lunar module *Aquarius*, where the life-support systems were still intact, and continued to fly toward the Moon, moving thousands of miles farther away from the safety of Earth every hour.

15

Mary generally woke Jackie at seven o'clock. Jackie would stay in bed as long as she dared. Then she would dress, brush her teeth and hair, and join her father in the kitchen for a bowl of cold cereal and a glass of milk before beginning her walk to school at seven forty-five.

That Tuesday, everyone in the Cone household was moving more slowly than usual. Bert had been awake most of the night working on their tax returns and had decided to sleep late. Mary was occupied with changing diapers and feeding the youngest children. After staying up past her bedtime to watch the broadcast from *Apollo*, Jackie struggled to get out of bed, and she was still combing her hair ten minutes before school started. She ran most of the way to school, but still arrived after the bell had rung to begin classes.

Hours later, as Jackie headed for lunch with her friends, she noticed a group of teachers circled around a television in the library, across the hall from the multipurpose room. She heard Walter Cronkite's voice and recognized pictures of Mission Control.

Jackie left her friends, walked into the library, and sat down on the floor in front of the television. Immediately, she realized something had gone wrong. The spaceship had exploded. Her breath failed. Images of the astronauts and her mother floated through her vision. She squeezed her eyes shut and stifled her cry in her sleeve, but she was unable to hold back the tears.

Walter Cronkite described the evolving crisis. No one yet knew what had happened or the extent of the damage. Reporters speculated that an asteroid might have hit the ship or that a fuel or oxygen tank might have exploded. Jackie thought about *Cosmos 248*, the Russian spacecraft that had attacked and destroyed a satellite in space several months before. In her mind, she saw a Romulan spaceship disintegrating after being hit by a phaser from the *Starship Enterprise*.

The astronauts were still alive, but the spacecraft was losing power and moving farther and farther from Earth. Their only hope was to continue on a path that would take them behind the dark side of the Moon, where they would try to fire rockets and redirect the crippled spacecraft back toward Earth.

The plan was perilous. The life-support systems on *Aquarius* were not designed to keep the astronauts alive for the length of time required to reach the Moon and return to Earth. They might not have enough air, power for heat, or water. No one knew if the rocket engines would still work, whether the guidance systems were still functioning, or whether the heat shields necessary for reentry had been damaged. The problems seemed insurmountable.

Jackie sat on the floor through lunch and recess, crying silently as she listened to the news. When the bell rang to resume classes, someone turned the television off and everyone quickly dispersed. She stood with the others but stopped before leaving the room. She could not go back to class. Her eyes were red and full of tears. Her sleeve was slick from wiping her eyes and nose. She could not let her classmates know she had been crying.

Jackie waited until the hallway was empty and then slipped across the hall into the restroom. She tried to compose herself by washing her face with cold water and brushing her hair with her hands, but she could not stop crying. It was hard to think clearly. She could not go back to class looking like she did. Everyone would know she had been crying. The only thing to do was go home.

Students with more experience knew how to slip out of school without being caught. They knew which teachers could see the hallway from their classrooms, which teachers watched the doors, and which assistant principals walked the halls. They knew which doors could be opened without setting off alarms, and how to get off the school grounds by climbing under the fence at the end of the playground, rather than walking out toward Main Street in full view of the principal's office.

Jackie had never thought about skipping school before. Now, it seemed to be the only thing to do. She slipped out of the lavatory and into the multipurpose room. There was a stage at the end of the room, and a door at the back of the stage that led to an alley on the side of the building. If she could get out that door, she would not have to walk through the halls without a pass.

She tried to walk calmly across the large room without arousing the suspicion of the cafeteria staff, who were cleaning up from lunch. Then, she darted up the stairs on the side of the proscenium and ducked behind the curtain. No one noticed her.

She moved cautiously to the back of the stage and pushed the handle to release the latch. The door opened, sounding an emergency alarm.

Jackie ran, letting the heavy metal door slammed behind her. Quickly, she ducked into a thicket of bushes along the side of the school and took cover under the branches. When the alarm stopped a moment later, she peered out between the branches. Seeing that she was alone, she stepped out from under the bush and paused to brush the mulch from her clothes.

Just then, Mrs. Owens, one of the secretaries from the principal's office, came out of the school to investigate the alarm. She recognized Jackie immediately.

"Miss Cone, what are you doing out here?" she asked, never expecting that one of the school's most delightful students would have set off the alarm. Other suspects came to mind first.

Jackie was frozen. "Nothing," she murmured.

"Did you see anyone else around back?" Mrs. Owens asked, still wondering who had set off the alarm. Suddenly, she realized it must have been Jackie. "Did you set off the alarm?"

"Yes, ma'am." Jackie looked at the ground in despair.

Mrs. Owens looked at Jackie and saw her free-flowing tears. "You're crying. Is something wrong?"

"Yes! Everything is wrong!" Jackie blurted out.

"Are you okay?"

"No," Jackie replied, struggling to stop her tears.

"Let's go back to the office and see if I can help you."

Jackie did not answer. Mrs. Owens put her hand on Jackie's arm and guided her toward the school. They entered through the front door, just as Mrs. Leslie came down the hallway toward the office to report that Jackie had not returned from recess.

"Miss Cone, is that you?" Mrs. Leslie called down the hallway.

"She was outside," Mrs. Owens said. "The exit alarm went off from the door behind the stage. When I went to investigate, Miss Cone was around the side of the building. She was crying."

Jackie looked at her with fury. Mrs. Owens had announced right in the middle of the hallway that she had been crying. Anyone could have heard her. Now the whole school would know!

"Let's go to the office and see what this is about," Mrs. Leslie said, taking Jackie's other arm firmly. They walked to the principal's office and sat down in a small conference room.

"What's going on?" asked Mrs. Leslie.

"I want to go home. Please let me go home! I can't go back to class!" Jackie blurted out.

"Can you tell me what's wrong?" Mrs. Leslie asked.

"They're going to die! I saw it on television."

Mrs. Leslie suddenly understood the problem. "The astronauts?"

"There was an explosion! They're going to die! They don't have enough air. They aren't going to be able to breathe. They're flying away from the Earth and are going to die! They're going to disappear."

"Jacqueline," Mrs. Leslie said, putting her hand on Jackie's shoulder to comfort her, "I know how much this means to you. But you can't just run away. You have to pull yourself together and come back to class."

Jackie exploded. "I can't go back to class! I don't care about class!" She stood and angrily shoved the papers and books from the table onto the floor, kicked her chair over, and continued shouting at the world. "They're going to die! I don't care about stupid geography or social studies or arithmetic or anything! I don't care about your stupid ideas! I don't want to go to class! I want to go home!"

The principal came into the room and stood silently beside Mrs. Leslie as Jackie's tirade continued.

"I don't care about school. I don't care about Vietnam or Ireland. I don't care about the environment. I don't care about anything! There isn't anything anybody can do. I don't care if a bomb drops on my head. I don't want to hide under my desk for the rest of my life. I don't want to live in a fallout shelter. I want to go home! Everything can go to hell—I don't care! You can go to hell! We are all going to go to hell. I want to go home. Please let me go home."

Finally, Jackie stopped and buried her face in her hands. "There isn't anything to do!" She continued her desperate sobbing. "There isn't anything to do!"

Moments before, Jackie had felt that the world's problems could be solved. She had had an idea that made sense, an idea that let her see beyond her fears. If people could land on the Moon, they could do anything. One small step, or perhaps a million small steps, but it had all been possible. Now it seemed overwhelming.

Mrs. Leslie and the principal watched helplessly as Jackie's fury ran its course. After several minutes, they stepped outside to confer about what to do. Mrs. Leslie recognized that Jackie was in no condition to return to class. Moreover, leaving school and cursing at a teacher required disciplinary action.

By the time Mrs. Leslie returned to the room, Jackie was sitting with her head down on the table, sobbing softly. Mrs. Leslie sat down beside her and put her hand reassuringly on her shoulder. "Jacqueline, look at me."

"Yes, Mrs. Leslie." Jackie raised her head and turned toward her.

"Your behavior just now was unacceptable. You are suspended from school for the rest of the day. The principal will call your parents and tell them to take you home. You are going to stay here in this room until they come. Do you understand?"

"Yes, ma'am."

"You will not be allowed back in school until you write a letter apologizing for your actions, have your parents sign it, and bring it to the principal's office. You can come back to class tomorrow if you are ready, but I do not want to see any more behavior like this from you ever again. Is that clear?"

Jackie nodded, then began to cry again.

* * *

Mrs. Leslie's classroom was buzzing with speculation about Jackie when she did not return from recess. It was not like Jackie to disappear. Her friends were worried.

When Mrs. Leslie came back into the room, Karen raised her hand immediately. "Is Jackie okay? Did you find her?"

"Miss Cone is okay. She is in the principal's office. She has been suspended from school."

Everyone in the room began talking at once.

"Jackie suspended?"

"How could Jackie Cone get suspended?"

"Did she do something really bad?" one of the school's perennial trouble-makers asked hopefully.

"Jackie didn't do anything bad," Danny snapped, rising to her defense. "Shut up and mind your own business!"

Mrs. Leslie waited until the chatter died down. "The circumstances of Miss Cone's suspension are a private matter between Miss Cone and the principal. Please be respectful of your classmate and allow this matter to remain private."

Mrs. Leslie turned to Danny. "Mr. Cohn, would you please gather up Miss Cone's belongings and take them to her in the principal's office?"

Danny was relieved to know where Jackie was and hoped he might be able to help her. He packed her things into her book bag and hurried down to the office.

He found her sitting in the conference room with her head down on the table and her eyes closed. "Jackie."

Jackie looked up and, seeing Danny, felt an intense desire to run to him and grab him and bury her face in his chest. But she did not move.

"Are you okay?" he asked.

"It's a nightmare, Danny. I want it to go away. It's like a nightmare."

"Young man, don't go in there," Mrs. Owens called out from her desk in the adjacent room before Danny could say anything.

"But Mrs. Leslie told me to bring Jackie's things to her." Danny turned toward her.

"You cannot go in there," Mrs. Owens repeated.

"But Mrs. Leslie said—"

"I'll take Miss Cone's things." Mrs. Owens guided Danny away from the door with a hand on his shoulder. "You can go back to class now."

"Can't I talk to Jackie for just a minute?"

"No."

Danny was stymied. "You can call me tonight, Jackie," he said over his shoulder, as Mrs. Owens hustled him from the room. "I'll come over if you want."

"Thank you," Jackie answered, forcing a meek and grateful smile, as Mrs. Owens closed the door behind Danny, leaving her alone.

By then, Jackie's panic had quieted. She realized that Mrs. Leslie had done her a favor; she would not have to go back to class that afternoon, but she could return to school the next day.

The principal called Mary and explained that Jackie had been caught trying to run away from school, had used profanity toward a teacher, and had been suspended. Mary had no idea what had come over her daughter and immediately drove to the school to bring her home.

During their short ride home, Mary tried getting Jackie to tell her what had happened, but Jackie did not feel like talking, and they drove home in silence. When they arrived at the house, Mary poured Jackie a glass of milk, brought out some cookies, and sat at the kitchen table with her, hoping she would talk. Jackie sat with her head buried in her arms, avoiding Mary's eyes. She told Mary that she had gotten upset when she heard about the explosion on *Apollo 13* and did not want her classmates to see that she had been crying; she refused to say anything more. After twenty minutes of stalemate, Jackie asked whether she could turn on the television to find out what was happening to *Apollo 13*.

"Absolutely not," Mary responded. "Not until your father comes home and we decide what your punishment will be for this behavior."

Jackie immediately burst into hysterical tears and ran upstairs to her room, slamming the door so hard that her plastic model of the *Apollo* spacecraft fell off the shelf and onto the floor. Jackie picked it up and hurled it violently across the room, smashing it into shards of pointed plastic. She grabbed her *Saturn V* model rocket in both hands and swung it at the mobile of the solar system that hung from her ceiling and the decorations on her walls until the Moon, the planets, and the stars were torn from the sky and lay shattered on the ground.

The destruction of her treasures made Jackie even more hysterical. She fell onto the bed, buried her face under her stuffed animals and pillows, and cried herself to exhaustion.

Mary heard the carnage coming from Jackie's room but had no idea what to do. She called Bert and told him to come home immediately.

It took Bert almost an hour to get home. By then, Jackie was lying despondently in her bed, hiding her head and her tears under the covers with her stuffed animals clutched tightly in her arms.

Bert sat on the side of Jackie's bed. "So, what happened today?"

Without looking out from under the covers, Jackie told him everything. She spoke in short, barely audible monotonic phrases. Bert listened attentively until she was done.

"Can you look at me?" Bert instructed her, gently lowering the covers off her face. Jackie did not look directly at him but remained curled up, looking purposefully at the stuffed animals in her arms. "You know your behavior was unacceptable," he chided her out of a sense of parental duty, not at all sure what had caused her uncharacteristic outburst. "The school was right to punish you."

"I know."

"Is there anything else you want to say?" Bert asked.

"I'm sorry," she said miserably, looking at him directly for the first time. "I'm really sorry."

"I know." Bert reached out for Jackie, who rolled into his arms and buried her face in his stomach. Having her father there helped. He was very brave. "This isn't going to happen again, is it?"

"No, Daddy. It won't happen again."

"Are you sure?"

"I promise, Daddy." She lay silently in his arms for several minutes.

"And what happened here?" Bert asked, looking at the devastation on the floor.

"I was upset."

"Can I help you pick up some of this mess before your mother sees it?"

"No. I can do it."

"Are you sure?"

"I can do it."

"Okay, then." Bert stood up from the bed. "See how much you can get cleaned up before dinner. After dinner, I want you to write the letter apologizing to Mrs. Leslie and the principal. Do you understand?"

"Yes, Daddy."

After Bert left the room, Jackie spent several hours collecting broken pieces of plastic and paper from the floor, intermittently breaking into tears at the destruction. At six o'clock, she heard Bert turn on the television in the living room and heard Walter Cronkite introduce the *CBS Evening News*. She desperately wanted him to tell her what was happening in space. She hesitated for a moment, then quietly slipped down the stairs and took her accustomed place in front of the television, hoping she would allow her to stay.

Seeing her come into the room, Bert put away the newspaper and the mail and went to sit beside her. Together, they watched as Walter Cronkite reviewed everything that had happened since the previous evening; the explosion, the efforts to determine what had gone wrong, the plan to bring the astronauts back to Earth, and the successful firing of a rocket to change their course. Jackie listened closely as Cronkite described the first leg of a suspenseful flight back to Earth with the astronauts huddled in the *Aquarius* without enough heat, food, or water. They were still in mortal danger, but there was hope.

"I'm scared, Daddy." Jackie put her head on his chest and felt his arms around her. "I'm really scared."

"Try to calm down, sweetie. It doesn't really affect you. It isn't the end of the world," Bert tried to reassure her.

"Yes, it is," Jackie pouted.

"No, it isn't," he corrected firmly.

"You don't understand. It's like your store, like what happened to Mommy, like what you told me about Ireland, and like what Danny told me about people who—" She began to tremble, and her voice failed.

"Shhh." Bert tried to comfort her. "Everything is going to be okay, sweetie."

"You don't understand."

Jackie and her father listened to Walter Cronkite describe the global reaction to the tragedy. While no one had seemed to care about *Apollo 12*, the world was mesmerized by the crisis aboard *Apollo 13*. Hundreds of millions of people around the world were watching and praying for the safe return of the astronauts. Ten thousand people joined Pope Paul in a special Mass at the Vatican. Thousands prayed at the Wailing Wall in Jerusalem.

Eric Sevareid's commentary that night on the *CBS Evening News* came closest to capturing Jackie's despair: "So the three astronauts head home through the desert of space, their oxygen and water running low. Perhaps the story will be seen one day as a parable; the Earth is also a spinning spaceship, all of us are astronauts, and our oxygen and water are also diminishing, but we have no place to go."

That night, Jackie cried herself to a sleep filled with nightmares. She was in the *Apollo* command module when the spacecraft exploded and began to disintegrate. Glass shattered around her. Bodies flew out the window. Sirens warned her to take cover. Her real and make-believe worlds faded into the distance. She watched; transfixed, paralyzed with fear, unable to fly, to move, to cry.

Jackie's tortured dreams took her to the family store in Hartford as gunshots shattered the windows, to hamlets under attack in Vietnam, skyscrapers being bombed in Manhattan, the bloody streets of Belfast, the battlefields of Boyne, the killing fields of Babi Yar, and the Temple Mount in flames in Jerusalem. Over and over, she had premonitions that an explosion was about to occur, then watched as apocalyptic explosions and mushrooming clouds exploded her world. She watched in helpless desperation as the astronauts, her mother, her father, and Danny disappeared into the blackness. She saw herself floating on a reed ship across the ocean, and felt the explosive winds and waves of an approaching hurricane. She struggled for breath as the oxygen seemed to ebb from the room. She tried to duck and cover, to take refuge in the lunar module, to cower in her father's arms, to fly or run away; but she could never move. She awoke repeatedly, hyperventilating, soaked in sweat, her mind overwhelmed with vertiginous delusions, frightened by visions that seemed so real and explosions that seemed so close.

Eventually, Jackie gave up trying to sleep. She turned on her light and sat at her desk. She wrote a letter to the principal saying that she had been very upset about the explosion on *Apollo 13*, that she was very sorry for the things she had done and said, and that it would not happen again. In the morning, her parents read the letter and added their signatures.

That morning, Jackie left for school at her usual time. Danny was waiting for her halfway to school.

"Hi, Danny," Jackie greeted him sheepishly as he approached.

"Are you all right?" he asked with evident concern. "I didn't know if you were coming back to school today or not. You didn't call or anything last night."

"I'll be okay."

"What happened? Why did you get suspended?"

"I tried to run away from school." She searched his eyes for his reaction.

"You tried to run away? Yikes! What were you thinking?"

Jackie took a deep breath. There were so many things she wanted to tell him; how she felt when she heard about the explosion, about her dismay and despair. She wanted to tell him about her nightmares the way he had told her about his, but she was afraid to do or say anything for fear she would cry.

"I sort of lost it," she said, trying to sound casual, as she explained what had happened the day before.

"That's not like you, Jackie."

"I just felt like I couldn't go on, that nothing was ever going to be the same. Everyone was acting like it was just another news story about things exploding and people dying somewhere, but it's not the same." She felt tears in her eyes and stopped abruptly. "It's different."

"I know," Danny said softly. "It's like when my parents get upset about the fighting in Israel."

Jackie looked at Danny, inhaled deeply, and exhaled in relief. Their eyes met for an instant. She did not have to say anything else. He understood. She felt an irresistible urge to put her arms around him, to have him hold her, to clutch him to be sure he would always be there. Instead, she turned her eyes away from his direct gaze.

"Wow! You got yourself suspended," Danny said, breaking the tension. "I really should have taped your mouth shut a long time ago for your own good!" He gave her a playful shove on the arm. It felt good when he touched her.

"Yeah, like *you* can teach me how to keep my mouth shut!" Jackie teased, nudging him back with her shoulder. "Come on, we better get to school." Jackie turned, and they walked the rest of the way in silence.

Jackie took her note to the principal's office and then went to class. She managed to sit through school on Wednesday and Thursday but was uncharacteristically quiet.

Danny stayed close to her throughout the week, running interference from her classmates and protecting her from their prying questions. Jackie was grateful.

Over the next several days, Jackie and the world watched and waited as the crisis in space played out. They watched and waited as Earth's gravity caught hold of the spacecraft, and it began accelerating toward home. They watched and waited as the astronauts huddled in *Aquarius* for warmth and made midcourse corrections to ensure they would enter the atmosphere at an angle steep enough to prevent them from bouncing off into space, yet shallow enough to keep from burning up in the atmosphere. They watched and waited as the astronauts returned to the *Odyssey* to prepare for reentry and jettisoned *Aquarius*, which fell to Earth in flames.

The astronauts were scheduled to reenter the atmosphere and splash down in the Pacific Ocean early Friday afternoon. No one knew whether the crippled spaceship could survive reentry.

Bert thought it prudent to bring Jackie home from school early on Friday, rather than risk a repetition of Tuesday's events if the reentry failed. Jackie was relieved that she would be able to watch the splashdown alone with her father.

Bert picked Jackie up at school at 12:30. They arrived at home and sat down in front of the television, just as the astronauts were scheduled to enter the atmosphere. As the television cameras scanned the horizon for the three parachutes that would bring the craft down safely in the ocean, Jackie held her father's hand so tightly that it hurt. The minutes of silence and searching seemed interminable. When the three parachutes finally appeared beneath the clouds and the voices of the astronauts were heard on the radio, Jackie breathed deeply again. She felt warm and released her grasp on her father's hand. They had survived!

That night, Jackie slept soundly. In her dreams, she flew a spaceship around Earth and the Moon, looking down on all the places she had seen on the evening news and studied in class. This time, there were no explosions, and the three parachutes set her back gently in her bed before dawn.

* * *

Ten days later, the impending fall of Cambodia prompted a major escalation of the war in Vietnam. American warplanes began saturation-bombing the Cambodian countryside, and American troops crossed the international border to attack communist forces.

Antiwar protests exploded on the streets and campuses throughout America. At Kent State, the National Guard shot and killed four students. Days later, more students were killed at Jackson State.

At one time, Jackie would have found such news agonizing. Now, she was able to watch the evening news without struggling. She knew the world would survive.

There would be times of cold and times of peril; oxygen and water and heat might be in short supply, but there would be solutions. *Aquarius* would crash in flames. The *Odyssey* would continue.

Book Two: The "Me Generation"
June 1970

16

Jackie and Danny finished sixth grade in June 1970. There was a short graduation ceremony on the playing field behind the school. They sat next to each other on folding chairs, exchanging mischievous glances and whispered comments throughout the short program.

There was little gravity to the proceedings. Most of the students were concerned only with escaping to the playground. Their parents were occupied with finding the best angle to take pictures of their children. Few of those present appreciated the extent to which the children had acquired a vision of the world and assimilated a set of ideas that would carry them through adulthood.

Like Lewis and Clark beginning their journey toward the Pacific, youth journey on a set path toward adulthood, following streams of ideas, yet unaware of the obstacles that lie ahead. Like astronauts on a trajectory to the Moon, there is often little that can be done to change direction except making minor course corrections or executing perilous abort strategies when life itself is at risk.

The graduation ceremony began with the principal leading the Pledge of Allegiance and the pastor of the Congregational Church leading the Lord's Prayer. Mrs. Leslie then talked for several minutes. She asked the parents to think back on the growth of their children who had come to elementary school as six-year-olds and were leaving on the verge of adolescence. "Try to remember how much your children have grown, how much they have learned, and how much they matured during the past six years. Try to realize, too, that they will grow and learn and mature just as much over the next six years, before they graduate high school, as the class of 1976.

There was a murmur among the parents at the words "class of 1976." Few had thought that far ahead.

"Your children have learned skills they will use throughout their lives. More importantly, they are well on their way to acquiring a set of ideas that will guide the way they think."

The principal then handed each student an informal certificate and invited everyone to stay for refreshments. Most of the children grabbed a handful of cookies and ran off to play. Their parents stayed to talk to the principal and teachers. Sixth grade was over.

Jackie and Danny walked over to talk to Mrs. Leslie. Jackie gave her a hug, and Danny shook her hand. Ruben joined them, along with Danny's parents.

"It's good to see you, Ruben," Mrs. Leslie greeted him. "I hear you've done well in high school."

"It hasn't screwed my mind," Ruben answered sullenly.

"And you were admitted to Juilliard. Congratulations."

"No big deal."

"I'm so glad to hear you are going to stay with your music. Good for you."

"It's all cool," Ruben mumbled, burying his hands in his pockets and walking away with a studied slouch.

"You should be very proud of him," Mrs. Leslie commented to Danny's parents.

"We are. He worked hard to get into Juilliard."

At that moment, Jackie's parents joined them. Danny and Jackie stood self-consciously several feet away from each other as Mrs. Leslie told their parents how pleased she was to have had them in her class, how wonderful they had been, and how successful she expected them to be in junior high school and beyond. Then she moved away to convey similar sentiments to the families of other students.

The two sets of parents exchanged pleasantries about how fast the kids were growing and what a good teacher Mrs. Leslie had been. Danny's father asked Bert when he would be able to reopen the store. Mrs. Cohn and Mary talked about their vacation plans for the summer. Then they went their separate ways; they didn't have much in common.

"I suppose you won't see Danny as much in junior high school," Bert began, as they headed home.

"We won't be in the same class all the time anymore," Jackie said with some sadness.

"You should get to know other boys, not just Danny—maybe some of the boys who go to our church," Bert suggested.

Mrs. Leslie's reference to Jackie being in the Class of 1976 was preying on Bert's mind. He had met Jackie's mother, Beth, at a summer camp for Catholic youth when he was entering his senior year of high school and she was a rising sophomore. By the time school started that fall, he had already given her his varsity pin and they were going steady.

Bert had enlisted in the Navy immediately after graduation and served through the Korean War in stations off the coasts of Korea and Japan. Weeks before the armistice was signed in May 1953, he was reassigned to Norfolk, Virginia. From there, he was able to arrange leave to take Beth to her senior prom, and he proposed to her that night. The photograph taken at the prom of Bert in his military dress uniform and Beth resplendent in a billowing gown and beehive hair was one of the pictures that was always beside Jackie's bed.

Bert and Beth were married in the spring of 1954. Bert continued to serve in the Navy, until his discharge in January of 1957. Jackie was born ten months later.

"You should get to know some of the boys at our church," Bert repeated.

"Daddy, I'm only twelve!"

17

Jackie and Danny did not see each other over the summer. Danny went to summer camp for six weeks and then on vacation with his family. Jackie spent her time hanging out with her friends at the local pool, babysitting her younger siblings, and helping her father prepare his new store for an opening in the fall. Danny sent her one letter from camp, asking whether she had received the invitation to his Bar Mitzvah and saying that he really hoped she would come.

She had received the formal invitation in the mail and asked Mary whether she could go. Mary did not like the idea of her daughter going to a synagogue, and told Jackie that she wanted to talk to Danny's mother before deciding. Several weeks had passed, and Mary had not yet made the call.

Jackie pestered Mary for several more days until she finally called Mrs. Cohn and agreed that Jackie could go. Once Jackie had permission, she carefully completed the response card that had come with the invitation, and wrote a letter to Danny at camp saying she would be there.

Karen told Jackie that she needed to have a nice outfit for the Bar Mitzvah service in the morning and a fancy dress for the party that evening. Jackie begged Mary to buy her new clothes for the occasion. After much pleading, Mary took Jackie to the mall to buy the clothes she wanted. Karen came along to be sure Jackie picked the perfect dress.

Danny celebrated becoming Bar Mitzvah on Labor Day weekend in 1970. The invitation said the service started at nine o'clock. While Mrs. Cohn had suggested that Jackie come around ten, Jackie was dressed in a short, flowered skirt, a white blouse, stockings, and starter heels at eight forty-five and insisted that her father take her immediately.

Jackie's father dropped her off in front of the synagogue promptly at nine o'clock. The building seemed deserted. She gingerly walked into the lobby and stood alone for several minutes, wondering what to do. It did not look like St Patrick's. She peered through the window into the sanctuary, where several adults were praying, but there was no magisterial dais, no stained glass, no statuary, no crucifix, and no pews. For a moment, Jackie was not sure she was in the right place.

Suddenly she heard Danny's voice behind her. "Jackie!"

She turned and saw him walking into the building with Ruben and his parents. "Danny!" She ran over to him and gave him a quick hug. Danny looked embarrassed, and Jackie stepped back quickly. "I'm so happy to see you. How was your summer?" she began happily.

"It was great. You're early."

"I wanted to talk to you—to hear all about your summer. Tell me everything!"

Danny's mother had no time for small talk. "Danny, we have things to do. You can talk to your friend later."

"I guess I have things to do." Danny shrugged. "I'll see you later, Jackie."

Jackie felt lost. "What am I supposed to do?"

"Wait here in the lobby," Danny said. "Lots of people will show up. Just do what they do." Danny's mother took him by the arm and led him toward the back of the building for last-minute preparations.

Jackie sat on a chair in the lobby and waited. It was not long before people started arriving. A few went into the service. Most stood around, greeting relatives and friends with hugs and formal conversation. Jackie felt out of place.

After about twenty minutes, a girl came up to her. She was around Jackie's age, with long, black curly hair, and she looked a little bit like Danny. "Are you Jackie?"

"Yes," Jackie answered uncertainly. "Who are you?"

"I'm Sarah—Sarah Rosen," the girl said, speaking so quickly that even Jackie had to pay attention to understand what she was saying. "My mother is, like, Danny's aunt, because his mother and my mother are, like sisters, so Danny's mother is, you know, my aunt, which makes Danny my cousin, like a first cousin or something, which is cool, though I never really understood the difference between first cousins and second cousins and removed cousins or anything. Anyway, I just saw Danny, and he said that you, like, didn't know anybody here and that you didn't know what you were supposed to do. He said it would be, like, cool if I would sit with you and tell you what to do and stuff like that. Cool?"

"Cool," Jackie agreed with a sigh of relief. "I have no idea what to do. I've never been in a synagogue."

"I know how you feel. I went to a Catholic church last year with a friend. I, like, had no idea what to do. You're not Catholic or anything, are you?"

"Yeah, I am," Jackie answered awkwardly.

"That's cool," Sarah continued. "Anyway, it felt so, like, totally weird being there, since I'm not Catholic, you know. I'm, like, Jewish, and I didn't have any idea what to do, and I didn't know if it was cool to kneel down when everyone else did and, you know, whether I should go with everyone else when they went down the aisle for the cracker—"

"For Communion," Jackie interjected knowingly.

"Yeah, that. I guess I wasn't, like, supposed to go— anyway, I guess you know all that stuff." Sarah noticed that the doors to the sanctuary had opened and that people were starting to go in. "Hey, let's get seats in the back row where we can, you know, talk during the service. It's pretty boring. Just follow me and do everything I do. It'll be cool." Jackie followed Sarah to seats in the farthest corner of the hall, where they spent much of the morning talking in animated whispers.

Several minutes after Sarah and Jackie had taken their seats, Danny entered the sanctuary with Ruben and his parents and sat in the first row. Soon, the room was filled with several hundred people.

After a while, the ancient scrolls of the Torah were taken from the Ark, carried with great ceremony around the room, and then placed on a table at the front of the room. One by one, people went up to the table and said a Hebrew prayer, after which one of the older men would read from the scrolls. Sarah tried to explain what was going on and kept turning the pages in Jackie's prayer book so that she would be on the right page. Jackie was grateful.

Finally, it was Danny's turn. He walked up to the front, said the Hebrew prayer, and then began singing in Hebrew, as the older men had done before. Jackie watched intently, wincing silently every time his voice cracked on a high note. When he was done, he sat back down with his family.

"I would be afraid to sing in front of all these people," Jackie whispered to Sarah.

"He was really good," Sarah replied.

Jackie was pleased.

Soon Danny was up again. This time he spoke in English. Jackie squirmed in her seat and sat up straighter, hoping she could catch his eye, but he was completely focused on his task. "What is he going to do now?"

"He is going to give, like, a sermon about what he just read in Hebrew, you know, what it means to him."

"In the Torah portion I read today," Danny began, "God says, 'Justice, justice shall you pursue.' God tells the people, 'Appoint yourselves judges and police for your tribes,' and he says, 'Make sure that they administer honest judgment for the people.'"

"When I read this portion, I wondered why God said the word *justice* two times. The rabbis say that the word *justice* is repeated two times to emphasize that this commandment is twice as important as the other commandments. Justice is more important than prayer, more important than eating the right foods, and even more important than going to services." Danny's voice conveyed a child's dislike of religious ritual and elicited laughter from his friends.

"I think this is a good commandment. It tells us that we need to have judges and police. It tells us we not only need to be against injustice, but to pursue justice. We should pursue justice in the South where civil rights leaders are afraid they will be killed and where black people can't vote, get jobs, or go to good schools. We should pursue justice for farm workers who pick lettuce. We should pursue justice for Jews who are not free in Russia, for Ibo who are not free in Biafra, and for Africans who are not free in South Africa.

"I learned from my portion that, now that I am an adult, it is my responsibility to pursue justice. How can I do this? I will protest for freedom for Jews in Russia. I will protest for civil rights. I will protest to end to the war in Vietnam. I won't eat lettuce." He purposely grimaced as he said the last word, and his friends broke into laughter. He then finished with a formal ending: "I pray that everyone will pursue justice and that justice, justice will bring us peace. Amen."

Danny immediately opened another book and began singing in Hebrew. Jackie turned to Sarah. "Did Danny write that?" she exclaimed.

"The rabbi helps," Sarah replied.

He may have had help, Jackie thought, *but the ideas were unmistakably Danny's.* They were the same ideas he had expressed in class every time the issues of justice and injustice were raised in current events.

"He was good," Jackie whispered, happy for Danny's accomplishment. She really did care that he had done well.

Eventually the service ended and lunch was served in an adjacent room. Jackie saw Danny only long enough to say, "You were great!" Otherwise, he was monopolized by his relatives.

Disappointed that she did not get to talk with Danny, Jackie stayed close to Sarah throughout the luncheon.

"Will I see you at the party tonight?" Jackie asked Sarah, when Mary arrived to take her home.

"Sure. It should be a good time!" Sarah replied. "Bye."

All afternoon, Jackie was restless in anticipation of the party that evening. She washed her hair twice because she did not like the way it dried the first time. Then she called Karen and asked her to come over and help her get dressed.

Jackie had never been so dressed up. Mary had bought her a long, light-blue dress with a ballerina neckline and white lace accents on the bodice, sheer stockings, and brand-new shoes with heels. From Karen, she borrowed a necklace of shining white stones and a matching bracelet.

Karen thought Jackie should wear makeup and showed her how to put on eyeliner, eye shadow, and lipstick. When Jackie looked at herself in the mirror, she thought she looked like a clown. She frantically scrubbed her face with soap and water to take it off, and then took another shower to be sure it was gone.

The result was inadvertent but stunning. Her eyes sparked; her freckled complexion was radiant; her hair, streaked with gold from the summer sun, seemed weightless.

Danny's party was held in a large hall at a local country club. There were seemingly endless courses of food, ceremony, games, and dancing to a four-piece band.

Sarah taught Jackie how to dance the Hora, and they joined in lines doing the Swim, the Pony, and the Bunny Hop. Jackie tried the Limbo but was worried about tearing her new dress and allowed herself to be eliminated immediately. Several times, Danny came over to talk to her, but a relative always pulled him away.

Shortly after dessert, the bandleader announced that the next dance would be "ladies' choice." Sarah turned to Jackie. "You should ask Danny to dance."

"No way!" Jackie was appalled at the suggestion.

"You heard the band guy. This dance is ladies' choice. That means the girls are supposed to ask a boy to dance. It's something you do at a Bar Mitzvah. It's, like, part of the tradition," Sarah said with a sly smile, taking advantage of her assigned role as Jackie's guide. "Anyway, Danny really likes you," she finished offhandedly.

Jackie looked at Sarah in disbelief. "He said that? He said he likes me?"

"He's always talking about you. 'Jackie this—Jackie that—Jackie said.' He was really worried when you got in trouble last spring. He likes you plenty."

"But it's not like he's my boyfriend or anything," Jackie protested.

"It's just a dance," Sarah pressed her. "If you want, I'll ask Ruben to dance at the same time."

"But Ruben is in college."

"I know. He thinks I'm just a little kid, but I think he's really cool. Anyway, he's my cousin so it's, like, okay to dance with me. Do you want to dance or not?"

"Okay," she said, feeling a little mischievous. "Let's do it."

They walked together across the dance floor to where Danny and Ruben were talking to several adult relatives. Jackie gingerly tapped Danny on the elbow. "Do you want to dance? Sarah said that girls were supposed to ask a boy."

"Sure," Danny said without breathing.

The band was playing *Rock Around the Clock* as they moved self-consciously onto the dance floor. They began to rock and roll, close enough to talk but not close enough to touch. Jackie was happy to have a chance to talk to Danny, even if it was hard to hear over the music.

When the song ended, the band immediately transitioned into a slow dance, the Carpenters' *Close to You*. Most of the young people left the floor. Danny and Jackie looked at each other uncomfortably for a moment. Danny held out his hands. "Do you want to keep dancing?"

"Sure," Jackie murmured. She stood frozen, forgetting her years of dance lessons.

Danny took the lead. He gently reached out to her, put his right hand properly on her waist, placed her left hand on his waist, took her right hand in his left, and held their arms out awkwardly as he began to dance a simple two-step, back and forth. They were barely touching, moving uncomfortably, careful to keep several inches apart and not step on each other's feet.

Jackie felt a surge of emotion. She squirmed inside her clothes, uncomfortably aware of the texture of the fabric against her skin. She felt Danny's jacket swing against her breasts, her dress brushing against his legs, his hand touching the small of her back, her hand on his waist. She felt the blood rush to her face. Her mouth was dry.

She saw Ruben dancing with Sarah, frolicking through a slow-motion swing of twisting turns and tangled arms. She watched how the adults were dancing as well, the women nestled in the arms of their boyfriends and husbands. Spontaneously, Jackie lowered her head onto Danny's shoulder and put her arm around his back. She felt him tighten his arm around her waist. Their bodies touched. Jackie was afraid; afraid to move her body against his, to hold too tightly, to pull away, to breathe too deeply, to dance or to look as if they were not dancing; she was afraid everyone was watching, but mostly she was afraid that the dance would end. As the band hit the last note, Jackie impulsively gave Danny a kiss and then stepped away. They looked at each other for an instant, too absorbed in sensations to speak.

Sarah interrupted their silence almost immediately. "Good going, Jackie! Cool!" She applauded her new friend, then turned to her cousin. "So, Danny, will you still dance with me, or are you two going steady now?"

"Sarah! We are not—" Jackie protested. The band began playing *I'll Be There*, and Danny and Sarah started to dance. Jackie backed away slowly.

18

Junior high school began on the Tuesday after Labor Day. For the first time in their lives, Jackie and Danny did not have class together. He was in the most advanced section of each course, and her grades put her on an average track.

Several times each week, Danny would walk home with Jackie, and they would share a snack, study, and do homework together at her house. They would talk for hours about the things they were learning at school and things in the world around them.

Danny would test his ideas on Jackie, expounding on all the things that were unfair about the world and propose solutions to every problem. Jackie would listen intently as he thought aloud, and then offer her commentary. Sometimes they would have heated arguments, when Jackie didn't think his ideas made sense or he was taking himself too seriously. Sometimes she would simply tease him by saying, "Who cares?" to everything he said, forcing him to redouble his efforts to make her care.

But she did care. She cared what Danny thought, and she cared about Danny.

Her ideas were different from his. It did not matter to her whether or not everything in the world was fair. She was interested in exploration, invention, and discovery. Jackie told Danny about things she read in *National Geographic* or saw on the *Wonderful World of Disney*. Danny sometimes retaliated for her taunts by responding, "So what?" to everything she said, until she got frustrated and attacked him, tickling him until he asked for mercy.

Mary was always present when Danny was in the house, keeping an eye on her daughter and the boy who was spending time with her. She was always close enough to know exactly what they were doing, but far enough away to be inconspicuous.

Once, Mary was not at home when Danny stopped by the house. Jackie knew that she was not allowed to have a boy in the house without supervision, but she did not want Danny to go away. He stayed and they went about their routine, taking a snack from the refrigerator and doing their homework at the kitchen table. They were hard at work when Mary came home an hour later.

Mary fumed until Danny was gone. She then gave Jackie a stern lecture, reminding her that she was forbidden to have a boy in the house alone, and that she should learn to be careful around boys in general now that she was becoming a woman.

"It's just Danny," Jackie protested.

"I don't care if it's Danny. Boys will be boys," Mary warned.

"This is silly," Jackie responded, staring purposefully at the ceiling.

* * *

Jackie gradually matured from a spunky child into a stunning teenager. By the time she was sixteen, she was almost as tall as her father; a bit taller when wearing heels. She was slightly built, with small breasts and hips and long, light-brown hair that was parted in the middle and flowed down past the small of her back. She moved with a dancer's lightness and energy, well aware that she turned heads with the swish of her miniskirts.

Danny was approaching six feet tall, though his unruly black hair standing on end often made him look even taller. Unlike Jackie, whose presence could captivate a room, he often seemed to get lost behind his reticent and restive mannerisms.

One summer at camp, he began playing competitive tennis. When he returned in the fall, he taught Jackie how to play, and they began spending afternoons together on the tennis court. The first months were spent giggling at errant shots and picking up wayward balls. Eventually, Jackie developed into a solid player. While she could never hit the ball as hard as Danny, she played well enough to give him competitive practice. Occasionally, she would even win a set, much to his chagrin.

They enjoyed playing mixed doubles together and were wonderful to watch. Jackie was lovely in her white tennis dresses. She went after every shot with unbridled energy, her unbound hair flying wildly. Danny, in contrast, played with a quiet intensity and power. He studied the court position of his opponents, calculated the angles of his shots, and spent hours practicing how to hit the ball harder and more precisely at the corners. They played to win, but they were always gracious, cheering each other's good shots, consoling each other's errors and, at the end of each match, pausing to hold each other in a tight embrace before congratulating their opponents.

Jackie and Danny also liked to go on long walks in the woods where they talked, explored, and self-consciously held hands. They looked for excuses to touch each other and to engage in battles with water, leaves, or snowballs that usually ended with one wrestling the other to the ground, where Jackie could rest her head on his chest. Often she came home with bouquets of wild flowers that she placed in a vase by the side of her bed, next to her mother's picture.

Sometimes, they went to a local amusement park. Jackie would take Danny on rocket rides designed for much smaller children. They would squeeze themselves into the seats and feel the centrifugal force of the ride pushing their bodies together as the rockets spun in circles. He made her go with him on the roller coasters, where she screamed and held on to him for dear life.

Karen and Jackie also remained friends and they both attracted a lot of attention from boys. Karen reveled in courtship, and was the first of Jackie's friends to have a steady boyfriend and the first to have sex. Jackie had little interest in dating and became adept at parrying the attention without hurting anyone's feelings.

During their first year of high school, Karen and Jackie joined the cheer-leaders. Soon, Jackie's schedule was filled with cheerleading practices, sporting events, pep rallies, and parties. She always invited Danny to join her social activities, but he usually declined. Many of her activities were on weeknights, when he wanted to study. Moreover, when he agreed to go with her, he often went home unhappy. He did not enjoy being in a group where Jackie was at the center of activities and everyone competed with him for her time and attention.

On occasion, he would agree to go on double dates with Karen and one of her boyfriends for pizza and a movie. Inevitably, halfway through the movie, Karen and her date would begin necking and petting, while Danny and Jackie sat uncomfortably with their eyes glued to the screen, pretending not to notice.

Danny much preferred spending time with Jackie alone, and they went out of their way to find things to do together. They worked to organize Earth Day events and start a student chapter of the Connecticut Public Interest Research Group. Jackie joined Danny in working for the McGovern-Muskie campaign in 1972 and the reelection campaign of Connecticut senator Abraham Ribicoff in 1974. When Jackie tried to start an astronomy club at Spring High School, Danny was one of the few students who joined.

Danny developed his own circle of friends. He was active in the National Honor Society, the student government, and the school newspaper, and played on the varsity tennis team.

At the beginning of his junior year, Danny was elected captain of the debate team. He begged Jackie to join the team with him. After years of arguing his ideas with her, he knew no one was better at articulating an opinion or finding weaknesses in his positions.

Jackie protested that she was already busy with too many other things, and that she was not smart enough to compete with the brainy kids on the debate team. Danny persisted until she finally agreed. What convinced her was the topic for the junior year: "New technologies will raise the Third World." She could not resist arguing the topic, or the opportunity to spend more time with Danny.

Danny and Jackie spent months preparing for that first debate. They collected information on the Green Revolution that had dramatically reduced world hunger during the 1960s. They studied the World Health Organization's program to eradicate smallpox, which had successfully eliminated this disease from all countries in the world except for a small desert region in East Africa. They learned about the Aswan High Dam that was under construction across the Nile, and how this enormous project would control flooding, stimulate agriculture, and generate power once it was completed.

They studied the book *The Limits to Growth,* published in 1972, which described the first computer models of the resources required to support human populations. The model predicted that there was not enough energy, water, or arable land to support continued population growth. If the Earth's population continued to grow, the authors proposed, essential resources would be depleted by the end of the century. This would lead to a collapse of populations and the disintegration of civilization, possibly within their lifetimes.

Jackie's faith in the potential of science and technology made her conclude that apocalyptic predictions in *The Limits to Growth* were probably wrong. She took the lead in arguing that technology would improve conditions around the world, citing the potential for developing renewable sources of energy, improving agricultural methods, and reducing population growth by using oral contraceptives.

Danny reached a different conclusion; namely, that the Earth's population was at risk due to the absence of a fair system for allocating resources to those in need. He argued that technology alone would not solve endemic problems of poverty, hunger, and disease, unless there were fundamental changes in the social order and could, in fact, make things worse. Ultimately, he feared that the ominous predictions of *The Limits to Growth* could come to pass.

As their teachers had long predicted, Danny and Jackie formed the core of a great debate team. The hours they spent together discussing and disputing the topic between themselves prepared them for everything their opponents raised in competition. They complemented each other well and challenged each other to be better. Jackie was an articulate front person, disarming with her charisma, confidence, quickness, and command of the facts. Danny was the attacker, thoughtful, incisive, intimidating, and sometimes sarcastic. They reached the finals of the state competitions before losing for the first time.

Several weeks before Thanksgiving of their junior year, Jackie asked Danny if he would take her to the homecoming dance, where she would be a member of the homecoming queen's court. Danny was chagrined that he had not asked her first, but was pleased that she wanted to go with him. Since neither was old enough to drive, Danny asked his father to take them to the dance, but asked Ruben to pick them up when it was over to avoid the embarrassment of having one of his parents waiting for him outside the school.

The evening was a bewildering whirlwind of music and activity. There were pictures to be taken for the yearbook, a ceremony to crown the homecoming queen and her court, and staged events by the cheerleaders, athletes, and student government to psych the team for their Thanksgiving Day game against their traditional rival.

It seemed like everyone at the dance wanted to talk to Jackie, and Danny spent most of the evening standing helplessly by her side. It was past ten o'clock before they moved out onto the middle of dance floor to escape the incessant demands of Jackie's friends and classmates.

The dance floor was lit only by the lights flashing off the mirrored ball on the ceiling, which constricted their pupils and made the room seem even darker than it was. They danced amidst the crush of students and the pounding rhythms of the rock band until midnight, when the tempo slowed for the final dances of the evening. This time, there was no hesitation as Danny held out his arms and Jackie nestled her body close to his. She felt her breasts pressing against his chest and his body rubbing gently against her stomach and legs as they swayed to the sounds of *Touch Me in the Morning*. She closed her eyes and savored the sensations. Their bodies pressed closer with each step and each breath, until there was nothing between them but the thin fabric of her dress, the cotton of his shirt, and the blood and sensation pulsating through her skin. When the last dance was over, they held each other motionless for a moment, then stepped apart as the lights came on. Danny reached for her hand and held it firmly as she deftly dealt with a last flurry of conversation before finally saying good night to her friends.

Ruben was waiting for them when they emerged hand in hand from the dance.

"Hi, kids," Ruben greeted them gaily as they climbed into the backseat of the car, which smelled of sweat, beer, and marijuana.

"Thanks for picking us up," Jackie answered.

"Yeah, thanks," Danny echoed.

"I didn't know you two were lovers. No wonder you wanted me to pick you up instead of Dad," Ruben teased.

"We're not lovers," Danny protested.

"Did you actually go to the dance, or did you spend the night making out underneath the bleachers like everyone else?"

"We went to the dance," Danny responded, irritated.

Jackie ignored the banter and snuggled close to Danny with her head on his shirt between the lapels of his jacket. She felt him brush the hair off her face, smooth it down her back, and put his arms around her. She was content to lie quietly in his arms, listening to the rhythm of his heart.

"I thought the only ones who actually danced were those who couldn't get laid." Ruben's teasing continued.

Ruben should have been in his final year of college. He had enrolled in Juilliard after high school, intending to pursue a career in music, but quit abruptly in the middle of the spring term before the end of his first year. Had he stayed to finish the term, he would have failed.

During his first year of college, Ruben became consumed by the idea that the essence of art and music was unfettered, free expression. He came to believe that organization and orchestration could only compromise creativity and consciousness. If everyone in the world had the freedom to express themselves through music, art, literature, poetry, and drama, he argued to anyone who would listen, the world's problems would end in an era of consensual peace, harmony, and love.

Ruben became active in a revolutionary organization dedicated to using art to advance radical causes. They sponsored street performances and teach-ins in the subways and staged protests demanding that cultural institutions boycott performers, products, and venues whose ideology they contested. They denounced the contributions of wealthy individuals, institutions, and industries that conflicted with their ideal of art, and they conducted sit-ins on campus to demand that teachers who disagreed with their views be fired.

After leaving school in the spring of 1971, Ruben spent a year teaching music and radical politics in the poorest neighborhoods of New Haven. Then, he moved to Berkeley, hoping to find a place where his radical views would be more widely accepted. Even there, however, he found the structure of school and study to be stifling, and he drifted away, alternately living in communes along the California coast or at home with his parents in Spring.

Ruben made no effort to hide his drug use. During the year he worked in New Haven, his parents routinely smelled marijuana coming from his room and found drugs in plain view on his shelves. He readily admitted to using psychedelic drugs, including LSD and mescaline.

Drugs, in fact, played a central role in Ruben's ideology. He did not consider drug use to be an illicit activity. Rather, it was a tool for breaking down inhibitions and enhancing the freedom of expression and achieving peace. When his parents insisted that he meet with a psychologist known for his work with adolescent drug users, he reluctantly agreed and spent the time arguing that his drug use was a social statement rather than a psychological problem.

"So, Jackie," Ruben started again, interrupting her reverie. "Danny said you were part of the homecoming court. So you're, like, royalty?"

"It's silly, I know," Jackie laughed self-consciously.

"When I was in high school, the homecoming queen had to sleep with everyone to get their votes."

"Ruben!" Danny exclaimed with embarrassment.

"Our band played at a homecoming dance once," Ruben continued, his speech pressured and his sentences running together. "The principal insisted that we cut our hair before he would let us play. We needed the gig, so we got these square haircuts that made us look like fifties geeks. Then, he made us give him a list of all the songs we were going to play and told us which songs were allowed and which ones were banned. I guess he was afraid we would screw with people's minds or something."

"Ruben, we're really not interested," Danny tried to interrupt him.

"Then he wouldn't even let us onto the stage, until he had inspected our instrument cases to be sure we didn't have any joints or booze or anything. Like half the class wasn't stoned that night and hung over the next morning."

"The funny thing was that one of my friends had a condom in his guitar case. You should have seen the principal when he found it—he turned red like he was going to let one loose himself. Like he didn't know why half the cars in the parking lot were rocking all night."

"Ruben, stop it!"

"It wasn't like that at Woodstock, you know. That was a real trip. No one told the bands what to wear or what they could play. That was real freedom. Hey, do you guys want some weed?" Ruben asked suddenly, holding up a small plastic bag with dried leaves. Danny looked at Jackie and shrugged helplessly. "Some people call them rockets, you know. I thought you liked rockets, Jackie."

"There's nothing wrong with a joint, you know," Ruben continued. "It's great with sex. If you're planning to screw back there, you should try some—it gets rid of all your inhibitions. It makes you free."

Jackie felt the blood rush to her face and the pressure of Danny's arm relax. The smell of Ruben's sweat, beer, and marijuana suddenly overwhelmed the sensation of being close to Danny. She sat up and looked at Ruben, revolted by his smell, his torn clothes, his unruly hair, and his incessant talk.

"Do you know why everyone is afraid of weed? Because they are afraid to be free, afraid everyone might want to be free."

Jackie looked at Danny's ashen face, silently pleading for him to make Ruben stop.

"But it's not like dropping acid," Ruben continued relentlessly. "Now, that's really a trip. You can fly without feeling bound by gravity or space or air or food or anything. It's like total freedom. You should try it if you're still into all that space stuff, Jackie. You feel like you are flying at warp speed. You see things that no one would even believe."

Ruben's verbal barrage continued, until they arrived in front of Jackie's house. Danny helped her out of the car and walked her to the front door, but the moment of intimacy had passed. He walked several feet away from her, looking down at the ground, ignoring the entreaty of her hand as it brushed his, unaware of her disappointed eyes.

"I'm sorry about Ruben," he mumbled when they reached the front door. "I'm sure he didn't mean to embarrass you. He's been very strange lately."

"Yeah, what's with him?" Jackie asked, irritated. "Does he have any idea what he's saying?"

"No, he has no idea."

"What happened to him?"

"I don't know. He's in trouble—probably drugs. We don't talk much anymore. I hope he didn't ruin your evening." Danny changed the subject. "I really wanted you to have a good time."

"I had a good time," she answered, reaching purposefully for his hand. "I hope you did too."

"Yeah, it was fine," he answered distractedly. They looked at each other awkwardly for a moment.

"I like dancing with you." Jackie tried to salvage the evening.

"I'm not much of a dancer. I've never had dance lessons or anything."

"You're a good dancer. It was fun." She squeezed his hand to keep his attention focused on her. "I had a good time."

"So did I," he admitted.

"Well, I better go in. Good night." Jackie leaned forward to give Danny a kiss but pulled back when she saw Ruben leering at them from the car.

"Good night."

19

Jackie and Danny graduated from high school on June 4, 1976. Danny was the class valedictorian, having maintained a perfect A average. The yearbook cited him as "Most likely to be a Supreme Court Justice." He was accepted at every college he applied to, and registered at Harvard for the fall.

Jackie had never shaken her childhood habit of being inattentive in class and distracted by extracurricular activities. She graduated with a low B average and was cited in the yearbook as "Most likely to kiss Captain Kirk." She planned to go to the University of Connecticut in Storrs.

Everyone knew Danny and Jackie were a couple. They were always an item at school dances, and at football games on cold nights, Jackie would snuggle close to Danny and pull a blanket over them to keep warm. There was gossip when Danny and Jackie fell asleep together in a sleeping bag during an Astronomy Club stargazing party. The yearbook had a picture of them dancing together at the senior prom, with the caption, "Most likely to have a child who is Miss America and wins the Nobel Peace Prize."

As Jackie approached the end of high school, her parents became increasingly concerned about their daughter's relationship with Danny. While they were courteous to Danny, they encouraged Jackie to meet Catholic boys and periodically arranged dates for her with boys from St. Patrick's or neighboring churches. Jackie willingly went along on these arranged dates, and, on one occasion, even met someone whom she liked well enough to date several times.

Danny's parents were preoccupied with Ruben's problems and genuinely liked Jackie's wholesomeness in contrast to the friends Ruben brought home. They occasionally reminded Danny that it would be good if he met a "nice Jewish girl," but they never forced the issue. They understood that Danny was going away to college in the fall and that Jackie probably would not be part of his life after he left.

Jackie had always known that Danny wanted to go to Harvard. She had helped him prepare his applications and essays, adding some of her lightness to his impressive list of accomplishments, and she waited anxiously with him for a letter from the admissions office. When the thick letter arrived, he waited until they could open it together.

Reading over Danny's shoulder, she realized immediately that he had been accepted. She let out a cry of happiness and gave Danny a tight hug, holding him firmly as her cry devolved into the realization that he was really going away.

They sat next to each other in alphabetical order at graduation, just as they had throughout their early school years. She took Danny's hand in both of hers when they first sat down and held it tightly throughout the ceremony. When it came time for his valedictory address, she squeezed his hand and whispered, "Break a leg," as he stood to ascend the podium.

Jackie knew Danny's speech by heart. He had been working on it for an entire semester. She had listened to new drafts almost daily, and they had spent hours together trying to make it perfect.

"In exactly one month," Danny began in a dramatic voice, "on July fourth, 1976, our nation will celebrate two hundred years since the signing of the Declaration of Independence. The diplomas that the class of 1976 receives today gives each of us independence, just like the Declaration of Independence two hundred years ago.

"Just as the wars that England fought in the 1760s led colonists to challenge English law and ultimately to rebel, the war in Vietnam led many of us to challenge the American legal system and led some to rebel. Just as the English's attempt to retain their power through actions that violated the rights of the colonists led to the fall of English rule, Richard Nixon's attempt to retain power through actions that violated our rights led to his fall. Just as the aftermath of the Revolutionary War made Americans think more about freedom and justice, the end of the Vietnam War can do the same. Just as the removal of the British crown from the colonies led to the Constitution, the Bill of Rights, and a new democracy, the resignation of our 'Imperial President' gives us an opportunity to renew our democracy. Just as the Revolutionary War paved the way for the settlement of the American West, we will have the opportunity to settle the Moon and the planets."

Jackie smiled broadly at the last line, which she had written. Danny had never thought it was relevant to his speech, but he left it in because it made her happy.

Danny concluded with a flourish. "As you come up for your diplomas today, try to imagine that you are members of the Continental Congress and that you are not just receiving a diploma, but affixing your name to a Declaration of Independence. What will you do next? How will you ensure that the inalienable rights of men and women to life, liberty, and the pursuit of happiness are protected? After today, we are all independent! We are all free! What will we do?"

He spoke with passion, poise, and the idealism of youth. Jackie hung on every word and was the first to begin clapping when he finished. The teachers offered their congratulations. His classmates offered only polite applause. Few appeared to be listening. No one seemed to care.

There was little idealism in the class of 1976 that day, and little interest in history, government, or politics. It was a generation that had grown tired of talking about war, peace, and civil rights. In August of that year, Tom Wolfe would famously dub the era of the 70s the "Me Decade" or the "Me generation."

When the Vietnam War ended in 1975, few Americans cared that Cambodia and South Vietnam quickly fell to the communists. When reports surfaced of atrocities in Cambodia, where the Khmer Rouge killed more than one-fifth of the entire population, the press and public looked away. Many in the class of 1976 would never even bother to vote.

Communism and capitalism continued to engage in a long cold war. America continued to be the target of terrorist attacks by radical, Arab, and nationalist groups. The world continued to be torn by revolutionary, racial, and religious conflicts. Sectarian violence continued in Northern Ireland, Israel, and Lebanon. Yet, few feared that civilization itself teetered on the brink of extinction.

The next speaker was Bob (Boomer) Stevens, who had been elected to speak for the class. Boomer was the school's star athlete and the captain of both the football and baseball teams, which had won regional championships their senior year.

Boomer talked about the high points of his high school experience. His talk was filled with stories about victories on the playing field, broad innuendoes about who had been sleeping with who, reminiscences of alcohol-induced high jinks, pointed jokes about his friends, and generally disparaging remarks about various teachers. His talk elicited laughter, cheers, and jeers from the audience, which energized him to move beyond the text that the principal had approved to more ribald language and stories. Then he turned to Danny.

"Danny, you gave a wonderful speech," he said with scorn. "I basically have no idea what you were talking about, but what the hell, it sounded good." Many students laughed. "The problem I had with your speech, Danny, is that you never told us the only thing we all want to know—did you ever sleep with Jackie?" The rowdy taunt elicited a burst of laughter and scattered catcalls from his friends and teammates.

Jackie was mortified. Her parents were there! Danny's family was there! How could he say something like that at her graduation? She wished she could pull the plug on the microphone or make Boomer disappear.

The principal had heard enough. He walked over to the podium and deftly edged Boomer away. There were scattered boos and cheers as Boomer jaunted off the stage waving to the crowd with both arms over his head and giving the V sign for victory.

Eventually, the principal began handing out diplomas and awards. Karen Altman walked across the stage at the head of the class. She had maintained a B average and was headed to the University of San Diego, where she would be far from her father and close to boys and the beach. Danny received the award for the highest grade point average, as well as awards for being the best student in social studies. Jackie was recognized for her contribution to school spirit.

As soon as the ceremony ended, Jackie walked disconsolately away from Danny without saying a word. She had desperately wanted to share graduation with him, to give him a celebratory kiss, to hold his hand, to hear people congratulating him on his speech. Boomer's talk had ruined everything. She could feel people looking at her as she walked around the room, silently asking the same question Boomer had asked. Everything was ruined.

20

In the fall of 1976, Danny started Harvard. Jackie drove to Cambridge with him and his parents to help him move into the dorm. They spent several hours setting up Danny's room, exploring the campus, and having ice cream at Steve's.

It was late afternoon when Jackie and his parents said good-bye and started driving back to Hartford. Danny's parents tried to make polite conversation on the way, but Jackie spent most of the two-hour ride crying softly in the backseat, hoping they would not hear.

Classes began the following week at the University of Connecticut. To save money, Jackie planned to live at home and commute fifteen miles each day to the campus in Storrs.

Jackie had not thought much about what to study in college or what she might do after she graduated. When she had to fill out a form listing her major, she wrote "astronomy" without giving it much thought.

By 1976, public interest in the space program had declined dramatically. There had been four successful landings on the Moon after the drama of *Apollo 13*, but three additional landings, planned as part of the *Apollo* Program, were canceled due to budget constraints and a lack of public interest. When *Apollo 17* left the Moon in December 1972, NASA had no plans for future lunar missions and was focused instead on building a reusable space shuttle that would not be able to fly beyond Earth's orbit. Neither the launch of *Skylab* in 1973, nor the much publicized docking of the American *Apollo* and Soviet *Soyuz* spacecraft in 1975, generated any popular enthusiasm for further space exploration. The last two *Saturn* rockets, which had been built to take men to the Moon, were decommissioned and laid on the ground outside the Kennedy Space Flight Center and the Johnson Space Flight Center in Houston; Earthbound monuments to the *Apollo* program.

In July of 1976, NASA announced that it would begin soliciting applications from women to fly in the space shuttle, which would be completed in the early 1980s. Jackie sent away for the application forms, only to learn that NASA was looking for women with advanced professional degrees in science or aeronautics who could serve as mission specialists. While she knew she did not have much chance of being chosen, she could not resist the temptation to apply. Shortly after school began in September, she received a form letter rejection encouraging her to apply again after completing her graduate studies.

Through the first months of the fall term, Jackie and Danny tried to stay in touch by telephone but found it frustrating. They tried to arrange times when he would wait for her call by the phone in the hallway of the dorm, but often he would not get there in time, or someone else would be using the phone and she would get a busy signal. It was also hard for Danny to call her, since she spent most of her days on campus and generally returned home only late in the evening. After weeks failing to connect by telephone, they both stopped trying.

It was even harder to spend time together. Jackie was still living at home, and her parents made it clear they would not approve of her staying overnight with Danny in Cambridge. Several times, she drove to Cambridge for a day but found the four-hour drive exhausting and the limited time together unsatisfying. Eventually, they settled on exchanging long letters, until they both became too inundated with schoolwork and extracurricular activities to communicate on a regular basis.

Jackie spent much of her free time that fall volunteering for Jimmy Carter's presidential campaign. In high school, she had become involved in politics only because it was a way to spend time with Danny. Carter, however, was someone who appealed to her. He had been a nuclear engineer in the Navy and had worked on the development of America's nuclear submarines before entering politics. He had a reputation as a technocrat, someone who sought technical solutions to problems, rather than engaging in rhetorical contests. Jackie liked his approach.

Through the fall, Jackie worked for the Carter campaign between classes, passing out campaign materials, staffing telephone banks, and helping at the polls. She enjoyed campaigning. It gave her an outlet for her energy, introduced her to a group of friends who shared her enthusiasm and energy, and reminded her of time she had spent with Danny. She was melancholy when the campaign was over, the campaign office closed, and her new friends returned to schools and jobs across the state. She found it hard to turn her attention to her classes.

The week before Thanksgiving, Jackie received a short note from Danny saying that he would be home for the holiday and that he looked forward to spending time with her. She was eager to see him.

Danny picked Jackie up just after breakfast on Friday morning, and they drove out to a park in the Berkshires. They spent the day walking in the woods, holding hands, telling each other about their experiences in college, and reliving high school memories. For two people who had spent years discussing every idea and sharing every thought, there was not nearly enough time for all the things they wanted to say to each other.

Shortly after Thanksgiving, Bert suggested that Jackie work part-time to offset the cost of her tuition and pay her share of the family's expenses, so she began working at the family store several evenings each week and on weekends. As the Christmas season and final exams approached in December, Jackie found herself overwhelmed. It was hard to limit her working hours without offending her father. She struggled to complete her term papers, failed to study for several final exams, and barely managed to get Cs in her courses. When school resumed in January, she took a job as a waitress near the campus in Storrs, where she made more money, was able to work more circumscribed hours, and could call in sick when she was overwhelmed.

Danny rarely came back to Spring, except over holidays. When he was home, they always tried to escape to a park or a museum, anywhere they could hold hands and talk. Jackie anticipated each visit for weeks in advance, making mental notes of the things she wanted to say. When they were together, they had time only for the most superficial discussion of the ideas, events, and emotions that were shaping them into adults. There was no time for the carefree spontaneity and the emotional intimacy they had shared for so many years.

By her second term at Storrs, Jackie recognized that majoring in astronomy was not about watching stars in the sky or exploring the solar system. Rather, the study of astronomy was dominated by the application of modern physics and mathematics to explain the structure and even the origins of the universe.

She had never done well in math or physics. She received Cs in the courses required for an astronomy major and was forced to drop several of the classes just before the deadline to avoid receiving a failing grade. At the beginning of her sophomore year, her advisor gently suggested that she consider majoring in a different field.

Jackie recognized that she was not the proverbial rocket scientist. Moreover, the space program no longer captivated her imagination the way it had as a child. While the unmanned missions of *Mariner, Pioneer, Viking,* and *Voyager* to the Moon, Mars, and Venus provided stunning pictures and scientific data about the solar system, they seemed to mark a denouement for an age of space exploration, not a beginning. After the *Pioneer* missions to Venus in 1978, it would be more than a decade before any American spacecraft was launched beyond Earth's orbit, and half a century before astronauts would return to the Moon.

Knowing she needed to find something else to do with her life, Jackie enrolled in introductory courses in biology, psychology, and sociology, searching for something she found interesting. Nothing was interesting. She dropped several courses after the first week while she could still register for something else. In other courses, she would find herself daydreaming in class, ignoring homework assignments, and taking tests unprepared. More than once, she stopped attending class altogether and accepted an "Incomplete."

For the first time in her life, Jackie also found herself socially isolated. It was hard to become engaged in the college community while she lived at home and worked twenty or more hours each week. She had no interest in talking to her classmates about courses they took seriously while she let her studies slide. When she was asked out on dates or went to sporting events on campus, she found herself longing wistfully for the camaraderie of the cheerleaders and the comfort of snuggling with Danny under a warm blanket. Increasingly, she spent the hours she was not working sitting alone in her room staring aimlessly into space.

Throughout her life, she had turned to Danny when she needed help. Now, there was no one to talk to, no one to listen to her, no one to contest her thoughts. No one challenged her or helped her maintain a sense of direction, and no one pushed her to do better.

It takes time and effort for two people to forge a relationship that enables them to talk meaningfully about their innermost ideas. With Danny, it had been an accident; their names juxtaposed in alphabetical order in a system that imposed order. Nevertheless, by the time they graduated high school, they shared a bond that embodied a lifetime of shared experience.

Jackie wondered whether she would have become friends with Danny if they had met in a classroom at Storrs. He was a studious, dark presence who internalized the torment, teaching, and tradition of his heritage. She was impulsive and bright, with expansive energy and missionary zeal. What would she have said if he had asked her out on a date? Would she have dated a Jew? Would she have been patient with his long silences, his need to carefully construct his thoughts before speaking, and his brooding moods? Would she have let him challenge her most cherished ideas, and would she have cared to challenge his? Would he have become a regular feature in her dreams?

Probably not.

The realization made her even more depressed. What was the point of making friends and dating if she would never have dared to befriend and date the one person in the world she had come to love? It had taken years for Jackie and Danny to learn how to talk to each other, how to touch each other, how to hold hands, and how to kiss. She thought back; the first time he had shared his nightmares with her and the first time she had shared her dreams with him; the first time she had cried in his arms and he had comforted her.

Jackie drifted into a deep depression. She went for days at a time without talking to anyone. She skipped classes regularly and was often inattentive and despondent at work. She ate irregularly and began to lose weight. At home, she was moody and temperamental.

Mary could do nothing to console her. Every conversation they had seemed to end in an argument. Bert tried to be understanding, but teen angst was not part of his experience. His life had moved seamlessly through school, military service, work, marriage, and family. He felt helpless seeing his daughter so unhappy.

He was also preoccupied with his own problems. Business was not good. Years of inflation and economic stagnation had made it harder to support the family. At home, he was overwhelmed with four adolescent and preadolescent children vying for his attention. Jackie would have to find her own way.

At the end of her sophomore year, Jackie received a letter from the dean's office placing her on academic probation. She had failed to complete required assignments for several courses and received grades of "Incomplete." She could register as a full-time student in the fall only if she arranged to complete the missing work and received passing grades in these classes. Jackie barely acknowledged the letter and buried it at the bottom of a desk drawer.

21

Jackie and Karen spent the summer after their sophomore year working and rooming together at a resort in the Catskills. Danny was in Europe for the summer on a foreign exchange program. Karen's latest boyfriend had stayed in San Diego to take summer courses. Jackie had no interest in spending the summer in Spring with her tween brothers and sisters.

"I might as well just drop out," Jackie complained sadly the first night she was alone with Karen in their small dormitory-style room. "Maybe I can get a job running rides at the carnival. Remember that ride with the rockets that flew around in circles? I used to like that."

"You're not dropping out of school," Karen rebuked.

"I can't imagine going to school for two more years. It's so boring. I just want to run away."

"Stop it, Jackie. So you didn't turn in your homework and have some incompletes. What's new? I don't think you've turned in a single homework assignment in your whole life."

"That's not true."

"You just never cared."

"I *don't* care! That's the point! The only time I ever did homework was when Danny made me."

"A smart boyfriend is a good strategy," Karen answered cynically. "Get a boyfriend to do your homework for you."

"I miss Danny."

"Get over him."

"I miss him!"

"I never understood what you saw in him. He isn't that good-looking. That hair always standing on end—ugh! And you never slept with him, so you don't even know if he's good in bed."

"Stop it, Karen!"

"What's the big deal? Find some guy to do your work for you. All you have to do is promise them sex," Karen continued playfully.

"Karen!" Jackie was aghast.

"You know guys will do almost anything for sex."

"Karen, stop!" Jackie insisted.

"It's a good way to get laid without having to hang around bars. You might even find yourself a husband. Guys with brains make a lot of money you know."

"That's not what I want," Jackie protested.

"What do you want?"

"I don't know. I don't know what I want to do. I just have no idea."

"So you're just going to sit around feeling sorry for yourself all summer? You're not going to be much fun. Look, you're not going to solve this by staring into space. Loosen up. Lose your virginity already."

"That's helpful." Jackie laughed scornfully. "Should I make a living selling my body?"

"You don't need a college degree to turn tricks," Karen teased.

"Go to hell!"

"That's the idea!"

Jackie hurled a pillow at her head. In a second, they were having a furious pillow fight, screaming and laughing as they slugged each other harmlessly with the pillows from the bed and cushions from the couch. It was exactly what Jackie needed. She felt much better when they stopped to catch their breath and clean up the mess they had made.

"So what are you going to do when you graduate college?" Jackie asked later that evening when calm had been restored.

"I don't know, and I don't care. You don't have to figure out your whole life. No one in our generation knows what they want to do."

"But aren't you supposed to learn something in college, something that will get you a job?"

"That's what my father keeps saying. He's always telling me what I'm supposed to do—go to medical school and become a doctor."

"He's done that your whole life. So what's new?"

"Now he's threatening to stop paying for college unless I enroll in premed courses. I don't want to be a doctor. I don't want to be like him. All he does is worry about work. I want to have a life! I want to have fun. I want to be happy!"

"Do you tell him that?"

"I tell him every time I see him."

"So what does he say?"

"He gets angry and yells at me. Then my mother gets angry with him for yelling at me. Then they start yelling at each other. Then I start yelling at them. It hasn't changed since I was a kid." She paused. "That's why I'm spending the summer here with you, working for minimum wage, rather than sitting by the pool at my father's country club, charging food, drinks, and sun tan lotion to his credit card. I didn't want to spend all summer yelling. That, and the fact that they don't allow me to have boys in the house. Can you imagine a whole summer without sex?"

"You're asking me that question?" Jackie laughed incredulously.

It helped Jackie to spend the summer with a friend, to worry about someone else's problems, and to know that she was not alone in trying to find herself. It helped having someone to talk to about her own adolescence and uncertainty. But it did not help her decide what to do about school.

Toward the end of the summer, Karen and Jackie had dinner with Karen's parents. It was an uncomfortable evening. Karen argued with her parents throughout dinner. Her father continued to push his daughter toward medical school. He described his fascination with human physiology and psychology. He described the progress being made in the war on cancer and about new machines called CT scanners that could see inside a living body. Karen stubbornly said she did not want to go to medical school and that it was her life and her decision, not her parents'.

There was no discussion, only declarations of long-standing views. If Jackie had not been there, the evening would certainly have dissolved in anger.

After hours of stalemate, Karen's father turned to Jackie. "So, what do you think my daughter should do, Jackie?"

"That's not fair, Daddy," Karen protested.

"Why isn't it fair?" He turned to Karen. "You're not listening to me. You never listen to me. Maybe your friend was listening. So—" he turned back to Jackie, "what do you think my daughter should do?"

"You don't have to answer, Jackie," Karen tried to intercede.

"I don't know, Dr. Altman," Jackie answered for herself. "Karen has to have her own idea of who she is and what she wants to do."

"Well, what do you think? Doesn't it make sense to earn a living and be part of something exciting and important?"

"It might make sense if—"

"Of course it makes sense," he interrupted.

"Maybe it isn't Karen's idea. Maybe it doesn't make sense to her."

"Nonsense. What would you do if your father offered to pay your tuition and room and board so you could go to medical school?"

"I don't know. It might be a good idea," Jackie answered reluctantly.

"So there!" Dr. Altman exclaimed in triumph. "See, Karen, your friend listens. She thinks it's a good idea. You're the only one who doesn't listen."

While Jackie loyally defended Karen's right to make her own decisions, she found herself intrigued by Dr. Altman's passion for medicine. She had taken an introductory biology course during her first year at college and found it somewhat interesting. It was the only course in which she had received a grade higher than a C. Over the next several days, the idea of pursuing a career in medicine began to intrigue her.

When Karen returned to California in the middle of August, Jackie turned her attention to completing her overdue coursework so she could resume school in the fall. It took her several weeks to complete the required assignments, contact the professors to convert her incomplete grades into Cs, and apply for reinstatement.

The first day of school, she registered for the second course in the biology curriculum; a course in cell and molecular biology. For the first time since starting college, she found herself completely engaged in a subject. She worked hard the entire semester, attended every class, completed all the assignments, and studied for the tests. She was particularly intrigued when the professor, Dr. Mary Singer, described her own research with the newly developed methods for recombinant DNA and genetic engineering. When a work-study position became available in the professor's laboratory, Jackie applied for the job.

The hourly wage for work-study was less than she made as a waitress, but the position paid her tuition and gave her more time to do homework and to study. Jackie's role in the laboratory was to perform menial work of growing bacteria and cleaning glassware. Nevertheless, she liked the people who worked in the laboratory and the powerful new technologies for genetic engineering and cloning that Dr. Singer was using.

The principle of cloning had emerged from the research that Karen had described in a current events presentation during elementary school. Those experiments demonstrated that, if the DNA from a virus was purified and then injected into a cell, the cell responded as if it had been infected with a complete virus. This included taking over the machinery of the cell to produce thousands of copies of new infectious virus, each of which could, in turn, infect other cells. If this process continued, enormous quantities of virus would be produced, each containing perfect copies of the DNA molecule that had been injected into the first cell. In this way, a single DNA molecule could be copied, or cloned, into innumerable identical copies.

In the 1970s, scientists learned how to construct and clone novel DNA molecules through genetic engineering. This involved cutting DNA into precisely defined pieces, purifying them in the laboratory, and then putting these pieces back together in different combinations to create new molecules, a process called *recombinant DNA*.

Dr. Singer's laboratory was trying to isolate and clone the gene that codes for human growth hormone from the tens of thousands of different genes in human cells. The ultimate goal of the research was to use recombinant DNA technologies to produce large amounts of growth hormone, enough to treat people with growth hormone deficiency.

The potential of genetic engineering seemed limitless. Not only was it theoretically possible to produce large quantities of human growth hormone to treat children with short stature, but also to produce human insulin to treat diabetes, human interferon to fight infections, and human blood clotting factors to treat hemophilia. Scientists also thought it might be possible to genetically engineer plants to be more nutritious, more resilient to spoilage, or more resistant to insects. Others thought it would be possible to genetically engineer animals as models for human diseases, or even use genes to treat human disease through gene therapy. Jackie was fascinated by the possibilities.

Genetic engineering was controversial in 1978. It had been only five years since the scientists who discovered recombinant DNA had, themselves, called a moratorium on their research to fully consider the social, ethical, and environmental implications of the new technology. While many people were excited about the prospect of exploring new treatments for disease, others were afraid that genetic engineering could accidentally create dangerous new strains of bacteria or even Frankenstein-like monsters. At many universities, neighborhood activists, students, and even faculty joined protests to ban genetic engineering and cloning from their campuses and communities.

The dialectical arguments about the potential benefits and risks of genetic engineering captured Jackie's interest even more than the research itself. When the campus paper ran an article describing the potential environmental and social hazards of cloning, Jackie wrote a letter to the editor describing how genetic engineering might make people's lives better. Several days later, she was asked to participate in a debate on the campus radio station with students who were trying to ban cloning from the campus. Jackie expounded on the boundless potential of genetic technologies to save lives and improve nutrition. Her opponents were not nearly as enthusiastic or skilled in debate, and Jackie was widely considered the winner of the encounter.

As Jackie became increasingly engaged by the controversy over genetic engineering, she gradually lost interest in the day-to-day work of the lab. Recombinant technologies were exciting but inefficient. Dr. Singer's laboratory had been searching for the growth hormone gene for more than two years without success. After working in the laboratory for six months, the repetitive work of purifying genes, cutting and recombining DNA, and growing bacteria became tedious.

22

In the spring of 1979, Danny wrote to Jackie that he was coming home for Passover with a friend whom he wanted Jackie to meet. He invited her to his parents' house for their Passover Seder, but did not say who he was bringing.

The next day, Jackie called Mrs. Cohn to say she would be coming. When they had finished discussing the arrangements, Jackie asked if she knew who Danny was bringing.

"He's bringing a girl. I think her name is Rachel," Mrs. Cohn answered directly.

Jackie caught her breath quickly. "Is she someone who—" Jackie stopped, unsure she wanted to hear the answer.

"I think they've been dating for a while," Mrs. Cohen answered gently. Jackie was not surprised. "We've never met her."

Danny and Jackie had always dated other people, and they often shared stories about bad dates and uncomfortable experiences. Instinctively, however, Jackie knew this was different.

Jackie dressed for the Seder in a short patterned skirt and sweater, bought a box of Passover candy as a house gift for Mrs. Cohn, and arrived at the Cohn's about an hour before the Seder. Danny met her at the door with a warm hug and immediately introduced her to Rachel Fiedler, who was standing next to him.

Rachel put out her hand and gave Jackie an uncomfortably firm handshake. "It's great to finally meet you, Jackie," Rachel said, holding on to Jackie's hand and speaking in a somewhat guttural English accent. "I've heard so much about you from Danny. He talks about you all the time. For the longest time, I thought you were his sister or something." Rachel's tone was frank and friendly.

Jackie had worried about the moment she would meet Danny's girlfriend. Instantly, she realized the moment was much more difficult for Rachel. She hadn't even known Rachel existed until several days ago. Rachel knew that Danny and Jackie had been intimate friends for years.

124

"I'm glad to meet you, too," she answered, being careful to sound sincere. "Danny has told me a lot about you too," she lied.

Danny's mother came out from the kitchen and greeted Jackie with a warm hug. "It's so good to see you. We're not going to start for a while. There's so much to do. Go sit with everyone else in the living room."

"Can we help?" Danny offered.

"No, there are already too many people in the kitchen."

Danny took Jackie by the arm, led her to the living room, and introduced her to the dozen relatives congregated there. Jackie saw Ruben sitting at the piano, fingering a silent melody on the closed keyboard. His torn jeans, sandals, and stained tunic contrasted with the holiday clothes everyone else was wearing.

"Hi, Ruben. I haven't seen you in years. How are you?" she greeted him simply.

Ruben did not acknowledge her. His eyes seemed to retreat even further into his already sunken features.

Jackie turned toward Danny, unsure whether she should try again. He shrugged and turned her toward the other side of the room.

"Jackie, you remember Sarah Rosen."

"Sure, we met at your Bar Mitzvah."

"Sarah is a student at the University of Connecticut, too," Danny added. "Maybe you've run into each other on campus."

"No, we haven't. It's a big campus," Jackie answered. Even if they had crossed paths, Jackie thought, it was unlikely she would have recognized Sarah. She was no longer a skinny kid, but a mature woman with elaborate makeup, big hair, and sophisticated clothes.

"We should try to get together on campus," Jackie offered.

"Sure, that would be nice," Sarah answered sincerely.

Danny guided Jackie to an empty chair on one side of the room, and then sat beside Rachel on the couch. Jackie studied her intently. Rachel was several inches shorter than Danny, with a broad, almost stocky build, dark complexion, and cropped black hair. Her manner was assertive and almost grating, even when expressing sentiments that were genuinely warm, open, and sometimes humorous. Jackie saw how they glanced knowingly at each other, how their fingers were intertwined, and how their shoulders and legs touched constantly. She wondered whether Rachel had been Danny's first lover.

Rachel was the center of attention. No one in Danny's family had met her before, and she was subject to an amiable but aggressive barrage of questions about her background and her family. Rachel had been born in South Africa, the daughter of refugees from Nazi Germany. Her mother left Germany with her family shortly after the Nazi party came to power, arriving in South Africa in 1934. Her father escaped from Germany on a kindertransport, days after Kristallnacht, and had been surreptitiously moved into South Africa by relief agencies. After the war, when it was determined that everyone in his family had been killed in German concentration camps, he was legally adopted by a Jewish family in Johannesburg.

As a young adult, he had become a lawyer fighting against racism, anti-Semitism, and apartheid, and had spent time in jail for his support of the African National Congress. With the racial situation in South Africa deteriorating, he had sent Rachel to college in the United States where he thought she would be safe.

Jackie was silent while Rachel fielded questions from Danny's family. It was easy for her to see what attracted Danny to Rachel. Rachel shared her father's activist political views and was an energetic, impassioned woman who had been on the front lines of the fight for justice, where Danny had always wanted to be. Listening to Rachel expound angrily on the injustice of apartheid was almost like listening to Danny.

They talked for about an hour before Mrs. Cohn called everyone to the table. Jackie took a seat next to Sarah and across from Danny and Rachel. Mr. Cohn led the ceremony celebrating the ancient exodus from slavery in Egypt to freedom in the Promised Land. Sarah again played the role of interlocutor, explaining the ritual and traditions as they went along.

They took turns reading aloud ancient prayers, in which each participant was asked to believe that they had been slaves in Egypt, and would still be slaves, if not for the wonder of the Exodus. They sang Hebrew psalms and Negro spirituals. They talked about slavery, struggle, and salvation in both the past and present tense. They recalled exiles returning to a promised land, receiving manna from heaven, and planting roots in a land of milk and honey. They talked earnestly about the civil rights movement and civil liberties, the fight against apartheid, the struggle of Soviet Jews for freedom, and reclaiming the land of Israel.

Only Ruben did not participate. He sat sullenly through most of the service without opening his prayer book. When it was his turn to read a paragraph celebrating the passage from slavery to freedom at the Red Sea, he refused.

"It's your turn, Ruben," his father urged gently.

"I don't want to read," he answered rebelliously.

"Ruben" his father's voice turned stern.

"I'm not going to read some stupid story about some bad trip. So they escaped from Egypt and crossed the Red Sea without getting wet? So there was fire and smoke on the mountains and manna on the ground every morning and some dude who talked a good line about freedom, and then made up a bunch of stupid rules so that no one would be free. Who cares anyway? They didn't end up free. They all died in the desert. That's the way it ends, isn't it? It was a bad trip, and they all died in the desert. Great story!"

"That's enough, Ruben," his father scolded.

"Now if the manna had been dope or acid—man, that would have been a real trip!"

"Ruben!"

"If there really is a God, and God wanted to do some miracle, how come God didn't just give everyone wings to fly out of Egypt and be free? Why would a God make people go through plagues and a bunch of dumb commandments and then leave everyone to die in the desert anyway? Why didn't God just let them fly?"

"Ruben, shut up!"

"Don't tell me to shut up," he responded with rising disgust. "What do any of you know about freedom? Woodstock was about freedom, you know. No one told you what to say or what to sing. No one told you what to wear or what to eat. There's no freedom here. Just a bunch of damned rules. This is stupid! I don't know why I even came. I'm out of here." He abruptly stood from the table and noisily left the house, slamming the door behind him.

There was a moment of uncomfortable silence as everyone looked around the table. "I'm sorry," Mr. Cohn apologized for his son. "It has been a difficult time for Ruben. Should I go after him?" Mr. Cohen asked his wife.

"Let him go," she answered sadly. "I think we should continue."

It took several minutes to regain the rhythm and reverence of the service. By the time they finished the rituals half an hour later and were ready for dinner, Ruben's outburst was largely forgotten and Rachel was once again the center of attention.

Dinner was festive, with enough food for three times the number of people and a cacophony of competing conversations. Jackie felt out of place. She was keen to talk to Danny but did not want to interrupt the family's absorption with Rachel or call attention to herself. She feared she would not have a chance to talk to him at all. She fought the impulse to stand up and walk out the door the way Ruben had, but she knew she would not be able to close the door behind her. Instead, she listened to the conversations around her and chatted amicably with Sarah.

When dinner was over, Danny, Rachel, and Jackie helped Mrs. Cohn clear the table, while everyone else gravitated back toward the living room. When the table was almost clear, Danny touched Jackie on the arm and asked, "Would you like to take a walk?"

Jackie was surprised. "Just you and me? What about Rachel?"

"My family's not done grilling her yet. She can hold her own."

"I'd love to take a walk." Jackie smiled.

Danny went over to Rachel and whispered something in her ear. Jackie saw her nod approvingly and give him a quick kiss. Danny then retrieved Jackie's coat and they went outside. They exchanged insignificant pleasantries for the first few minutes and then walked in silence for a while before Jackie asked, "Is Ruben okay?"

"No. He's not doing well. He's been living in some commune in California and is doing a lot of drugs. He was high on something tonight. I don't think he knew what he was saying."

"I saw," she answered sympathetically, though she was not thinking about Ruben. There were so many things she wanted to say to Danny, but somehow the time didn't seem right.

"Do you like her?" Danny asked after another silence. Jackie was surprised at the question.

"Rachel?" she asked, buying time.

"Yeah."

"She's very nice. You two seem happy," she answered sincerely.

"We are," he said haphazardly. Then he continued more carefully. "I was hoping you would like her. It means a lot to me, you know, what you think." Danny seemed unsure of what he was trying to say.

"It does?"

"I guess it's kind of strange, but I really wanted you to like her. You and I have known each other so long. I'm accustomed to knowing what you think about everything." He paused. "I hope it wasn't an awkward question since, you know, you've always been my girlfriend."

128

"I've always been your girlfriend?" Jackie asked, startled at his choice of words.

"You were my girlfriend," he repeated. "Why do you sound surprised?"

"I'm just surprised you said it that way. We've never used the word. We always hated when other people talked about us as boyfriend and girlfriend. It always seemed to mess everything up."

"You were the only girlfriend I had until I met Rachel."

Tears began to well up in Jackie's eyes. "Danny, I would have loved to have really been your girlfriend. I was just always so afraid that—well, whenever anyone started treating us like boyfriend and girlfriend, everything seemed to get weird. For years, we couldn't even talk to each other without being teased. Then—" Her voice trailed off.

"I remember." Danny supported her gently.

"I was always so afraid." Jackie paused until she could control her voice without crying. "You have no idea how much I've missed you. I've missed being able to talk with you, to tell you my ideas, to know what you think about things. I always depended on you for so many things, and now—" She started crying. "I really miss you."

"I know. I miss you too." Danny put his arm around her as they walked.

"Danny, can I ask you a question?"

"Sure."

"If you really thought of me as your girlfriend, why didn't we—" Boomer's mean-spirited jest at graduation came to mind, but that wasn't what she wanted to say. "How come we never talked about it? We talked about everything else in the world—how come we never talked about us?"

"We were just kids."

"At some point we grew up. We're not kids now," she challenged him.

"Maybe we could have talked about us at some point," Danny agreed. "Maybe we should have. I just don't know when."

They both thought back through their long friendship that had started with the play of grade-school children and gradually matured into a partnership of young adults.

"We were probably the only ones who didn't talk about our relationship," Jackie said with quiet humor. "Everybody else was always busy gossiping about whether we were sleeping together."

They walked along again in silence. Then, Danny said, "Jackie, would you do it differently if we had the chance to do it over again?" He measured his words carefully.

"I don't know," she responded. She had asked herself that question ten thousand times since leaving high school without ever knowing the answer. "I don't think so. We were so happy. I really love you, Danny."

This time, it was Danny who was startled by the choice of words; a word they had never used before. Jackie saw his discomfort and hurried to correct herself. "I don't mean I love you the way you and Rachel—" She stopped awkwardly. "I mean, I love being with you. I love talking to you and doing things with you."

Danny searched for words but found only silence.

"How about you? Would you do it differently?" Jackie returned the question.

"I've thought about that over and over. I don't know. Maybe we—"

Jackie looked at him expectantly, hoping he had an answer to the question; but he let the thought drift without completing it.

"There were so many times over the past several years that I really wanted to talk to you." Danny took a deep breath. "You know, about us—but it never seemed right. I really missed you when I first started college."

"You missed me?" She was surprised.

"You can't believe how intense and insane everyone is at Harvard. I really missed having you around to keep me thinking straight. Every time I came home, I planned to have a serious talk with you—but everything was always so crazy. We never had time to really just talk. You were here in Spring. I was in Cambridge. We couldn't connect on the telephone. It was awkward when you visited. When I was home, my parents wanted me to spend all my time with them or with Ruben. When we were together, you always had so much to say that there was never enough time. You always have loved to talk." Danny teased her gently to break the tension.

"I know." Jackie laughed self-consciously.

He waited to be sure his emotions were under control before continuing. "Several times I had it all worked out in my mind exactly what I would say to you and what I hoped you might say. Then I would see you and—I don't know—somehow I never managed to say any of the things I planned. I'm not sure I ever really tried." Danny stopped again. "Maybe we could have, like, gone away together somewhere for a couple of days to talk things through. Maybe we could have done something different. I don't know."

Jackie wanted to ask him what he would have said, but she was afraid to know. Instead, she simply said, "It's been the same for me."

"Then I met Rachel. She's wonderful. We have a lot in common."

"I understand," Jackie said warmly.

"I really love you, too, Jackie. But—"

"But what?"

Danny paused for words and then blurted out the thoughts that had been on his mind for years. "You had this idea that you wanted to be the first girl on the Moon. I had this idea that I wanted to join the Peace Corps. I was afraid we would always be going in different directions."

Jackie stared into his eyes, knowing he was right.

He turned his eyes away, took a deep breath, and returned to his original thought. "I really wanted you to like Rachel. It was important to me."

"I like her. I really do."

"I'm glad."

Again, Jackie wondered if Rachel was the first woman Danny had slept with. She had always imagined she would be his first. Perhaps she should have acted on her aching desire to touch him while they were lying under a blanket gazing at the stars, or asked him to touch her, or led him up to her bedroom when her parents were away and asked him to make love to her, or simply showed up at his dormitory in Cambridge, invited herself in, and made love to him.

They continued walking around the block in silence. Jackie wanted to find a place to sit alone and cry. But she did not want to miss any time that she could spend with Danny.

Just before they got within sight of the house, Jackie stopped and embraced Danny tightly with her head on his chest. "I love you, Danny. I really love you. But I'm also happy for you—for you and Rachel." Tears were rolling down her cheeks and onto his shirt, but she meant what she said.

"I love you, too, Jackie." Danny was flustered. This was not the way he had imagined their talk ending. He had not expected them to declare their love for each other now, after spending so many years without saying the word. Once, it had not been important to talk about such things. Now it was too late. "But we never—"

Jackie placed her hand gently over his mouth. "Danny, I know. It's okay. It really is okay." The tears running down her cheeks contradicted her words.

"But, Jackie, we never said—" He wanted to find a way to ease her tears.

"Are you going to marry Rachel?" Jackie interrupted suddenly.

"We've talked about it. Rachel wants to get married. I'm hoping to get a Rhodes scholarship so I can go to England for a year. Then, we would both like to spend time in Africa, maybe with the Peace Corps or UNESCO. I think we'll wait to see where we're going before we decide."

"Just promise to invite me to your wedding." She tried to make it a joke but began crying again, realizing she would not be the bride. "Promise me!"

"I promise."

As they walked back into the house, Jackie wiped her face and tried to make herself presentable. Danny's relatives had finally run out of questions for Rachel and were beginning to tell her stories about his childhood. Danny pulled up a chair next to Rachel and took her hand.

Jackie sat in the background, where her tears would not be noticed. She was jealous, but not of Rachel. She was jealous of Danny.

He was right. He had always wanted to plant trees in the deserts; she had wanted to build colonies on the Moon. Now their paths had diverged. Danny knew where he was going and how he would get there. She doubted she would ever get to the Moon.

* * *

Later that night, she lay uncomfortably in her bed for hours, uncertain whether she was awake or asleep. There was always a full Moon on the first night of Passover, but Jackie could not find it through the clouds. She saw herself at the command of an *Apollo* spacecraft, unable to set a course to her destination, to sight the stars, correct her course, or respond as the fuel gauge fell to empty and the space craft crashed on the rocks. The explosion tore her world apart. She saw Danny, her mother, and her father disappear, out of touch, out of reach, out of sight. She struggled to find them, to follow them, to hold them and bring them back. She gasped for air as the life-support systems failed, and she awoke shivering, breathless, and soaked in sweat and tears.

23

In the summer of 1979, a team of scientists working at a newly formed company, Genentech, announced that they had successfully cloned the human growth hormone gene that Dr. Singer's laboratory had been trying to clone for years. They also announced success in genetically engineering bacteria to make large amounts of growth hormone, and had made enough of the hormone to begin testing its effectiveness in humans. Genentech predicted that the market for human growth hormone would bring the company billions of dollars in profits each year.

Genentech was one of a wave of technology companies that emerged in the late 1970s to develop new drugs through genetic engineering. These companies hired leading scientists from universities and raised hundreds of millions of dollars for research aimed at bringing the promise of technology closer to reality. To the public, companies like Genentech became the most visible symbols of technological progress.

In June, Dr. Singer was offered a job at Genentech as a senior research scientist with a salary many times higher than she would ever make at the university. They also offered to hire the other members of Dr. Singer's laboratory, including Jackie, so that the work of the laboratory could continue without interruption.

Jackie visited Genentech with Dr. Singer in midsummer. She was awed by the scale of the Genentech campus in South San Francisco, laboratories staffed by hundreds of scientists, hundreds of millions of dollars worth of equipment, and manufacturing facilities for cloning genes and purifying their products on an almost unimaginable scale. She was enthralled listening to the company's founding scientists and executives describe how genetic technology would provide radical new treatments for disease and revolutionize the practice of medicine. They made it sound easy. There was so much power, promise, and optimism that Jackie sensed they could do anything.

Dr. Singer accepted the offer, and prepared to close her laboratory and move to Genentech that fall. She did not encourage Jackie to move with her. Instead, she counseled Jackie to finish college so she could get a higher-level position as a technician, maybe become a teacher, or, if she could improve her grades, consider going to graduate school.

By then, Jackie had tired of working in the laboratory and had no interest in being a technician. She also could not imagine herself as a teacher in a classroom of children. Graduate school sounded interesting, but it would take two more years to graduate college and at least five years to get a Ph.D., before she could even begin postdoctoral studies. It had taken less time to launch men to the Moon! By the time she finished, Jackie thought, scientists at Genentech would have already done everything worth doing.

Moreover, Jackie had finally concluded that she had no particular aptitude for science. Like the public in general, she was enamored of the idea of science and technology but found its substance beyond her grasp. She was not one of those students who walked around with a slide rule sticking out of her pocket or reveled in being one of the first to have a pocket calculator.

As a child, she had always imagined herself going to the Moon but had never given much thought to how rockets or guidance systems worked. She had celebrated the Green Revolution and the eradication of small pox, but had only a limited concept of what had been done to achieve these goals.

Science was too complicated and required too much concentration. Her attention span was too short. She would have to find something else to do with her life, and she still had no idea what that might be.

When Dr. Singer left Storrs in August, Jackie received another letter from the dean's office stating that she had to designate a new advisor and have a plan of study for her major approved by the department before she could register as a full-time student in the fall. This time, Jackie had no idea what to do. The only choice was to quit.

Every night, her sleep was interrupted by recurring dreams in which she was flying in the *Apollo* command module on the way to the Moon, sitting on the deck of the *Starship Enterprise* in search of distant suns, sailing on the *Ra* across the oceans, or walking the streets of Hartford, Saigon, Boyne, Belfast, or Manhattan when bombs and waves and wind exploded the windows and walls, and everything around her disappeared. She struggled desperately to hold on to Danny, her mother, and her father, only to find herself paralyzed, mute, and alone as they faded into the impenetrable darkness. The ending was always the same.

Bert was sympathetic when Jackie told him she was not returning to school. He told her she could always work at the family store if she needed money. Mary told Jackie that graduating college was not that important and that she should think about getting married and starting a family. Karen invited her to come live with her in San Diego.

Jackie really wanted to talk to Danny. She picked up the phone dozens of times to call him. Sometimes she actually dialed. Once, she stayed on the line long enough to hear him answer, but she hung up immediately. What would she tell him? What would he say? What could he do? What did she want him to say or do? She had no idea.

24

In late August, Jackie received a letter from Peter Williams, an organizer for the Carter–Mondale reelection committee whom she had met during the 1976 campaign. Peter had been a law student in 1976 and, in the ensuing years, had become a congressional aid and experienced political operative. His letter asked whether she would be interested in working full-time for the committee in preparation for the 1980 primaries and general election.

Despite the growing sentiment against President Carter in the press, and the public's perception that the country lacked leadership and direction, Jackie still liked Carter. She even liked the speech he had given several weeks before, in which he had spoken about the "crisis of the American spirit" and outlined his plans for a national energy policy.

Most pundits considered the speech a debacle. Jackie had personalized Carter's words, recognizing her own malaise and crisis of confidence. Carter had reminded the nation, "We ourselves are the same Americans who just ten years ago put a man on the Moon. We are the generation that dedicated our society to the pursuit of human rights and equality. And we are the generation that will win the war on the energy problem and in that process rebuild the unity and confidence of America." Carter's appeal to the triumph of the space program as a model for recapturing confidence in the future was a clarion call, but one that Jackie, like the nation as a whole, had no idea how to answer.

Jackie gratefully accepted the invitation to work for the reelection committee. It was something to do, something that would get her away from home, away from Storrs, away from everything. She spent a month in Washington at the end of the summer training for the campaign. When her training was complete, she was assigned to move to New Hampshire to begin preparing for its first-in-the-nation primary in February of the following year.

At the end of September, she moved into an apartment in Concord, New Hampshire, with Peter and several other members of the campaign staff. Through the fall, the team worked closely to organize the campaign. Jackie learned firsthand how to plan and manage a major political campaign, raise money, coordinate events, and work with broadcast and print media to disseminate the candidate's message.

The first weeks of the campaign were difficult. She had to find ways to answer the question, "Where do you go to school?" without saying that she had dropped out. She had to find ways to answer, "Do you have a boyfriend?" without confessing that she was alone.

Jackie was assigned to set up the offices of the reelection committee in Dover, New Hampshire. She worked with local party members to secure space for the committee's office, set up facilities, and recruit employees and volunteers to run the office, staff telephone banks, and canvas the community. She arranged local fund-raising events and media coverage. Several times, she was part of President Carter or Vice President Mondale's entourage as they campaigned through the state.

As the campaign progressed, her mood improved. Campaigning came easily to Jackie, who had always enjoyed talking, debating, and organizing. Gradually, her confidence increased, and she found herself slipping naturally into a leadership position among her peers, as she always had before. By year's end, she was part of a small core of political operatives running the campaign, and had made many contacts among local and national Democratic Party officials and media outlets in New England.

Nationally, President Carter's reelection campaign was floundering. Carter was widely perceived to be a weak president who had failed to redress the country's problems. Moreover, he had been unable to secure the release of the American diplomats who had been taken hostage by Iran in November of the previous year.

Senator Edward Kennedy of Massachusetts took the unusual step of challenging the incumbent president for his party's nomination, and he was expected to provide a strong challenge in the New England primaries. The reelection committee was concerned that if Kennedy did well in New Hampshire, he could pose a serious challenge to Carter. Kennedy's entrance into the race forced everyone in the campaign to redouble their efforts to ensure their candidate won that all-important first primary.

Jackie worked tirelessly on the campaign throughout the fall, through Christmas and New Year's, and through the early winter without taking time off. At the end of February, Carter easily won the New Hampshire primary. Jackie and her colleagues allowed themselves a night of buoyant celebration in a Concord hotel ballroom in front of the national media. Once the media was out of sight, they continued their celebration back at their apartment with fewer inhibitions.

There had never been much physical attraction between Jackie and Peter during the campaign. That evening, however, the shared joy of victory, complemented by overflowing champagne, celebration, and accolades, led them toward something else. Congratulatory hugs took on more intensity; casual touches had more intention; caution succumbed to impulse.

Her head was spinning from exhaustion and spirits when Peter led her to his room and began to remove her clothes and make love to her. She wanted to struggle against him, to cry out, to run away to safety, but she could not.

It was a familiar dream, but this time it was not a nightmare. In this dream, she could move, scream, reach out, and cry out in pain and ecstasy. In this dream, when the inevitable explosion ripped through her body and she gasped for air, she could let everything around her bleed into nothingness without concern. When it ended, she could still see the awe-inspiring loneliness of the universe, soar effortlessly across the Earth and among the luminous stars, and sink into a peaceful sleep.

When she awoke the next morning, Jackie was sore and had a piercing headache. She left Peter's room while he was still sleeping, then showered and packed most of her belongings before he awoke. They had several awkward exchanges that morning as everyone joined in closing up the apartment and packing for their next destinations.

Jackie was going to Connecticut to help mobilize for the state's primary at the end of March. Peter was returning to Washington to work at campaign headquarters.

Peter found Jackie alone in her room, just as she was stuffing the last of her belongings and campaign mementos into her knapsack. He sat on the corner of the small desk next to her and gently brushed his hand over her hair and shoulders.

She bristled and turned away.

"Are you okay, Jackie?"

"I'm fine," she answered curtly.

"Do you want to talk about last night?"

"No."

"Are you upset?"

"No."

"We should talk."

"I don't want to talk."

"We should talk. I didn't mean to take advantage of you."

"It doesn't matter," she answered with irritation.

"Was that your first time?" he explored gently.

"That's none of your business!"

"Jackie, I'm concerned."

"Look, Peter—" she turned to him with determination in her voice, "—we did what we did. I'm okay. I don't want to talk about it. There's nothing to talk about. That's it!"

"That's it?"

"Yeah, that's it! Leave me alone, okay?"

"I'm not sure you're okay." Peter was perplexed by her response. While he did not expect their night together to lead to a relationship, he also did not expect her to be quite so cold.

"Well, I'm fine!" she said dismissively, slinging her knapsack over her shoulders. "See you around." She gave him a collegial kiss on the cheek and walked briskly out of the apartment and down the stairs to her car. Peter thought about following her, but her behavior was inscrutable. He did not know what else to do or say.

Before starting the car, Jackie let her head fall back against the seat, closed her eyes, and took several long, deep breaths. The last thing she wanted to do was talk to Peter. Maybe Peter had taken advantage of her. Maybe she had taken advantage of him. It really didn't matter. What mattered was that, for the first time in years, she had seen a different ending to her recurring dream, an ending in which the inevitable explosion had not brought tragedy, an ending in which she was able to fly away before crashing on the rocks, an ending in which she was not left grasping for the fleeting images of the people she loved, but was capable of taking control and continuing alone. She felt more serene and more secure than she had for years.

* * *

At the end of March, President Carter lost the Connecticut and New York primary to Senator Kennedy. The reelection committee immediately asked Jackie to go to California to help organize for its primary in June, an event that pundits predicted would ultimately decide the nomination.

Jackie was exhausted. She had been working nonstop on the campaign for seven months and was ready to move on to something else. This time she knew exactly what she wanted to do.

Throughout the campaign, she had been drawn to public relations and work with the media. She liked the dialectic of ideas, issues, and policies. She enjoyed the care that went into constructing and communicating the candidate's message, the attention that went into polling the public to assimilate their views, and the process of working with media to disseminate their stories.

She decided to return to Storrs and complete a major in communications. She met with the chair of the Department of Communication Sciences to develop a study plan that gave her credit for many of the courses she had taken during her first three years at Storrs and some of the fieldwork she had done with the Carter campaign. Her plan was to take a full course load during the summer of 1980, take leave in the fall to work on Carter's national reelection campaign, if he were the candidate, and complete the course work for a bachelor's degree during the spring and summer of the following year.

Jackie rented a tiny efficiency apartment on the edge of campus and found a job waiting tables to pay the bills. Each night, she spent hours on the telephone with friends who had stayed with the campaign, keeping abreast of their activities and offering her advice. She was relieved when Carter swept the Democratic primaries in the South and Midwest and was able to lock up the party's nomination before the California primary.

* * *

In May, Jackie received an invitation to Danny's graduation from Harvard and a celebratory dinner afterward. She had often considered stopping in Cambridge to visit him while she was working in New Hampshire but had never made the time. Now she was afraid that she would be out of place at a commencement that he was sharing with Rachel.

Jackie spent many futile hours trying to draft a letter to Danny, describing her feelings and wishing him well. Finally, she settled on sending him a store-bought graduation card with a short note saying only that she would not be able to attend.

The week before Danny's graduation, Jackie ran into Sarah in the lobby of her apartment building. Sarah told her that Danny had received a Rhodes scholarship and that he and Rachel were leaving for Oxford the week after graduation.

"You know—" Sarah seemed to interrupt herself awkwardly, "—you should come to Danny's graduation. I'm going to drive up there for the graduation—you can come with me if you want."

Jackie declined gently, but Sarah was persistent.

"Danny is going to miss you. You should come and surprise him. It would be fun!"

"Fun?" Jackie did not think anything about Danny's leaving would be fun.

"He really wants to see you," Sarah offered uncomfortably.

"Did Danny tell you to invite me?" Jackie challenged her, suddenly realizing it was no accident that she had encountered Sarah in the lobby of her apartment building.

"Yes," Sarah confessed. "He asked me to talk to you. He really wants you to come."

Over the next week, Sarah ran into Jackie several more times to repeat her invitation. Sarah even called Jackie the morning of graduation to give her one last chance to change her mind. Jackie thanked Sarah for the call, but this time told her bluntly that it would be better if she did not get involved. When she saw Sarah on campus several weeks later, Sarah told her that Danny and Rachel had left for Oxford and that he had asked her to communicate his love.

In July, Jackie received a long, handwritten letter from Danny. He wrote about receiving a Rhodes scholarship and his plans to study for a year at Oxford. He also wrote that he and Rachel had been admitted to law school at Stanford, but had decided to defer their admission for several years to work for UNESCO at a school in East Africa.

The letter's last page was very different from anything Jackie had ever received from him. From the numerous eraser marks on the page, Jackie recognized that it had been a difficult letter for him to write.

"I was disappointed that you could not come to my graduation." He wrote. "I have never graduated without you. It didn't feel right. I have always been afraid that we would end up on different paths in life. Now that it has happened, I am sorry. While I cannot imagine undertaking the path ahead without Rachel, I would not be the person I am if you and I had not traveled as far as we did together." He signed the letter, "Love always, Danny," words he had never written to her before.

Jackie folded the letter carefully and placed it at the bottom of her jewelry box, under the pictures of her mother that had sat on the night table beside her bed through childhood.

* * *

During the summer of 1980, Jackie completed a semester of coursework, then rejoined Carter's national campaign at the beginning of September. It was a melancholy campaign against a Republican candidate, Ronald Reagan, who had an overwhelming lead in the polls.

Jackie was asked to work in Massachusetts, a state that was traditionally a Democratic stronghold, but one where there was lingering resentment against Carter for defeating their favorite son, Ted Kennedy, in the primaries. Moreover, a liberal Republican, John Anderson, had launched a third-party campaign for the presidency, and his candidacy had considerable appeal among the young voters, who were an important Democratic voting bloc in the state. If John Anderson received enough of the progressive vote in Massachusetts, the Republican Party could win the state for the first time in memory.

Jackie moved into an apartment in Boston with several other members of the campaign staff for the fall campaign. They spent difficult months struggling to maintain a viable campaign organization and motivate the Democratic faithful to support their party's candidate.

Many traditional donors to the Democratic Party were reluctant to contribute to a candidate whom they believed had no chance of winning. There was also an acute shortage of volunteers, since many students, normally the backbone of a political campaign, were supporting John Anderson.

Throughout the fall, Jackie met with the party's traditional donors to solicit contributions and arranged events to raise desperately needed money. She met with the old-money Brahmins who controlled the political apparatus of the Democratic Party. She met with the leaders of New England's traditional industries, with the entrepreneurs behind the state's new high-technology companies, and with community leaders, academics, clergy, and elected officials. She arranged fund-raisers at elegant hotels, rallies on college campuses, prayer meetings at churches, public endorsements from local officials, and media events with the candidates and their representatives.

Jackie was an attractive, articulate, and energetic spokesperson for the party, an effective fund-raiser, and a fearless champion for her candidate. She made a lasting impression on many of the people with whom she worked, and by the end of the campaign, she had built a personal network of acquaintances that included many of the most influential citizens in New England.

In November, Ronald Reagan won a landslide victory. He carried the traditional Republican strongholds in the South and West, as well as traditionally Democratic states, including Massachusetts, where John Anderson siphoned votes away from the Democratic candidate. Jackie spent election eve with hundreds of others from among the party faithful at the Park Plaza Hotel in downtown Boston, watching helplessly as Ronald Reagan was declared the winner in one state after another. Then she went home alone.

In the days after the election, Jackie received numerous job offers from prominent New England media outlets and public relations firms. She declined each of the offers and returned to Storrs to finish school.

In the spring and summer of 1981, she took a heavy course load to complete the requirements for her major. She was totally engaged by her studies, anxious to apply the lessons she had learned during the campaign, and interested in learning how she could have done better. For the first time in her life, she had no difficulty achieving an A in every course.

By September, Jackie had enough credits for a bachelor's degree in communications. She decided to remain at Storrs for one more semester to complete a master's degree and write a thesis based on her work with the Carter campaign. She received her bachelor's and master's degrees just before Christmas in December 1981, five and a half years after starting college.

That summer, Jackie received another letter from Danny. He and Rachel had completed their year in Oxford and were going to Kenya as part of a UNESCO program to teach in a rural school. They planned to spend two years in Kenya before returning to the United States for law school. Danny wrote that it might be hard for Jackie to send letters to Kenya and suggested that, if she wanted to write, she should send the letters to Rachel's parents in Johannesburg, who would have the letters delivered. He finished by saying he was anxious to know how she was. Again, he signed his letter, "Love always, Danny." Again, Jackie placed the letter in her jewelry box without responding.

After graduation, she accepted a job with Fernald Partners, a public relations firm in Cambridge, Massachusetts, that provided support to companies in the emerging high-technology and biotechnology industries.

25

Jackie had met William Fernald, the Managing Partner and President of Fernald Partners, early in the course of the fall campaign. William was a wealthy executive, and a leading figure in the Massachusetts Democratic Party. He had been a supporter of Ted Kennedy during the primary campaign, and was slow to become involved in the national campaign after Carter won the party's nomination.

They met when Jackie accompanied the Chair of the reelection committee to a meeting at William's home in Weston, asking him to assume a more prominent role on behalf of the Democratic presidential candidate. Jackie sat silently through most of the meeting as the two graying party figures reminisced over past campaigns and debated political strategies, the chances of victory in November, and the consequences of either success or failure. William felt a sense of responsibility to the party, but he did not like Carter and did not think he could win.

After an hour of stalemate, he turned to Jackie. "So, young lady, you have been listening to two jaded old-timers talk about politics for an hour. Why does a lovely young woman like you support Carter?"

"I think he's the right man," Jackie answered confidently.

"Why? Young people are supposed to be optimistic. At your age, you're not supposed to believe in a crisis of confidence or a lack of spirit," he said, challenging her with one of the political attacks being used against President Carter.

"I don't know about that," Jackie said self-consciously.

"Why aren't you supporting Reagan or Anderson?" William pressed.

"I think Carter is right. There is a crisis of confidence in the country. There is a lack of spirit, a lack of direction. That is a big part of the problem."

"Why is it part of the problem?"

"Carter said it in his speech last July. Ten years ago, we put men on the Moon. People talked about building colonies in space and sending missions to Mars. We believed we could do anything."

"So what?" William was intrigued with her answer and prompted her to continue.

"If we could land men on the Moon, we should be able to solve our energy problems. We have the technology. We can generate energy from nuclear power, from the Sun, the wind, the tides, even our trash. We can make energy from corn and other crops. We can improve the efficiency of our cars. We can build more energy-efficient buildings, factories, offices, and cities. If we can land men on the Moon—if we can land men on the Moon, then these things—"

"But why Carter?" William interrupted.

"Because he understands that the limitations are really political, not technical. He understands that problems can be solved if we have the will, the confidence, the spirit."

"I wish Jimmy Carter sounded half as convincing as you do." William sat back in his chair and tested Jackie again. "The problem, young lady, is that while I agree with you, the public doesn't. Carter has been unable to get his ideas across to the public."

"That's our job," Jackie answered quickly. "That's what a campaign is all about—to both communicate his ideas and also instill confidence—to make people see that his ideas make sense. We have to do what President Kennedy did when he proposed sending men to the Moon. We have to get people to accept the idea."

William nodded approvingly. He understood the power of public relations. It was one answer he could not contest.

William had started his career working in the public relations department at Digital Equipment Corporation, one of the first high-technology companies in the corridor around Boston. In the early 1970s, he left Digital to start Fernald Partners, a firm that specialized in public relations and marketing for the many technology-based companies in the Boston area.

The idea that technology could play a central role in society was exactly the message that Fernald's clients were struggling to communicate to a skeptical public. William had never met anyone who expressed these ideas more simply and sincerely than Jackie. He knew immediately that he wanted her to work for him at Fernald Partners.

Despite his lack of enthusiasm for Carter, William found himself being drawn into the campaign by Jackie's persuasion and persistence. Within weeks of their first meeting, he not only agreed to make a substantial personal contribution to the party, but also to host a major fund-raising event at his home in Weston, which Jackie would organize.

The event at William Fernald's home was one of the most important fund-raisers of the Carter campaign in Massachusetts. For a minimum contribution of ten thousand dollars per person, donors could meet personally with Vice President Mondale, Senator Kennedy, Governor King, and members of the Massachusetts congressional delegation. Jackie managed every aspect of the event, which raised over a million dollars for the Carter-Mondale campaign and reinforced William Fernald's position as a leader of the Democratic Party in Massachusetts. The evening was a triumph for the party, for William, and for Jackie.

When the celebrities and major contributors had left, and congratulations had been offered all around, William invited Jackie to meet some of his colleagues and clients who had attended the event. Mrs. Fernald brought out some of the leftover food and wine, and they sat in his living room talking informally about politics and business until late in the evening.

William delicately prompted Jackie to describe her perspectives about technology to his colleagues and clients. Jackie was in her element. The long hours she had spent refining and refuting ideas with Danny had given her a formidable fund of knowledge, passion, and power of persuasion. Before the evening was over, several clients asked William if she would be working at Fernald Partners and told him they would be pleased if she worked on their accounts.

Several days after the election, William and Jackie met for lunch at the Harvard Club. They spent a long afternoon talking about the lost election and Jackie's plans for the future. William told Jackie that he would like her to work at Fernald Partners, but he also advised her to complete a bachelor's and master's degree in communications. He offered her part-time work with Fernald Partners while she finished school, so she could pay her living expenses and tuition, and he promised to offer her a permanent job when she graduated. Jackie accepted immediately.

Jackie worked intermittently with Fernald Partners over the next year, getting to know William's colleagues and many of their clients. She attended the annual Christmas party, the St. Patrick's Day party at the office, and the July Fourth barbecue at William's summer home on Cape Cod and began to feel like a member of their team. Several months before Jackie graduated, William presented her with a formal job offer as he had promised.

William's offer to work at Fernald Partners was by far the best of the many offers that Jackie received in the months leading up to graduation. In addition to offering her a signing bonus and a salary that made her immediately affluent, William offered to give her a significant role on several important accounts. There was also the possibility of her becoming a vice president within three years. Privately, he told Jackie that he would consider making her a partner if she was as productive as he expected.

Jackie was thrilled with the offer. She liked William and the people at his firm. More importantly, she was excited about being involved in promoting the potential of technology.

Several weeks before Christmas, Jackie bought a newly renovated, two-bedroom condominium in an old brownstone in Boston's Back Bay. The condominium had a large living room with a fireplace and a picture window that overlooked the Charles River. She spent the week before Christmas buying everything she needed to furnish a new home; a queen-sized poster bed with matching dresser and night tables for her bedroom; a mahogany desk for the second bedroom, which she set up as a study; a large breakfront, table, and upholstered chairs for the dining area; a leather couch and console television for the living room; and two modern recliner chairs that she set facing out the window toward the river. Finally, she bought a Christmas tree, which she planted prominently in front of the window overlooking the river and the sky.

On Christmas morning, Jackie drove to Spring with presents for her family. When she returned late that evening, her car was overloaded with mementos from her childhood, as well as boxes of china, crystal, and heirlooms that had once belonged to her mother.

She spent the evening unpacking the boxes. The photographs of her mother were placed on the night table by her bed, several special stuffed animals were positioned as decoration on the shelves in her bedroom, and her mother's china and crystal were put on display in the dining room.

Jackie was puzzled by one of the boxes, which was filled with old Christmas ornaments. Her father had insisted that she take the box, but hadn't told her why. She didn't remember ever using the ornaments at her parent's house, and didn't understand why her father had been so insistent. Only when the box was nearly empty did she understand; they were the ornaments that were on the tree in the photograph of her first Christmas, sleeping in her mother's arms. Jackie retrieved the picture from her bedroom and, one by one, placed them carefully on the tree exactly where they appeared in the photograph.

It was long past midnight by the time Jackie was finished, but she was too energized to sleep. She kept walking around the condominium, rearranging things on the shelves and walls until they were perfect, and then doing it again an hour later.

When she finally lay down in her new bed and closed her eyes, she saw herself flying through the oceans of space to the Moon and beyond. Other spacecraft were flying around her, some powered by rockets, some by reindeer, some by the sun and the wind, and some by angels. She saw Danny wave to her through the window of a 747 on its way to Africa. She tried to wave back, but he was moving too fast in a different direction. She tried to change course so she could talk to him, but he faded out of sight before she could say a word.

After hours of drifting in and out of sleep, Jackie turned on the lights and sat down at her new mahogany desk to write a letter to Danny. It had been over two years since she had written to him.

Her letter was a long outpouring of emotion and relief. She wrote about everything that had happened to her over the previous years; her failures in college, the Carter campaign, finishing school, finding a career, and her sudden prosperity. She stayed awake the entire night to complete the letter. It took her two weeks, however, to decide how to sign her name. Finally, she signed her letter the way Danny had signed his: "Love always, Jackie."

26

Jackie joined Fernald Partners with the dawning of the age of technology. It was an age born with the launch of *Sputnik,* and nurtured by the massive investments in education and science that followed. However, it was not until the 1980s that technology began to have a significant impact on the general public.

The emergence of technology as a dominant social force in the 1980s was not the result of new, discontinuous innovations or dramatic inventions. Integrated circuits, which provided the foundation for modern computers, had been invented in the 1960s, and their power and speed had been doubling every eighteen months for more than fifteen years. By the early 1970s, researchers at Xerox had already built microcomputers small enough to sit on the desktop, and the ARPANET, an early version of the Internet, connected several hundred computers in the United States and England. By 1977, consumers could buy a TRS-80/model I computer at a Radio Shack outlet or an Apple I or a Commodore computer at an electronic store. Two years later, the more advanced Apple II and TRS-80/Model II computers were for sale, along with pioneering software programs such as WordStar, a word processor that enabled people to compose and edit documents, and VisiCalc, a spreadsheet that gave individuals advanced record-keeping and bookkeeping functions. By 1979, consumers could also equip their computers with modems that enabled these machines to communicate with one another and exchange electronic mail over telephone lines. In July of that year, CompuServe launched the first commercial computer network, MicroNET, which extended the concepts of computer networking to the public.

The year 1981, however, was a seminal point in time for emerging technology. In August, IBM introduced the first personal computer, the PC, powered by the Intel 8086 chip. In October, Microsoft introduced the first MS-DOS operating system. Together, the PC, Intel chips, and Microsoft operations systems would come to dominate society. In 1982, *Time* magazine would award their coveted "Man of the Year" award not to a man or woman but to "The Computer."

The early 1980s also saw the maturation of a vibrant industry focused on developing high-technology products for routine commerce, communications, and health. Over the next two decades, tens of thousands of new technology and biotechnology companies were founded, and the relentless growth of this industry would become the bellwether of the age.

The greatest challenge facing the technology industry in the early 1980s was not how to build smaller, more powerful machines, but rather how to translate the enormous capabilities of computers into products that American industry and the public believed they needed to buy. Even as the first microcomputers came to market in 1977, Ken Olsen, who had pioneered the development of small computers as the founder of Digital Equipment Corporation, was quoted as saying, "There is no reason for any individual to have a computer in his home." Without a change in public attitude, there would be no market for the products of the technology industry and no technological revolution for society.

Jackie's mission at Fernald Partners was to help technology companies convince a skeptical public that the products they were developing provided practical and necessary solutions to real-world problems. To achieve commercial success, the industry had to convince the public that they needed word processors to write their letters, spreadsheets to do their checkbooks, and troves of information immediately at their fingertips. They had to convince corporations that continuously upgraded, state-of-the-art computer systems and endless sources of information were essential for their competitive success. They had to convince investors that technology companies would succeed, and convince the government that the dissemination of technology was a national priority. Most importantly, they had to make the public believe that the stuff of science fiction, such as artificial intelligence, thinking and talking machines, databases with endless information, radios in watches, and telephones small enough to hide in shoes, was not only realistic, but, in fact, inevitable products of the future and essential accoutrements to personal and professional success.

Jackie understood that the raw power of the emerging technology did not guarantee public acceptance. She knew that President Kennedy had translated the potential for manned flight to the Moon into a national mission by tying it to America's fear of communism and sense of manifest destiny. She also recognized that Carter had failed to translate the potential for an endless supply of clean energy into practice by linking it with the appearance of weakness.

Jackie knew the public was fearful of technology. Computers were still perceived to be multi-ton monsters of tubes and flashing lights designed to solve inhuman problems. The media often portrayed computers as impersonal and potentially malevolent tools of big business and big government. As 1984 approached, she also knew the public would be thinking of George Orwell's hideous vision of a world that was subservient to technology.

The public was even more fearful of biotechnology. The illusory risk of creating Frankenstein monsters and swarms of lethal organisms often overshadowed the real potential of finding cures for disease. There were persistent grassroots efforts to restrict research on new technologies, to delay release of genetically engineered products into the environment, and to limit the distribution of biotechnology-based medicines and foods.

Jackie was not a scientist. She did not try to understand the arcane details of the science and technologies that her clients were developing. She had a different skill, namely the ability to see through the technology to its impact and implications. Her view was colored by an essential, almost innocent, optimism that technology was good and that virtually anything was achievable. She could project technologies through the prism of her faith to articulate their practical applications and their potential in a clear, credible, and convincing manner.

Jackie's teams worked with start-ups to translate the technological visions of their founding scientists into something that would attract investors. They worked with young companies to establish brands that were associated with progressive thinking, personal benefits, and profits, and they helped mature companies market and sell their products. Her teams advised universities and charitable foundations on how to disseminate news about their research to the public, develop the inventions, and raise money for new initiatives. They worked with the media, government, lobbyists, and social action groups to convert public skepticism about technology into acceptance. They helped newspaper and television reporters by providing background information and feature stories that cultivated public excitement about the age of technology as it continued to unfold.

Jackie sometimes worked with investors to help them evaluate potential investments in technology companies. Her insights into how companies could portray their technologies to the public and position their products in the marketplace helped investors assess the value of these companies and the opportunities for profit.

Tim Weber was the manager of a mutual fund that invested exclusively in emerging technology companies. His initial investments in the first-generation technology companies like Intel, Apple, Microsoft, Genentech, and Biogen in the 1970s had been phenomenally successful. The dramatic growth of his fund and his own personal investments had made him extremely wealthy by the time he was thirty-five.

In the fall of 1982, Jackie met Tim at a private reception she had organized for one of his portfolio companies. Tim was immediately attracted to her. He spent the evening watching her as she directed the event, noting her handshake and her smile, her featherweight hair and dancer's bearing, the lines of her tailored suit, and the confident tenor of her voice. He called her several days later with an invitation to accompany him to a black-tie benefit for a cancer charity the following month. Jackie accepted immediately.

Tim had a carefully cultivated reputation within Boston's social circles as one of the city's most eligible bachelors. He was six feet two and retained the bearing of a collegiate football player. He was always meticulously groomed and impeccably dressed in custom-tailored suits and the most expensive shoes and accessories. Professionally, he was known to be smart, aggressive, and often ruthless. Socially, he was known for his charity, connections, and confident sense of humor. Tim's box seats at Fenway Park and the Boston Garden were a well-known perquisite for his business associates and friends, as well as an important site for personal and professional networking. He regularly attended charitable events, and the tables he sponsored always provided substantial contributions to worthy causes.

For the event, Jackie bought a shimmering black evening dress, sparkling jewelry, and elegant shoes. She replaced her glasses with contact lenses, had her hair lightened and styled, and had her makeup done at a fashionable salon in the Back Bay. Tim proudly entered the ballroom with Jackie on his arm, aware that her eye-catching elegance made his already-important presence even more impressive.

The event was Jackie's first foray into Boston's formal society. From her work on the Carter campaign, she knew many of the old-money Bostonians, industry executives, entrepreneurs, and politicians who were attending the event.

Tim was accustomed to being the center of attention at such events. That evening, however, more people were interested in Jackie. Throughout the night, the rich and powerful elite of Boston's business and political worlds congregated around his table to welcome her into their company. Tim liked it that way.

The following day, he called Jackie to ask her to spend the weekend at his home on Cape Cod. She agreed. By the beginning of the Christmas season, Jackie and Tim were an item at innumerable parties thrown by the elite of Boston society and began appearing together in the society columns of the Boston newspapers.

They spent Christmas week together sailing the Mediterranean on Tim's yacht. When they returned, she moved into Tim's expansive penthouse looking over Boston Common, though she also kept her smaller condo in the Back Bay. They spent their weekends at his Bar Harbor–style house on Cape Cod, and vacationed on his yacht or at his condominium on the slopes at Vail. Together, they enjoyed the finest restaurants, clubs, and shows in Boston, New York, London, and Paris. They were among the suffering faithful at Fenway Park during the Red Sox's losing season in 1983 and had courtside seats for the Celtics' championship the following spring.

Tim showered Jackie with lavish presents of designer clothes, diamond jewelry, furs, and art. She found herself caught up in Tim's conspicuous lifestyle, which mirrored the extravagance of an age in which television shows such as *Dallas* and *Dynasty* were emblems of popular culture. They were a high-profile couple in a decade that would be known for ostentatious displays of newfound wealth and power.

Some of the more unkind gossip described Jackie as simply the latest of Tim's decorative girlfriends. She was sometimes self-conscious of the fact that he was ten years older than she was and that he had been involved in long, public relationships with other women before her. Nevertheless, she was having too much fun to worry. She was genuinely fond of Tim and was living a dream.

With Tim, she could sail across the seas with the waves and the wind and explore distant lands. She could fly in the Concorde through the stratosphere, ten miles above the Earth, and observe its curvature through the portals. She did not know or care whether Tim would ever be interested in marriage. She was at the epicenter of an age of technology, doing something exciting, something she loved. She was happy.

* * *

Danny responded warmly to Jackie's first letter with a long letter of his own, recounting his experiences during the years they had not communicated. They began to exchange letters regularly. His letters described working at a residential school UNESCO had established in rural Kenya and the hopelessness of a population caught between the dissolution of their traditional cultures and the distant dreams of modernity. He wrote about the impact of the modern world on family and tribal structures, the interruption of traditional routes of commerce and travel, and the loss of time-honored methods of agriculture and industry. There was enough land, labor, and talent in the Third World to feed everyone and to produce goods to bring them out of poverty. He argued that this could all be achieved through education and ensuring that emerging nations established just systems of economics and justice.

In addition, Danny described Rachel's interest in the children of Africa. In the 1980s, more than one in ten children born in East Africa died within their first year of life. Rachel believed that the future of underdeveloped countries lay in the potential of their children, not the parents. It was hard to reeducate adults who were already entangled in traditional occupations and obligations by the time they reached adolescence. Children represented an unconstrained future. With proper education, health care, nurture, and protection, they could provide the leadership and the strength to lift their societies out of poverty and into a more productive future.

Jackie, in turn, told Danny about the technological revolution that was blooming around her and how it would eventually provide solutions to the problems they were confronting. Things would be different, she suggested, when even the most remote corners of the world would be connected by computer networks, when biotechnology could provide vaccines for endemic diseases, and genetically engineered crops could improve nutrition.

She reminded him of how they had once watched a computer being delivered to the third floor of a bank building in Spring. The computer had been too large to fit through the building's front door or into the elevator, and a construction team had to cut a hole in the brick façade and use a crane to hoist the computer into the building. Now, fifteen years later, the computer on which she wrote her letters was more than a million times more powerful and had been delivered to her home in a cardboard box by the U.S. Postal Service.

Their letters were always signed "love," but they were more concerned with the dialectic of their ideas and experiences than their emotions. Between letters, Jackie rarely thought about Danny. She was totally engaged by her work and enamored by her affair with Tim.

27

In April of 1983, Jackie received a large envelope with a return address in Johannesburg, South Africa. Within the larger envelope were two smaller envelopes. One had her name in elegant calligraphy. The other had her name in Danny's handwriting.

Jackie opened the formal envelope first and found an invitation to a wedding.

Mr. and Mrs. Isaac Fiedler
request the honor of your presence
at the marriage of their daughter
Rachel Ester

to

Daniel Aaron Cohn
on August 6, 1983
at Temple Beth Zion
Johannesburg, South Africa

Jackie smiled at the invitation and then turned her attention to the letter from Danny. He and Rachel were still in Kenya, and they had become engaged over New Year's, during a visit with Rachel's parents in Johannesburg. They would finish their work in Kenya in July and would marry in Johannesburg in August before heading back to the States. Danny's parents would fly to South Africa for the wedding, but no one else from his family would be there. Even though he knew it was unlikely that Jackie would come, he wanted her to know he remembered his promise to send her an invitation.

She sent her formal regrets to Rachel's family and a letter to Danny, telling him that if they were stopping in Boston on their return, she hoped they could get together. In the middle of August, Jackie received a letter from Danny postmarked in Johannesburg saying that they would be stopping in Spring for several days at the beginning of September before flying on to California to begin law school. He suggested that they get together for dinner one night. Jackie made reservations for four people at a country inn near Spring. She was happy he was coming back.

Tim was not pleased about driving for two hours to a restaurant in Connecticut that had no Zagat rating. He expressed his irritation by driving toward Hartford at speeds that tested the capabilities of his Jaguar convertible. When they arrived, Jackie stopped to brush the effects of the wind from her hair and fix her makeup. Then they sat in the lounge and ordered drinks to tide them over until Danny and Rachel arrived.

Jackie saw Danny immediately when he walked through the door. He was thinner and darker from his years in Africa, but otherwise he looked the same.

Danny did not immediately recognize Jackie. She looked different. She was not wearing glasses, and her makeup masked her freckles and altered the contours of her cheeks and eyes. Her hair was also lighter, shorter, and fuller than he remembered.

Jackie jumped up and enthusiastically embraced Danny, then Rachel, congratulating them on their wedding and welcoming them back. Tim shook hands politely and immediately ordered a round of drinks.

Dinner conversation was lively as Danny and Rachel recounted their experiences in Africa and everyone debated the future of that continent and its people. Danny and Rachel had strong feelings about the social and political future of Africa. Jackie had ideas about applying technology. Tim was interested in whether there was money to be made by investing in Africa.

By the time the main course was served, Tim was tired of talking about poverty, economics, and politics and began to focus his attention on the wine list. He ordered lavishly, as was his usual habit, carefully selecting a vintage to go with each course, then formally tasting and critiquing the wine as it was served. Jackie saw Danny's concern as Tim ordered bottles of wine that cost hundreds of dollars, and she quickly reminded everyone that Tim was treating for dinner in honor of their wedding.

After dinner, they retired to the lounge. Tim ordered port for everyone and a cigar for himself, and pontificated on how the flavor of port matured with age. The others sat back on the couches simply enjoying each other's company and conversation. They were still there an hour later when the bartender announced last call.

"Will I see you again before you leave for California?" Jackie asked hopefully, as they prepared to leave.

"I don't think so. We have a lot to do," Rachel said. "For one thing, I need to buy clothes before we leave for school."

Danny started laughing.

"What's so funny?" Rachel said, hitting him playfully. "Stop laughing at me! It's not funny."

"Jackie, when some women say they need to buy clothes, it's just a cliché. Rachel really means it!" Danny said, still laughing. "We left *all* of our clothes in Africa for the students and teachers at the school. You have to understand, they don't have anything, not even clothes. We decided to leave everything we had—shoes, socks, even underwear—everything. We only kept the clothes that we actually wore onto the plane to Johannesburg."

"It wasn't a hard decision," Rachel interjected. "I could never have worn those clothes again in public after washing them in stinking water for two years. After a while, we got used to the smell, but I don't think it ever really comes out."

"We bought some things in Johannesburg, you know, for the wedding—" Danny started to explain.

"—but I figured it would be easier to buy everything else I needed in Boston," Rachel finished his sentence. "I know my way around the stores in Boston, and it's expensive to ship things from South Africa and get them through customs. Also, we didn't have much time in Johannesburg, and I wanted to spend the time we had with my family, not shopping. I don't know when I'll see them again."

"You have to buy everything?" Jackie asked, measuring in her mind her own dressers and closets full of clothes for every season, occasion, and degree of formality.

"Hey," Rachel said suddenly. "Do you want to come with me? It might be fun shopping, you know, just girls. Danny is a terrible shopper. I'm sure he would be happy not to come."

"Sure, why not?" Jackie answered immediately.

"We were going to drive one of my parents' cars to Boston for the day." Danny was thinking ahead. "You two could go without me. Ruben is in town, and my parents really wanted me to spend some time with him. If I don't have to go to shopping with Rachel tomorrow, I could have more time with him."

"How is Ruben?" Jackie asked.

"Not well. He's been in and out of rehab programs since I left."

"I'm sorry."

"I haven't talked to him at all since we left for Africa. My parents are hoping that talking might do him some good. I doubt it, though."

"Good luck," Jackie offered.

"So, what are we going to do?" Danny changed the subject abruptly.

"Well, I can probably stay at my parent's house tonight—that's the easiest thing. Rachel and I can drive to Boston in the morning, and she can drive back when we're done."

"Great!" Rachel responded.

Jackie turned to Tim. "Tim, would you mind driving back alone? It would be a big favor." She gave him a solicitous kiss. Tim was relieved not to be included in the plans and quickly took his leave. Danny went to retrieve his car, while Jackie called her parents from a pay phone outside the restaurant to tell them she would be staying overnight.

"Why don't you drop me at your parents' house first," Rachel told Danny, as they climbed into the car. "I'm really jet lagged, and I'm sure you two have plenty to talk about without me."

"Are you sure?" Danny asked.

"Of course."

Jackie sat in the backseat until Rachel got out at Danny's house. He walked her to the door and gave her a kiss. Jackie moved up to the passenger seat for the short ride to her parents' house.

They had not been alone for almost four years. Neither of them knew where to start the conversation.

"I like Rachel," Jackie began sincerely. "You two seem happy."

"Yeah, I'm very lucky," Danny answered.

"Was she the first one you ever slept with?"

"Jackie!" Danny exclaimed, shocked. "What kind of question is that?"

"I've wanted to ask you that for years," Jackie said, slightly embarrassed. There was a moment of silence before she prodded him again. "So?"

"Yes, as a matter of fact, she was my first. I didn't date that much in college. I wasn't looking to get married or anything." Danny glanced over at Jackie to see if she had any reaction. "How about you? Are you sleeping with this guy?"

Jackie looked at Danny sheepishly. "Would you think less of me if I was?"

"As a matter of fact, yes, I would."

"Well, I am. We don't have much in common, but we have a lot of fun. He has a great house on the Cape and a yacht that—" She let the sentence trail off, knowing Danny would not be interested. "We have a lot of fun."

"You can do better," Danny chided gently.

"I can do better?" She mocked his voice. "You, maybe?"

"That's not what I meant."

"I know."

"Was he your first?" Danny asked, earning a disapproving look from Jackie. "You started it," he reminded her.

"No," Jackie answered thoughtfully. "My first was someone I worked with during the Carter campaign. It wasn't really a relationship—just one night actually." She stopped and looked at him, hoping he would say something so she would not have to say more.

"It's funny," he said abruptly. "All those years, you and I talked about everything in the world, but we never talked about our relationship or about sex or anything even close. Now we haven't seen each other in three or four years, and we're sitting here asking each other about our sex lives, as if it is the most natural thing in the world."

"Maybe it is," Jackie challenged him.

"What do you mean?"

"Maybe it is the most natural thing in the world, you know, talking about sex. Maybe that's what we should have been talking about all those years. We were always caught up in some world where all we did was talk and all that mattered were big ideas. This is the 'me decade,' haven't you heard? We're the 'me generation.' What's wrong with that?"

"Because that's not who we are," Danny answered.

"I don't know, Danny. Maybe that's who I am now. Maybe it is all about sex and vacationing where it doesn't rain."

"That's not you, Jackie."

"How would you know?" Jackie tested him.

"I can tell," he answered confidently. "You know, I almost didn't recognize you when I walked into the restaurant."

"You didn't recognize me?" Jackie was shocked.

"You look different—all the makeup, the blonde hair, the jewelry and clothes. At first I was afraid that you might have changed. But as soon as we started talking, I knew that underneath it all, you haven't really changed."

"I've changed a lot!" she protested.

"Maybe on the surface maybe, but you still sound like the same Jackie Cone who thought the only reason to go to school was to prattle about the space program—the same Jackie Cone who could win debates arguing that technology would solve all the world's problems. You've grown up and dressed up, but nothing's really changed."

"Everything's changed," Jackie answered uncomfortably. "I'm not some perky little kid who walks around with my head in the clouds any more. I have a job—a career. I'm really good at what I do."

"That's not what I mean."

"I'm not the same," Jackie insisted.

"Do you remember Mrs. Leslie?" Danny asked.

"Of course."

"Remember the things she used to say—how she wanted to teach us how to think, how we would find ideas that would give us direction in life and make us who we are?"

"So what?"

"She was right. Your ideas haven't changed. Maybe you don't talk about space all the time, but now it's computers and telecommunications and biotechnology."

"So what's wrong with that?" Jackie got defensive.

"Nothing at all," Danny answered warmly. "I love the person who used to believe there would be colonies on the Moon and Mars—the person who could actually make me think about whether Martians would have civil rights." Danny stopped and looked at her affectionately.

Jackie thought back to sixth grade, to her fears of riots and war, the ecstasy when *Apollo 8* circled the Moon and when *Apollo 11* landed, the panic when she told Mrs. Leslie that going to the Moon made humans more like God, the despair at the explosion on *Apollo 13*.

Maybe Danny was right. Her ideas had not changed. Maybe the accidents and coincidences that had finally carried her over the troubled waters of adolescence and dissidence were neither accidents nor coincidences. Maybe there was a common thread to the ideas that had attracted her to the Carter campaigns, the science courses she had continued to take long after she knew she had no aptitude for science, and her success representing companies at the frontier of science and technology.

"*You* certainly haven't changed much." She sought a comparison. "You still sound just like you did at your Bar Mitzvah."

"Hopefully, my voice doesn't crack anymore." They both laughed.

Danny pulled up in front of her parents' house and stopped the car. Jackie turned in her seat to look at him. "It's really good to see you, Danny. I really missed you."

"I missed you too."

"So, what do we do now?" she asked pensively.

"What do you mean?"

"I mean, I haven't seen you in four years. You're married. You're moving to California. Am I ever going to see you again?"

"Sure. Why not?"

"I don't know. It feels weird. You and I had this amazing friendship growing up. You were my best friend. We did everything together. We could almost read each other's thoughts. We once tried to convince a teacher we were twins, remember?" They laughed together at the memory of an old prank, but Danny did not say anything.

"Then everything changed," she continued. "You went to college. You did great, as usual. You met Rachel. You got your scholarship. You went to Africa, as you always wanted. I don't think you knew how much I missed you, how desperate I was, how unhappy. I had no idea what I wanted to do. I failed at everything. I was really miserable."

"I knew," Danny answered gently.

"It took me years to get over the idea that you were still out there somewhere, that you would come back like you had always came back from summer camp, that we would talk, that I would tell you everything and you would understand, that we would—" Her voice trailed off into melancholy.

"Look, Jackie, it's never going to be like when we were kids."

"I don't need that anymore." She corrected her tone of voice quickly. "Things are different now. Things worked out pretty great. I'm really happy."

"But we don't have to be strangers, either," Danny continued. "I don't want to be strangers."

"Neither do I." She thought for a moment. "But the day I met Rachel, you said I was your old girlfriend. That's not fair to Rachel. She's your wife."

"It's okay with Rachel," he interrupted. "She actually thinks we might really be twins!" They laughed again.

"You and Rachel could become friends," he offered. "She doesn't have any family in the States, and she doesn't have many friends. She's a little like me. I'm not always the easiest person to be around."

"I remember."

"You were one of the few people who ever put up with me."

"I remember that, too," Jackie laughed.

"You might enjoy shopping with Rachel tomorrow. Give it a chance."

"I will."

Jackie leaned across the seat to give Danny a kiss on the cheek and then rubbed a spot of her lipstick off with her thumb. "We'll figure something out. Good night, Danny."

"Good night."

* * *

The next morning, Jackie and Rachel drove to Boston. They shopped all day, repeatedly carrying shopping bags back to Jackie's condominium and heading out again to buy more. Rachel bought a complete wardrobe: underwear, socks, and pajamas; sweaters, coats, and hats; casual clothes for school and business suits for internships; and shoes to go with everything. Jackie got caught up in the buying frenzy and added to her already ample wardrobe.

As they shopped, Jackie saw a different side of Rachel. They shared a mischievous sense of humor, enjoyed trying on clothes together, and delighted in tormenting salespeople with spirited pranks.

By late afternoon, they were exhausted but still had not bought everything Rachel needed. Rachel called Danny to tell him she would stay at Jackie's condominium overnight, so they could finish their shopping in the morning.

That night, Jackie and Rachel went out for seafood and beer at the No Name restaurant on the waterfront. Then, they returned to Jackie's condominium and stayed up most of the night talking, trying on clothes, and telling incriminating stories about Danny.

Jackie had never felt so comfortable talking to anyone before, except Danny. Rachel was a lot like him. She shared his inquisitive and insightful intellect, his idealism, and his commitment to ideas. It helped that Danny had already told Rachel a lot about her, and they could skip over the awkward introductory exchanges of new acquaintances.

Rachel talked a lot about her family. She had left her home in Johannesburg when she was eighteen, and had only seen her parents a few times in the ensuing years. She talked about her intense loneliness starting at Harvard with her family thousands of miles away.

"Did you plan to stay in America forever when you came?" Jackie asked.

"I didn't think about it much," Rachel reflected. "My father probably knew all along that I was not coming back. He tried talking to me about it at the airport just before I left, but he got very emotional. At the time, I didn't understand why he was so sad. I remember telling him over and over again not to worry, that I would see him soon, that I would be back. I was just a teenager. I couldn't conceive of being separated from my family forever."

"Would you go back now if you had the chance?"

"No. Not now. My family is here now."

"Your family?" Jackie was confused for a moment.

"Danny."

"Of course." Jackie was embarrassed at her oversight.

"I really missed my parents," Rachel reminisced quietly. "I was so lonely that I sort of adopted my roommate's family. Erin, my roommate, came from western Massachusetts. I used to go home with her every weekend. I don't even know whether I was invited, but I went there whenever I needed a break, for holidays, whether or not Erin was there—even for a summer one year. I was at their house so much that I started calling one of the rooms in their house *my* room, and her brother started introducing me as their long-lost sister. But it wasn't the same as having a real family and a real home."

"It will be different for our kids." Rachel's thoughts began to drift. "They will always have a home. My mother says that her family lived in the same town in Germany for more than two hundred years. They had traditions, family, community. I have a picture of my grandmother's wedding. There were hundreds of people there. My mother says they were all relatives. At our wedding, there were maybe ten people I knew. It's going to be different for our kids."

Jackie listened to the rapture in Rachel's voice as she described her idealized vision of a family. She recognized that this was the idea that had driven Rachel to marry at an age when few of her friends had any interest in making a similar commitment.

"Do you ever think about having kids?" Rachel asked.

"No!" Jackie replied in a tone more definitive than she intended. At some level, she recognized Rachel's feelings of loneliness, though she did not share Rachel's longing for a family. "Not really." She qualified her answer in a softer tone.

"Danny said you have a nice family. He says you are close to your father."

"He remembers when we were kids."

"You're not close now?"

"We've drifted apart. I don't see them much. We don't have much in common anymore. You know, my real mother died when I was an infant."

"Danny told me. What happened?"

"I don't really know. My father never talked about her much," Jackie answered with resignation. "My stepmother was—*is*—a fine mother. I love her and all that, but she had four kids after she married my father. It seemed like she was always pregnant or taking care of a baby. I was a lot older. Her kids never felt much like brothers or sisters. Mostly, I remember trying to avoid babysitting so that I could go out with my friends." Jackie paused for a moment. "I don't know if I want to have kids."

"Of course you want to have kids," Rachel responded automatically.

"I don't know if I do or not," Jackie answered adamantly. "I know everyone expects me to get married, have a family, kids. My parents think I should have started looking for Prince Charming as soon as I graduated high school. The only thing they care about is whether Tim is going to ask me to marry him. Personally, I don't care. I can't imagine being pregnant and having children. There isn't enough time in my life."

"Children will change your life."

"That's all I need! It's taken me ten years to get my life in order," Jackie laughed. "I'm very happy the way things are, thank you!"

It had been years since Jackie had had such an intimate conversation with anyone. By the time Rachel left the following evening, they were fast friends.

28

Danny and Rachel left for Stanford several days later and moved into a small, third-floor apartment on the edge of campus. Jackie and Rachel talked regularly, often spending hours on the phone. Danny had never been comfortable talking on the telephone and rarely joined the conversation. He preferred to listen in the background, sometimes asking Rachel to repeat what Jackie was saying and prompting her to ask his questions. When Jackie had business on the west coast, visiting clients in California's burgeoning Silicon Valley, she would often stay for an extra day to visit with Danny and Rachel. Sometimes she would also see Ruben.

Over the years, Ruben had been admitted repeatedly to rehabilitation programs for alcohol and drug addiction, and had been jailed more than once for drug possession. When Danny and Rachel moved to California, Ruben began showing up on their doorstep hungry, strung out on drugs, and begging for money to buy more.

Rachel was uncomfortable around Ruben, whose behavior was often crude and out of control. But Danny could never turn his brother away. Each time Ruben appeared, he would let him stay in their Palo Alto apartment, sleep on the couch in their living room, and share their one bathroom, while their parents tried to arrange for Ruben to be admitted to yet another rehabilitation program. Most of the time, Ruben would stay at their apartment for several days, and then simply disappear back onto the streets before any arrangements could be made for his care.

In the fall of 1983, the Democratic National Committee offered Jackie a position in Walter Mondale's 1984 presidential campaign. She was unsure how to respond. The 1980 Carter campaign had been one of the highlights of her life, and many of her old friends were likely to be involved in the fall campaign. On the other hand, she was overwhelmed with an expanding portfolio of clients, and was hoping to be promoted to vice president in the firm. No one thought the Democrats had any chance in 1984, and she did not want to compromise her career for a lost cause.

More importantly, Jackie was secretly considering voting for Reagan. She admired Reagan's ability to communicate and his Star Wars strategy for national defense, which complemented her own ideas about technology. Moreover, many of her clients had technologies that could be applied to national defense, and she was developing public relations and marketing plans that would position them to profit from the billions of dollars Reagan proposed to spend on the program.

Jackie knew that many scientists did not believe an anti-missile defense system was feasible. Yet, she remembered the Russian anti-satellite weapon *Cosmos 248*, which had destroyed a target in space in 1969, and she thought it was unlikely that technology would be a limiting factor. She never doubted that the same spirit of invention and ingenuity that enabled men to land on the Moon would meet the challenge laid down by Reagan. She admired the way Reagan, like Kennedy, had successfully positioned technology at the center of the nation's destiny.

She met with William Fernald to talk about the 1984 election. While William was committed to backing the Democratic candidate, he agreed that the firm should not be too closely associated with one party. He suggested that it would be better if Jackie were not directly involved in the campaign. She was relieved.

Jackie's workload increased dramatically through 1983, a year that became another defining point in time for technology. After more than a decade of feeble economic growth, the major stock markets began a hectic rise, nearly doubling in little more than a year. There were more IPOs in 1983 than ever before, led by a wave of young technology and biotechnology companies. These IPOs raised billions of dollars for research and development, and established the value of technology stocks as a measure of public faith in technology in general.

Throughout 1983, the public eagerly bought technology and biotechnology stocks, and the value of these stocks rose dramatically. Those who had been involved in founding these companies made fortunes, as did Jackie. Her ever-expanding list of clients gave her the highest bonus of anyone at Fernald

Partners, and she had shares in many of the companies whose stock prices were rising rapidly.

Tim made enormous profits for his investors, which, in turn, made him a celebrity. *Boston* magazine ran a feature article about him, describing his financial success and generous support of local charities, and characterizing Tim and Jackie as one of the city's most attractive couples. She was featured in many of the photographs that accompanied the article; dancing with him at charity functions, sitting in his arms in front of the fireplace of his Boston town home, and lying with him in a hammock overlooking the ocean at his house on the Cape. While Jackie professed to be embarrassed by the exposure, she secretly enjoyed the notoriety it brought.

Jackie faced an intricate challenge in helping her clients mature from start-up enterprises to public corporations. Like Jefferson soliciting money from Congress to fund Lewis and Clark and the Corps of Discovery, or Kennedy selling the voyage to the Moon to taxpayers, Jackie knew that she had to do more than sell the vision of invention and ingenuity. Now, she had to show shareholders how they would get acceptable returns on their investment. While her work increasingly focused on detailed metrics of products and profits, she never lost sight of her expansive vision. She understood that Lewis and Clark, *Sputnik*, and *Apollo* had set ideas in motion that continued to influence the world long after their temporal, geopolitical goals were forgotten.

It had never been hard to sell the American public on the excitement of invention and ingenuity. The public has always been enamored of the image of a creative genius working in a laboratory or garage to make inventions that would change the world. The Wright Brothers, Thomas Edison, and Alexander Graham Bell were national heroes. In the 1980s, this adulation was transferred to a new set of heroes: Steve Wozniak, Steve Jobs, and Bill Gates. Reality was more complicated. Each of these inventors was also an opportunistic entrepreneur who applied for patents, raised capital, and built companies to translate their inventions into marketable products.

It was investors like Tim and their multibillion-dollar investment funds that provided most of the capital required to develop inventions into marketable products. These financiers did not invest in technology because they had any particular interest in innovation or invention. They invested in technology only because they calculated that the value of technology companies would grow faster than traditional businesses. In fact, such investors often forced their companies to curtail development of futuristic products to focus on those that were most likely to provide certain profits. Investors did not want to hear that the company would create new markets; they wanted to see products that would succeed in existing markets. They did not care whether the company's technologies could change the world, because they understood that the world did not always change in predictable ways. If Tim thought the price of pork bellies, wheat, or copper would rise faster than the value of technology, he would invest in commodities rather than the companies Jackie represented.

29

Public interest in technology stocks was historically cyclic. By the summer of 1984, interest began to wane. Companies that investors and the media had loved only months before were suddenly subjected to intense, critical scrutiny. Stock prices, which had risen based on the promise of future market opportunities, began to drop precipitously.

As the appeal of technology and biotechnology companies waned, even more companies turned to Fernald Partners to help. Public relations became increasingly important, as each company tried to differentiate itself from its competitors and convince investors that their stock would continue to rise, even as the stocks of similar companies declined.

Jackie was promoted to vice president in the summer of 1984, a position that gave her greater responsibility within the firm. She found herself working long hours, seven days a week, to meet the needs of her clients and manage her staff.

Tim was also working harder to take advantage of the dwindling number of IPOs and to profit from technical fluctuations in the prices of stocks that were no longer consistently rising. There was little time for anything except work. It became more difficult to escape to the Cape or their yacht for long weekends, and there were fewer extended holidays for sailing, skiing, scuba, and sex.

In June 1984, Jackie received an invitation to Karen's wedding. Karen had successfully resisted her father's pressure to go to medical school and had majored in marketing. Her fiancé was a medical student whom she had met working at the marina in San Diego, and she had moved with him to San Francisco when he began his residency.

Karen was married in an informal afternoon ceremony at a vineyard north of the Golden Gate Bridge in October. Many of the guests were her fiancé's classmates from medical school or colleagues from his residency, and the boisterous celebration was filled with drunken pranks and scatological humor that Jackie found repulsive.

Jackie felt alone and out of place. Tim had not wanted to fly to California for the wedding, so Karen spent the afternoon introducing Jackie to her single male friends, all of whom Jackie found irritating. Moreover, she had not realized the ceremony would be quite so informal, and she was overdressed in heels and a sheer silk dress. She stayed only long enough to be polite, and then left to meet Danny and Rachel for dinner in Chinatown before her overnight flight back to Boston.

She was in a bad mood before she sat down for dinner. She snapped at the hostess about the location of their table, found fault with the crispness of the duck and the stickiness of the rice, and sent the vegetables back to the kitchen because the MSG gave her a headache. She argued with Danny throughout dinner, pointedly contradicting everything he said and uncharacteristically insulting him for his views.

The most intense arguments were about the upcoming election. Danny was appalled when Jackie told him she planned to vote for Reagan. He had supported Reverend Jesse Jackson in the Democratic primaries and only reluctantly decided to support Walter Mondale, once he won the Democratic Party's nomination. When Mondale nominated a woman, Geraldine Ferraro, as his running mate, Rachel had also become involved in the campaign, which she saw as a historic opportunity to support a woman for national office.

Jackie was not in the mood for a reasoned debate. She denounced Danny's views about Jackson as naïve and idealistic. She dismissed Rachel as a foreigner who had no right to an opinion about American politics. Danny, in turn, accused her of selling out her ideals and her conscience for wealth. Before he completely lost his temper, he angrily left the table and took a short walk around the block.

"You're really on edge tonight," Rachel said with concern after Danny had left. "Are you okay?"

"It's been a lousy day."

"You're not making it any better. I've never seen you and Danny go at each other like this."

"He's being impossible."

"You are certainly doing your part to make it unpleasant. What's wrong?"

"I'm not looking forward to flying all night to get home." Jackie dodged the question. "I never get enough sleep on these overnight flights."

"Do you want to stay here in San Francisco overnight? You can take a flight in the morning if it would make you feel better. Our place is small, but you are certainly welcome to stay. I'm sure Danny would take you to the airport in the morning."

"Thanks, but no. Tim is planning to meet me at the airport early in the morning. We're hoping to get out to the Cape for a day. We've been so busy lately that we've hardly been there all summer. We haven't spent a day together in weeks. I can't remember the last time we had sex."

Rachel knew there was more to Jackie's foul mood than the prospect of a long flight home and not enough sex. "I've never seen you in a mood like this before. You can't be this angry with Danny just because he doesn't agree with your politics. You're going to win in November anyway. Did something happen at the wedding?"

"The wedding wasn't much fun," Jackie mused. "I mean, it was nice to see Karen. We go way back. But I don't know—I just felt uncomfortable the whole time."

"And how's Tim?" Rachel continued to probe. "We thought he might come out with you for the wedding."

"Tim is great. He's working hard. We're both working hard. I talk to you more than I talk to him."

"We're always here for you. Of course, the way you're treating Danny tonight, he may never want to talk to you again," she warned in jest.

Jackie smiled halfheartedly for the first time. "I don't think I can chase Danny away that easily after all these years. I guess I owe him an apology."

"If you want to talk, you know, just girls, we can send Danny home. It might be safer for him," Rachel teased.

"Let the poor guy stay. He doesn't have to be lonely just because I am."

"Are you sure?"

"Tim is great." Jackie's rambling thoughts returned to the previous question. "We're very happy together. Things have just been hard lately."

"Are you going to marry him?"

Jackie looked at Rachel in surprise. "How did that come up?"

"Your friend's wedding really bothered you, didn't it?"

"I guess," Jackie said offhandedly. "I don't know."

Jackie knew there were growing rumors within their social circles that she and Tim were planning to get married. Many people thought they were an ideal couple. No one had ever seen them fight, and they both went out of their way to express their affection by buying each other expensive gifts, organizing lavish parties, and arranging exotic vacations. As Tim approached forty, many people thought he would be wise to marry someone as attractive and accomplished as Jackie.

But Jackie also knew that he would never propose to her. While they were genuinely fond of each other, they were not in love. Tim was someone to play with, but he never probed her ideas. One reason they rarely fought was that neither of them cared enough about the other's ideas to fight about them. It was not the same kind of relationship she once had with Danny.

The question about marriage was left dangling as Danny came back to the table.

"I'm glad you came back," Jackie said with some life in her voice for the first time that evening.

"Am I going to need rabies shots to sit next to her?" he asked Rachel before sitting down.

"She won't bite," Rachel answered. "I offered to send you home for your own safety, but Jackie said you could stay."

"No biting?" He turned to Jackie with mock concern.

"I promise. No biting," Jackie laughed.

"So what's going on?" Danny asked with real concern once he was seated. "I've never seen you act like this before."

"I had a hard day. I'll be okay. Just don't start beating on me again about voting for Reagan," she said with a weak laugh.

"Jackie, you know I would do anything in the world for you. I would personally fly you to the Moon, if I could. But please don't ask me to let you vote for Reagan! Anything but that!" They all laughed together for the first time that evening. Jackie needed their company and their laughter. She felt much better when she boarded the flight home later that night.

* * *

In November of 1984, Jackie was not alone in voting for Reagan. The election was a landslide. Reagan won every state in the nation except Mondale's home state of Minnesota and the District of Columbia.

Just before Thanksgiving, Jackie told Tim she thought it was time they both moved on with their personal lives. He did not disagree.

It was not hard for Jackie and Tim to make the transition from lovers to friends. They agreed to spend the Thanksgiving weekend together at Tim's house on the Cape, as they had done in previous years. After a long, relaxing weekend, Jackie collected her things from the Cape house and from Tim's in-town condominium and moved them to her own place in the Back Bay. Tim insisted that she keep all the gifts he had given her, the souvenirs and mementos of their travels, and much of the art and antiques they had purchased together. It was impossible to fit everything into her small two-bedroom condominium, so she donated many things to charities and put others in storage.

It was harder to disentangle their social lives. Jackie and Tim had been together long enough that they often received invitations to social events as a couple. Neither wanted to be subjected to matchmaking or gossip through the holiday season, so they made a point not to talk about their separation and continued to attend holiday parties, benefits, and social events together.

Jackie also agreed to accompany Tim to Washington in January for Ronald Reagan's second inauguration. Tim was a major donor to the Republican Party, and he had been invited to one of the many inaugural balls. Jackie thought it would be fun.

30

For the first time since graduating college, Jackie spent Christmas with her family in Spring. Tim had never wanted to spend time with her family, and she had been more than happy to spend the holidays sailing or skiing with Tim at resorts far away.

The entire Cone family came together in Spring for Christmas. Mary's two daughters still lived at home. The youngest, Allison, was a junior at Spring High School. The oldest, Cathy, lived at the house with her husband, who had been without a job for several months, and their two young children.

Mary's two sons no longer lived at home. Her older son, Bert, Jr., was a student at the University of Texas and was bringing his girlfriend home to meet the family for the first time. The younger son, Corey, had moved to New York after graduating high school, where he worked as a waiter in the theater district. A year later, he and his roommate had moved to San Francisco, where they rented a small apartment in the Castro district and worked as waiters in some of the city's many eclectic restaurants. He was coming for Christmas alone.

Jackie had never felt close to her half-siblings. Time and circumstance had created even more distance. There was an evident disparity between her jet-set lifestyle and her family's lower-middle-class sensitivities and persistent economic concerns.

It was also disconcerting to be introduced to the smelly infants as their "Aunt Jackie" and hear Mary and Bert being called "Grandma" and "Grandpa." She had to resist the urge to run away every time someone handed her a squirming baby to hold. Jackie could not figure out how to hold a baby without getting her clothes soiled, her jewelry chewed or mangled, or the baby slipping to the floor. She was thankful when the toddlers climbed out of her awkward grasp and wandered away, or when someone mercifully took the struggling infant off her lap.

Mary tried to accommodate the entire family in the house. She moved the babies into the room with Cathy and her husband so that Bert, Jr., and Corey could sleep in their old room, arranged for Jackie to sleep on a cot with Allison in her room, and put sheets on the couch in the basement for Bert, Jr.'s girlfriend.

Jackie was relieved when no one objected to her choosing to stay at a nearby inn where she could have her own bathroom, clean linens each morning, and decent coffee with fresh breads for breakfast. She was accustomed to the convenience, services, and quality that her affluence afforded.

Bert did not know how to react to Jackie's blonde hair, makeup, designer clothes, and formal manners. He found it hard to recognize his little girl in the sophisticated woman she had become, yet her animation, enthusiasm, energy, impatience, and zeal were still familiar.

He listened attentively as she described the innovations and inventions that were unfolding around her, and her work promoting the products and promise of technology. He saw the sense of accomplishment in her face when she described successfully convincing people to believe in technologies and her disappointment when she described her failures.

"You sound like a missionary," he mused when Jackie paused in her monologue. "It must have been in your Irish blood after all."

"What are you talking about?"

"It's in the Irish blood to be missionaries, to spread our ideas and faith around the world."

"I haven't been in a church since Cathy's wedding." Jackie was appalled at the suggestion.

"I know—I wasn't talking about religion. The way you believe in what you are doing, the way you work so hard to spread your ideas—you are a missionary."

"It's different," Jackie concluded dismissively.

"I'm not sure it's so different. I know the Irish blood," Bert answered.

* * *

On Christmas Eve, Allison stayed home to babysit, while the others went to the early Mass. Sitting in the church pews where she had spent every Christmas Eve of her childhood made Jackie feel like an impatient and inattentive child. Nothing had changed. The service was still long and tedious. The Holy Trinity still looked down on the congregation from the window over the dais, their heads surrounded by circles of light and the stars of the firmament. Now, however, she was expected to pay attention, and people around her gave her irritated looks every time she began to play with her jewelry.

Father O'Brien was almost seventy. While he no longer led Mass, he still delivered the homily. He began by recalling the miracle of the Immaculate Conception. Then he turned his attention to reproductive technologies: "The birth of Christ brought the love of God to the world. The sacred marriage of a man and a woman brings us closer to experiencing the union of Christ with his Church. Reproductive engineering brings us freezers full of abandoned embryos and lawsuits in which life is merely property."

He quoted Pope John Paul II who, several weeks before, had reaffirmed the church's opposition to any form of artificial reproductive technologies in a teaching, entitled "Redemption of the Body and the Sacrament of Marriage."

Father O'Brien read from the Pope's writings: "'Throughout all modern civilization, especially in Western civilization, there is an occult and at the same time an explicit enough tendency to measure this progress on the basis of things—that is, material goods.' In contrast, the church seeks to 'measure man's progress on the basis of the person—that is, of what is good for man as man, what corresponds to his essential dignity—This development in fact is measured to the greatest extent on the basis of ethics and not only on technology.'"

As Father O'Brien approached the end of his homily, his voice rose to an impassioned pitch. "I have always wondered how a child conceived in a test tube understands the Lord's Prayer." He asked, "To whom are they referring when they say, 'Our Father, who art in heaven, hallowed be thy name?' Our Lord Jesus Christ, who brings blessing to each child in His name, or a nameless scientist who conceives the child for vainglory?

"What do they mean when they say, 'Thy kingdom come, thy will be done, on Earth as it is in heaven?' Are they praying for the kingdom of God who loves Man as he loves his own son? Or are they praying for a kingdom of inhuman machines?"

"Whom are they praying to when they say, 'Give us today our daily bread?' The Creator of the Heavens and the Earth, or a genetic engineer who has the hubris to alter God's holy creation? Who do they think had the capacity to 'forgive us the wrong we have done' other than our Savior Jesus Christ? Does mortal man presume to grant himself salvation and deliverance?" Father O'Brien's voice became softer and more compassionate. "And when a child conceived in a test tube says, 'Amen,' whom does he hope will hear his prayer if not our Heavenly Father, his Son Jesus Christ, who was graciously given to us on this Christmas Day, and the Holy Spirit—the one God."

Jackie sat smugly through the homily, silently rebutting each of Father O'Brien's rhetorical questions and solemnly affirming her faith in technology with every verse. She had no doubt that reproductive technologies gave life, that agricultural technologies could provide populations with their daily bread, that there was beneficence in the magisterium of technology. She was not concerned with Father O'Brien's skepticism. He had not believed that men had reached the heavens on Christmas Eve in 1968. She believed with perfect faith that they had.

When the service ended, Jackie had an almost irresistible urge to jump down the steps and run home, as she had so often as a child. Instead, she patiently greeted Father O'Brien and stood awkwardly beside her parents as they talked with their fellow congregants. Her parents' friends took turns marveling at how the sparkling and active child had matured into a stunning and accomplished young woman.

Everyone asked the same questions: "Where are you living? What are you doing? Are you married yet?" Jackie patiently answered each question dozens of times. Many commented that with her beauty, she should not have trouble catching a man. Several offered to introduce Jackie to single men they knew. Eventually, the crowd dispersed and Jackie walked home with her family under a full Moon that shimmered through the bare branches of trees.

By the time they arrived home, Allison had already put the children to sleep with promises that Santa Claus would come. The adults assembled in the living room to finish wrapping presents. Mary opened the liquor cabinet and brought out platters of Christmas cakes and cookies.

Jackie had a car full of professionally wrapped presents for everyone in the family. She had spent lavishly without a second thought. Among the presents was a small box containing the keys to a new Volvo for Mary and a large box with an IBM PC/AT personal computer, the first personal computer with a built-in hard drive, for her father. There were high-tech gadgets and toys for each of her siblings, in-laws, and their children. Jackie was content that she had done her part for Christmas.

It was past midnight when the last presents were wrapped and placed under the tree. By that time, too many beers and too much gin and tonic had loosened the better social inhibitions of Jackie's family, and the conversation began to delve into personal matters.

Jackie's breakup with Tim and her prospects for marriage were the most popular topic for everyone except Jackie. Mary started the conversation by asking whether there was any chance they might get back together. Cathy bluntly stated that there was nothing wrong with marrying someone for money, pointedly saying she would have been better off if she had married someone rich instead of someone who could not hold a job. Her husband then turned on Jackie, complaining bitterly that technology was taking away jobs by replacing employees with computers and machines.

Jackie tried to change the conversation by asking Bert, Jr., and his girlfriend about school and what they planned to do after college. Bert, Jr., said he wanted to go into sales. His girlfriend said she wanted to have a large family, and that she did not think she would be able to take care of kids and have a career at the same time. Mary agreed and pointedly said she hoped all of her daughters would put their families ahead of their careers.

Allison jumped in to argue in support of women's rights, announcing that she did not plan to give up her career to sit at home and do nothing when she had a family. Everyone looked at Jackie expectantly, waiting for her to defend her own choices, but she stayed silent.

Corey began to describe a strange new disease called AIDS that was spreading through his neighborhood in San Francisco. It crippled the immune system, leaving the sufferers susceptible to unusual infections, cancers, and, seemingly inevitably, death. One of his close friends had recently died. Several others were gravely ill.

Cathy said she heard that the disease affected only homosexuals, and that it might have something to do with their unnatural sexual behavior. Mary interjected that she did not think a good Catholic family had to worry about such problems, and admonished her children on the importance of chastity outside of marriage. Bert, Jr., agreed with her. Allison unwisely challenged them both, defending the right of people who cared about each other to have sex without marriage, which led to a free-for-all argument with her parents and siblings about premarital sex, birth control, homosexuality, marital responsibilities, and how Jackie and Corey needed to set a better example for their youngest sister.

Jackie refused to be drawn into the fray. She let her family argue among themselves for some time without comment. Eventually, she found a polite opportunity to announce that she was tired and was going back to her hotel to get some sleep.

That night, she dreamed she was soaring over the surface of the Moon in an *Apollo* spacecraft, drawn by remote-controlled reindeer. She saw the Moon's cratered surface passing below her, just as she had seen it on television sixteen years before. She heard the voice of Astronaut Lovell repeating the words of his Christmas broadcast: "The vast loneliness is awe-inspiring, and it makes you realize just what you have." She heard the voices of Mission Control crackling over the radio with instructions on how to land the spacecraft on the rocky surface, except the voices were those of her parents, Father O'Brien, Danny, Rachel, Tim, and many others. They were all talking, teaching, arguing, debating, laughing, and crying at once. As the voices grew louder and more insistent, Jackie tried to follow the cacophony of competing commands, until a large rock loomed in the path before her. Calmly, she threw a switch on

SPUTNIK'S CHILD

the control panel that turned the voices off. Then she took the controls of the powerful spaceship in her own hands and flew confidently over a landing site strewn with boulders to a spot where the surface was tranquil and the Earth could be seen from the heavens.

31

In January, Jackie and Tim flew to Washington for Ronald Reagan's inauguration. They stepped out of the terminal at National Airport into a shivering cold that shattered seventy-year-old records.

Inauguration day was no warmer. It was so cold that President Reagan took the oath of office inside the Capitol Rotunda before a small crowd of dignitaries, rather than on the west portico of the Capitol in front of the American people, and the inaugural parade was cancelled.

That evening, the inaugural balls in Washington were the most extravagant in history. Jackie and Tim attended the ball at the National Air and Space Museum, several blocks from the Capitol.

The museum's enormous galleries and corridors were filled with men in graceful tuxedos and women in designer gowns. Just before nine o'clock, President and Nancy Reagan made a brief appearance at the ball. President Reagan made a few prepared remarks from the bandstand, thanking the organizers of the event and the crowd for their support, praising the American spirit, expressing his faith in the future, and invoking God's blessing on America. After ten minutes, he waved to the crowd and danced off to another inaugural ball, as the band played *Fly Me to the Moon*.

After the president left, the crowd dispersed throughout the museum. Tim quickly found that the venue was too noisy for networking. Instead, he and Jackie spent most of the evening strolling through the museum's exhibit halls.

The National Air and Space Museum was a colossal edifice, built to display America's leadership in the developing flight and exploring space. The Atlas and Saturn rockets, which launched the *Mercury* and *Gemini* astronauts into space, stood upright beneath the ceiling. The *Enola Gay*, which dropped the first atomic bomb on Hiroshima, hung suspended between its walls. Jackie and Tim walked under the original Wright Brothers *Flyer*, Lindberg's *Spirit of Saint Louis*, and Earhart's *Lockheed Vega*. They walked past a replica of the original *Sputnik* and the rockets that had sent generations of satellites into space.

176

The centerpiece of the National Air and Space Museum was an exhibit titled *Apollo to the Moon*, which chronicled the history of the *Apollo* Program. Jackie was in awe seeing the space suits that Neil Armstrong and Buzz Aldrin had worn on the Moon's surface, the shovel that had cut into the lunar soil, and the black-and-white television camera that had captured the iconic image of Armstrong's first small step. She marveled at the Command Module *Columbia*, which had brought the *Apollo 11* astronauts back to Earth, and she tried to imagine how the primitive metal capsule, smaller than the cabin on Tim's yacht, could have carried men millions of miles to the Moon and back.

In the main hall outside the exhibit, a rock that the *Apollo* astronauts had taken from the Moon was displayed on a pedestal of polished granite and glass. An aisle flanked by velvet ropes led congregations of people toward the platform, where they could touch the precious artifact from the heavens.

As a child, Jackie had often imagined holding a Moon rock in her hand. Now she approached the relic with a reverence usually reserved for Communion. She could hardly breathe as she reached out to touch the rock. She ran her manicured hand cautiously over the surface, shivered slightly, then felt a warm glow radiate through her body and took a deep breath. She pressed her glistening nails onto the rock to feel its hardness, and then surreptitiously turned her hand over to scrape her multifaceted diamond rings against its surface, which remained perfect.

Her hand lingered on the rock. She looked around at the rockets standing along the walls, their nose cones pointing toward the heavens like the arches of a great Gothic cathedral, the artifacts enclosed in the consecrated place, and the celebrants massed around her. Her gaze and her spirit turned up toward heaven.

The early Church had transformed the story of Christ walking on the waters of the Sea of Galilee into a symbol of God's power and a missive to the world that the coming of Christ brought great goodness. In the late twentieth century, America had translated the history of men walking on the surface of the Sea of Tranquility into a symbol of the power of free men and the message to the world that humankind could accomplish great goals. In commemoration, America had built a temple no less in stature and significance than the soaring cathedrals of Europe. It was a place designed to inspire wonder and reverence, a place of pilgrimage for common people and presidents, and an oracle showing the faithful the way to the heavens.

Jackie had long ago consolidated her sense of wonder and awe at humankind's ability to reach the heavens into a personal faith. In childhood, the image of men walking on the Moon had helped her find order and optimism in a disorderly and distressed world. Through adolescence, these ideas had provided her identity and her opportunity. As an adult, she had channeled her restless energy into shaping her world in accordance with these ideas.

Tim watched as Jackie stood in transcendental bliss with her hand on the relic from the Moon, her eyes turned toward heaven, and her hair straying across her face. He gently brushed the hair from her eyes, lifted her hand from the rock, and led her back to Earth.

Book Three: Irrational Exuberance
January 1985

32

S everal weeks after Reagan's inauguration, Jackie received a rare telephone call from Danny. "Rachel wanted me to call you," he said, after they exchanged a few pleasantries. Jackie sat down at the kitchen table with the long, twisted cord from the wall phone stretched back behind her.

"What's up?" she asked, immediately suspicious that Danny would initiate a call at Rachel's request.

"We have an idea for you," he said uncertainly.

"What is it?"

"Did you ever meet Rachel's college roommate?"

"I thought *you* were her college roommate," Jackie teased.

"Jackie, I'm serious. Her roommate was a girl named Erin Brennan—they were very close. Anyway, Rachel used to spend a lot of time with her and with her family."

"Rachel told me. She said they used to introduce her as their long-lost sister."

"That's a good description. Anyway, Erin has an older brother named Steve—Steve Brennan—who is not married, and—"

"And Rachel wants to set us up on a date," Jackie surmised immediately.

"Let me talk, Jackie, will you?" Danny said, sounding even more uncomfortable. "I was saying—Rachel and I had dinner with Erin last night. She was out here for a meeting. Anyway, she said that Steve just moved to Boston to work at the Massachusetts General Hospital. He's a doctor."

"Isn't that a basic requirement for a good marriage prospect for Jews?" Jackie continued to tease him, enjoying his evident discomfort.

"Jackie!"

"I never could figure out why Rachel married you. You're not a doctor."

"Would you shut up for once in your life?" Danny pleaded.

"I'm sorry," she laughed, "but I've never heard anyone sound so uncomfortable arranging a blind date. Do you only have trouble talking about dates when they involve me?"

"Jackie, give me a chance, please!"

"Go ahead," she relented with another laugh.

"Anyway, Erin said something about setting you up on a date with Steve. As soon as Erin said it, Rachel went, like, totally crazy! They didn't talk about anything else all evening except how to arrange for you two to meet. Rachel didn't sleep all night. Then she woke me up this morning and insisted that I call you immediately. It's five o'clock in the morning here, you know. She is totally nuts, Jackie. I've never seen her like this before." Danny sounded relieved to have delivered his message. "You don't have to do this if you don't want to."

"I trust Rachel. She found a passable husband," Jackie admitted. "So, are you going to tell me anything about this guy?"

"Rachel knows him better than I do. I've met him a number of times. He's nice."

"Is that all? He's nice?"

"You really need to talk to Rachel. I know he graduated from medical school the year before we finished college, so he's probably something like five years older than we are. Like I said, you really have to talk to Rachel. She knows him better than I do."

"So when do I meet this guy?"

"Well—" Danny again sounded uncomfortable, "you have a date Saturday night."

"What!" Jackie was incredulous.

"This wasn't my idea, Jackie," Danny pleaded. "You have to understand, Rachel and Erin went completely nuts. They were running back and forth to a pay phone all through dinner talking to her brother. I think they even made a reservation for you at some restaurant."

"What makes you think I don't have a date already for Saturday night?"

"Do you?" Danny paused, suddenly sounding worried.

Jackie heard Danny talking to Rachel in the background. "Come on, Rachel, I really don't need to be in the middle of this. Talk to her yourself."

"Do you mean Rachel has been there with you the whole time?" Jackie exclaimed. "Tell her to get on the phone!"

"I'm sorry, Jackie. I didn't want to do this, but Rachel—"

"Put her on the phone!" Jackie demanded.

She heard Danny passing the phone to Rachel.

"Jackie, you've got to believe me!" Rachel blurted in a voice bubbling with excitement. "You're going to marry this guy!"

"Rachel!" Jackie exclaimed in disbelief at her forwardness.

"Just believe me. He's perfect for you!"

Over the next hour, Rachel gave Jackie an animated and detailed recitation of everything she knew about Steve. Over the next several days, Rachel called repeatedly with more information about Steve along with advice on what Jackie should wear, how she should fix her hair, how she should act, and what she should say. As the week went on, Jackie became more and more caught up by Rachel's excitement, but also more concerned that, when the date finally happened, it could be anticlimactic.

* * *

Jackie had been on many first dates, but never one like this. When Steve finally rang the doorbell on Saturday night, it felt like a curtain rising on a well-rehearsed play, rather than a first date where every move is uncertain and uncomfortable. She was more nervous about forgetting all Rachel's instructions, than she was about meeting Steve.

Steve dissipated her nervousness immediately with his gracious manner as he introduced himself, opened the door for her as they left, and led her to the waiting taxi. Rachel's description of him had been accurate in every detail. Steve was tall and acutely thin with fine facial features, fair skin, and silky white hair that swept across his forehead and stood obstinately in a cowlick on his crown. He wore gray woolen pants and a gray tweed sport coat with a bow tie. His straight posture and polite gestures projected a formal manner, though Jackie also saw a shy smile and subtle sparkle in his blue eyes.

They exchanged comfortable conversation on the short ride to the restaurant where Rachel and Erin had made reservations. Jackie told him how Danny had been a childhood friend and how she had come to know Rachel after they returned from Africa. Steve described how Rachel had spent so much time at their house in Pittsfield while she was in college, that he began to treat her like a younger sister.

As they talked, Jackie found herself unconsciously finishing Steve's sentences in her head even before he could speak the words. It was a strange sensation, as if she had already heard what he was going to say. Then she realized, she had; from Rachel!

In Rachel's manic, controlling excitement, she had completely ignored the common boundaries of personal privacy and communicated an enormous amount of intimate information about Steve, even anticipating what he would say and what stories he would tell. Almost simultaneously, Steve recognized the same thing; that Jackie was saying things he had heard from Erin.

Rachel and Erin had tried to leave nothing to chance.

"I can't believe they told you so much about me." Jackie laughed self-consciously, as they began comparing notes on their matchmakers' tactics.

"—or that they told you so much about me!"

"Sometimes a woman is supposed to be a little bit mysterious on a first date."

"I'm afraid it's too late for that!" Steve laughed. "I don't know if either of us has any secrets left."

"I'll get those conniving finks!" Jackie threatened mischievously. "We have to get even."

"I'm game. What do you have in mind?"

"I'll think of something." Jackie's mind raced. "We could make them believe they messed everything up by telling us too much. I could—" Jackie burst into laughter as an idea came to her "—I could tell Rachel that because they told you so much about me, you didn't ask any questions about me the whole night, so I got the impression that you weren't interested in me."

"That's good," he laughed. "It's not true, of course," he added quickly. "I have another idea. I could tell Erin that we both found each other so completely predictable that the evening was boring."

"Or—this is good!" Jackie began laughing so hard she could hardly talk. "I could tell Rachel that you have some really dark personal secret that you've never told Erin because you knew she was an incorrigible gossip who couldn't keep a secret!"

"That is good," Steve laughed. "I would love to see her face when she hears that."

Their ever more imaginative schemes for reprisal and their laughter quickly became infectious. Jackie's sides hurt from laughing by the time they got to the restaurant. Their discovery of Rachel and Erin's scheme to control every aspect of their date set a tone of conviviality that Rachel and Erin had not planned.

Jackie and Steve had a leisurely dinner at one of Boston's finest restaurants. It did not feel like a first date. They did not have to begin by talking about the weather, the traffic, or human interest stories in the news. They did not have to skirt around issues of politics or religion, not knowing each other's sensitivities. The intimate knowledge that Rachel and Erin had given them about each other enabled them to explore ideas, ideals, ambitions, and emotions that are rarely broached on a first date. They talked comfortably, as if they had known each other for years.

After dinner, they took a taxi back to Jackie's condominium, where she invited him in for a drink. Jackie had never met anyone with whom she connected so quickly and completely. She opened a bottle of wine, and they continued talking earnestly for hours.

They had already finished one bottle of wine and opened a second when the telephone rang at eleven thirty.

"I'll let it ring," Jackie said quickly, not wanting anything to interrupt the evening.

The telephone rang again at twelve midnight, then again at twelve fifteen, twelve thirty, and twelve forty-five. By then, Jackie and Steve both suspected who was calling. When the telephone rang again fifteen minutes later, Jackie silently picked up the receiver and held it several inches away from her ear so they could both listen. They immediately recognized Rachel's voice. "Hello, Jackie? Jackie? Are you there? Hello?"

Steve put his fingers to his lips, gesturing for Jackie to be quiet, and took the phone from her. Disguising his voice in a thick South Boston brogue, he angrily expressed his irritation at being awakened in the middle of the night by repeated telephone calls.

Rachel did not recognize Steve's voice. "I'm—I'm so sorry," she stammered, and hung up immediately. Steve and Jackie turned toward each other, laughing at Rachel's discomfort.

The phone rang again immediately. This time Steve answered and, in the same affected accent, launched into a heated harangue, threatening to call the police if there were any more calls. Rachel still did not recognize Steve's voice and began to apologize profusely.

Jackie listened, standing closely behind Steve so she could hear both sides of the conversation. As Steve continued his tirade, and Rachel sounded more and more embarrassed, Jackie could not control herself. She buried her face heavily into Steve's shoulder to stifle her amusement and then abruptly burst into giddy laughter.

Rachel recognized Jackie's laugh immediately.

"Jackie! Oh my God! Steve! It's you! You're still there!" she exclaimed, suddenly knowing both that they had tricked her, and that the date she had arranged had been a success. She hung up the phone without a word and called Erin to tell her what had happened.

Jackie and Steve fell back onto the couch. She was light-headed from the wine and laughter. Her head fell on Steve's chest, and his arms folded around her, as their bodies continued to shake with pleasure.

There were no more phone calls that night. They would not have answered anyway.

Steve left just before 5:30 that morning to make rounds at the hospital. Jackie let him out the door with a soft embrace and a kiss. When he was gone, she collected her clothes from the living room floor and eased contentedly back into bed.

33

When Jackie awoke again, just before noon, it occurred to her that she had never slept with anyone on a first date, and that it might not be the best way to start a promising relationship. But Steve had completely captivated her. After hours of talking, several bottles of wine, and the mischief with Rachel, they had eased into lovemaking that had been more vibrant and vital than anything Jackie had ever experienced or even imagined.

She felt buoyant as she showered, made the bed, and retrieved the Sunday paper from the lobby. She spent the morning contentedly reading the Sunday *Times* in front of the large window overlooking the frozen river.

Rachel called several hours later. "So you slept with him?" she said gruffly without even offering a greeting.

"How did you know?" Jackie answered sheepishly.

"You don't cover your affairs very well," Rachel teased. "For one thing, he answered your telephone at one in the morning. It's not hard to figure the rest. How could you?"

"I'm not saying I did." Jackie tried to maintain a semblance of dignity. "I guess you didn't plan for me to have sex last night?"

"I did not!"

"You forgot to tell me that part of the plan! I'm surprised you didn't think of it. You thought of everything else," Jackie laughed. "So, what did Steve think of our date?" she said, turning more serious.

"How would I know?" Rachel feigned ignorance.

"Let's see," Jackie mused, "if you are true to your meddlesome form, I'm guessing that as soon as you hung up on us last night, you called Erin to tell her that he was still in my apartment. Erin probably called her brother by six this morning to see if he was home, which he wasn't, so she probably paged him at the hospital to ask him about the date. I'm also guessing that, as soon as she hung up the phone with Steve, she called you, even though it was three-thirty in the morning in California, to tell you everything she heard from Steve. I also assume that you spent at least half an hour on the phone with Erin deciding what you would each tell us. Am I close?"

"You're good," Rachel admitted with a laugh. "Of course, Steve didn't tell Erin he slept with you—he is a gentleman. He did say that he liked you, that you are very lovely and very interesting, that he had a wonderful time, and that he wanted to see you again. Erin and I have some ideas about your next date. It didn't occur to us, though, that you might both prefer a cheap hotel to a five-star restaurant," Rachel teased.

"Stop it!" Jackie demanded. "You've been married too long if you think *my* sex life is any fun." They both laughed. Then Jackie's tone became more subdued. "I didn't mess things up, you know, by sleeping with him, did I?"

"I don't think so," Rachel said seriously. "There are certainly worse things to a guy than getting laid on a first date by a rich, beautiful woman!" Rachel couldn't help teasing.

"Rachel, stop it! I'm already embarrassed enough! You are not being helpful."

"I'm sorry. I'm just trying to figure out what happened. It's not like you to sleep with someone on a first date. You've never done that before, have you?"

"No."

"And Erin thinks her brother is practically a virgin."

"He's no virgin. I can promise you that," Jackie laughed.

"I won't tell her. Spare me the details. So, what happened?"

"I don't know." Jackie tried to analyze her own behavior. "There was something about the way we connected. We both felt so alive. It just felt so natural, almost necessary."

"Jackie Cone! You're in love," Rachel gloated.

"Stop it, Rachel. We've only been on one date!"

"Trust me," Rachel said conclusively. "You are going to marry this guy."

"Rachel!" Jackie protested.

"Be sure you invite me to the wedding."

* * *

Steve called Jackie that afternoon and invited her for a walk along the Charles River Esplanade. Jackie met him on the Fiedler Bridge that led over the highway to the water's edge. They spent hours strolling along the river before the Sun began to set and they realized how cold they were. Then, they retreated to a coffeehouse in the Back Bay so they could continue talking.

If Jackie was not completely in love with Steve by the time she returned to her condominium late that evening, she fell in love with him over the next weeks and months in a way that she had never experienced before. There was none of the caution and awkwardness of her childhood affection for Danny, none of the emotional catharsis of her night with Peter, none of the conspicuousness of her long affair with Tim. For the first time in her life, Jackie wanted to immerse herself totally in the emotions, expectations, and experiences of a man. For the first time, she found a man who wanted to do the same with her.

Jackie fell in love with Steve's astute manner and the sense of adventure that lurked just below the surface. She fell in love with someone who could wear a conservative tweed jacket and bow tie over fine wool pants to the theater, and over blue jeans while walking in the park, and never look out of place; someone who could quote both Shakespeare and Seuss; someone who could debate science and politics with passion, yet also play practical jokes with a straight face. By Easter, Jackie and Steve were inseparable, and he was spending more time at Jackie's condominium in the Back Bay than at his own small apartment near the hospital.

Steve was unlike anyone Jackie had ever met. He was a throwback to the gentlemen scientists and physicians of the nineteenth century, who were at once the bastions of the conservative Victorian establishment, and the harbingers of a radical new age of science. He had followed his father's footsteps in choosing a career in medicine. His father had graduated from Johns Hopkins Medical School in 1929; the year penicillin was discovered. He was a general practitioner in an era when physicians made house calls, when their ability to appreciate the subtle signs and symptoms of disease were the most powerful tools for diagnosing a patient's ailment, and when rest, fresh air, nutrition, and simple medications to control pain and bowel irregularity were the most potent remedies a doctor could offer.

Steve was fourteen when his father died. He remembered following his father on weekends, as he made rounds through his patients' homes, and standing by his father's side to hand him items from his large black medical bag. He recalled the smell of infection and antiseptic as well as the sound of his father's voice, soothing people in pain and joining them in prayer. He watched his father as he laid his hands on patients to probe their ailments and provide assurance. He remembered elderly patients reaching for his hand to hold on to the feeling of youth.

Steve attended medical school at Johns Hopkins, his father's alma mater. The medicine Steve learned in the 1970s, however, was fundamentally different from the medicine his father had learned half a century before. The introduction of penicillin into medical practice in the 1940s had virtually eliminated the historical scourges of puerperal, scarlet, and rheumatic fevers. More importantly, penicillin's success established the principle that simple chemical compounds could cure complex diseases. It was the first miracle drug.

By the 1970s, physicians had a broad arsenal of miracle drugs. There were antibiotics for infection, antihypertensive medicines for heart disease, bronchodilators for asthma, anti-metabolites for cancer, immune suppressants for arthritis, minor tranquilizers for anxiety, and major tranquilizers for psychosis. The practice of medicine had been transformed from an art based on the appreciation of disease to a discipline focused on the application of drugs.

Despite Steve's training in modern medicine, he never forgot how his father had practiced the medical arts. He saw for himself that there was something about touching a patient and taking the time to listen to their stories that made people improve, even before the drugs he prescribed could take effect. He came to believe that patients who prayed had measurably better outcomes than those who did not.

Steve's specialty was research on human subjects, and he had moved to Boston to head a clinical research center at the Massachusetts General Hospital. He was interested in how a lifetime of unique experiences contributed to disease, health, and healing. He was interested in finding new ways to treat and prevent disease, as well as ways to improve the quality of life for those with incurable diseases.

Steve introduced Jackie to a different world of social, intellectual, and leisure activity than she had known with Tim. They spent their time together walking around the city, bicycling through the parks of Boston's Emerald Necklace, and attending open-air concerts on the Esplanade and productions of Shakespeare on the Common. They frequented science and art museums and worked to raise money for numerous patient-advocacy groups.

Jackie gradually eased into Steve's unpretentious lifestyle. She began declining invitations to formal society events that were unrelated to her work. She stopped wearing makeup on a regular basis, let her hair revert to its original honey color, and grew it longer than it had been in years. She retained, however, her penchant for short skirts and high heels, which were even more arresting next to Steve's always-conservative gray tweeds and bow ties.

That summer, they spent a month traveling through Europe by rail, visiting the museums, cathedrals, and castles in great capitals and small towns throughout Western Europe. Steve liked to stay in rustic inns that were often centuries old, and to dine in small restaurants and pubs situated off the tourist routes. He enjoyed spending evenings trying to order meals and communicate with the local patrons in rudimentary French and German, and he reveled in the memorable adventures that resulted from misreading menus and missing connections on local trains.

Jackie enjoyed having the time to talk with Steve, read, and leisurely explore their surroundings. They learned how to sleep together in the cramped compartments of passenger trains and how to make love on fragile beds in creaky inns without their activities being exposed to patrons in adjacent rooms. Periodically, however, Jackie tired of shared bathrooms, worn sheets, and improvised showers, and would insist that they spend one night at a five-star hotel where she could wash her hair under a hot shower, send her clothes to the laundry, and order room service in English.

In each town they visited, they would first find the great Gothic or Roman-esque churches in the town's center, where they would admire the architecture, statuary, and stained glass, and climb the bell tower to view the countryside. Jackie was particularly intrigued with the elaborate mechanical clocks that, for centuries had measured the time, seasons, and phases of the Moon. She loved watching the ancient machines announce the hour with intricate chimes and miniature centurions, which danced around the clock face to celebrate the technical prowess, power, and prosperity of another age.

Steve marveled at the great organs that graced even the most modest churches with elaborate pipes and ethereal sounds that resonated through time. They made it a habit to attend Vespers at the end of each day to hear the organs. Jackie would rest her head peacefully on Steve's shoulder, gaze skyward at the Gothic columns pointed at the heavens like rockets, and wonder how such magnificent structures could have been created during a dark age of learning and technology. Steve would close his eyes to concentrate on the overtones of the great organs, his lips moving in silent prayer.

Shortly after they returned from Europe, Steve asked Jackie to attend Mass with him Sunday morning. She was uncertain how to respond. Jackie had no interest in spending Sunday mornings in church. She had come to recognize, however, that spirituality was important to Steve, and that her own indifference to religion was something they had to work through before they could consider marriage.

Steve and Jackie began to talk earnestly about their views on religion. Steve described a religiosity that differed from her parents' Catholic faith. He had little devotion to the canons of scripture or the liturgy of the church. Rather, he was inspired by the sense that there was more to humanity than what was revealed by science. He believed there were everyday occurrences in medicine that could only be considered miracles by a reasoned mind. He believed that there was a space beyond the trained senses and tools of scientists that could only be touched by intuition, emotion, and prayer.

"I don't understand you sometimes," Jackie challenged him. "You are a scientist, yet somehow you don't believe in science. You are a doctor, but you don't believe that you heal people. What do you believe in?"

"I never said I didn't believe in science or medicine, only that I believe that there is something more. It's hard to describe."

"Try."

"There is something amazing about medicine, about health and healing that isn't purely scientific. I find that when I pray for my patients, I see things about them I hadn't seen before, and I understand things I didn't understand. It gives me a sense of—I don't know what to call it—amazement, awe, wonder, maybe God?"

"What does God have to do with this?" Jackie tried hard not to sound argumentative.

"Maybe nothing. Maybe everything. You've told me how you feel when you look up at the Moon and how you felt when you touched a Moon rock for the first time. How do you describe that feeling?"

"Amazement. Awe. Those are good words."

"That's what I'm trying to describe."

"What is?"

"That sense of amazement and awe, that it's all a little unworldly."

"But what does it have to do with God?" Jackie was beginning to tire of the conversation.

"Why did the astronauts read from Genesis the first time they circled the Moon?" Steve replied.

Jackie trembled slightly as she recalled the words of Genesis coming from lunar orbit on Christmas Eve and the vision of the Moon's cratered surface with the Earth rising in the heavens. "I don't know," she replied. "I never thought about it. It was very emotional—maybe spiritual," she admitted, sensing a glimmer of what Steve was talking about. At the same time, she remembered how the voyages of *Apollo* had finally dispelled her childhood illusions about heaven. "But I still don't see why it has anything to do with God, with prayer, with communion."

"Because, the way you feel when you look at the Moon—that's how I feel when I pray. The way you felt when you touched the Moon rock—that's how I feel when I take Communion."

Jackie's face contorted in an expression of studied disbelief. "Look, Steve, I don't mind going to church with you," she said with a tone of finality. "I understand it's important to you, and I like sharing things with you. But I just don't believe there is some omnipotent, supernatural being out there in heaven somewhere. I don't think you do either. Whatever the astronauts felt when they reached the Moon, no matter why they chose to read from Genesis, the Earth is just a planet in orbit around the Sun—the Moon is just a rock circling around the Earth—and the astronauts were only there because scientists, engineers, and politicians decided to build rockets that could take men to the Moon."

"But you still found it awe-inspiring."

"I did," Jackie agreed readily. "But, tell me one thing. Even if you feel there is something spiritual or awe-inspiring about health and disease, at the end of the day, you still have to believe that you can cure people by diagnosing what is wrong and giving them a drug to treat it—don't you?"

"Yes, I believe that," Steve answered, with some equivocation in his voice.

"Do you believe it?" Jackie asked again, searching his eyes for the certainty she did not hear in his voice.

"I do." Steve reached for her and brushed her hair away from her eyes.

That Sunday, they attended Mass together for the first time. Over the next several months, they attended Mass at several different churches in Boston and Cambridge, until they found one where they both felt comfortable. Even then, Jackie would sit through services impatiently, measuring time by the kaleidoscopic colors of the Sun moving through the stained-glass windows. Sometimes, she would watch Steve as he prayed and wonder what he was really thinking.

34

Jackie introduced Steve to her family at Thanksgiving. Bert immediately saw a glow on his daughter's face in place of the affected and aloof façade he had seen the year before. He was thrilled to see her full of life and spirit.

Allison and Corey liked Steve immediately. Mary, who assumed that Tim had abandoned Jackie after their long affair, gave Jackie a halfhearted admonition to be sure this boy did not take advantage of her before he committed to marriage. Cathy took every opportunity to remind Jackie that she would have been extremely wealthy if she had married Tim.

The family spent most of the day talking in the living room, while Cathy's children played at their feet. As the room became crowded, Steve gave up his place on the couch and sat down on the floor where the youngsters immediately adopted him as a playmate. Watching Steve cavorting with the children, Jackie had a vision of what it might be like to have her own family.

On an impulse, she joined Steve on the floor. He showed her how to hold a child securely in her arms and demonstrated stages of child development with the tricks that physicians use to perform a physical exam. Within an hour, Jackie found herself laughing uncontrollably, as Steve encouraged the children to climb up on her chest and knees, and then slide down her legs as if she were a slide at the playground. Eventually, the children tired of the game and ran off in search of their mother. Jackie rolled over onto her side and laid her head contentedly in Steve's lap.

On Monday after Thanksgiving, Steve gave notice to his landlord that he would vacate his apartment at the end of the year. Jackie contacted a real estate agent to put her condominium on the market. Together, they bought a four-bedroom duplex in a historic building in Boston's Back Bay.

By then, the mutual attraction that Jackie and Steve had felt on their first date had matured into profound affection and attachment. Steve had become a regular fixture in her dreams, sitting beside her as she steered spaceships through the heavens. Incrementally, they had begun to envision themselves as part of the other's future. Ineffably, they became a family.

Jackie spent Christmas with Steve, Erin, and their mother Elaine at the Brennan family home in Pittsfield, Massachusetts. During the year she had been dating Steve, Jackie and Erin had become friends, though they were not close. After the frenzied enthusiasm leading up to Jackie's first date with Steve, Erin had become suspicious of the speed at which their relationship had developed. It had taken her some time to get to know Jackie and trust her.

On Christmas Eve, they shared a quiet family dinner. They talked about Elaine's health, the repairs the house needed, and news about old friends in the community. Erin talked about finishing her Ph.D. in clinical psychology. Jackie and Steve described their travels and their work. Elaine had prepared numerous courses of food, each of which was served with a story concerning the origin of the recipe, how she had chosen the ingredients, or a reminiscence of holiday dinners in years past. Steve and Erin knew each of the stories by heart, and they helped Elaine fill in any forgotten details so that Jackie would be familiar with the family's traditions.

When the meal was over, Jackie excused herself to get dressed for church. It took her only a few moments to brush her hair and put on a short, black-velvet dress with an assortment of ruby and emerald jewelry reflecting the colors of Christmas. When she was dressed, she wandered down the stairs to the living room. Steve was standing alone in front of the Christmas tree. She walked up behind him, put her arms around him, and rested her head on his shoulder. He turned to give her a kiss, and then stood holding both of her hands in his.

"I have something for you," Steve said, smiling self-consciously.

"I sort of guessed."

"I could do something theatrical like get down on my knees and ask you to marry me?"

"No need," Jackie almost whispered. She could feel his hands trembling, and she held them more tightly in her own, until they were still. "You already know my answer."

"I know, but there is something I need to say," he continued.

"From the night we met, I've felt this truly amazing connection with you—your energy—your sense of wonder at the universe—the way you think about things."

Steve's voice struggled against his emotions. Tears filled her eyes as he slipped one hand out of her grasp and reached into his jacket pocket. Taking out a gold and diamond ring, he placed it on Jackie's finger. "I love you, Jackie Cone. I feel blessed to ask you to marry me, to share my life with you, to make you my wife, to be your husband."

Without even glancing at the ring, Jackie stepped forward to hold Steve in a tight embrace. It was all she could do to say, "I love you," before the tears started flowing onto his shirt. She struggled to find her voice. "I'm so happy."

Elaine and Erin, who had been watching secretly from the top of the stairs, could not wait any longer and bustled into the room, taking turns hugging Jackie and Steve and sharing their tears of joy. It was several minutes before Jackie had the chance to look at the two-carat diamond ring Steve had placed on her finger. When she did, she was again overcome with uncontrollable tears. Before they left for Mass, Jackie saw Erin slip away to call Rachel and tell her the good news.

Jackie cuddled next to Steve throughout Mass. She spent most of the service staring at the heavenly stone that graced her finger and the colored stars that it projected around her. Her mind drifted in a celestial bliss. She saw the Earth rise over the curvature of the Moon and felt the warmth of the Sun rising from its winter solstice.

Steve prayed as he watched the spectrums of light refracting on Jackie's face and the radiance of her eyes. Nothing in his knowledge of humanity or nature could explain his sense of joy. There was something wondrous, something ineffable, something gracious about his feelings of love that, like the psalmists and saints, he could acknowledge only through prayer.

In his homily that night, the pastor talked about the recent meeting of the Synod of Bishops, called to reassess the teachings of Vatican II. He read portions of the statement issued by this Second Extraordinary Synod: "In the wealthy nations we see the constant growth of an ideology characterized by pride in technical advances and a certain immanentism that leads to the idolatry of material goods. From this can follow a certain blindness to spiritual realities and values." He reiterated that the role of the church was to stand in opposition to this view: "But we are speaking of something totally different from the secularism that consists of an autonomist vision of man and the world, one which leaves aside the dimension of mystery, indeed neglects and denies it. This immanentism is a reduction of the integral vision of man, a reduction which leads not to his true liberation but to a new idolatry, to the slavery of ideologies, to life in reductive and often oppressive structures of this world."

* * *

On New Year's Day, Jackie and Steve drove to Spring to celebrate their engagement with the Cones and talk about plans for a wedding in May. Jackie knew that it was important to her father that she be married at St. Patrick's Parish, but she had specific ideas about the ceremony and reception. Mary tried to be helpful but was quickly overwhelmed by Jackie's energy and the expense of what she had planned. She was grateful when Jackie declined her offer of assistance.

The following weeks were a blur of frenetic activity. It took Jackie only a week after New Year's to reserve St. Patrick's Parish for the ceremony, hire a wedding planner, and book a nearby historical mansion for the reception. By the end of the next week, she had tried on virtually every wedding dress in the boutiques along Newbury Street without finding one that she liked, and had found a dressmaker who would make a dress to her exact design.

Steve vicariously shared in Jackie's near-manic activity. He cautiously admired her appearance in dozens of different wedding dresses and listened attentively as she talked about flowers and food, music and menus, always careful to preempt her more egregious excesses before they became set in stone. Each evening, he let Jackie unwind in an animated monologue about the progress she had made during the day before taking her in his arms, silencing her with gentle kisses, and making love with her until she was tired enough to sleep.

35

On Monday the following week, Jackie's attention turned from wedding planning, to the launch of the space shuttle *Challenger*. It had been many years since Jackie, or the public, had paid much attention to the space program, but this flight promised to be different. The *Challenger* mission in January of 1986 was a bold public relations effort by NASA to rekindle interest in the space program by including a grade school teacher, Sharon "Christa" McAuliffe, among the astronauts.

Christa McAuliffe was the face of a high-profile Teacher in Space Program that would broadcast lessons about science and space exploration directly from orbit to students around the world. In the months leading up to the flight, there was a barrage of publicity about the Teacher in Space program, space exploration, and Christa McAuliffe. The public was enamored of Christa; her all-American character, her life story, and her selection from among more than eleven thousand other teachers who had applied for the program.

The launch of *Challenger* from Cape Canaveral would be a grand media event, intended to attract media from all over the world. Jackie planned a series of public relations events, press releases, receptions, and presentations at the Cape that would advertise her client companies and their products to the hundreds of reporters that would cover the launch. Among the notable announcements that week was the release of Microsoft's first Windows operating system, the launch of IBM's first laptop computer, agreement on an international standard for electronic mail, and the invention of a machine capable of automatically sequencing DNA.

The launch of *Challenger* was scheduled for Wednesday, January 22, 1986. Technical difficulties, however, prevented the shuttle from launching on Wednesday, again on Thursday, and again on Friday.

The launch was rescheduled for Saturday, only to be cancelled, yet again, due to bad weather at an emergency landing site in Africa. With unusually cold weather and storms predicted at the launch site over the next several days, it seemed likely that the launch would be postponed again, possibly for several weeks. Everyone was frustrated by the delay.

Jackie decided to return to Boston. She was exhausted. Since Christmas, she had been flying on the emotional energy of her engagement and planning for the wedding. A week of chaperoning clients through a maze of media events in Florida had left her completely drained. Moreover, she needed to be in San Francisco for an investment conference the following week, and she desperately wanted to spend some time with Steve and collect a change of clothes before flying off again.

Steve picked Jackie up at the airport Saturday afternoon, and they spent a quiet evening in front of the fireplace before falling asleep in each other's arms. They slept late Sunday morning, and spent the rest of the day taking down the Christmas decorations and putting away the ornaments from the Christmas tree, which, as always, had been arranged on the tree exactly as they appeared in the photograph Jackie had treasured since childhood.

By the time Jackie and Steve went to bed Sunday night, the Christmas decorations had been carefully packed into boxes and put away in the basement. It was not until Tuesday morning, after Jackie left for the airport to catch a six o'clock flight to San Francisco, that Steve finally took the denuded Christmas tree down to the curb to be taken away by the garbage truck.

* * *

NASA tried to launch *Challenger* again on Monday, but equipment malfunctions forced yet another postponement. There was extraordinary pressure to launch on Tuesday. The persistent delays in front of the world's media had become a public relations embarrassment. Moreover, on Tuesday night, President Reagan was scheduled to give his State of the Union address, in which he planned to highlight Christa McAuliffe, *Challenger*, and the Teacher in Space program.

Tuesday morning in Florida was unusually cold and windy. Temperatures overnight had dropped as low as 8°F. Water pipes on the launch pad had been opened to prevent them from freezing, which led to an accumulation of ice on the launch platform. NASA managers spent the night in tense teleconferences with the engineers who had designed the shuttle, debating whether the spacecraft could be launched safely in subfreezing conditions. Many of the rocket's components had never been tested under such extreme conditions, and there was no consensus that the spacecraft could be launched safely. When the launch director decided to proceed with the countdown, several of the engineers responsible for the shuttle's construction refused to sign off on the plan.

There were more delays during the countdown on Tuesday. This time, however, the difficulties were overcome and, at 11:38 a.m. EST, the *Challenger* blasted off.

One second after ignition, puffs of smoke emerged from the side of the booster rocket where an O-ring, brittle from the cold, failed to contain combustible gases from the rocket engine. One minute into launch, *Challenger* experienced a sudden wind shear that further loosened the seal around the frozen O-ring. Seconds later, flames burned through the external fuel tank. A half million gallons of liquid oxygen and hydrogen fuel exploded. Crowds of people on the ground in Florida and millions of schoolchildren watching on television around the world witnessed the shuttle disintegrate a mile above the earth and saw the shattered fragments fall into the sea.

* * *

Jackie was in a good mood on the flight to California that morning, unaware of the disaster that had transpired in Florida. The weekend at home with Steve had rejuvenated her. She was looking forward to the investment conference where the buzz would be about Microsoft's upcoming Initial Public Offering. Many analysts predicted that this IPO would be the harbinger of a long-awaited boom in technology stocks. She was also looking forward to seeing Danny and spending a day shopping with Rachel when the meeting was over. It was going to be a good week, Jackie thought, undaunted by the clouds that hung over the Golden Gate Bridge and the rain falling on the tarmac as they landed at the airport.

Jackie rented a car at the airport and immediately started driving toward downtown San Francisco. The radio was tuned to a popular music station, and Jackie had already turned north on the interstate, when the first set of songs ended and the announcer began reading the news bulletin about the *Challenger* disaster.

The news hit Jackie like a bullet. She went numb, hardly aware of anything as her car began to veer across the highway toward a truck in the right lane. Too late, she kicked frantically for the brake and flung the steering wheel one way, then the other, trying to avoid a collision. Her car spun on the slick pavement, surged across the shoulder, and crashed sideways into the guardrail. The windshield exploded. The alarm sounded. The steering wheel jerked violently in her hands and pressed harshly into her chest. Her head whipped forward until everything faded into darkness.

A driver who had been behind her as she swerved across the highway pulled onto the shoulder and ran toward her. He saw columns of steam shooting from the ruptured radiator and Jackie sitting motionless in her seat, her face pressed against the steering wheel. He started banging on the side window with his hands, trying to get her attention. She did not move. For a moment, he thought she was dead.

Jackie was unconscious for several moments before the piercing sounds of the alarm reverberating in her head and the flashing lights exploding behind her eyes brought her back to consciousness. She felt centrifugal forces spinning her chaotically into space and the force of gravity pulling her back to Earth. She struggled for breath and tried to swallow the mixture of blood and tears that was accumulating in her mouth.

The man continued banging on the door. "Can you hear me? Open the door!" he yelled.

She felt nauseous. Her head hurt. It was hard to think. With effort, she turned her head toward the sound of banging on the window. She wished it would stop. The noise was hurting her ears.

"Open the door!" the man yelled again. "Let me help you! Open the door."

Jackie pushed herself back against the seat and looked around. She brushed the hair from her face and felt the blood on her face, wincing when she touched the welt forming on her forehead. She tried to move her legs, but they were twisted uncomfortably underneath the crumpled dashboard.

"Open the door!" he shouted again.

She reached hesitantly for the latch and pulled. The door swung open. The man grabbed Jackie awkwardly by the arm and held her as she extracted her legs from under the dash, staggered to the shoulder, and collapsed limply onto the grass.

"Are you okay?" he asked, as he draped his coat over her to protect her from the rain.

"I don't know," Jackie answered hesitantly, taking deep breaths to ward off the nausea.

"You must have hit your head on the dashboard. Your face is bloody."

"Is it?"

"Do you need to go to a hospital?"

"I don't know," Jackie answered, still dazed and unable to focus on the barrage of questions.

"You hit the guardrail pretty hard. You're lucky no other cars hit you. You're lucky I didn't hit you." He thought himself fortunate to have avoided an accident. "What happened?"

"I guess I lost control." Jackie's voice was barely audible.

"Were you changing lanes or something?"

"I don't know."

"Do you need to go to a hospital?" the man asked again, concerned about Jackie's well-being but also anxious to get on his way.

"Just give me a minute." She took several deep breaths, which made the nausea finally recede and her head clear.

"What do you want to do?" he asked again, when he thought Jackie might answer.

"I don't know. That car isn't going anywhere," she said, looking around for the first time at the crumpled metal of the car and columns of steam coming from the engine.

"I can drive you somewhere, maybe to the next exit. We can find a phone and call for help—the police or an ambulance or something. There might be a service station that can take care of your car."

"It's a rental."

"That's easy. Call the rental company. They'll have an emergency number and will take care of everything."

"That's a good idea," Jackie answered, grateful that she did not have to think for herself.

"I'll drive you in my car. Can you walk?"

"I'll try."

He reached out to help her stand. As she stood, her legs wobbled for several seconds, and she leaned heavily on the man's elbow as he helped her to his car.

"Do you need anything from your car?"

"My purse. Thanks."

The man ran back to the wrecked car to retrieve Jackie's purse. Then he drove several miles to the next exit and turned into the driveway of a Holiday Inn hotel. "This will be a good place to call for help."

By that time, Jackie was feeling more lucid, though her head hurt and even the filtered light coming through the clouds seemed to burn her eyes. "Sure, thanks."

"I'm sure someone at the front desk will help you if you need anything. They can call the police for you or they will certainly have a pay phone. At least you'll have somewhere to wash up and wait for help out of this rain."

"That sounds good."

"Is there anything I can do for you? Anyone I can call for you?" he asked, still unsure about Jackie's health.

"Like you said, I'll call the car rental company."

"Do you have a friend you can call, someone to come get you?"

"I have friends. That's a good idea."

"Call your friends," he encouraged. "Do you want me to come in with you or make a call or anything?"

"No. I can do it," Jackie responded with determination, as she opened the car door and prepared to exit. "Thank you for stopping. I'm very grateful. I don't know what I would have done alone on the side of the highway."

"I hope you're okay." He was still unsure of whether he should stay with her, but he was also anxious to go about his business. "Call your friends. You probably shouldn't be alone."

"I'll do that." She stood from the car, holding on to the doorframe to be sure she did not fall, and then closed the door behind her. "Thank you again."

"You're welcome. Good luck."

Jackie walked into the hotel and went directly to the restroom behind the front desk. She washed her face and tried to rinse the drops of blood from her blouse. She studied the purple and red welt on her forehead and thought about trying to cover it with makeup, but found it hard to keep her head still and her eyes focused. Instead, she returned to the lobby to find a pay phone.

There were several televisions in the lobby showing continuous coverage of the *Challenger* disaster. Jackie stopped, transfixed by the pictures of the launch and the explosion, the tubes of white smoke shooting across the sky, and the faces of onlookers watching in horror and disbelief. Tears welled up in her eyes. She felt unsteady and quickly sat in the nearest chair.

Jackie watched for several minutes before trying to stand again and walk to a pay phone mounted on the wall. She called the emergency number on the car rental agreement and reported the accident. The operator said that they would contact the police and told Jackie to stay where she was, cautioning that it might take some time for the police to arrive because of the slick highway conditions and an unusually large number of accidents around the city. Then, Jackie dialed Danny and Rachel's apartment in Palo Alto, but there was no answer.

Disappointed that Danny and Rachel were not home, Jackie sat back on the couch to wait for the police. But there was no way to escape the endless replays of the astronauts' last walk to the shuttle, the explosion, and the crowds of people struggling with their emotions. Each repetition made her head hurt worse.

On an impulse, she stood up from the couch, walked out of the hotel to the taxi stand on the curb, and climbed into the backseat of the first car in line. She gave the driver Danny and Rachel's address, closed her eyes to contain her tears, and promptly fell into a restless sleep, oblivious to the sound of sirens on the highway.

It took an hour to drive through the rain from South San Francisco to Palo Alto. Jackie was groggy when they arrived at Danny and Rachel's apartment. She paid the fare and climbed the two flights of stairs on the outside of the building to the door of their unit. From the landing, she heard the telephone ringing behind the closed door, but no one answered. She rang the bell, but there was no response. She banged on the door with her hand and called out Danny and Rachel's names, but there was no one home. Exhausted, she sat down on the floor with her back against the door and, protected from the rain, buried her head in her arms and immediately fell asleep again.

A half-hour later, Jackie was still sleeping in front of the door when Ruben arrived at the top of the stairs. "Look what the bad Moon brought in," he grunted, stomping his feet loudly on the metal landing to shake the water from his boots. Jackie looked up, hardly recognizing Ruben's once-handsome features in the bony face, glazed eyes, bushy beard, and wet, unkempt hair. The bottoms of his blue jeans were frayed and brown with mud. He was struggling to hold a rain-soaked paper bag of groceries together with both arms.

"Rachel made me to go to the grocery store," Ruben continued without acknowledging Jackie directly. "Damn her if she didn't know it was going to rain and I would get all wet. It's always like that. Woodstock was like that, you know. You would see the Sun and lay all your things out to dry and go to find some food, and then it would start raining again, and by the time you came back, the food would be soggy and your clothes would be all wet. It's always like that."

"Hello to you, too," Jackie interrupted sarcastically, as Ruben reached directly over her head to put the key into the lock, while juggling the fragile grocery bag on his knee.

"Yesterday the Sun was out. Today it's raining. Woodstock was like that, you know." Jackie watched silently as Ruben continued to struggle with the lock.

"Where's Danny?" she demanded.

"Not here," Ruben answered without interest.

"Where's Rachel?"

"They're either at class or studying. That's all they do. They go to class, then they study, then they go to class, then they study. Do you want to know what their problem is? No sex. They never do it. Have you ever seen them do it?"

"When will Danny be home?" Jackie asked, ignoring Ruben's obscenities.

"How would I know? They don't tell me anything. They don't even tell me when they're going to send me away to dry out. Of course, if they really wanted me to dry out, they wouldn't send me out in the rain for groceries."

"I'll wait."

"Suit yourself," Ruben answered dismissively, as he pushed the door open and stepped around her into the apartment. "Do you want to come in?"

"That would be nice," she answered sarcastically.

"Whatever."

Jackie stood up from the floor. As she did, she felt the pain again in her head. The room faded, and she felt herself begin to fall. She braced her hands on her knees, and then slowly pushed herself erect against the doorframe until her sight returned and she could stand securely. Then she followed Ruben into the tiny apartment.

Ruben managed to take two steps toward the kitchen before the rain-soaked paper bag gave way, sending the contents crashing to the floor. "Damn. It's always like that!" Ruben growled in disgust, kicking at the grocery items on the floor. "Woodstock was like that, you know. You would go to find some food, then it would start raining and everything would get wet." He kneeled down to pick up a half empty bottle of scotch, a copy of *Andante* magazine, an incomplete six-pack of beer, a container of milk, and an assortment of fruits and vegetables.

"You've been drinking," Jackie responded contemptuously, the pain in her head and Ruben's intemperate behavior making her irritable.

"Among other things," Ruben answered casually. Just then, the telephone rang, accentuating the pulsating pain in Jackie's head. Ruben ignored the phone and continued methodically picking up the things that had fallen on the floor.

"Are you going to get it?" Jackie demanded.

"No, they don't like when I answer the telephone."

The telephone continued to ring, stopped, and started again several seconds later. "Should I get it?" she asked impatiently, still standing awkwardly in the center of the room.

"No one is calling here for you," Ruben answered curtly. He finished collecting the groceries from the floor, opened another beer, and turned to look at Jackie. For the first time, he noticed the dried blood and bruising on her face.

"What happened to you?" he asked with genuine concern.

"I had an accident."

"You look terrible."

"You don't look good yourself."

"No, I mean—you're hurt." He struggled against his inebriation. "Do you need help?"

"I need to sit down."

"Here, let me make some room for you." Ruben put his beer down on the counter and helped her to a chair in the kitchen. "What can I do? You're hurt. Can I get you something to drink?"

"I don't think scotch will help, if that's what you're offering," she answered sarcastically.

"That's not what I meant." Ruben sounded embarrassed. "You're hurt. What happened?"

"I was driving downtown from the airport when I lost control of the car. The road was wet. I was thinking about other things. The next thing I knew, my car crashed into the side rail and there was some guy pounding on the windows telling me to get out."

"What can I do? Are you okay?" Ruben asked awkwardly.

"No, I'm not okay. I crashed my car. The shuttle exploded. My head is exploding."

"I heard that the shuttle crashed," Ruben interrupted, suddenly, with a cackling laugh.

"What are you laughing about?" Jackie stared at him incredulously.

"That's how it ends. That's how everything ends," Ruben continued with a knowing laugh.

"There's nothing funny about this," Jackie snapped.

"Don't you see how perfectly absurd this is? They spend billions of dollars for some teacher to trip out, and it all blows up."

"Have you completely lost your mind? Christa McAuliffe was going to teach everyone about space, about science, about exploration, about the future—"

"Come on, Jackie." Ruben interrupted with an edge in his voice. "You don't believe all that insipid space stuff anymore. That's all you ever talked about when you were a kid—astronauts and rockets and space and colonies on the Moon and going to Mars and all that fantastic nonsense. It was all so insufferably cute and annoying. But you're all grown up now, Jackie. No one is going to the Moon. Nobody believes the future is going to be like some *Star Trek* flick."

"I do, Ruben." Jackie was indignant.

"Don't give me that pubescent innocence—you know what the world is really like." Ruben turned aggressively toward Jackie. "You knew what it was like when you started screwing that rich boyfriend of yours so you could fly with his diamonds."

"Shut up!" Jackie demanded.

"You know what the world is like," he taunted.

"I know you're high on something!" Jackie dismissed him.

"So are you!" Ruben mocked her.

"Go to hell!"

"You're just like me, you know," Ruben exploded in a bellicose rave. "You think you're different. You think you're better—but I'm just like you. I can fly just as well as you. I have wings and I love rockets and the Moon and Moon rocks and stars and stardust and emeralds and rubies and diamonds just as much as you do. I know what it is like to reach for the Sun and the Moon and the stars expecting to touch them and then—POW!—everything blows up in some big fucking explosion and suddenly there is no more Sun or Moon or stars or precious stones—no more light and no more life—and you feel your body burn, the air around you consumed, and your wings melt in the fire. Suddenly, you can't see and you can't fly and everything crashes around you and it all becomes nothing but a bad trip."

"You're insane!"

"Woodstock was like that, you know. There was this light—this fire that made everything in the universe so crystal clear that you could see things you had never seen and imagine things that you had never imagined. Everything was alive. Everything was real. You could see it. There was this stairway to heaven with this awesome light shining down—then it was gone and there was nothing but thunder and explosions of lightning and clouds and rain and everything was pulling you down, down onto the rocks and into the sea. That's how it ends. That's how it always ends. It always ends up being a bad trip."

"Stop it, Ruben! Just stop it!" Jackie's head was throbbing. She desperately wanted Ruben's diatribe to end.

"They're all the same, you know—drugs, diamonds, your precious Moon and stars. They take over your brain. They make you see some great light, some great ecstasy, some heaven you can fly to—something so real that you can walk on it and touch it and hold it in your hand—but every time you come close, it explodes. But even then, you can't stop reaching for it, you can't stop trying to fly toward some heaven that may or may not even exist, even though you know there is no God, no goddamn light—only lightning and thunder and rain—only another bad trip."

"And by the time you realize it is raining and that the lightning is not going to light up the sky, you learn that the only thing that matters is not getting wet. You want to forget that you ever saw a light, that you ever tried to reach for the Sun or the Moon or the stars, that you ever tried to fly. But you can't. You can't stop reaching for it. You can't stop flying toward the light, even though you know it is always nothing but a bad trip. Woodstock was like that."

"You know what it's like, don't you, Jackie?"

"Go to hell!"

"You're just like me," Ruben mocked her.

"I'm nothing like you!"

"You're always reaching for a fix."

"I am not!"

"It really hurts when you don't have a fix," he taunted. "You're just like me. You thought you had a fix. You thought you could fly. You felt it, didn't you? You thought it was real. You saw the light. You wanted to go there. You wanted it to be real, something you could step on and touch and hold in your hands—but then it was gone. It was just a bad trip. You saw it explode. It was on television. You saw it. Now you're afraid. What if there aren't any more lights? What if there aren't any more fixes? What if there aren't any more diamonds? What if there aren't any more rockets? What if there are no more Moon rocks? What if it's all gone? What if it just keeps raining? You and me Jackie—we're the same."

"I'm nothing like you!" Jackie suddenly shouted at Ruben. "I'm not looking for a fix."

"Sure you are. You always think there's a fix out there."

"Damn you, Ruben!" Jackie began screaming hysterically. "I'm nothing like you! Yes, this is a stinking bad trip. I'm hurt! I'm scared. You have no idea how scared I really am. You have no idea."

The telephone rang. Jackie was thankful for the interruption and reached for the phone without hesitation. "Hello?"

"Jackie! Thank God!" Steve exclaimed on the other end of the phone as soon as he heard her voice. "We've been looking everywhere for you!"

"What?" Jackie was confused for an instant, not expecting to hear Steve's voice.

"The San Francisco police called me hours ago. They said that you had called for help and that they found your car abandoned on the highway, but no one knew where you were. The police have been checking all the hospitals in the area. I've called this number a dozen times thinking you would probably go to Danny if you needed help, but there's been no answer. Are you okay?"

"No."

"What happened?"

"I had an accident. I was driving out of the airport when I heard about the shuttle. I must have lost control of the car."

"Are you hurt?"

"I hit my head on something."

"Are Danny or Rachel there with you?"

"No, just Ruben."

"How badly hurt are you?"

"I have a bruise on my forehead and a horrible headache."

"How did you get to Danny's apartment?"

"I don't remember."

"You need to see a doctor. Can Ruben take you to an emergency room?"

Jackie looked over at Ruben who had picked up a guitar and was strumming harsh, discordant chords with one hand, while thumbing mindlessly through his newly purchased copy of *Andante* magazine with the other.

"Ruben," she called. He turned his head toward her with a vacuous stare that looked past her into space. "Ruben, can you take me to the hospital?"

"It's raining," he answered helplessly, shrugging his shoulders. "You'll get wet."

Jackie turned her attention back to the telephone. "No, he can't help." Suddenly, Jackie was overcome by a wave of fear and confusion. "Steve, I'm scared." she almost whispered. "Just talk to me."

"Should I call the police or an ambulance?"

"Danny should be home soon. Just talk to me."

Jackie was still on the phone a half hour later when Danny and Rachel returned from class. Danny immediately took her to the emergency room, and waited with her until she was examined first by the emergency room physician and then by a staff neurologist. The doctors ordered a CT scan, which showed swelling and a trace of blood on the surface of her brain.

By the time the CT scan was completed, Jackie's headache was worse, the ceiling lights were hurting her eyes, and her neck was so stiff that the nurses had given her a neck brace and narcotics for comfort. The neurologist recommended admitting her to the hospital for observation.

Danny sat with Jackie that evening as she drifted in and out of sleep. Several times, she tried to start a conversation but found it difficult to stay focused. Instead, Danny passed the time making small talk while listening to the television in the background. She was vaguely aware that President Reagan cancelled his State of the Union Address that evening and instead, talked to the nation about the *Challenger* disaster, saying, "We'll never forget them, nor the last time we saw them this morning as they prepared for their journey and waved good-bye and slipped the surly bounds of Earth and touched the face of God." He spoke directly to the millions of children who had seen the explosion on television in their classrooms. "I know it's hard to understand, but sometimes painful things like this happen. But they're all part of the process of exploration and discovery, all part of taking a chance and expanding man's horizons. Man will continue his conquest of space. To reach out for new goals and ever greater achievements—"

Shortly after President Reagan's speech ended, the nurses announced that visiting hours were over and Danny had to leave. Jackie spent the remainder of the night uncomfortably on the edge of consciousness. When she was awake, she was acutely aware of the constant beeping of the heart monitor beside her bed and the discomfort of her head and neck. When her eyes closed, she could feel the g-forces pressing down on her head and the neck brace holding her into her seat on the deck of the shuttle as she lifted off from Cape Canaveral. She felt herself soaring through space and steering around the rocks in their path until the fuel tanks were empty and the walls of the spacecraft began to disintegrate around her. She reached for the brakes and spun the steering wheel, trying to regain control. She reached for the emergency oxygen supply and tried to crawl toward the cold darkness of the lunar module, but nothing could prevent the explosion. Nothing could prevent her from spinning feverishly across the highway into the barriers designed to keep her on course and crashing into the guardrail. Nothing could prevent Christa McAuliffe and the others from disappearing in the fire and the smoke and crashing into the ocean.

As the explosions and the pain became inevitable, she would hear the wind, the rain, the thunder, and the dissonant chords from Ruben's guitar closing in on her. The rhythm of her heartbeat on the monitor over her bed merged with the telemetry from *Sputnik*, the sound of footsteps shuffling uncertainly along the sidewalk, pendulums swinging on ancient clocks, and fists pounding on the windows.

She tossed and turned, until the electrodes on her chest came loose, triggering the heart monitor's alarm. She listened unconsciously for the pattern of the siren, the steady blasts that would signal an alert or the wailing tone that would signal an impending attack, and instinctively covered her head under her pillow for protection. Her nurse responded a moment later by resetting the alarm, reattaching the electrodes, and offering Jackie a dry nightgown to replace the one that was soaked in sweat.

The next morning, Jackie still had a headache and a stiff neck. Her doctors said the danger from the concussion had passed and she no longer needed to be in the hospital. They fitted her with a neck brace and cautioned that she needed to rest and should wait at least one more day before flying home.

Danny and Rachel insisted that she stay with them and offered to let her sleep in their bed so she could have a real mattress, while they would sleep on the couch.

"What about Ruben?" Jackie asked, as Rachel described the arrangements.

"He's gone."

"Gone? Where did he go?"

"I don't know. When we got home from the hospital last night, his stuff was gone. He didn't tell us he was leaving or where he was going or anything. He never does."

Rachel helped Jackie check out of the hospital, while Danny spent the day filling out accident reports for the San Francisco police and trying to recover Jackie's luggage from the wrecked car. That evening, they ordered Chinese takeout and ate in front of the television, where they could watch the continuing news coverage of the *Challenger* disaster.

"I don't know how you go on after something like this, how anything will ever be the same," Jackie said, as they watched yet another replay of the *Challenger* disintegrating over Cape Canaveral.

"These things stay with you, but you also learn that the world goes on pretty much the same," he responded sadly.

"You've always been so depressing," she chided him gently.

"It is depressing," Danny said in self-defense.

"But this is different. Christa McAuliffe was going to teach everyone that—that we could—so many things—" She stopped without finishing the sentence. "I don't know how to say it."

"I understand," Danny said gently, his eyes catching Jackie's. "I remember you had plenty to say when *Apollo 13* exploded—enough to get yourself suspended from school."

"But this is worse. They're not coming back. There's no *Aquarius*. There's no *Odyssey*. There's no parachute," Jackie whispered, staring back into the silence of Danny's eyes. She felt an old urge to put her arms around him, to clutch him to be sure he would always be there. Instead, she turned her eyes away and looked down at her plate of food. "I guess I'm not very hungry," she murmured, as she pushed her food around the plate. "Maybe I'll just turn in early."

36

Jackie took a flight back to Boston the next morning. She was uncomfortable throughout the flight. The plane was noisy, the bright lights hurt her eyes, the neck brace was uncomfortable, and she fidgeted constantly trying to find a position that did not make things feel worse. By the time Steve met her at the airport that evening, the only thing she wanted to do was close her eyes and sleep. She was grateful when Steve led her directly to bed, arranged the pillows to support her back and neck, turned off the light, and left her alone.

But Jackie could not sleep. She lay in bed for several hours, endlessly shifting from one uncomfortable position to another, drifting in and out of the same, recurring nightmare, and counting each hour as it was announced by the grandfather clock in the hall. Eventually, she gave up trying to sleep, pushed herself out of bed and, after pulling a sweatshirt over her nightgown, wandered from the bedroom.

She stopped in the kitchen, where she placed a kettle of water on the stove and turned the flame on high. While waiting for the water to boil, she automatically began sorting through the pile of newspapers and mail that had accumulated on the kitchen counter. Identifying several pieces of mail that required attention, she walked to the study and placed them in the in-box on her desk.

In the center of her desk was a copy of NASA's press kit for the *Challenger* mission, which she had brought back from Florida. On an impulse, she began reading: "The launch of a high school teacher as America's first private citizen to fly aboard the shuttle in NASA's Space Flight Participant program will open a new chapter in space travel—" Her eyes began to tear as she came to the official portrait of the seven astronauts who had died and read their brief biographies. Jackie felt herself shiver and flush as she recalled how she had applied to be an astronaut. She began to sweat. NASA had not said how the astronauts had died, but she had seen it in her nightmares hundreds of times. She could feel her pulse pounding and pain building in her head. When the kettle on the stove began to whistle, it pierced her ears like a shard of broken glass.

Jackie turned toward the kitchen to respond to the kettle's urgent whistling. As she did, she noticed that the Christmas tree was no longer standing in the living room in front of the window. Her fists clenched immediately. Angrily, she walked past the kitchen directly to the bedroom and abruptly ripped the covers off the bed where Steve was sleeping.

"What happened to the Christmas tree?" she demanded.

"What?" Steve turned toward her, half asleep and unsure what she was asking.

"What did you do with the Christmas tree?"

"I took it down to the curb."

"You what?" Jackie was enraged.

"After you left, I put it out with the trash."

"Why did you do that?"

Steve sat up in bed, now fully awake and aware of her fury. "We took the decorations down last weekend when you were home, remember?"

"Why did you throw the tree away?"

"Most of the needles were already gone. It was a fire hazard," he tried to reason with her.

"Who said you could throw it out?"

"What should I have done with it?" he asked, still confused by her anger.

"That's not the idea."

"What is the idea?"

"You threw it out. Now it's gone."

"So?"

"It was important to me."

"The Christmas tree?"

"Yes, the Christmas tree! You had no right to just throw it out!"

"I'm sorry," Steve answered, not at all sure what he was apologizing for. "Christmas was more than a month ago."

Jackie did not answer.

"I've never seen you like this before, Jackie. What's this all about?" Steve asked.

"It's about you throwing out my Christmas tree!" she shouted.

"Come on, Jackie. This can't just be about a dead tree."

211

"No!" Jackie's anger intensified. "It isn't about a dead tree. It's about a Christmas tree that suddenly doesn't mean anything to you so it's just thrown into some incinerator to burn up."

"Jackie, calm down." Steve urged, bewildered by her rant.

"You don't care, do you?"

"Care about what? I have no idea what you're talking about, Jackie."

"I'm talking about everything I care about exploding and burning!" Angrily, she turned and stomped out of the room, leaving Steve sitting on the edge of the bed.

She returned to the kitchen, where she took the kettle off the stove, fumbled to make a cup of instant coffee, and cut a slice of leftover fruitcake. Then she sat down at the kitchen table. The fruitcake was stale. The coffee was no better. After one bite of cake, she pushed them both aside and buried her head in her arms on the table, sobbing uncontrollably.

Steve sat on the bed for a moment until he was fully awake, put a robe over his pajamas, and followed Jackie into the kitchen. He came up behind her and began to massage her neck gently. Jackie winced from the first pressure on her sore muscles, but Steve persisted, and the pain began to recede under his fingers.

"Can you tell me what that was all about?" Steve asked, as he felt her muscles relax and heard her breathing assume a normal cadence.

"I'm sorry. I didn't mean to act like that."

"What's wrong?"

"I just keep thinking about the *Challenger*. What's going to happen now? How can anyone ever have the faith to do it again, knowing that it can just blow up like that?"

"Shhh. Try to relax," Steve interrupted, feeling her back muscles tightening.

"And Ruben was so horrible and so vulgar. Why did he do that? Why did he say those things? And why does he always smell so bad?"

"Shhhh."

"Is Ruben right? Is this how it ends?" Jackie asked.

"Shhhh."

"And what about the children who saw it? What are they going to think when they look up at the stars? How can they believe in anything? All they're going to remember is the explosion."

"That's not what they'll remember," he answered reassuringly.

"But that's what they saw."

"Maybe, but they'll get over it and learn why Christa McAuliffe and the others were there in the first place."

"How?"

"You'll tell them."

"I don't know. I don't know if I'll ever get that picture out of my mind," Jackie answered miserably.

"You will."

"How?"

"If you're up to it," Steve suggested, "today was declared a national day of mourning for *Challenger*, and there's going to be a memorial service in Houston this afternoon and a special Mass at our church tonight. Maybe going to church would help."

"How does that help?" Jackie pushed Steve away and turned to confront him with irritation in her voice. "Tell me. Is it going to bring Christa back? It is going to fix whatever was wrong with the shuttle and make it fly again?"

"That's not the idea." Steve raised his palms in retreat.

"What is the idea?" Jackie demanded.

"People find that prayer can be helpful."

"What does it help? I don't understand."

"You don't have to go to the service," Steve said, retreating. "It was just an idea."

"I don't get it. Tell me?" she answered argumentatively.

"I'm sorry I brought it up. I didn't mean to upset you." Steve looked toward the clock on the wall for a distraction. "Look, Jackie, it's late. I have to get up in several hours and go to work. We should try to get some sleep."

"You go to bed. I don't think I can sleep right now. I'm going to sit for a while," Jackie answered.

When the alarm clock sounded several hours later, Steve found Jackie asleep at the kitchen table with her head in her arms. He gently led her to bed, tucked the covers around her, and left for work.

Jackie slept until mid-afternoon. When she awoke, she turned on the television just as Ronald Reagan was eulogizing the *Challenger* astronauts at the Johnson Space Flight Center in Houston: "We think back to the pioneers of an earlier century, and the sturdy souls who took their families and the belongings and set out into the frontier of the American West. Often, they met with terrible hardship. Along the Oregon Trail, you can still see the grave markers of those who fell on the way—Today, the frontier is space and the boundaries of human knowledge. Sometimes, when we reach for the stars, we fall short. But we must pick ourselves up again and press on despite the pain."

* * *

Jackie did not go to work that day, nor did she go to work in the days and weeks that followed. She continued to have severe headaches, stiffness and tenderness in her neck, and occasional episodes of dizziness and nausea. She was unable to sleep for more than three on four hours at a time and did not feel rested when she awoke.

When the symptoms persisted into the second week, Steve took her to a neurologist who performed an MRI, which showed a small blood clot where the bleeding had been before, as well as persistent swelling in the tissues of her neck and spine.

"Is it serious?" Jackie asked the neurologist.

"No, you should be okay," the doctor answered.

"But there is a blood clot in my brain?"

"You had a contusion—it's like a bruise with some swelling and some bleeding. As long as your blood clots normally, it's just like having a black and blue mark. It will go away. The swelling in your neck, the whiplash injury, is what is giving you pain."

"So how do you fix it?"

"You need to keep wearing the neck brace, and I will refer you to a physical therapist who can give you exercises to help regain normal motion. I can also give you some prescriptions for Tylenol with codeine to help with your pain and some Valium to relax your muscles."

"Can I go back to work?"

"If you feel like it."

But Jackie did not feel like going back to work. She found it hard to sit at her desk without her headache recurring. The medicines helped ease her pain, but they also made her lethargic. When she took enough codeine and Valium to be comfortable, she could not sit on the couch and read the newspaper for any length of time without falling asleep.

Jackie also found it hard to concentrate. Everything reminded her of *Challenger.* Every time she turned on the television or radio or opened a magazine or newspaper there were new revelations about what had happened in the hours leading up to the ill-fated launch. She became preoccupied with news stories of the disaster and gradually abandoned her efforts to catch up on work or even household chores. Plans for the wedding also lapsed as Jackie missed the deadline to confirm the wedding date with the priest and neglected to make an advance payment to the caterer.

"I think we should postpone the wedding," she told Steve one evening. "I'm still not feeling well, and I don't know how long this is going to last. I'm not going to get married wearing a neck brace under my veil!"

"You'll be fine by May," Steve answered casually.

"But there's so much that has to be done if we're going to get married in May. I have to put together a guest list, address the invitations, drive down to Spring to talk to Father O'Brien—he may have made plans to do some other event that day. I have to meet with the florist and the photographer at the church. I'm in no mood to start running around to stores for all the things we need to buy. I don't know how I could even begin."

"I can help," Steve offered.

"No. I want to do it," Jackie insisted. "I want to enjoy doing it. I just can't think about it right now."

"Is it your sore neck that's making it hard?"

"Sure," she answered noncommittally.

"Nothing else?"

"No. Why do you ask?" Jackie sounded surprised.

"You've been very distracted lately."

"I know. I'm sorry."

"And we haven't slept together since the accident."

"My neck hurts. It's uncomfortable."

"I know."

"Really, Steve," Jackie responded, taking his hand in hers. "I just think we should postpone the wedding. I'm just not ready."

"Okay," Steve agreed reluctantly.

* * *

In February, the government-appointed Rogers Commission began a formal investigation into the cause of the *Challenger* disaster. Jackie followed every detail of the investigation on television and in the newspapers. She returned to work at the beginning of March, but within days suggested to William that the Commission's investigations were likely to affect public perceptions of technology, and that she should be in Washington to hear the testimony firsthand.

Jackie spent much of the next several months in Washington, listening as the Rogers Commission considered many possible explanations for the disaster. She heard theories that the shuttle might have been sabotaged, that there may have been flaws in the shuttle's design or construction, that shuttle components might have been damaged or inadequately maintained, that there may have been mistakes in preparation for launch, or that the weather conditions at the time of launch may have been too extreme for flight. She listened to testimony about the urgent discussions held in the hours before the flight among engineers, managers, and even the White House, as well as the circumstances that had led flight directors to waive safety concerns and allow the countdown to proceed.

The Commission issued its report at the beginning of June. It identified an O-ring on the booster rocket, which failed in the freezing temperatures, as the immediate cause of the accident. More importantly, the Commission concluded that the disaster was a human failure, which could have been avoided if NASA managers had heeded the warnings of their engineers not to fly in subfreezing temperatures, if there had been greater emphasis on safety, if there had been better communication between engineers and managers, and if there had been less pressure to launch in adverse conditions.

Jackie and the public interpreted the report as concluding that there was nothing fundamentally wrong with the space shuttle technology or with space flight. A new, improved shuttle would be built to replace the *Challenger*. Manned flight into space would continue.

A week after the Rogers Commission completed their report, Jackie suggested to Steve that they reschedule the wedding for the end of September. Steve agreed.

37

Jackie and Steve were married in September at St. Patrick's Parish in Spring. Erin, Rachel, and Danny were in the wedding party along with Jackie's brothers and sisters.

Jackie was resplendent in a white gown with pearls, sequins, delicate lace on the bodice, and a long train of shining silk. A pearl tiara framed her face, which radiated like the Sun, and her long veil trailed to the ground behind her. Steve wore a gray morning suit and ruffled shirt that seemed to reflect his unruly hair. A videographer captured every moment as Bert walked Jackie down the aisle, and Father O'Brien led them through traditional wedding vows, accompanied by Jackie's happy tears and Steve's silent prayers.

The reception that followed was a spirited affair. There were seemingly endless toasts to the newly married couple and a six-piece band for dancing. For Jackie and Steve, it was a soaring whirlwind of emotion and excitement. When it was over, they dashed through a cloud of rice and flower petals into a long white limousine that took them to the piers in New York harbor where they boarded the Queen Elizabeth II for their honeymoon.

* * *

The first years of marriage were extraordinarily busy for both Jackie and Steve. In March 1986, the tremendous success of Microsoft's IPO and the booming economy had ignited another cycle of public stock offerings as well as investments in new start-up technology companies. Jackie's reputation as a creative leader in the field grew, and a large number of new companies joined her already ample portfolio of accounts. In the spring of 1987, William Fernald made her a partner in the firm.

Steve was increasingly recognized as an expert in clinical research. He was involved in a large number of studies at the Massachusetts General Hospital, investigating basic mechanisms of health and disease as well as testing new drugs and biological products for therapy. He was promoted to full professor at Harvard Medical School in the summer of 1987.

Danny and Rachel graduated from Stanford Law School in May 1986 and moved to New York. Danny took a position with Helsinki Watch, an organization dedicated to monitoring international compliance with the Helsinki Final Act and promoting human rights throughout Europe.

The Helsinki Final Act was a landmark agreement among thirty European nations, the United States, and the Soviet Union, intended to establish a long-term basis for peace in Europe. The Final Act created the Organization for Security and Cooperation in Europe as a forum for ensuring both the security of member states and peaceful cooperation on multinational issues. Importantly, the Final Act identified human rights as a central principle for preserving peace by calling for "respect for human rights and fundamental freedoms, including freedom of thought, conscience, religion, or belief."

The Final Act promised greater freedoms to the restive populations of communist Eastern Europe, including freedom of speech, the right to travel and emigrate without restrictions, and the right of self-determination. Danny's job was to work with Helsinki Committees in the countries of Eastern Europe that were signatories to the Final Act. The goal was to promulgate human rights, and to protect those individuals who were working to promote human rights and democratization. By the end of the decade, the Helsinki Committees and human rights provisions of the Final Act would play a decisive role in the dissolution of the communist governments of Eastern Europe, and would contribute to the final collapse of communism in the Soviet Union soon thereafter.

Rachel took a job with UNESCO, where she was involved in negotiating the Convention on the Rights of the Child, a landmark agreement that extended the principles of human rights to children; the right to survival and full development; protection from harmful influences, abuse, and exploitation; and participation in family, cultural, and social life. The agreement committed the signatory nations to prevent discrimination, provide health care and education, and protect children's political, personal, economic, social, and cultural rights. In 1989, the Convention on the Rights of the Child would be ratified by virtually every country in the world, and hailed by human rights activists as the most universally accepted human rights agreement in history.

Danny and Rachel spent many weekends with Jackie and Steve to escape their cramped Manhattan apartment. They spent their time together in animated debates about politics, public affairs, philosophy, religion, and world events. While they frequently disagreed, and it was rare for anyone to voluntarily cede a point, they debated out of affection for the dialectic of ideas, knowing that their debates enabled them to more effectively articulate their perspectives and defend them to others.

During the summer of 1987, Steve took a sabbatical to work at Guy's Hospital in London. Jackie went with him, working from the office of a London-based investor, and communicating with her office in Boston via the newly omnipresent facsimile machines or telephone modem on her computer. They spent their weekends that summer traveling through Cornwall and southern Wales, visiting ancient monolithic sites, castles, and cathedrals, and staying at quaint inns. When they returned to Boston in September, Jackie was pregnant.

Jackie had always wondered how she would respond to pregnancy, childbirth, and motherhood. She worried how pregnancy would alter her body, how she would bear the pain of labor, and what it would be like to breast-feed. She also worried about whether she could have both a child and a career, and whether she would be a good mother.

Steve had taught her to see children as more than the smelly siblings she remembered from her childhood, and encouraged her to look forward to motherhood. As Jackie approached thirty, any ambiguity she had felt about having children was gone.

A month later, in October 1987, a dramatic stock market crash ended another cycle of economic expansion and optimism. Following the largest one-day drop in stock market history, the stock market continued its downward slide, losing almost one-third of its value over a period of weeks. It would be almost five years before there would be renewed economic growth. Many of Jackie's clients did not survive the downturn.

Over the next several months, Fernald Partners was forced to reduce its staff. Jackie took the opportunity to restructure her work and her schedule. Many of her day-to-day activities were assigned to associates so that she could focus on bringing in new clients from her extensive network of academics, entrepreneurs, industrialists, and investors. At the same time, she was able to create a more flexible schedule that she hoped would accommodate both motherhood and her career.

Pregnancy was difficult for Jackie. She found it hard to adapt to the changes in her appearance and limits on her distinctively boundless energy. In addition, while she had never been shy about being the center of attention, she was offended by the attention that her pregnancy attracted from family, friends, business associates, and even strangers. Several times, she lost her temper when a colleague or client made a comment about her pregnancy, appearance, or motherhood that she considered unprofessional.

Rachel had spent years dreaming about having children and was just as excited as Jackie. She had certain ideas about how everything should be done and tried hard to impart her ideas to Jackie. Rachel believed in natural childbirth and felt a midwife should deliver the baby at home rather than in a hospital. She also thought Jackie should breast-feed for at least the first year, before introducing foods or formulas.

While Steve was supportive of natural childbirth and breast-feeding, he adamantly opposed the idea of giving birth at home or the involvement of a midwife. Jackie was caught in the middle as Rachel and Steve argued their perspectives, experiences, and passions.

Finally, she told them both to shut up. She wanted her child to have the best medical care that modern technology could provide, and she arranged to give birth at Harvard's Brigham and Women's Hospital. Moreover, she announced that she planned to have an epidural and as much painkiller as the doctors would give her, because she did not see any reason to feel the pain of labor. Jackie's pronouncement only ignited more debate as both Rachel and Steve tried to convince her that she would miss something wonderful by forgoing natural childbirth. Jackie was unconvinced.

* * *

When Jackie was three months pregnant, she had her first ultrasound. She was awed by the technology that could peer into her uterus and provide images of the life that was growing inside her. Jackie was so moved by the image of her baby that she decided it would be fun to have an ultrasound at home so she could see the baby grow day by day.

"You can't have an ultrasound machine at home," Steve laughed when Jackie told him.

"It's all arranged," Jackie said matter-of-factly. "I called one of my clients who makes ultrasound machines. I've worked with them for years, and they were more than happy to lend me one. They're even sending a technician over to show me how to use it."

"Are you serious?" Steve was incredulous. "You really want to have an ultrasound machine in our bedroom?"

"Think about it. We could see the baby whenever we want."

"No way!"

"Why not?" Jackie was surprised that Steve did not agree.

"Because, I don't know—" Steve was flustered as he tried making a rational argument against what seemed like a completely irrational idea. "That's not why you use technology."

"I don't see anything wrong with it."

"Everything is wrong with it. That's not the way I want to know our baby."

Eventually, Steve prevailed, and Jackie had to make do with the video recordings from each check-up. By the fifth month, the fetus was sufficiently mature for the ultrasound to reveal that she was carrying a girl.

Jackie and Steve began preparing their home for the birth of their child. They converted one of their bedrooms into a nursery with brightly colored murals on the walls. They spent thousands of dollars buying the latest baby furniture, clothes, toys, swings, mobiles, music, and strollers recommended by child-care experts.

Katie was born uneventfully in April. The first pains of labor convinced Jackie that she had made the right decision about having an epidural. Steve was constantly by her side, holding her hand, coaching, and offering comfort. He was the first to hold Katie, taking her from the nurses and placing her gently on Jackie's breast.

Any residual uncertainty Jackie may have had about being a mother was gone the instant she gazed down at Katie's face and played with her tiny fingers. When Katie began to suckle tentatively at her breast, Jackie's heart beat faster and a rush of blood made her head spin and her spirit soar through space before coming to rest on a bed of tranquility.

Despite months of preparation, Jackie and Steve were totally unprepared to take care of Katie when she first came home from the hospital. While they had bought every conceivable technical contrivance to help them with baby care, they quickly learned that none of their preparation would help them survive.

Survival did not depend on the diapers' advanced stay-dry design, but on being able to reach the diapers from the side of the changing table, and knowing how to fold a dirty diaper and drop it in the trashcan with one hand while keeping the other hand on the slithering infant to ensure that neither the infant nor the diaper's contents ended up on the floor. Survival did not depend on having electronic toys to rock the baby or music boxes to play soothing music, but on unplugging the telephone, stereo, and television, and even silencing the grandfather clock in the hallway to be sure nothing distracted Katie from eating or sleeping. It meant taking the Cabbage Patch Dolls and brightly colored Disney characters out of her crib, leaving only a soft white dog-shaped pillow. For Jackie, survival depended on being able to curl up in

Steve's arms when she was exhausted, and have him hold her tightly until Katie wanted to be fed again.

Jackie had help. Elaine came several days after Katie was born and stayed through the summer and into the fall. She quietly dismantled Jackie's neat, technologically-efficient organization and discarded most of her modern gadgets in favor of more time-tested and practical solutions.

At the beginning of September, Jackie hired a live-in nanny from Ireland, Beatrice. Beatrice had already brought up children for two families in England, caring for the children when they were infants and toddlers, and moving on to a new family when they entered school. America was new to her, and it took Beatrice some time to adjust to the rapid pace of Steve and Jackie's world. As Jackie gained confidence in Beatrice, she gradually weaned Katie from the breast and returned to work. By the time Katie was six months old, Jackie was working full-time, though she often worked from home, using the computer, telephone, and fax in her study.

The new parents were transfixed by everything that Katie did. They thrilled at her infantile grasping and stepping reflexes. They spent hours gazing in awe at her delicate hands and feet and the ever-changing expressions on her sleeping face. They celebrated her first smile and helped her explore tastes, temperatures, smells, and sounds. Before she learned how to sit, they lay with her on the floor; when she was learning to crawl, they crawled along with her; and they led her by the hand as she learned how to walk. Together, they explored sand and earth, plants and animals, wind and rain. They shared her wonder at the brightly colored leaves that fell from the trees in the fall, the snow that fell in the winter, and the colorful flowers that emerged in the spring.

Months before Katie's second birthday, Jackie was pregnant again. The first ultrasound showed she was carrying twins, a boy and a girl.

The town house in Boston was already too small for their growing family. Moreover, Elaine was finding it increasingly difficult to maintain the house in Pittsfield alone, and Steve thought that she should live with them.

Jackie and Steve put their town house on the market and, just after New Year's, bought a large Victorian in Concord with six bedrooms, five baths, and a separate apartment for Beatrice. The house had a gabled entrance, round turrets on the corners, and a roofline crowned with peaks and chimneys. It was set several hundred feet back from the road on four acres of land that sloped sharply down into the forested wetlands behind their property. From the back porch was a beautiful view of the steep, rocky slope and granite outcroppings, which led down into the woods.

The twins were born in June of 1990. The boy they named Steven, Jr., whom they called Stevie. The girl was named Stephanie.

Jackie's second pregnancy was more difficult than the first. She gained more weight than expected and, from the middle of her second trimester, was forced to severely curtail her activities. By the third trimester, she had high blood pressure and swelling in her legs. Her doctor insisted that she stop working and stay in bed. At eight months, an ultrasound and amniocentesis showed that the twins were sufficiently mature to be delivered. Jackie and Steve met with their doctor, who recommended a cesarean section. Jackie was relieved to skip the last month of a difficult pregnancy and a protracted labor with twins. She also decided that three children was enough, and had the surgeon perform a tubal ligation to ensure she would not get pregnant again.

Jackie had hoped it would be easier to take care of an infant the second time around. She was not prepared for twins. The babies were small and weak, and they were unable to nurse effectively. The presence of a loquacious and jealous toddler in the house demanding her share of the attention made things even harder. After two weeks of trying, Jackie quit nursing in frustration.

Jackie was also anxious to return to work after spending months at home. When the twins were one month old, she began to leave them with Beatrice during the day and resumed her responsibilities at Fernald Partners.

By the time Katie began preschool in the fall of 1990, she was a confident and energetic child, who commanded more than her share of attention with her penchant for climbing into the nearest lap for an affectionate hug when she felt ignored. Stevie and Stephanie were fascinated by Katie, and did their best to emulate the other little person in the house who knew how to walk and talk. Their favorite game was to follow Katie around the house, imitating every motion she made, touching everything she touched, and mimicking her every sound until they drove Katie crazy and she would run into the woods behind the house to get away from them.

* * *

For Danny, the rapid collapse of communism after 1989 began a period of frenetic activity. He began spending virtually all of his time in the formerly communist countries of Eastern Europe and the former Soviet Union, helping the newly liberated populations establish democratic governments and systems of law. Never before in history had the world witnessed an opportunity to affect the civil rights and freedoms of so many people. Time was critical, as the fledgling nations struggled between the competing pressures of democracy, totalitarianism, nationalism, tribalism, and fascism. Danny was exhilarated by the chance to experience this seminal moment in history and was totally absorbed by his work.

Rachel's work changed after the Convention on the Rights of the Child was signed in 1989. She stayed with UNESCO to help the member countries enact laws that would protect the rights of children, as anticipated under the Convention. Her work, however, was increasingly overshadowed by AIDS, which was approaching epidemic proportions among women and children in Africa and much of the Third World.

AIDS was first recognized in isolated communities in the United States in the early 1980s. In less than ten years, scientists had discovered the HIV virus that caused the disease, described its epidemiology, and developed drugs that could control the disease's progression. The infection itself, however, remained stubbornly resistant to public health efforts to prevent its spread, vaccines that might protect uninfected individuals, or drugs that would provide a cure.

Rachel saw AIDS undo much of the progress that had been made toward improving the welfare of women and children in Africa. She began to spend most of her time pleading with African governments to recognize the scope of the epidemic and take public health measures to stop its spread. It was difficult and depressing work, and she became drained by the futility of trying to stem the rising tide of death and disease.

Danny and Rachel were working on two different continents and rarely saw each other. They wrote long letters to each other almost daily, though often it took weeks for their letters to arrive. Occasionally, they would spend several days or a week together in Europe or Israel as they traveled between destinations.

Rachel was lonely. When she was in the States, she spent most of her time with Jackie, Steve, and the children in Concord, rather than at her cramped Manhattan apartment. It had always been her idea to have children, a family, and a home. As she approached thirty-five, she was desperately afraid she might miss the chance.

38

Ruben died in the fall of 1991, days before his fortieth birthday. Danny was in Budapest when his parents called to tell him the news. He flew home for the funeral, which would be the next day, according to Jewish custom. It took Danny half a day to contact Rachel, who was in a remote region of Zambia, and it took her several more days to fly back to New York through Lusaka, Johannesburg, and London.

The funeral was a private graveside event, attended only by Ruben's immediate family. Following the funeral, the family sat Shiva at their home, where they received friends and extended family and said Kaddish, the prescribed prayers of mourning.

Steve and Jackie were the first to arrive at the Cohn home after the funeral. When they entered, Danny rose from his low chair to greet them, giving Jackie a tight hug and Steve a formal embrace as they expressed their condolences.

"I'm so glad you're here, Jackie," Danny said, sounding relieved. "I was afraid nobody would come who knew Ruben before he—"

Danny's parents rose to greet Jackie before he could finish the sentence. They had not seen her in many years, and had never met Steve. Danny stood quietly while Jackie expressed her condolences, courteously introduced Steve, answered questions about herself and her family, and, when prompted by Mrs. Cohn, brought out pictures of Katie and the twins from her purse. Mrs. Cohn gushed over the pictures until she was called away by the arrival of other visitors. By then, the house was overflowing with people and animated conversation.

Danny led Jackie and Steve to his old bedroom, where they could sit quietly and talk. Danny sat on the edge of the bed, while Jackie sat in his desk chair and Steve propped himself on the edge of the dresser.

"Are you okay, Danny?" Jackie asked.

"Yeah," he answered offhandedly. "We all knew something would happen to him eventually."

"So, what happened?"

"It doesn't really matter. He had so many problems," Danny replied evasively.

"Was it drugs?"

"I don't know. I don't want to talk about it."

"Is there anything we can do for you?"

"No. I'm just glad you're here."

"I didn't know whether we were supposed to bring flowers or food or something—"

"My parents are asking people to make a contribution to the Jewish National Fund to plant trees in Israel in Ruben's memory."

"That's a nice idea," Jackie replied.

"It is a nice idea," Danny echoed sadly. "Ruben was always obsessed with the Sun and the rain—planting trees in his honor seems somehow appropriate." Tears welled in Danny's eyes as he became lost in thought.

"We'll certainly make a contribution," Steve responded promptly.

"I'm sorry about the baby pictures," Jackie apologized, trying to preempt an awkward silence. "I wasn't sure if it was appropriate, but your mother asked."

"My mother asks everyone for baby pictures. She really wants grandchildren," Danny said, his tone discouraging any further discussion on the subject.

"You and Ruben were very close when you were kids." Jackie tried again to make conversation.

"Not so much in recent years. He had so many problems. Sometimes, I felt like I didn't know him anymore," Danny said bitterly.

"I remember when we were in elementary school," Jackie said, trying to be supportive, "you used to follow him around and repeat everything he said. You thought it made you sound grown up."

"And now everyone talks about him like he was just some hippie drug addict," Danny complained.

"He changed a lot," Jackie said poignantly, thinking back to their encounter in the hours after the *Challenger* disaster.

"So, tell me about him," Steve interjected in his best clinical manner. "I didn't know him, but Jackie's told me how close you were as kids."

Danny was relieved that someone had finally asked him to talk about Ruben, and he began an often rehearsed, but never expressed, monologue about the brother whom he had loved and the inexplicable tragedy that had consumed his final years. He described Ruben's youthful accomplishments as a musician and the brotherly bond they had shared. He described the events of the summer of 1969, how Ruben and his friends had gone to Woodstock, and how he had watched the accomplished artist he so admired morph into an angry adolescent and addict. He described Ruben's failure at Juilliard, his move to Berkeley, and the tragic spiral of radicalism, rebellion, retreat, and resignation that he had never been able to escape.

"I am so tired of people saying that Ruben was a child of the sixties, as if he were some caricature," Danny finished bitterly.

"We were all children of the sixties," Jackie offered.

"I have no idea what that means," Danny said argumentatively.

"The sixties were scary," Jackie recalled. "Do you remember the air-raid drills, the riots, the war, and all the protests and terrorism? It seemed like the whole world was going to explode. We all had to find a way to deal with it."

"I remember," Danny agreed.

"It must have been worse for Ruben," she continued. "By the time we got to college, the war was already over. Nixon was gone. Things were beginning to settle down. We never had to worry about the draft."

"There was more to the sixties than that," Steve interjected. "You two probably don't really remember most of the sixties."

"I remember the sixties!" Danny protested.

"Ruben was closer to my age—he was eleven or twelve when President Kennedy was assassinated." Steve said, pressing his point.

"Something like that," Danny replied.

"We were six," Jackie mused. "I don't remember very much." Danny did not disagree.

"Those years make a big difference," Steve continued. "When you are eleven or twelve, ideas are beginning to be fixed in your mind. I remember the sixties differently. It was a time of incredible hope and optimism. A boy hero had become president talking about courage and freedom. There was this idea that he could pull an entire world to safety, just as he had rescued his crew from a sinking ship. Amazingly, it seemed to work. He found a way to avoid war over Berlin. He was able to prevent missiles from being stationed in Cuba. The country began to make progress toward civil rights. We were going to land a man on the Moon. Then, suddenly, he was gone."

"Kennedy was Ruben's hero, too," Danny recalled. "He must have read *Profiles in Courage* aloud to me a dozen times."

"Do you think things would have been different if Kennedy had not been assassinated?" Jackie asked, turning to Steve.

"No!" Danny answered emphatically. "It was Kennedy who got us involved in Vietnam in the first place!"

"I disagree," Steve countered with some gravity. "I think things might have been different. I don't know if Kennedy could have avoided the war in Vietnam or prevented Martin Luther King from being assassinated and everything else that followed. But I remember how people seemed to change when he was assassinated. My parents and my teachers were apoplectic—people lost hope. When President Kennedy died, it was as if his ideas and idealism died too. My generation came away feeling empty."

"Is that what happened to Ruben?" Jackie asked, turning to Danny.

Danny hesitated before answering. "Maybe. I don't know what he believed in. He had this mystical vision of a world caught in an endless cycle of suffering. He believed music and art and drugs could change everything. He thought he saw it at Woodstock and was never really the same after that. He came back in this euphoric state, talking about having looked at the Sun and having seen a seventh heaven." The conversation lapsed into silence.

Those who came of age in the 1960s grew up in an era dominated by the dialectic of ideas. Time-honored structures that, for centuries, had imposed certain well-ordered nationalistic, religious, or cultural ideas on populations were weakened. Vatican II revised the basic canons of Catholicism, and the theologies of all faiths grappled to understand the unfathomable immorality of the Holocaust and prospect of nuclear annihilation. The world was torn by a cold war between the forces of capitalism and communism, radicalism and conservatism. Nations searched to understand the meaning of independence and interdependence. Populations searched for the balance of civil rights, civil liberties, and civic responsibilities.

The complex debates that raged among philosophers, theologians, politicians, artists, and scientists were largely incoherent and inaccessible to young people. Instead, a generation tried to find its way based on caricatures of great ideas expressed in sound bites on television and the lyrics of folk music and rock and roll.

"So how did you feel about Kennedy's assassination?" Jackie turned to Steve.

"I had nightmares for years. I would dream that I was in the car with Kennedy when he was shot. My father was there too, and he would try to save him and would ask me to hand him things from his medical bag, but I could never find the right instrument—or I would drop things or something would always go wrong," Steve answered, but he was thinking about something else.

In his mind, Steve was recalling his own experiences at Woodstock. He, too, had made the pilgrimage to Yasgur's Farm in search of peace, love, and harmony. In the chaos of the first day, he had run into someone he knew, a nurse who had once worked in his father's medical office. While most local health professionals had shunned involvement with Woodstock, she had volunteered to work at the medical facility on the festival grounds. By the end of the first day, the facility was already inundated with thousands of people who needed medical attention. Steve offered to help, and spent the rest of the festival laboring in the understaffed and overwhelmed medical tent.

Steve's memory of Woodstock was of three horrible, sleepless days and nights, helping the medical staff as they struggled to treat drug overdoses, bad drug trips, feet torn by broken glass, wounds, infections, dysentery, and dehydration. One entire tent was set up for people who had burned their eyes staring at the Sun. He ran errands, distributed food, cleaned up vomit and blood, emptied bedpans, and helped restrain addicts as they writhed through the agony of withdrawal. By the time the festival ended, he had seen two people die of drug overdoses and one crushed by a tractor. It was the first time Steve had watched someone die.

He also witnessed two births. It was the first time he had witnessed a life begin and the first time he had felt the urge to pray.

Before the conversation could resume, Danny's father came into the room to announce that the rabbi had arrived to lead the mourners in the evening prayers and the Kaddish. They joined the others in the living room for the service, which was followed by a smorgasbord of food, the traditional gift brought to a house of mourning.

As the crowd began to disperse later that evening, Danny pulled Jackie aside. "Can you do me a huge favor?" he asked. "Rachel is flying into Kennedy Airport tomorrow from London. I told her that I would meet her at the airport. I really want to be there, but I think I need to stay here with my parents. I'm the only one left, and I don't think they should be alone right now. Can you meet Rachel at the airport and bring her here? I know this is asking a lot."

Jackie agreed without hesitation.

39

The following day, Jackie drove to New York to meet Rachel's plane. Rachel was exhausted from almost forty hours of traveling and was disappointed that Danny was not there to meet her. It had been three months since she had seen him. Even then, they had only spent a weekend together in a hotel near

Heathrow Airport, while she was in transit to Africa. Rachel poured out her fatigue and frustration to Jackie in a continuous monologue as they stowed her bags in the trunk of the car and began the two-hour drive to Spring.

Rachel not only missed Danny, but she was also increasingly dissatisfied with her work. Negotiating the Convention on the Rights of the Child with the educated leaders of Africa, who shared her idea of improving the well-being of women and children, had been exhilarating. It was frustrating, however, dealing with the provincial bureaucracies of each country and the canons, customs, and cultures that often placed little value on women and children. It was depressing dealing with the overwhelming tide of AIDS. She was also envious of Jackie, who had a family and children.

It was an hour before Rachel's cathartic rambling was complete. "Thanks for listening, Jackie," she said finally. "I really needed to get some of this off my chest."

"I'm always here for you," Jackie answered sincerely.

"Thanks. So," Rachel changed the subject abruptly, "you drove all the way down here to pick me up, and I haven't even asked you about my nieces and nephew. Tell me all about them!"

"They're wonderful," Jackie said with a mother's joy. "Steve showed Katie how to kick a soccer ball the other day. It was the funniest thing we'd ever seen. Katie would run up to the ball and give it a huge kick. Half the time she would fall down and the ball wouldn't move at all. When she did stay on her feet, the ball would move maybe two feet. In either case, she thought it was hilarious and Steve and I couldn't stop laughing, which just encouraged Katie to keep doing it again and again."

"Has she been getting my presents? I try to send her something special from every place I go."

"She loves getting things from you. She's always asking me to show her where Aunt Rachel is on her globe. She was all excited when I told her I was picking you up. You'll have to come up later in the week to see her."

"I will. And how are the twins?"

"They're so much fun. They drive Katie absolutely crazy!"

"You sound happy."

"I am. You always told me that children would change my life. I never believed you."

"You told me once that you weren't sure you wanted kids."

"I wasn't. Kids didn't appeal to me much. When I was growing up, there was always a smelly baby in the house. It took me years to get that horrid smell out of my mind! All I remembered about kids was having to change diapers and babysit when I wanted to be out with my friends. I probably was not a very good sister."

"It's funny how things turn out. When Danny and I came back to the States, and I got to know you for the first time, I thought you might decide not to have children. You had this great career, that incredibly rich boyfriend, gorgeous clothes and jewelry, a penthouse, a mansion on the Cape, a yacht. You were always busy attending some charity event or jetting off to some amazing resort somewhere in the world. You've changed."

"I have changed," Jackie agreed. "Those were great times, but this is better."

"You could have more kids," Rachel teased.

"No way! After the twins, I had the surgeon make sure that would never happen again!"

"Why would that stop you? I'm sure you could arrange to have your eggs fertilized in a test tube and your baby grown in an incubator. That's probably what you would have done in the first place if Steve and I hadn't argued some sense into you!" Rachel continued to tease.

"I would not!" Jackie protested with a laugh. "I hope you have the experience of walking around pregnant with twins someday!" she responded, knowing this was exactly what Rachel wanted. They drove along in silence for several minutes.

"I want to have children. I'm thirty-four already," Rachel said, breaking the silence with a tone of melancholy. "But with my travel schedule—and with Danny so totally preoccupied by work, I don't know if we're going to have kids before I get too old. This isn't what I expected."

"Danny can't be busy in Europe forever."

"I can't wait for forever. I'm thinking of leaving UNESCO."

"You told me you weren't happy with your work."

"I never thought I would be thirty-four and childless. I wanted a normal life, a family, a home."

"Danny might be ready for that too," Jackie offered.

"Did he say anything?" Rachel's voice lifted.

"Not really. You know how hard it is for him to talk about anything before he has a chance to think it all through."

"I know," Rachel answered, resigned to Danny's ways.

"Ruben's death has been very hard for him."

"He sounded bad on the phone," Rachel agreed.

It was already dark when they arrived at the Cohn's house. Jackie stayed long enough to take a break from driving, have something to eat, and call Steve to ask about the kids. Danny tried to convince her to stay overnight and drive back in the morning when it was light, but Jackie was anxious to get home.

Rachel and Danny stayed in Spring for the week of prescribed mourning. When it was over, he returned to Hungary to continue his work. Rachel went to Boston to spend a week with Jackie and Steve.

Jackie immediately noticed that Rachel's mood was lighter than it had been the week before. Rachel busied herself with the kids and a bag full of toys that she had brought. It was several hours before the children tired of playing with Aunt Rachel and moved on to other activities.

"We're going to do it!" Rachel whispered excitedly when they were finally alone. "We're going to have a baby!"

"That's great!" Jackie exclaimed, embracing her. "What changed?"

"You were right. Danny was tormenting himself, trying to rationalize everything that has ever happened in his life. You know how he is."

"I know."

"Anyway, you aren't supposed to do anything during the week of mourning, so we had a lot of time to just talk. We haven't talked so much in years. It was good for both of us. We agreed that our work is out of control and that we want to start a family before it's too late. We're going to have a baby!" Rachel finished with glee.

"I'm so happy for you!"

"Danny wants to have a little Ruben. You know, there's a Jewish tradition that naming a child after a deceased relative keeps their name alive—keeps part of them alive."

"I hope that's not why you decided to have a child," Jackie cautioned.

"No. Actually, neither of us said anything about it at the beginning. I suggested naming the child after Ruben after we had already talked through everything and agreed that it was time to have children. It meant a lot to Danny, you know, that I would want to name our child after his brother. We all try so hard to be reasonable and rational, but traditions still matter—you named your first son Steve."

"It is a tradition," Jackie agreed. "So, what are you going to do now?"

"I've been talking to some friends about joining their law firm in New York City. I'll visit them next week. I'm sure we can work something out. Danny would like to find a faculty position where he can stay involved in human rights issues without traveling all the time. He'll find something. If we both have jobs in the city, we might finally earn enough money to get a decent apartment. We'll probably have to pay for a nanny and schools and—" Rachel's mind raced ahead to the hundreds of things that would change in their lives. "We're really going to do it!" She grabbed Jackie's hands in hers.

"So, when is all this going to happen?" Jackie asked.

"Well, you're not supposed to have sex when you're in mourning." Rachel stopped with a coy smile. "But it was sort of the right time of month."

"Rachel!"

"Don't tell anyone."

"Does Danny know?"

"You don't do this alone, you know," Rachel teased.

"That's not what I meant." Jackie was chagrined.

"Yeah, he knew. It was the greatest sex we ever had."

"Rachel!"

"Don't tell anyone, promise?"

* * *

Six weeks later, Rachel called to tell Jackie she was pregnant. Soon thereafter, she resigned from UNESCO at the end of the year and joined a law firm that specialized in family law. Her position gave her the opportunity to remain involved in advocating for women and children in the political and legislative arenas. Danny joined the faculty of Columbia University Law School, where he taught and wrote books on international law and human rights.

Rachel was radiant throughout her pregnancy. She had a natural childbirth in the bedroom of their Manhattan apartment with only Danny and a midwife present. They named their baby girl Ruth, though everyone would come to know her as Ruby in Ruben's memory. A year later, Rachel gave birth to a son, Benjamin.

From the beginning, Rachel struggled in her role as a working mother. She was torn between her sense of responsibility to continue advocating for women and children, and the sheer joy she felt being around her own children. Each case she accepted at work made boundless demands on her emotions and her time. Each moment she spent away from her children was filled with regret. She went to work every day with an aching desire to be at home.

Shortly after her son was born, she quit her position at the law firm. She channeled her energy in different directions, joining the boards of her children's school, their synagogue, and non-profit advocacy groups in their community. It had always been her idea to put family and children first.

40

Katie began first grade at Concord Elementary School in the fall of 1994. She was vivacious, smart, and impatient; much like her mother had been at the same age. She retained the platinum-blonde hair of her infancy and had her mother's sparkling eyes and freckles along with her father's more delicate facial features.

Katie was an active child who often had difficulty paying attention in class and was sometimes disruptive. More than one teacher suggested that Katie had Attention Deficit Disorder and recommended that she be treated with Ritalin to improve her attention span.

"It sounds like a good idea to me," Jackie told Steve, after a meeting with Katie's teachers. "Her teachers say she has trouble sitting still. If there's a drug that can help her, it might be a good idea."

"I'm not going to give my daughter drugs to make the teacher's job easier." Steve was dismissive.

"But what if the teachers think it would be good for her, that it might help her grades?"

"You don't give kids drugs to get better grades."

"I was a lot like Katie at her age," Jackie persisted. "In retrospect, I probably had ADD too. Maybe Ritalin would have helped me."

"She doesn't need drugs."

"I thought you believed in medicine," she challenged him.

"I do believe in medicine, when it's appropriate. But Katie doesn't have a disease. She's just a fidgety kid—a lot like her mother. In case you didn't notice, I rather like the way fidgety kids grow up." Steve affectionately took Jackie in his arms and definitively ended the conversation with a kiss.

By the time Katie was ten, much of her energy was channeled into playing soccer, which she found much more interesting and engaging than school. Her bedroom was decorated with posters of Mia Hamm and Kristine Lilly, the stars of the United States National Women's Soccer Team, which was preparing for the upcoming Women's World Cup in 1999. She rarely wore anything to school except soccer shorts and a jersey with Hamm or Lilly's name and number. She spent hours practicing with her soccer teams and playing keep-away with the twins, who would gang up on her in pesky double-teams and tackle her to steal the ball.

Like many American parents, Steve and Jackie did not know much about soccer. They could only cheer loudly for Katie during Saturday morning games, complain about fouls perpetrated by the other team, provide rudimentary instruction about sportsmanship, and pay the tuition for a variety of soccer clinics and camps.

In contrast, Beatrice had grown up with the European obsession for the sport and taught Katie everything she knew. As Katie began to show interest and talent, Beatrice invited one of her former wards, who had played semiprofessional soccer in England, to spend a summer with the family in Concord and teach Katie the more advanced skills of the European game.

Katie quickly learned techniques and strategies that were significantly more sophisticated than those of her teammates. She also learned to be a determined combatant, unconcerned about colliding with other players on the field to wrest control of the ball. While her aggressive and physical play was rarely unsportsmanlike, it contrasted with the more deferential style of most girls her age. During the course of a game, Katie would often be called for several fouls or given a yellow card for playing too rough. Once, she was even given a red card and ejected from a game for a collision that the referee considered unnecessary. Katie routinely came home from games and practices with bruises, mud, and grass stains on her legs, and sometimes even blood on her face.

Katie was not a team player. She preferred to dribble the ball through the defense and shoot at the goal rather than pass the ball to teammates who played without her skill or intensity. Her coaches were often torn between trying to teach her to be a team player and simply taking advantage of her standout ability to win games. Those who tried to lecture Katie on teamwork and sportsmanship found it hard to challenge her sincere determination to excel and win. Most decided that it was better just to let her play. With Katie taking the lead, their teams rarely lost.

* * *

In the early 1990s, the country entered a period of expansive economic growth that would prove to be the longest and greatest economic boom in history; a boom driven by the consummation of an age of technology. The stock market tripled. The value of technology and biotechnology stocks increased ten times faster. Tens of thousands of new technology companies were started to commercialize computer and communication technologies and launch new applications of the Internet. In addition, hundreds of new biotechnology companies were founded to develop novel drugs, devices, and diagnostics.

The public became infatuated with technology. Personal computers and cellular phones became ubiquitous. High-speed Internet services began to reach into homes as well as offices and businesses. People began to buy books, art, clothes, medicines, food, cars, and even homes through the Internet, rather than from conventional sellers. High technology suddenly came to be incorporated into every aspect of daily life, just as Jackie had always expected.

In medicine, the most striking change was the integration of drugs into the routines of healthy people. There was growing acceptance of drugs to treat depression and anxiety. There were new drugs for lowering cholesterol and controlling blood pressure that were sufficiently safe to use even in people who had no symptoms, but only a calculated risk of disease. Powerful antacids, pain relievers, and allergy medicines became available without prescriptions. Lifestyle drugs were approved to treat baldness and even improve sex.

The Internet spawned a wave of globalization. In the information age, workers in any corner of the Earth could participate in the global economy. Many pundits believed that information technologies would succeed in bringing economic growth to regions where traditional industries had failed. The information superhighway would become the medium through which developing countries could become global consumers and producers.

In addition, the clouds of geopolitical uncertainty, which had hovered over Jackie's youth, seemed to finally recede. At the outset of the decade, Francis Fukayama published a widely acclaimed book, entitled *The End of History,* in which he proposed that the traditional conflicts of history had been finally resolved. He argued that the great conflicts between liberal democracy and totalitarianism, which had dominated the nineteenth and twentieth centuries had resulted in the unequivocal triumph of the principles of liberal, capitalist democracy. As the end of the century approached, more people around the world lived under liberal democracies and enjoyed basic human liberties than ever before.

The last decade of the century was remarkably free of military conflict. There was a short war in 1991, when Iraq invaded Kuwait, only to be pushed back to its frontiers by a broad alliance of civilized nations. There were simmering conflicts in remote countries, such as Afghanistan, Angola, Rawanda, Congo, Sudan, Somalia, and Serbia, that stopped short of igniting larger conflagrations or global concerns. Even Israel enjoyed a decade of peace, engaged in a scripted process of negotiations with its Arab neighbors. The United States and the states of the former Soviet Union began to dramatically reduce their stocks of nuclear weapons and decommission the military infrastructure built for mutually assured destruction in a world war that had never occurred.

For Jackie, the explosive growth of technology and prolonged economic boom brought waves of new clients, products, and initial public offerings. As the technology industry globalized, Fernald Partners decided to expand their operations. The firm opened new offices across the street from the World Trade Center in New York, as well as in London and San Francisco.

41

Katie was eleven years old in the spring of 1999 when she graduated from junior soccer, a game played on small fields with six players on a team, to the mature game played on a full-size soccer field with eleven players on each side. She adapted immediately to the large fields, which extended her advantage against less committed and skilled players. She routinely scored several goals in every game. As a result, her team was undefeated going into the last game of the season and was invited to a regional tournament over Memorial Day weekend.

The last game of the regular season was played on their home field against the team from the nearby town of Belmont. Belmont had a strong team and a star player whose skill level and intensity matched or surpassed Katie's.

Katie had a cold all week, with a runny nose and a low-grade fever, but she was not going to let anything keep her from playing soccer. She scored one goal in the first few minutes of the game and a second one just before halftime. In the second half, Belmont's star player was assigned to shadow Katie everywhere she went on the field. For the rest of the game, Katie was locked in a physical, one-on-one contest with an equally talented and spirited defender. There was a lot of pushing and shoving as both girls fought for the advantage on the field.

The score was tied at three to three through the second half. With almost ten minutes to go, Katie finally captured a loose ball and broke away from her defender and toward the goal. The defender, while momentarily out of position, slid forward into Katie's path, tackled her, and kicked the ball away. The two girls collapsed onto the ground in pain.

The game was stopped for several minutes so the two girls could compose themselves enough to stand up. When they did, the referee instructed them to shake hands and then sent them to their respective sidelines to nurse their injuries. The game ended minutes later in a tie.

On the way home, Katie was still in pain. When they arrived, Beatrice helped her shed her clothes, comb some of the mud and grass out her hair, and climb into a hot bath. Several minutes later, Beatrice came down to find Jackie.

"You need to look at your daughter," Beatrice said, her deep brogue filled with concern. "She has an awful lot of bruising, more than I like to see on the lass."

"It was a rough game," Jackie answered casually.

"That's what your daughter said too. But she has a lot of bruising. You ought look at her."

Jackie followed Beatrice up to see Katie, who had bruises on her arms and legs, back and torso, and a large bruise over her knee, which was red and swollen. She impatiently ascribed each bruise to a specific incident on the playing field and then, annoyed by the attention, sent her mother and Beatrice away so that she could bathe and dress in private.

Jackie told Steve about the bruises. He looked cursorily at several bruises that Katie unwillingly showed him on her arms and legs and concluded that she was probably right about the game being unusually rough. He suggested that she take Tylenol for her pain and hold an ice pack on her swollen knee.

All week, Katie's knee hurt. On Tuesday, she was in so much pain that Jackie kept her from practice. On Thursday, she went to practice, but uncharacteristically chose to sit on the sidelines through most of the drills. By Saturday, she felt well enough to play in the tournament.

The tournament involved playing three games, two on Saturday and another Sunday morning, followed by a championship game between the two teams with the best records Sunday afternoon. On Saturday, Katie's team easily won both their games. Katie scored one goal in the first game and three in the second. That night, Beatrice found even more bruises. Again, Katie reluctantly showed her parents some of the bruises on her arms and legs and convinced them that she was okay.

She did not feel well on Sunday, but wanted to play in the tournament anyway. It had rained all night, and the morning game was played in intermittent drizzle and mud. Katie played without much energy, and the game ended in a zero-to-zero tie. The tie, coupled with their two wins on Saturday, was good enough for Katie's team to advance to the championship game that afternoon.

After lunch, more Tylenol, and a shower, Katie felt better. The championship game was against a team that had been undefeated all year and had several top-level players. Katie played hard and scored two goals early in the first half, but her team was losing four to two at halftime.

In the second period, Katie's team continued to be pressured by their aggressive opponents. Midway through the period, with the score was six to two, the opponents were awarded a corner kick after the goalie prevented yet another goal by punching the ball to the side of the net. Katie lined up with her teammates in front of the goal to defend. There was a lot of pushing and shoving for position as the ball was kicked. Katie leaped forward, trying to head the ball away from the goal. At the same instant, her opponent leaped toward her, trying to head the ball for a score. The ball ended up in the goalie's arms, but the two girls' heads collided in midair, and they fell to the ground.

Both girls quickly recovered from the shock of the contact and jumped up to resume play. Katie turned to run ahead to an offensive position, took ten steps toward midfield, and then collapsed limply to the ground, unable to prevent her face from falling into the mud. The goalie's momentum carried her forward, and she kicked the ball over Katie. For several moments, play swirled around Katie, who lay motionless on the ground, until the screaming parents and coaches on the sideline caught the referee's attention and he whistled for play to stop.

Jackie and Steve saw Katie fall awkwardly to the ground and ran out onto the field. Katie was not unconscious, nor was she fully awake. She was able to turn her head so her face was off the ground, but her vision was blurred. Her head and neck hurt. She was embarrassed to be lying in the middle of the field, but she could not move her arms or legs.

Steve automatically took over as he pinned Katie to the ground, keeping her neck immobile, and told everyone else to stay away. Jackie heard the urgency in Steve's voice and instinctively reached for the cell phone in her pocket to call 911.

Katie was still lying motionless on the ground ten minutes later when the ambulance arrived. The paramedics worked over Katie for twenty minutes, checking her vital signs, placing a support around her neck, and easing her onto a stretcher before carrying her gently into the ambulance. Steve jumped into the ambulance with them, as they raced toward Children's Hospital, the sirens sounding a wailing tone punctuated by a series of short blasts.

Jackie's head was spinning. Her pulse exploded in her ears. The flashing lights of the ambulance flickered like flames through her terrified tears. She tried to call out to Steve as they drove away, but no sound came from her lips. She wanted to run after them, to hold Katie securely in her arms, to press her head against her breasts, to kiss away her pain; but she could not move. She was hardly aware when Beatrice took her firmly by the elbow, led her off the field to the car, and drove her home.

She managed to walk weakly into the house and collapse into a chair next to the telephone, without removing her raincoat. She checked the messages on the phone, hoping that Steve might have called to tell her everything was all right, but there was no message. She dialed Steve's cell phone, but he did not answer. Finally, Jackie called Children's Hospital and was told that Katie had been admitted to the intensive care unit. An ICU nurse confirmed that Katie and Steve were there and promised to tell Steve to call home as soon as possible.

It was more than three hours before Steve called. "I'm sorry I didn't call sooner," he apologized immediately, his speech revealing more tension than his words. "Things have been moving so fast."

"What's going on?" Jackie was terrified by his tone of voice.

"Katie is in a coma. She had a seizure in the ambulance as soon as we left the field. They gave her medicines to stop the seizure and put her on oxygen, but she's been unconscious ever since."

"Oh my God!" Jackie hardly had the strength to hold the receiver in her hand. "Do they know what's wrong? What happened? Why did she fall? Why did she have a seizure? What's happening? Is she going to be okay?"

"They don't know what's going on yet," Steve said. "She must have hurt herself when she bumped heads with the other girl. She may have a concussion."

"They didn't hit that hard. That's happened before." Jackie was bewildered. "She seemed okay at first."

"There's more," Steve continued ominously. "Remember the bruises we saw last week and last night?"

"Yes."

"When they took off her clothes in the ambulance, she had even more bruises. They want to do an emergency CT scan and be sure she doesn't have any bleeding in her head."

"My God! Is my baby going to be okay?" Jackie started to cry.

"I don't know," Steve answered.

"Tell me she's going to be okay!" Jackie begged. "Tell me she's going to be okay!"

"This is the best children's hospital in the world. They'll take good care of her," Steve answered without conviction. "I don't like the bruising," he added gravely.

"Can I see her? Should I be there?"

"Things are still somewhat chaotic here. They probably will not let you see her for some time. They really don't want me here either, but they haven't kicked me out yet. Why don't you stay home with the twins for now? They need you too. I'll call you when you should come down."

"Take good care of my baby." Jackie was now sobbing. "Make sure they take good care of my baby."

42

Several hours later, Jackie arrived at the hospital. By then, the initial phase of frenetic activity was subsiding. Samples of blood and urine had been sent to the laboratory for tests, and a CT scan had been performed to look inside Katie's brain. She had been treated with intravenous drugs to prevent seizures, medicines to prevent swelling of the brain, and antibiotics in case she had an infection. She had received transfusions of blood and plasma to prevent her from bleeding and fluids to maintain the metabolic balance of her body.

Jackie immediately broke into tears when she saw her daughter in the ICU. Katie was lying unconscious on the bed, covered only by a strategically draped sheet that barely covered her chest and pelvis. Her wrists and legs were secured to the bed frame. Her soiled and torn soccer uniform had been tossed onto the floor in the corner of the room. Plastic tubes protruded from the bend of each arm, just above her wrist, and from the side of her neck. An oxygen mask obscured her face. Electrodes were pasted across her chest and her scalp, where patches of long blonde hair had been crudely shaved away. A bag of urine hung at the foot of the bed. Bags of pale-colored blood and plasma hung from a pole at the head of the bed, connected to tubes that ran into each of her arms and the base of her neck. Blood and iodine stained the sheets and the floor.

Steve was sitting by the side of the bed, holding Katie's hand. Jackie came up beside him and grasped their hands tightly in hers. He responded with a reassuring squeeze; Katie did not.

"She's unconscious," Steve whispered.

"Is she going to wake up?" Jackie asked urgently.

"She may be unconscious for a while."

"Why?"

"It could be from the injury. More likely, she's unconscious from the seizure."

Jackie reached to stroke Katie's hair, which was encrusted with dirt and blood from the soccer game as well as disinfectant and gel from the electrodes.

"She needs a bath," Jackie observed.

"They'll clean her up. It was hectic here until several minutes ago."

"Do they know what happened?"

"The CT scan showed some bleeding around her brain."

"My God! Is she going to be all right? Is her brain going to be all right?"

"Hopefully. There was some swelling along with the blood, but it didn't look like she was still bleeding. If the bleeding stops, she'll probably wake up. If it continues, they may need to operate. They had a neurosurgeon see her several minutes ago, just in case."

"A neurosurgeon?" Jackie asked. "She's going to need brain surgery?"

"It's just a precaution."

"Is all of this just because she bumped heads with the other girl?"

"No." Steve paused and took a deep breath. "One of the tests showed that her platelet count is very low," he said, trying to minimize the concern in his voice.

"What's a platelet?"

"Platelets are little cells that circulate in the blood and make it clot. If you don't have enough platelets, even a minor injury can cause bruising or bleeding. That's probably why she started bleeding when they bumped heads."

"Is that why she had so many bruises last week, why her knee has been so painful—because she didn't have enough platelets?"

"Probably. Her platelet count could have been low for some time without anyone knowing."

"What was her platelet count?"

"Less than three thousand," Steve answered ominously.

"What should it be?"

"More like three hundred thousand."

Jackie took a deep breath. "Can they just give her platelets?" she said, hoping there was a simple answer.

"That's what they're doing." Steve gestured toward the pale blood bags hanging from the head of the bed.

"What causes the platelet count to be too low?"

"They need to do more tests to find out," Steve answered evasively. "Right now they are just trying to make sure she's stable."

Jackie heard gravity in Steve's voice and did not pursue the question.

"Is she going to wake up? Is she going to be okay?" she asked again.

"We just have to watch her."

Katie remained in a coma for the rest of the day and through the night. Jackie never left her side. After her initial dismay at seeing Katie's bruised body in the ICU, Jackie began to acclimate to the surroundings and even derive a certain comfort from the commotion around her. There was something awe-inspiring about the medical machine that was caring for Katie. There was so much power, so much potential, and so much promise. Without knowing anything about her daughter's illness or the treatments she was receiving, Jackie had faith that Katie would be cured.

She watched bags of platelets, blood, fluids, and medicines flow into Katie's veins like vital elixirs. She watched every beat of Katie's heart on the electrocardiogram and blood pressure monitors on the walls, noting every change in rate or rhythm. She noted the fluctuations of Katie's brain waves on the electroencephalogram, trying to guess which pattern registered dreams, which reflected fear, and which revealed a response to a squeeze of her hand or a stroke of her hair. Jackie began recognizing repetitive rhythms in the cacophony of beeping monitors and buzzing machines that provided assurance that Katie was still alive. Even when Jackie fell into a fitful sleep in the chair at the foot of the bed, she was unconsciously aware of the sound of Katie's beating heart on the monitors and was startled awake every time the regular cadence was disturbed.

In Jackie's dreams, she huddled with Katie in the cold of the lunar module as they struggled to stay alive after an explosion rocked their ship on the way to the Moon. She heard the series of short blasts from the siren and tried to duck and cover, and she listened to the voices around her trying to determine what had happened and a way to bring Katie back. She relived the feeling of panic, the passage behind the dark side of the Moon, the prayers said around the world, and the critical corrections that adjusted their course so they would not burn up on reentry or be forever lost in space. Over and over again, she lived the end of their journey; three parachutes appearing softly beneath the clouds and Katie climbing out of the capsule alive.

The next morning, Katie was still in a coma. Another CT scan showed that there had been no further bleeding. There was nothing to do but wait and see if she would wake up.

Jackie helped the nurses change the sheets under Katie and give her a sponge bath. She lovingly combed and sponged the mud, grease, and disinfectant out of her hair, touched away the crust that had accumulated in the corners of her eyes, and gently moistened her dry lips. Katie's eyes fluttered open briefly. She tried to move against the restraints that bound her to the bed.

Jackie saw fear and pain in her eyes and leaned down to kiss a tear before it could run down her cheek. "I'm here, baby."

"I don't feel good, Mommy. My head hurts," Katie mumbled faintly.

"I know. Everything will be okay."

"Mommy."

"Everything will be okay." Jackie tried to sound comforting as Katie drifted back into a deep sleep.

Katie did not awaken again until after midnight. When she did, she was able to open her eyes for several moments and look at her surroundings. She spied her favorite stuffed animal sitting on Jackie's lap, and her eyes smiled appreciatively as Jackie placed the worn, white dog in her arms. Then she fell asleep again.

The next day, Katie awakened more often and stayed awake longer each time. She began reaching for Jackie's and Steve's hands, as soon as she was awake, holding them tightly to be sure they would not get away. She tried to talk several times but struggled to form any sensible words.

Two days later, Katie was more alert. She complained of a headache, pain in her eyes from the light, and a stiff neck if she tried to move. She was in pain but out of danger. One by one, the tubes and monitors were removed. By mid-afternoon, she had only a single IV in her arm, a catheter for her urine, and electrodes on her chest to record her heartbeat.

Each day brought rapid improvement. She was moved out of the ICU to a regular hospital room and was able to use the bathroom with the help of a nurse. She tried to sit in a chair to watch television, though the light from the television hurt her eyes, and Katie asked that it be turned off almost immediately. A physical therapist tried to help her walk, but she was too unsteady to stand alone for more than an instant.

Five days after she was admitted, Katie woke up famished, though she complained that everything she tried to eat tasted bad. Jackie and Steve eagerly took turns going out to buy candy, donuts, cookies, soda, ice cream, French fries, potato chips, pretzels, and pizza; anything that Katie might find palatable, all of which quickly ended up in the trashcan next to her bed after one bite.

That evening, Stevie, Stephanie, Beatrice, Elaine, and Erin were allowed to visit for the first time. Over the next several days, Katie's friends and teammates came to visit. Soon, the ceiling of her room was covered with dozens of brightly colored balloons, and the sparse furniture was buried under mounds of stuffed animals and flowers. A pile of electronic games also began to grow next to her bed, although her sight was still too blurred and her reflexes too slow for her to use them.

It took several more days of physical therapy before Katie was strong enough to walk alone to the bathroom and her vision clear enough to play computer games or watch DVDs on her laptop. Soon, Katie's biggest complaint was boredom.

43

As the emergency resolved, the doctors began to focus on diagnosing why Katie's platelet count was so low. Making a diagnosis was the essential first step in the process of predicting what would happen in the future and determining the proper course of treatment.

One of Katie's doctors explained that leukemia could stop the body from making enough platelets, so he performed a biopsy of her bone marrow to look for malignant cells. Jackie panicked at the mention of leukemia, and was relieved when the biopsy showed no evidence of this dread disease.

Another doctor explained that certain infections could shut down the production of platelets in the body, so she performed a battery of tests, which showed no evidence for any overwhelming infectious disease. Yet another doctor suggested that a toxic drug reaction might have reduced the number of platelets, though no one could identify any drugs that Katie might have taken that would cause this side effect. Others considered whether a systemic disease, such as rheumatoid arthritis or lupus erythematosus could have lowered Katie's platelet count, though there was no other evidence to indicate that she had these chronic, debilitating diseases.

Over the next several days, one medical specialist after another examined Katie. Each would propose a different explanation for her disease, prescribe a new series of often-painful diagnostic procedures, and then disappear without reaching any conclusions. For every diagnosis that the specialists suggested, some symptoms and circumstances seemed to fit, while others did not. One by one, every suggested diagnosis was discarded.

After ten days in the hospital, Katie was strong enough to begin resisting the indignities of people walking in and out of her room, watching her while she slept and showered, and escorting her to the toilet. One morning, she refused to let the nurse draw blood, and threw a temper tantrum when she was taken to the X-ray department for yet another diagnostic procedure. Still, there was no diagnosis, and her platelet count was too low for her to be safely sent home.

"I can't believe all these Harvard doctors can't figure out what is wrong with Katie," Jackie complained bitterly to anyone who would listen. "I just can't believe it."

As Katie's doctors continued, unsuccessfully, to look for answers, Jackie began to hear a strange term used to describe Katie's illness: *idiopathic*. Soon,

Katie's doctors began referring to her diagnosis as Idiopathic Thrombocytopenic Purpura, or ITP.

The daily meetings that Steve and Jackie had with Katie's doctors rarely provided Jackie with any comfort, and she became increasingly frustrated with the lack of a diagnosis. "So what is this disease I hear you talking about, ITP?" she challenged Dr. Rafael, who had become Katie's primary doctor while she was in the hospital.

"Idiopathic thrombocytopenic purpura, ITP. It is really a description of her disease, not really a name," he answered. "*Purpura* means 'bruising,' *thrombocytopenia* means that there are not enough platelets, and *idiopathic* refers to the fact that we don't know what causes it."

"You don't know what causes it?"

"It's what we call a 'diagnosis of exclusion.' It is diagnosed by excluding every other disease that can cause a similar problem. If we don't find anything else wrong, we assume it is ITP."

"Is she the only kid in the world with some disease that doesn't even have a name?"

"No, it's actually rather common. Something like two hundred thousand people get the disease every year."

"That doesn't make any sense. If you can't find anything wrong, you just call it *idiopathic*?" Jackie said skeptically.

"I'm afraid that's it."

"How could any self-respecting physician call something *idiopathic* and expect to be taken seriously? Medicine is not supposed to be like that anymore."

"I know it isn't a very satisfying answer," Dr. Rafael said, waving his hands helplessly.

"Do you know how to cure it?"

"We know how to manage it. I wouldn't say we have anything that can be called a cure. The good news is that it usually gets better on its own."

Jackie turned helplessly toward Steve, her eyes begging for a better explanation, but he had little to add to what Dr. Rafael had already said. Even an Internet search later that night failed to provide any satisfying answers.

The little research that had been performed on ITP, suggested that there was something in the blood of patients with the disease that was destroying their platelets. In the early 1950s, one foolhardy researcher had purposely given himself a transfusion of blood from a patient with ITP, and promptly suffered a severe loss of platelets himself.

Over the years, more rational experiments revealed that patients with ITP had antibodies attached to the surface of their platelets, and that these antibodies seemed to trigger the destruction of the platelets in the spleen. These results led some doctors to begin calling the disease *immune thrombocytopenia purpura* rather than *ideopathic thrombocytopenia purpura,* a change that conveniently retained the ITP acronym, and enabled physicians to avoid admitting that anything in medicine remained idiopathic. The cause of the disease, however, remained unknown, and no one had discovered a cure.

Two weeks after Katie was first admitted to the hospital, she was stable enough to be discharged. While her platelet count was still below thirty thousand, Dr. Rafael thought this number would be sufficient to prevent further bleeding. He met with Jackie and Steve just before Katie left. "None of the tests we performed identified any definitive cause for Katie's disease, so we are definitely going to call it ITP," Dr. Raphael repeated.

Jackie desperately wanted a more definitive answer, but was beginning to realize none would be forthcoming. "So what's going to happen now?" she asked.

"Well, there are two forms of the disease. The childhood form generally occurs around five years of age and resolves spontaneously, usually within a year. There is also an adult form of the disease, which can be chronic, even fatal."

Jackie shuddered. "So what's going to happen to her?"

"My best guess is that Katie has the childhood form of the disease, though she's somewhat older than the typical patient. Seventy percent of children with ITP recover within six months. Only five percent have the disease for more than a year. The odds are on your side that she will get better."

"But what's going to make her better if there's no treatment?"

"We gave her steroids here in the hospital that will raise the platelet count for a while. We also gave her a drug called *anti-D*, which can slow destruction of her platelets. But these are only temporary measures. There is no evidence they actually cure the disease. The disease usually resolves spontaneously."

"Why?"

"We don't know."

"So what do we do in the meantime?"

"The most important thing is to prevent her from bleeding again. I recommend that we check her platelet counts every week. If her counts drop, we can give her steroids or anti-D again. In an emergency—if she's bleeding, we can give her more platelet transfusions."

"What's going to happen?" Jackie asked again, hoping for a different answer.

"I think she will get better. The best thing is to do as little as we can and wait for the disease to resolve."

"And what if it doesn't?"

"We can try other things. Sometimes it helps to surgically remove the spleen, though that has serious long-term complications. There are drugs that will suppress the immune system, but sometimes the drugs can be as bad as the disease itself."

"So what are we supposed to do?"

"As I said, the most important thing is to avoid injuries, particularly anything that might cause her to bleed again into her head."

"But she's a kid—an active kid. Kid's fall down, they play ball, they push and they shove. We can't control everything that happens to her."

"You don't have to. Katie should go about her normal activities as much as possible. Most of the little things will not be a problem. She may bruise more easily, and some of the bruises may be more painful, but the most important thing is to guard against head injuries. Bleeding into the brain can be life-threatening."

"But she could hit her head in a car accident."

"You can't protect against everything."

"Can she go out at recess and play with the other children?"

"As long as she is careful."

"Can she ride a bike? How about rollerblades or a scooter?"

"She has to be careful, and I suggest she wears a helmet."

"Can she play soccer?"

"No contact sports. Soccer is particularly dangerous because of the headers."

"No soccer," Jackie sighed. "That's going to be hard. She lives for soccer."

"I realize that," Dr. Rafael concurred. "The hardest part of managing the disease is that she may not feel sick, even when her platelet count is low. But she has to be careful all the time."

"It would be easier if you could simply give her a drug that would cure it," Jackie said sullenly.

"I wish I could."

Jackie was thankful that Steve was with her when they took Katie home that evening. There were so many questions that the hospital had been unable to answer and so many things she needed to talk to him about. Over the ensuing days, they spent endless hours discussing how their lives needed to change, how to care for Katie, what activities they would need to curtail or let continue, what to tell their families and friends, and what to tell the school. When Jackie's childhood nightmare began to recur, and the explosions tore at her world and Katie began to fade into the darkness, she needed to be able to roll over to Steve and press her head tightly against his chest and listen to the regular cadence of his heart.

While Katie was happy to be out of the hospital, it was another week before she felt strong enough to go to school. When she returned to school for the last days of the term, she still had intermittent headaches and blurred vision and found it harder than usual to sit still and pay attention in class.

Katie had been looking forward to spending the summer at an advanced soccer training camp. Instead, Jackie and Steve rented a house on Cape Cod, and the children spent the summer playing on the beach and at the community pool under Beatrice's constant supervision.

By midsummer, Katie had recovered her strength and coordination almost completely and had been weaned off the seizure medications. The stronger she felt, the harder it was to limit her activities. Beatrice was afraid to leave her alone for even a minute. Even at the pool, she had to monitor Katie constantly to keep her from diving headfirst into the water or joining her friends in pickup games of water polo or soccer. Feeling stifled by the strict supervision and limits on her activities, Katie became angry and argumentative.

Each week, Katie submitted to having blood drawn for another platelet count, hoping that the platelet count would be normal and that she could begin playing soccer again. Each week, she would be depressed when the results showed that her platelet counts were still low. There was no improvement during the summer. Several times, in fact, her platelet counts dropped below ten thousand, and Dr. Rafael treated her with steroids. Once she had a nosebleed and was given a platelet transfusion.

In late August, with her platelet count still hovering near the critical point, Jackie and Steve took Katie for additional medical opinions from experts at the National Institutes of Health and St. Jude's Hospital. Each expert gave them the same advice: most children get better, steroids and anti-D can control the disease, but there was no cure. The best course of action was to be patient and let the disease run its course.

When school started in September, Katie's platelet count was below thirty thousand. Dr. Rafael advised that she not play soccer. Katie threw a terrible temper tantrum when Steve told her she would not be able to play soccer in the fall. She ran to her room, crying hysterically. In her room, she began kicking soccer balls violently against the walls until everything on her shelves had crashed onto the floor, the folding doors to her closet had been knocked off their tracks, and the light bulbs on the ceiling and the glass in the mirror over her dresser had been shattered.

Steve and Jackie tried to ignore the sounds of carnage coming from Katie's room, until they heard the sound of breaking glass. By then, the room was in shambles. Steve had to carry Katie out of the room, and restrain his kicking and screaming daughter until she exhausted herself.

After putting Katie and the twins to bed, Jackie complained bitterly to Steve as they sat in the kitchen. "I don't get it! We're on the verge of the twenty-first century. Billions of dollars are spent on medical research. Every day you hear about a new cure for cancer, and no one knows anything about this disease! It's not just idiopathic—it's idiotic!" Jackie's frustration was growing. It was difficult coming home every day to a depressed and angry child. She was not used to feeling impotent, and she found it hard to accept that there was no solution to Katie's problem.

"It's not that simple, Jackie," Steve said calmly.

Steve was always calm. It was one of the things that Jackie had always admired about him, but now it was becoming one of the things that annoyed her the most. She wished he shared her agitation and anger and showed more animation and ardor on Katie's behalf.

"Why isn't it simple? Why isn't anyone studying the disease? Why isn't anyone trying to figure out what to do, how to make it go away, how to cure it? Why isn't the government studying this? Why aren't drug companies trying to find a cure? Why isn't it that simple?" Jackie ranted.

"It just doesn't work that way. There are a lot of different diseases. Scientists work on diseases they think are important."

"It's important to me!" Jackie interrupted angrily. "I hope it's important to you too! Sometimes I'm not sure it is."

"It *is* important to me," Steve reassured her. "But it has to be important enough for someone to invest the time and money in the research. This is a relatively rare disease, and it tends to resolve without treatment, so there hasn't been a lot of interest in investing in research."

"Somebody should be working on a cure!" Jackie shot back, frustrated by the fact that Steve was right and by her inability to evoke his passion. "It has been three months already," she continued unhappily, "and her platelet count was down again today."

"So what exactly did Dr. Rafael say?" Steve preferred to talk about medicine.

"Nothing new. Nothing's ever new. Her platelet count is below thirty thousand, and he wants to give her another course of steroids. This happens, like, every other week. Can we keep giving her steroids like this? I thought they were dangerous."

"They can be, but they are necessary," Steve answered.

"Then he gave me the usual lecture about making sure she doesn't hit her head and trying to be patient." Jackie paused. "I've never been very patient. I can't stand not doing anything. I can't stand the idea that there's nothing to do!"

"I know," Steve said affectionately.

"There must be something I can do! I spent my entire professional life telling the world that science and technology can solve every imaginable problem."

"I wish there was something we could do too."

"What about the Human Genome Project?" Jackie abruptly raised a question that had been on her mind for weeks. "I sit through meetings almost every day with some scientist telling me that the Human Genome Project is the greatest thing since the discovery of penicillin, that it will lead to all sorts of miracle drugs, and that it's going to revolutionize medicine. I've probably written business plans for a hundred companies that claim they can find cures for diseases that I've never heard of, diseases I never want to hear of, diseases I'm not convinced even exist! Is any of this going to help Katie, or isn't her disease important enough?"

"There's a lot of excitement about the Genome Project. But it hasn't had much impact on medicine yet."

"Why not, if everyone thinks it is going to be so great?"

"A lot of things just take time."

"We don't have time! We have a sick child!" Jackie snapped.

"I understand." Steve sat beside Jackie and gently put his arm around her.

"I don't want understanding. I want to do something!" Jackie shrugged him away and turned to face him. Her eyes caught his in an intent stare. "Steve, I can't believe there's nothing anyone can do. I just can't believe it. There must be something I can do, anything!"

Steve pulled back, breaking eye contact. He took a deep breath. "Well, maybe—"

"Maybe what?" Jackie pressed hopefully.

"I heard an interesting lecture the other day," Steve began reluctantly, "by a professor from Harvard, Allan Marcus. I worked with him on a project some years ago."

"I've heard of him." Jackie looked up. "He's on the scientific advisory boards for some of the companies I work with. People say he's very smart."

"He is smart," Steve agreed. "Anyway, he gave a lecture about the Human Genome Project and his research on the immune system. He didn't talk about ITP, but he had some ideas that could be relevant. You might want to call him and ask what he thinks."

"I need to do something," Jackie answered with a lift in her voice. "Thank you."

Jackie called Allan the next day and made an appointment to meet with him.

44

The Human Genome Project was the last great scientific endeavor of the twentieth century. The project's goal was to decode all the genetic information of humanity, an endeavor that was frequently compared in scope and significance to the space program that had placed men on the Moon.

The science of genomics emerged in the late 1990s from decades of progress in understanding DNA and the function of the genetic code. Experiments in the 1960s demonstrated that the DNA of each organism comprises a genome containing all the information necessary to create a living organism and direct its functions. It was information written in a language comprised of four letters—A,G,C, and T—strung together in long DNA sequences that comprised words, sentences, and paragraphs.

The first genomes to be studied in the 1960s were those of simple viruses. By the 1970s, with the development of cloning and recombinant DNA technologies, scientists began to study the genomes of more complex organisms, including bacteria, yeast, plants, and animals. Hundreds of genes were cloned and characterized, providing dramatic insights into the essential mechanisms of growth, development, reproduction, immunity, healing, and even death.

Eventually, science turned to the study of the human genome. By doing this, scientists hoped to understand the instructions that enabled a fertilized human egg to develop the form, functions, and faculties of a human being, as well as determinants of health and disease.

The problem was one of scale. The simple viruses that scientists studied contained only a single piece of DNA, comprising only fifty thousand bases and less than twenty genes. The genome of a bacterium was one hundred times larger, comprising several million bases. The human genome is a hundred thousand times larger, comprising more than three billion bases and tens of thousands of genes. If finding one gene in a simple virus's genome was like sorting through a deck of playing cards to find one particular card, finding one gene in the human genome was like sorting through a deck of cards stacked more than a mile high!

In the mid-1980s, another idea emerged. Instead of trying to study the human genome one gene at a time, why not sequence every gene in the human genome in one grand experiment? One scientist joked that trying to find any one gene amidst the enormity of the human genome was like an angler trying to catch one particular fish in a lake using a pole and lure. It would be easier, he suggested, to drain the lake!

Scientists began developing plans to determine the sequence of the entire human genome. Some thought a program of this scope was impossible. Others, like Jim Watson, who had won the Nobel Prize for discovering the double helical structure of DNA, thought it was possible. It would be a massive undertaking, one that would require new technologies and investments of capital, time, and talent on the scale of the *Apollo* Program that had taken men to the Moon.

The Huntington's Disease (HD) Foundation, led by Nancy Wexler, made a critical contribution to the genesis of the human genome project. In the late 1970s, there was no known cause or cure for Huntington's disease, which ran in the Wexler family. Doctors knew only that the disease was genetic. The HD Foundation brought together scientists to consider strategies for finding the gene that caused the disease. They raised money to support their research, and recruited thousands of patients who donated blood samples for the scientists to study. In less than five years, this research would succeed in discovering the gene that caused this disease, thus validating the potential of genomics and the Human Genome Project.

In 1990, Congress authorized funding for the Human Genome Project. The project's goals were to "identify all the genes in human DNA, determine the sequences of the three billion chemical base pairs that make up human

DNA, store this information in databases, improve tools for data analysis, transfer related technologies to the private sector, and address the ethical, legal, and social issues." It would also determine the complete sequences of the genomes of other organisms, including certain bacterium, fruit flies, and mice. Jim Watson agreed to be the project's first director. The project was expected to take thirteen years.

By the fall of 1999, new technologies were in place for high-speed sequencing, and dozens of academic centers and companies around the world were vying to be the first to complete the sequence of the genome. Millions of bases were sequenced every day. Thousands of genes were being discovered. It was just a matter of time until the complete sequence of the three billion bases of the human genome was completed.

The Human Genome Project generated both excitement and hyperbole. Academic leaders declared that the Human Genome Project would revolutionize medicine, a sentiment that was widely repeated by biotechnology executives, public relations firms like Fernald Partners, and Wall Street analysts. Someday, they proposed, people would have their entire genome sequenced at birth and would carry a card with their gene sequence in their wallets. Someday it would be possible to develop customized drugs based on a person's genetic makeup, and it would be possible to identify genes that caused disease and to repair genes within the human body to eliminate the disease risk. Nothing appeared to be beyond the capabilities of genomic technology.

* * *

Allan Marcus was not involved in the race to sequence the genome. Rather, he was interested in applying genomics to understand how the immune system worked. Like many scientists in the age of genomics, he believed that the best way to study something as complex as the immune system was to start by characterizing all the genes that could be involved in its function.

Allan was particularly interested in understanding how an infection turned on the immune system, and how eradicating the infection turned it off. He also hoped to understand why these mechanisms sometimes failed; why the immune system could not eradicate certain infections like HIV or tuberculosis; and why it sometimes attacked normal tissues, causing diseases such as diabetes or arthritis. In listening to Allan's lecture, Steve realized that if ITP were caused by the immune system mistakenly destroying the body's platelets, then Allan's research might provide insights into the mechanism of Katie's disease.

45

Allan's office at Harvard was a large room furnished with an antique mahogany desk and credenza, leather desk chairs, a comfortable couch, and walls filled with books, pictures, pieces of data, and carefully framed awards that were the trophies of a successful academic career. There were two 40-inch LCD computer monitors on his desk. One wall was covered with a floor-to-ceiling whiteboard decorated with sketches, diagrams, and Post-Its. The opposite side of the room had a large window that looked out over his laboratory, where several dozen students, technicians, and postdoctoral fellows worked.

When Jackie arrived, Allan was dressed in an Abercrombie & Fitch sweatshirt, neatly pressed jeans, and tassled loafers. He had recently celebrated his fifty-fifth birthday, and his ambivalence toward ageing was evident in the graying, yet stylishly groomed, stubble on his jaws and chin.

Jackie was now in her forties. Wearing a tailored business suit cut several inches above the knee, no makeup, and her shoulder-length hair layered in its natural light-brown color, Jackie was a lovely woman who still exhibited the engaging energy she had in childhood. Allan took notice immediately.

They chatted amicably for several minutes about their mutual friends in the biotechnology industry before Jackie began discussing the purpose of her visit. She related the history of Katie's condition and her frustration that she had not improved after more than four months. She handed Allan a notebook with pages from Katie's medical record and articles that Steve had provided describing the disease.

"The question," Jackie concluded, "is whether you think the Human Genome Project can help Katie, and whether you know of anyone who might be using genomics to study her disease. We want to do anything, anything that we can to cure her."

Allan quickly skimmed the papers that Jackie had given him, and then leaned back in his chair thoughtfully. "I don't know much about ITP. I never heard of it until I ran into your husband the other day," he said. "Your husband is right—ITP is probably similar to the diseases we're studying in our laboratory, what we call an *autoimmune disease*, where the immune system is attacking the body by mistake. Some of the things we're doing could be relevant."

"What do you mean?" Jackie asked hopefully.

Allan rose from his chair, walked over to the whiteboard, slowly erased some of the scattered diagrams and, in the habitual manner of a professor, began drawing on the board as he spoke. "We try to understand what happens inside an immune cell, what people call a *white blood cell*, when it is confronted by something it is supposed to destroy—for example, bacteria. We know that each white blood cell in the body is preprogrammed to destroy a specific target. Some kill bacteria—others kill viruses, for example. When a cell senses its target, the cell will begin making antibodies against the target and do a variety of other things, like making more and more white blood cells, until the target is destroyed."

While he talked, Allan continued to lazily sketch on the board; a large triangle representing a white blood cell, colored dots representing bacteria and viruses, then more white blood cells surrounding the dots.

"Once the infection is eradicated," Allan said, as he erased the colored dots with his thumb, "the white blood cells that were responsible for the attack are supposed to die." He erased all but the original white blood cell with the palm of his hand. "And the immune response is supposed to stop. That's the simple form of the story."

"I understand so far," Jackie interjected.

"We know there must be a genetic switch in the white blood cell that turns the cell on when it encounters the particular target and another switch that turns it off after the target is destroyed. My laboratory is trying to find these master switches, understand how they work, and maybe understand why they sometimes fail. For example, why isn't the immune system turned on to attack HIV or tuberculosis? Why isn't the immune system turned off when it is causing damage in arthritis or diabetes? In your daughter's case, the immune system should not be attacking her platelets. Why was it turned on? Why isn't it turning off? Does that make sense?"

"I guess. But I'm interested in finding a cure."

"Fair enough," Allan responded, without interrupting the cadence of his thought. "In my laboratory, we use a genomic approach to studying thousands of genes—even the whole genome—to identify all the genes that are involved in the immune process. If we can find the genetic switch that turns the immune system on and off, and if we can understand how this switch works, then we should be able to find drugs that can do the same thing. For example, we want to find a pill that can turn on the immune system to kill the HIV virus, tuberculosis, or cancers." While he was talking, Allan again drew various objects haphazardly on the board; colored circles representing an HIV virus, a tubercle bacillus, a cancer cell being consumed by triangular white blood cells.

"In a disease like your daughter's, where white blood cells are attacking platelets," he said, as he drew a small black circle next to a triangle, representing a platelet being engulfed by the white blood cell, "we want to find a pill that can turn the immune system off." He picked up a red marker and emphatically drew a large red X, separating the black circle from the triangular white blood cell that was consuming it.

Jackie's heart skipped a beat. There it was! The drug that could cure the disease! It was only two red lines in ink on a laboratory wall, but it was hope. Expectation surged through her body. She took a deep breath to keep her voice steady. "Can you do that?" she asked, her eyes transfixed on the red X.

"In principle, yes." Allan walked back behind his desk and sat down. He stared for a moment at his own scribbles on the whiteboard. "I don't know anyone who is working on ITP, but it could be interesting."

"So, what would be the first step?" she asked cautiously.

"Well, you need some way to study the disease. We prefer to study diseases in mice. We don't work much on humans. It's much more difficult. Your husband is the expert in clinical research."

"I'm not terribly fond of mice, myself," Jackie interjected with a forced laugh. "Though I imagine it might be easier to keep a mouse happy than a sick child." Her humor failed.

"If you want to study diseases in humans, you need to collect blood samples and medical information from a lot of people who are affected. You said there were two hundred thousand people in the country who have this disease?"

"Something like that."

"That's a lot."

"And what would you do with the samples?"

"Several things. One is, you can scan the genome to find genes that are common in people who have the disease and rare in people who don't. If you can find a gene that is associated with the disease—"

"Then you'll know how to treat it?" Jackie encouraged him to complete the thought.

"That's certainly the idea," Allan answered haphazardly.

"How many people would you need for such research? Ten? A hundred?" Jackie asked intently.

"Thousands."

"What else would you need?"

"Money. Genomic research is very expensive. Every sample we study costs us several hundred dollars."

Jackie calculated quickly. "So if you need to study several thousand patients, you're talking about a project that could cost a million dollars."

"Probably several million. That's why I like working with mice!" Allan laughed. Then he paused, realizing that Jackie's affect had changed.

"Let me ask you something," Jackie asked, staring directly at Allan's face. "Would you study ITP if there was enough money for the research and enough patients willing to participate?"

"It could be an interesting problem."

"So, if you had two or three million dollars, it could be done?" she pressed.

Jackie's intensity suddenly troubled Allan. "This is an academic laboratory," he cautioned. "We do basic research. We choose projects that are good science."

"I respect that." Jackie tried to avoid sounding impatient. "You said that this problem could be interesting and that you were doing things that could be relevant. If I could raise the money?"

"We're talking about a lot of money," Allan answered dismissively.

"I appreciate that. But I'm trying to understand why no one in the world is studying ITP. Hundreds of thousands of people have the disease. There is all this genomic science, all this technology, all this knowledge—but no one is applying it to ITP. If the problem is simply money—" Jackie sensed that her tone sounded too demanding, and she stopped herself abruptly.

"It's not just money. It has to be good science," Allan cautioned again, feeling somewhat pressured by the direction of the conversation. "You have to understand, I'm not a physician. My laboratory does not get involved in diagnosing or treating people. We do science to understand how the human body functions when it is healthy and what goes wrong in various diseases. We do science," he repeated with emphasis.

Jackie realized that she was being rebuffed and deftly changed the direction of the conversation. "I don't know if you are familiar with what I do," she said, brushing her hand over the top of her head to push the hair off her face and forcing herself to project a more relaxed manner.

"A little." Allan was relieved that the conversation seemed to have taken a less serious turn and was anxious to know more about her.

"I'm a partner at a public relations firm called Fernald Partners. We handle public relations for many high-technology and biotechnology companies. I think we work for most of the biotechnology companies in Boston. I spend my life helping scientists and companies raise money for science, research, and development."

Suddenly, Jackie's forced affability disappeared. She sat forward on the couch. "I don't know whether the research you described is right or not. I *do* know that I can raise any amount of money—one million, two million, ten million dollars, anything it takes—to save my daughter's life."

Allan retreated deeper into his chair, closed his arms over his chest, and looked across the table at the attractive and aggressive woman whom he sensed was about to change his life. "I can't promise anything," he said defensively. "I don't know enough about ITP to know if it is worth studying."

Jackie knew that she needed to proceed more carefully. She gestured with her hands to interrupt him. "I'm not asking you to promise anything. I need to think about the things we talked about. I'll talk to Steve to see what he thinks. Maybe we can meet again soon?"

"I would like that."

After Jackie left, Allan read the articles Jackie had given him about ITP, and he searched the computerized databases of the National Library of Medicine for more information. He became intrigued with the curiosity of a disease that continued to be called *idiopathic* in the age of genomics. By the end of the day, he was convinced that his laboratory might have the tools necessary to uncover the cause of the disease, and he began to formulate a research plan in his mind.

Allan was at a crossroads in both his professional and personal life. He had been at Harvard for twenty years and had published over two hundred scientific papers. He was widely respected in his field and spent much of his time traveling around the world speaking at prestigious universities and conferences.

Lately, however, he was dissatisfied. He was tired of writing grant applications and asking people for money to support his research. Moreover, his laboratory and personal life were in transition. Several of his graduate students had recently completed their theses and were leaving. A post-doctoral fellow, with whom he had had a long affair, had left for a faculty position in California. Several new students and fellows had started working in his lab and were looking for projects. He was searching for something interesting, something dramatic.

Allan was consumed by science. He had been married and divorced twice and had been in many relationships with women who found they could not compete with his work. The only relationships that lasted more than several months were those with coworkers or colleagues, and these were sustained more by proximity and shared professional interests than by passion or intimacy. He felt himself fortunate that there were no children from any of his marriages or relationships to compete with his passion for science.

Maybe working on a disease that remained idiopathic would be interesting. Maybe Jackie could raise the money he needed so he could focus on research. Maybe Jackie could help him. In any case, he was interested in getting to know her better.

46

The Living Genome Foundation was inaugurated a month later over dinner at Jackie's home in Concord. She returned home from her first meeting with Allan, energized by the idea that there was something she could do to find a cure for Katie's disease. Over the ensuing weeks, Jackie met with Allan repeatedly to talk about his work on the immune system, how he might approach research on ITP, what samples he would need, and how much it would cost to do the work. She met with Steve's colleagues at the Massachusetts General Hospital to learn how human studies were performed and to understand the ethical guidelines that governed their work. She spoke with Nancy Wexler, who had successfully galvanized the scientific community to find the cause of Huntington's disease at the dawn of the genomics era, to learn how she had raised money and organized scientists to work on the disease that was her personal concern.

With each conversation, Jackie became more convinced that she could make a difference, more committed to a course of action, and more confident that a cure would be found. Allan became caught up in Jackie's fervor, and like many others before him, was drawn to follow her lead. Gradually, he committed himself to working with her to study ITP.

In early October, Jackie hosted a dinner for Allan as well as several dozen of her friends and colleagues. The guests included William Fernald, Tim Weber, Dr. Rafael, Danny, and Rachel, as well as the founders and executives of several successful biotechnology companies and their spouses. All the guests were familiar with Katie's illness as well as Jackie's frustration with its course.

After cocktails and hors d'oeuvres, Jackie called all her guests together in the living room and introduced the idea that had been germinating for several weeks. She announced she was starting a foundation that would raise money for genomic research aimed at finding a cure for ITP. She described how the HD Foundation had stimulated the scientific community to study Huntington's disease by providing support for its research, and declared that she hoped to do the same for ITP. The Foundation would be the channel through which the promise of the Human Genome Project would be realized for children with any idiopathic disease that had escaped the attention of government and industry.

"How much money do you think you can raise?" Allan asked.

"We are going to start by raising five million dollars," Jackie replied.

Allan looked at her in disbelief.

"That's a lot of money," Rachel interjected, thinking of how hard it was to raise even several thousand dollars to support programs to protect women and children or fight AIDS in Africa.

"It only sounds like a lot of money if you've never seen Jackie in action," William joked. "If you bet 'over/under,' be sure you take 'over' on this one!"

"I'll bet on Jackie anytime," Tim offered his support.

"Count my chips in, then," Allan laughed.

Everyone either added their voices in support or nodded in approbation, except Danny. "Are you sure you want to do this?" He was skeptical.

"I'm sure," Jackie answered nonchalantly.

"You're describing a colossal effort. Have you thought it through? Do you really think it will work?"

"It has to," she replied bluntly. "What other idea do we have?"

There was lively conversation about Jackie's plan as the guests moved toward the dining room for dinner. By the time dessert was served later that evening, Jackie had asked each of the guests to help her form the Foundation. Everyone agreed to make a contribution. Allan and Steve agreed to put together a research plan. William Fernald agreed that Jackie could use Fernald Partners for public relations and marketing, at no cost. Tim Weber offered to introduce Jackie to some of his wealthy clients. Rachel offered to do the legal work for the Foundation pro bono. Others agreed to make cash contributions. The Living Genome Foundation was born.

Jackie immediately began planning a campaign to raise money for the Foundation. For twenty years, she had been cultivating a network that included Boston's elite society; the old-money establishment, executives of traditional industries, New Age entrepreneurs, investors, and the media. She had made her reputation by introducing them to the age of technology at its inception. Those who had followed her lead had become extremely wealthy as the value of technology skyrocketed through the 1990s. Now she was asking for a favor in return. Few declined.

She had directed hundreds of fund-raising campaigns for politicians, universities, charitable foundations, and companies. Jackie knew what to do. She designed brochures describing the Foundation's mission, drafted press releases to announce its launch, and contracted with a local company to construct a Web site. She developed lists of high-net-worth individuals and foundations that might make large donations, identified companies that might consider sponsorship, and acquired mailing lists individuals to solicit through a mass public relations campaign.

Jackie's plan was to make Katie the poster child of the campaign. She arranged for Katie to have a photo shoot with a prestigious Boston photographer, who spent several days taking hundreds of pictures of Katie in different settings and attire. He took formal portraits of Katie in his studio, as well as pictures of posing at a school desk, playing in her bedroom, and sitting on the sculptured ducklings and the swan boats in the public garden.

Katie hated the attention. She resisted efforts to apply makeup, refused to let anyone arrange her clothes or hair, and would not smile or pose for the pictures. Often, she deliberately closed her eyes, distorted her face, stuck out her tongue, or changed position just as the picture was being taken.

The results of the photo shoots were awful. Few of the pictures were usable.

When Jackie studied the pictures closely with the photographer, she also realized that the shape of Katie's face had changed. She had always had her father's delicate features. Now her cheeks were subtly rounder, softer, and redder; a common side effect of steroids. Jackie had never noticed it before.

It took extensive work using digitized images and an airbrush to produce pictures that Jackie thought were suitable for the publicity campaign. The artist thinned Katie's cheeks and eliminated the redness. He digitized frames in which her eyes were open, and superimposed her open eyes onto images in which her eyes were closed. In the process, he made her eyes slightly larger than normal, made the sclera slightly whiter and the pupils blacker, and added a subtle glimmer of light to her irises. He removed the blemishes from her skin and digitally added makeup; a touch of color on her lips, a smooth blush on her cheeks, a sharper outline and colored shadow above her eyes, and more length and thickness to her lashes. When they were done, Katie's likeness was enlarged onto hundreds of posters, inked onto the Foundation's letterhead and envelopes, printed on thousands of brochures, and featured prominently on the Foundation's web site.

Once the plans for the campaign were in place, Jackie contacted a senior writer at the *Boston Globe* and promised him an exclusive story on the Foundation's launch in exchange for prime coverage of the story in the newspaper. She offered the producer of NBC's *Today Show* an exclusive opportunity to prerecord interviews with herself, Katie, and Allan if they would run the story the day the Foundation was launched. She hired freelance writers to write articles for popular magazines about Katie, ITP, the promise of the Human Genome Project, and the Foundation. She contacted the offices of Mayor Menino, Governor Cellucci, and Senators Kennedy and Kerry to obtain their formal endorsements.

In November, the official kickoff of the Living Genome Foundation was held at the Harvard Club. The event attracted print and broadcast media from all over New England, as well as the health and science reporters from several national publications. Everything was calculated for maximal media exposure and impact.

The pressroom at the Harvard Club was lined with giant posters of Katie. Mylar balloons with her likeness floated in the air. Jackie worked behind the scenes making sure the event stayed on schedule, while a popular Boston sports reporter served as the master of ceremonies.

The program began with a member of the United States National Women's Soccer Team, which had won the Women's World Cup the year before, presenting Katie with a soccer ball and a jersey signed by members of the team, and expressing hope that Katie would get better so she could continue playing soccer. Dr. Rafael then gave a brief description of her affliction.

Allan Marcus was introduced next. Speaking from a script Jackie had written, he talked about the promise of the Human Genome Project and how genomic research would help find cures for untreatable diseases. He finished by promising to work personally to find a cure for Katie so that she would be able to play soccer again.

Jackie spoke last, announcing that the Foundation's first grant of one million dollars would be made to Allan Marcus at Harvard for research to find a cure. She stood back and watched as Katie handed Allan a poster-size representation of a check for one million dollars and quietly told Allan and the cameras that she hoped this would help make her better. There was not a dry eye in the room.

Jackie then asked for everyone's help in raising money to find a cure, and ended the proceedings with her thanks. The event lasted exactly fifteen minutes and ended just in time for reporters to compose their segments for the evening news. Nothing was spontaneous. Every melodramatic moment was scripted. Everything went according to plan.

The kickoff event created a groundswell of media attention. The *Boston Globe* ran a feature article on the launch of the Living Genome Foundation on the front page of their *Style* section. Television stations showed footage of Katie receiving the ball and jersey from the United States National Women's Soccer Team and handing the million-dollar check to Allan. The *Today Show* broadcast the prerecorded segment in which Katie Couric interviewed Jackie, Katie, and Allan about the disease and how the Human Genome Project would provide a cure. Katie again handed the poster version of the check to Allan with her well-rehearsed lines of hope. Over the next several weeks, Jackie, Katie, and Allan appeared on several daytime talk shows, Allan was featured in a long interview on *NPR Science Friday,* and there were stories about Katie and the Foundation in popular magazines ranging from *Discovery* to *People.*

The campaign for the Living Genome Foundation told a story that Jackie had written hundreds of times before. In simple words and images, the campaign appealed to the promise of science to provide a solution to suffering and pain. In Jackie's campaign, the double helix melded into medicine and the melodrama of a child's need for healing and hope. ITP became a metaphor for every idiopathic ailment that people feared for themselves, their families, or their friends.

It was a propitious time for this story. It resonated with daily news reports about the race to complete the sequence of the human genome. It turned stories about the arcane science of genomics into a story about hope. Katie became the poster child for the promise of genomics.

Not everything, however, went according to plan. While Katie had been on her best behavior for the kickoff event, she soon reverted to the disruptive behavior that she had exhibited during the photo shoot. She would complain about feeling sick moments before a scheduled appearance, consistently refused to wear stage makeup, deliberately mussed her hair and clothes, and sat sullenly in front of the media or donors when she was supposed to smile and be charming.

Over time, the reporters began to write about Jackie rather than Katie. Jackie was the quintessential human-interest story; a passionate and compassionate mother who would stop at nothing to find a cure for her child. Moreover, she was an attractive woman and an articulate speaker who knew how to command a stage and distill the complex science of genomics into simple sentences and sound bites. As the campaign progressed, Jackie found herself becoming not only the spokesperson for the Foundation but also for the promise of genomics itself.

The launch of the Foundation in the fall of 1999 coincided with a period of phenomenal growth for the technology industry. In the last months of the millennium, the value of technology stocks soared beyond anyone's wildest expectations. Overnight, hundreds of technology and biotechnology companies were worth billions of dollars. Their investors, executives, and even their employees instantly became multimillionaires.

Jackie found it easy to raise money for the Foundation in this expansive economic environment. Many individuals who had made millions of dollars in technology over a period of months were willing to donate a small fraction of their newly minted wealth to a cause that mirrored their own values and ideas.

By Christmas, the Foundation already had pledges for more than eight million dollars, and the goal was raised to fifteen million. A small staff was hired to coordinate activities, make telephone calls, and handle contributions. Although the Foundation desperately needed office space, no one wanted to spend the time or money to find or equip an office. Instead, the Foundation continued to work from Jackie's house, gradually outgrowing the study, a playroom, and the enclosed deck that looked over the hill and down into the woods behind the house.

Finally, the Foundation's activities overtook the dining room. Computers were set up on the large mahogany dining table at the room's center, and the upholstered chairs were replaced by metal folding chairs. Over time, the china, heirlooms, mementos, and art that had decorated the room were supplanted by office supplies, brochures, and posters bearing Katie's likeness.

* * *

Thanksgiving marked six months since Katie's first hospitalization. Dr. Rafael decided it was time to reassess Katie's condition and diagnosis. His studies showed that she had recovered completely from the head injury and seizure she had suffered in May. Her platelet count, however, remained low, and her disease still had no diagnosis other than ITP.

Ominously, there was no sign that her disease was remitting. Her platelet count frequently dropped below ten thousand, requiring treatment with steroids. More ominous, in October she was hospitalized overnight after suffering a transfusion reaction against platelets administered to stop a nosebleed. Tests performed at that time showed that she had developed an allergic hypersensitivity to platelet transfusions, which would make such treatments more dangerous and less effective over time.

Katie's behavior was also becoming alarming. She was increasingly moody and disruptive, both at home and at school. At the end of the fall term, she received gentleman's C's in all her classes, though she was often inattentive in class, rarely turned in any homework, and did poorly on her tests.

At school, Katie no longer associated with her soccer teammates, but found a new group of friends. In early November, Beatrice found a package of cigarettes in Katie's knapsack. Several weeks later, she found an unopened six-pack of beer in the woods behind the house. Just before Christmas, one of Katie's new friends was caught shoplifting at a local mall. Jackie had to scramble to keep Katie's name out of the police report and the local news.

Katie began seeing a child psychologist at Children's Hospital, who helped her talk about her anger and anxiety. She readily accepted the opportunity to talk to the therapist but refused to participate in a support group with other children her age who had chronic diseases, such as diabetes or asthma. Katie argued angrily that she was not like these other children and that she was going to get better. She was tired of being treated as if she were sick.

47

Just after New Year's, the Foundation completed the first grants to researchers around the country who had agreed to join a consortium to study ITP. The largest grant was to Allan Marcus's laboratory at Harvard for genomic studies. Other grants were awarded to scientists at Johns Hopkins, St. Jude's Hospital, Texas Children's Hospital, and Stanford. A grant was also made to Steve's clinical research center at Massachusetts General Hospital, which would serve as the coordinating center for recruiting patients and collecting the samples and medical records required for the research.

The first step in any research involving human subjects is to submit the research plan to a hospital ethics committee, or Institutional Review Board, for approval. The most important question raised by the ethics panel was how the investigators planned to protect the privacy of individuals who donated genetic samples or personal clinical information to the study. The panel was concerned that the study participants could suffer from discrimination if information about their genetic makeup inadvertently became available to insurance providers or potential employers.

To avoid such problems, the ethics panel insisted that the samples and medical information had to be anonymized, meaning that the patient's name and all identifying information had to be removed from any blood samples or medical records before they could be used for research. The scientists who were conducting the study would receive only bar-coded samples and data, and would never know the identity of the individual whose materials they were studying.

Steve's clinical research center established a central repository for the samples, where they were collected, anonymized, and then distributed to research laboratories for their studies. The only way anyone could determine who had contributed any particular sample was by accessing a secure computer database maintained in Steve's laboratory.

* * *

In June 2000, scientists reported that the sequence of the human genome had been completed, several years ahead of schedule. President Clinton presided over a press conference at the White House to announce this giant step for humankind: "Nearly two centuries ago, in this room, on this floor, Thomas

Jefferson and a trusted aide spread out a magnificent map—a map Jefferson had long prayed he would get to see in his lifetime. The aide was Meriwether Lewis, and the map was the product of his courageous expedition across the American frontier, all the way to the Pacific. It was a map that defined the contours and forever expanded the frontiers of our continent and our imagination."

"Today, the world is joining us here in the East Room to behold a map of even greater significance. We are here to celebrate the completion of the first survey of the entire human genome."

"Today, we are learning the language in which God created life. We are gaining ever more awe for the complexity, the beauty, the wonder of God's most divine and sacred gift. With this profound new knowledge, humankind is on the verge of gaining immense new power to heal. Genome science will have a real impact on all our lives—and even more, on the lives of our children."

Jackie took advantage of the avalanche of news articles about the completion of the Human Genome Project to redouble the Foundation's fund-raising efforts. The day after the announcement at the White House, she arranged a photo-op for Katie with President Clinton and the scientists who had completed the human genome sequence. Within days, digitally enhanced pictures of Katie standing with the President were added to the Foundation's public relations materials.

Public interest in the completion of the human genome sequence helped the Foundation surpass its fund-raising goal by midsummer. With this milestone achieved, Jackie delegated the fund-raising responsibility to the Foundation's small staff and began spending more of her time tracking the Foundation's research.

Jackie began to attend the weekly research meetings in Allan Marcus's laboratory. She sat in the back of the room and listened as Allan's students, fellows, and technicians described the experiments they had performed the previous week and those they were preparing to perform. While Jackie did not understand all the science, she felt better knowing that the work was proceeding.

For many years, it had been known that the blood of patients with ITP contained antibodies that could destroy platelets. The question that had never been answered was, why? To answer this question, Allan's laboratory set out to find the genes that were responsible for the disease.

Early in the course of the Human Genome Project, it was observed that each person's genome is a mosaic made of hundreds of thousands of DNA segments, each one of which is shared with many other people in the population. Just as the characteristic features of a mosaic are created by incorporating tiles with different characteristics, for example, crafting the color of the eyes or contours of the face using tiles with different colors or shapes, scientists discovered that an individual's characteristics are determined by the assortment of gene segments that comprise their individual genome.

They also discovered that each of these segments had distinguishing markers, much like a barcode impressed on the back of a tile. Just as the pattern of a mosaic might be described by listing the barcodes of every tile and its position, so too the tools of genomics made it possible to scan all of the markers in an individual's genome, and list the hundreds of thousands of different segments that comprise the mosaic of that individual. In doing so, it became possible to identify segments of the genome that contributed to different features of an individual; segments that were involved in growth and development, segments that determined the color of the eyes, skin, or hair, segments that were associated with stature and strength, and even segments that influenced behavior. Similarly, genomics could identify segments associated with disease. Like a tile in a mosaic that might be subtly misshapen, contain an imperceptible defect in workmanship that made it fragile under stress, or have been glazed at the wrong temperature that distorted its color, segments of DNA might harbor elemental flaws, or mutations, that disrupted the picture of health.

The genomic approach to studying disease was to catalogue all the gene segments present in individuals with that disease, and to compare this with the catalogue of gene segments present in unaffected people. If one particular segment was found more often in those with the disease, it suggested there was something within that segment that might be responsible for disrupting the patient's health.

In July, Allan's laboratory began scanning thousands of DNA segments from people with ITP and from a matched set of individuals who did not have the disease. Millions of segments were scanned every day. Within a month, one segment caught the researchers' attention; a segment that was present in a large fraction of ITP patients, but few of the unaffected individuals. Allan thought this might represent the flawed segment that was contributing to ITP.

The next step was to examine the segment in detail to identify the flaw, the imperfection in the sequence of the genome that might disrupt the normal mosaic. With the Human Genome Project completed and the sequence of the entire human genome known, this was done using powerful computer programs to analyze hundreds of thousands of gene sequences looking for subtle differences in their composition.

Allan's research quickly focused on a specific gene that was present within the segment that seemed to be associated with the disease. The gene was called platB.

The platB gene was known to code for a protein found on the outer surface of platelets. Allan hypothesized that patients with ITP might have a mutation in the platB gene that caused abnormal activation of the immune system. He assigned a graduate student in the laboratory to determine the sequence of the platB gene from a number of patients with ITP and an equal number of individuals without the disease, looking for differences in the sequence that could cause the disease.

Comparing the genome sequences of dozens of individuals would inevitably reveal many individual variations. Most of the variations that Allan's student found were rare, occurring in only one or two isolated individuals. Others were found equally in affected and unaffected individuals, suggesting that they were simply innocuous, normal variations. One variation, however, stood out; a specific change in the base sequence of the platB gene that was present in forty-five of the first fifty patients with ITP, but only one of fifty unaffected individuals.

When rolling dice, the same number can appear several times in succession by random chance. When one number appears consistently, however, it suggests the dice are loaded. So too, when a specific sequence is consistently found in patients with a disease, but not in normal individuals, it suggests that this is not occurring by chance. Rather, it is evidence that such a sequence may be involved in causing the disease. This is what Allan had hoped to find.

Allan then began to study the mutation in more detail, using computer programs that enabled him to visualize the shape and structure of the normal and mutant gene product. Looking at the proteins that were coded by the two genes, he saw immediately that the mutation changed the structure of the protein in a way that might allow it to be attacked by antibodies circulating in the blood. Allan sensed he was close to understanding the cause of the disease.

He then turned to another computer program that compared the structure of the normal and mutant platB proteins with the structures of hundreds of thousands of other genes from other species, including infectious bacteria and viruses. Surprisingly, he found that the structure of the mutant platB protein looked tantalizingly similar to a protein that was part of a common cold virus. The similarity was subtle; a short piece of the mutant platB protein folded into a shape that resembled a short piece of an otherwise unrelated protein from the cold virus. Nevertheless, Allan thought that the two shapes might be similar enough to allow an antibody, which attacked the virus, to accidentally attack the similarly shaped, mutant platB protein as well. Allan had a hypothesis that could explain the cause of ITP.

"The hypothesis is," Allan began, describing the work to Jackie and Steve, "that when a child who has the mutant form of platB is infected with the cold virus, some of the antibodies the body makes against the virus coincidentally attach to the mutant protein on their platelets—it's like a case of mistaken identity. We know that if antibodies bind to platelets, they will be destroyed. So that would explain why the platelet count drops. It may also explain why the body keeps making antibodies."

"Normally, once the immune system successfully eradicates an infection, the body stops making antibodies. The problem here is that if the immune system mistakes the mutant platB protein for persistence of the cold virus, it will continue to make antibodies as if it were still responding to an infection. It's a vicious cycle. As the body makes more platelets with the mutant protein, it keeps activating the immune system to make more of the antibodies that are destroying these platelets. Anyway, that's the hypothesis."

"Can you test it?" Steve asked.

"I think so. We can genetically engineer mice so they have the same platB mutation we see in patients, and then we can infect the mice with the cold virus to see if they get ITP from antibodies against the virus."

"That's very clever," Steve mused.

"Does it help us find a cure?" Jackie asked.

"It could," Allan responded. "If the experiment works, and we see a disease like ITP in the mouse, then we can do experiments with different drugs to see if they will treat the disease—perhaps we can even design some experimental drugs to see what happens."

"That's great!" Jackie exclaimed.

"We're not there yet," Allan cautioned, "but I'm optimistic."

Allan's laboratory immediately began the experiment to test his hypothesis. They created two genetically engineered strains of mice; one that had the normal human platB gene inserted into its genome, and one that had the mutant human platB gene. The plan was to infect both strains of mice with the cold virus to see whether the immune response against the virus would also result in platelet destruction. Allan expected that the immune response in mice with the normal human platB gene would eradicate the infection, and the mice would recover without complications. In contrast, he predicted that when mice with the mutant platB gene were infected with the virus, the antibodies that attacked the virus would also react with the protein on the platelets and destroy them. If the experiment worked, the mice would have ITP.

A postdoctoral fellow began constructing two sets of genetically engineered mice. The first was made by injecting the normal human platB gene into mouse embryos so that the human platB gene was incorporated into the mouse genome in place of the normal mouse platB gene. The second set was made in the same way, using the mutant form of the human platB gene.

Jackie was restless with anticipation as the mouse embryos were harvested, injected with the recombinant genes, and surgically implanted into the uteruses of pregnant mice. She waited expectantly as the surrogate mothers carried their genetically engineered offspring through the twenty-one-day gestation and gave birth. Soon, there were dozens of genetically engineered mice in the laboratory.

As the research progressed, Jackie spent hundreds of hours with Allan in his office, listening to him explain the work being done and asking endless questions. She particularly enjoyed sitting with Allan while he worked at his computer analyzing the gene sequence data. Watching the three billion bases of the human genome scroll before her eyes was like watching stars through the window of a starship moving at warp speed. She almost felt like she was on the deck of the *Starship Enterprise* as it explored distant galaxies or at the controls of *Apollo* as it headed toward a landing on the Moon. She recalled lying in bed as a child, staring up toward heaven, wondering what it was like, wondering whether her mother was there and if a spaceship could bring her back. Now she dreamed about Katie. Somewhere in this magisterium, Jackie believed there was a solution. Somehow, the power that could send men to the Moon and rockets into heaven could provide a cure.

Sometimes, she felt an overwhelming sense of fear, the premonition of an explosion, and the encroaching darkness. Sometimes, she started to feel the panic that had overwhelmed her when she heard about the explosions of *Apollo 13* and *Challenger*. Sometimes, she would see Christa McAuliffe waving good-bye as she walked toward the launch pad.

273

When the terrible fears began overwhelming her, Jackie tried to concentrate on the end of the story; taking control of the spaceship to fly safely past the boulders, huddling in the cold and darkness of the lunar module as long as it took to survive, and finally riding three parachutes out from beneath the clouds and emerging alive.

When the genetically engineered mice were six weeks old, the experiment began. Two sets of mice were infected with the cold virus. In the genetically engineered mice with the normal platB gene, the viral infection was short-lived and the animals were healthy again several days later. In the genetically engineered mice with the mutant platB gene, the platelet counts began to drop several days after the infection. Within a week, several of the animals died from bleeding. The animals had ITP! All that remained was to find the cure.

48

The first months of 2000 were a time of holiday-like exuberance for technology as the stock market hit unprecedented new highs after a decade of continuous growth. There was a palpable sense that society was fundamentally changed. Technology was creating new communities in cyberspace and transforming commerce and communications. The power, potential, and promise of the Internet, computers, wireless communications, and biotechnology seemed limitless. Many predicted that there were years of extraordinary expansion still to come.

Some analysts, however, began to express concern that the exuberance was irrational and that that the unparalleled growth of technologies over the past decade could not continue. Some concluded that the rise had been too fast, and that there needed to be a correction. Others thought that the explosive growth was a speculative bubble, and that the bubble would inevitably burst.

Over the previous twenty years, Tim Weber had made billions of dollars for investors by investing aggressively in technology. With the abrupt surge in technology stocks in the spring of 2000, he was one of the first to conclude that the value of technology stocks could not be sustained, and he began to systematically divest his funds of technologies. Other investors followed his retreat.

By early summer, the value of technologies began to drop as precipitously as it had risen. The NASDAQ lost more than half its value. The extraordinary economic expansion, which had begun in 1992, suddenly ended. The economy sank into a recession.

Jackie and her teams at Fernald Partners struggled to fight the loss of faith in technology, but public relations could do little to stem the retreating tide. As the markets collapsed, companies that Jackie had represented for years scaled back their operations and their expectations. Many declared bankruptcy in desperate attempts to stop the bleeding. Others simply disappeared and died.

Work became depressing. Reporters no longer asked Jackie to comment on the future of the Internet or the potential of biotechnology. Instead, she was asked why her clients had failed to meet their earnings projections, why their expansive predictions of market growth had been wrong, and whether her clients were guilty of fraud. She was named as a defendant in several lawsuits by angry investors, who accused her of deliberately misleading them into making investments that had become worthless.

Boston Magazine ran a long feature story about how public relations firms like Fernald Partners had purposely hyped the promise of technology, and how the public had been misled into buying inflated stock in companies that had never made a profit. The article included a picture of Jackie speaking at an investment conference on behalf of a client who had subsequently declared bankruptcy. The picture was digitally enhanced with exaggerated contrast and artificial colors that made the flowers on her blouse look like flames, her eyes seem dark, and her lips unseemly red.

"They made me look like the devil!" Jackie complained when Danny and Rachel were visiting over Labor Day weekend. "Even I wouldn't buy anything from someone who looks like that."

"I'm not sure Steve would have married you if he knew you *could* look like that!" Rachel joked.

"It's certainly a picture I never saw while we were dating," Steve replied with a laugh.

Jackie, however, was not amused. "I can't believe people are giving up on technology. Computing power is still doubling every eighteen months. Genomics has only begun to revolutionize the way we discover drugs and practice medicine. There are markets all over the world that we are just beginning to reach."

"We love you, Jackie—even if you can be a devil sometimes!" Danny quipped, uninterested in a worn topic of conversation and trying to keep the talk light.

"You don't believe me?" Jackie challenged him.

"I believe you," Danny responded with resignation. "I'm sure you're right. I'm sure there are still great things to be done—and I certainly don't think you're the devil. You know I just don't believe in it the way you do."

Jackie bristled, as she always did, when he expressed his skepticism about technology. "What don't you believe?"

Danny had never shared Jackie's categorical enthusiasm for technology, though over the years he had come to appreciate its power. He recognized the fallacies in the early predictions of the *Limits to Growth,* which had drastically underestimated the ability of emerging technologies to provide essential resources, produce energy, and improve agricultural yields. He had witnessed how the dissemination of information had empowered subjugated peoples and encouraged social change and liberalization. But he had also seen the unintended costs and consequences of technology.

No society had ever embraced the idea of technology more completely than the Soviet Union, which had made scientific socialism and technocracy a unifying principle of national, social, economic, and human organization. In the end, however, the idea had failed. Rather than creating a new, sophisticated, and efficient social order, scientific socialism and communism had degenerated into autocracy, repression, and stagnation. Communism had become a new idolatry. Social progress, freedom, tradition, and religion had been stifled. Soviet industry and agriculture had collapsed. Chernobyl, the Aral Sea, and stockyards of rusting nuclear weapons were environmental disasters of unprecedented scale and scope. Danny had spent years working to rectify the social, human, and environmental nightmare that the Soviet Union had left in its wake.

Now, Danny was concerned about new challenges arising from the dissemination of technology. He was troubled by the spread of nuclear weapons to cultures without a tradition of restraint, the effects of global warming on agriculture and social stability, and the impact of expanding travel on epidemic disease. He was worried that the proliferation of shared databases compromised privacy, and that the Internet was being used as an instrument to promote demagoguery and hate.

"I just don't believe everything about technology is good," he repeated, drawn into the debate against his will. "You can't just extend the Internet into Africa and expect people to instantly become consumers. You can't just plant genetically engineered seeds and magically eliminate hunger. You can't just pass out drugs and cure AIDS."

"But why not?"

"Because it isn't just about technology. It is also about societies and their cultures. Not everyone wants your technologies." Danny sounded irritated.

"But why not?" Jackie persisted.

"Not everyone in the world shares your idea that technology is good."

"So you have to teach them that it is. That's what you and Rachel did in Kenya, isn't it?"

"We were just there to help people," Rachel disagreed.

"I just want to help people too," Jackie answered.

"But that's not the same," Danny interjected. "People have different ideas about what's important, what's right, what's wrong—about the value of things. You can't just march in and change everything."

"But what if they have no idea how to feed themselves? What if they have no idea how to treat disease? Do you just let people suffer and die?" Jackie's voice had a pleading tone.

"It's complicated." Rachel sounded resigned. "When we were in Africa, probably the most important thing we did was simply to plant trees and help people carry water from the wells to water them. I'm not sure that all the time we spent teaching math and science and social studies helped fix much of what was wrong. Sometimes there are limits to what you can do."

"I can't believe that," Jackie insisted.

"It doesn't matter whether you want to believe it or not," Danny interceded. "This isn't a high school debate, where you win points by arguing some extreme position and getting someone else to concede. There is reality, and the reality is that there are limits."

"I see!" Jackie threw her hands up in the air in frustration. "This is where you tell me I'm still the naïve little Jackie Cone you knew in elementary school who thought there would be space stations and colonies on the Moon and tourists on Mars and all the problems on Earth could be solved by blasting them into the Sun—that I should have learned my lesson already, because it was only true in fiction and didn't turn out to be reality, right?"

"But it didn't turn out that way, Jackie," Danny answered carelessly.

"What?" Jackie looked at him angrily.

277

"There aren't any space stations or people on Mars. I'm not sure there ever will be."

"Go to hell!" Jackie exploded. "I'm tired of all this pessimism. Don't tell me to give up!"

Danny and Rachel were stunned by her sudden rage. Steve had seen it before.

"No one is telling you to give up." Rachel tried to be reasonable.

"That's all I hear every day," Jackie continued angrily. "Everyone talks about giving up, about all our clients that are bleeding and dying, about everything I've worked for being bankrupt. Everyone is telling me now that I've done something wrong or that I don't know what I'm doing." Jackie stood up from the table and turned toward the wall so the others could not see how close she was to tears.

Steve came up behind her and put his hands on her shoulders. "No one is talking about Katie, here," he said gently.

"I know," Jackie sighed miserably. "But it's all mixed up."

"But they're not talking about Katie," Steve repeated carefully.

"They might as well be. It's all the same."

"No, it's not the same," Steve tried to sooth her.

Rachel overheard their conversation and realized her mistake. "I didn't mean it that way, Jackie. I'm sorry."

"I heard you!" Jackie turned on her irritably. "Maybe things can't be fixed—maybe it's all a fiction—maybe it's all a fraud—maybe my ideas are bankrupt—maybe I'm lying to myself and everyone else—maybe I'm stupid— maybe there isn't anything anyone can do—"

"I didn't say that," Rachel protested.

"I can't let her die."

"Jackie, calm down. This is not about Katie," Steve tried again.

"I'm tired of everyone telling me that I'm wrong all the time!" she continued ranting.

"Jackie, we understand the choice you're making." Rachel tried to be reassuring, but Jackie was not listening.

"I can't believe it—I can't believe there's nothing we can do. There must be some way to fix all of this!" Jackie burst into hysterical tears. Steve tried to put his arms around her, but she broke away and ran up the stairs to their bedroom. Rachel started to follow, but Steve gestured to let her go.

"Is she okay?" Rachel asked, bewildered by Jackie's outburst.

"She's fragile. It's hard to know what will set her off sometimes."

"Is Katie okay? Did anything happen recently?"

"Nothing happened. That's the problem. It's been more than a year. We hoped she would be better by now."

"Is she getting better?"

"No." He shook his head. "Not yet."

"But the doctors thought the disease would probably resolve within a year, right?" Danny asked.

"That's what we hoped."

"So what's her prognosis now?" Rachel asked.

"No one knows. We hoped she had the childhood form of the disease, which usually resolves by itself. But there is also an adult form that can become chronic, sometimes life threatening. We really don't know what she has anymore." Steve stopped to compose himself.

"What do you think?" Rachel asked.

"I think it's just going to take longer than we thought. Jackie's worried."

"Of course she is," Rachel commented, thinking about how she would feel if it were her child.

"Is there any treatment?" Danny asked.

"We've tried everything we can think of. We've had her on some experimental drug that we hoped would increase her platelet count."

"It didn't help?" Rachel asked.

"No."

"And all the work Jackie is putting into the Foundation?" Rachel asked.

"You know Jackie," Steve continued. "She's totally invested in the idea that there will be a cure, that she is going to be able to fix everything. Allan has her all worked up about his research and some of the things they've found. He does have some interesting results—"

"Will he find a cure?" Rachel asked hopefully.

"I don't know." There was no optimism in his voice.

49

Katie entered the sixth grade in September 2000. It had been sixteen months since her diagnosis, and her disease showed no sign of remission. Her platelet counts were lower than ever, and the transfusions of platelets she needed to prevent bleeding were becoming less effective and more likely to cause severe reactions.

Dr. Rafael began treating Katie with higher doses of steroids in an effort to reduce the need for platelet transfusions. With the higher doses of steroids, her appearance became more bloated and her growth began to slow.

Jackie continued taking Katie to specialists around the country, even though she knew more about ITP than the experts they visited. Some doctors proposed treating Katie with stronger immunosuppressive drugs that could have severe side effects, including infection, organ damage, and even cancer. Others suggested surgically removing Katie's spleen, a procedure that carried a lifelong risk of deadly infection. One suggested a bone marrow transplant to replace her dysfunctional immune system with new marrow, possibly from one of the twins.

Steve said no to every new intervention that was suggested. Jackie found it maddening, even though she trusted Steve's medical judgment.

Katie was also suffering emotionally. The confident child whose life had revolved around soccer became quiet and reclusive. She was embarrassed by her bloated appearance and alternated between steroid-induced eating binges and near-starvation to try to control it.

Beatrice was afraid to let Katie out of her sight. She didn't trust anyone other than the twins to play with her, and they were drilled to avoid any activities that could injure Katie and to report when Katie tried to do things that were forbidden. Katie, in turn, tried to avoid her siblings, refusing to walk with them to and from school and spending most of her time at home alone in her room.

Jackie began spending more and more time with Allan in his laboratory. She called him several times each day for updates on critical experiments and went to his office directly after work each evening. She had dinner almost every night with members of the research team, talking about their progress and their personal lives and, not incidentally, keeping them focused on finding a cure for Katie.

As Jackie became increasingly oblivious to everything except the search for a cure, her family tried to be accommodating. Beatrice kept the house running, making sure meals were served and that the children were sent off to school every day. Elaine took the children shopping when they needed clothes, toys, or supplies for school. Steve took the family to church on Sunday.

Steve and Jackie rarely talked to each other. There was not enough time. Jackie generally came home from the laboratory just in time to read stories to the children, put them to bed, and fall asleep herself. When she did spend an evening with the family, the three children competed for her attention. There was no time to be intimate, no time to talk about their relationship, no time to work through the growing tension or the direction of Katie's care.

Steve believed Katie would recover. He talked about "tincture of time" as if it were a medicine. He tried to convince Jackie to have faith in the restorative power of the human body and the resilience of children. He encouraged her to find comfort in prayer. Every effort that he made to calm Jackie's fears seemed to push her further away.

As a physician, Steve knew how to help families deal with the anguish of illness. He knew how to keep his composure when telling people that they were dying or that the death of a child, parent, spouse, partner, or sibling was inevitable. He could talk about the most horrible and tragic events in medicine with the same regular cadence and measured, rhythmic pattern of speech that he used to inquire about their hobbies and their health. Most patients found his manner reassuring. But Jackie did not want Steve to be reassuring. She wanted him to share her ardor and her anger. She wanted him to agree that the world was unfair. The more he tried to calm her, the more she tried to anger him. The more he tried to pacify her, the more she tried to upset him. Jackie accused Steve of being callous and condescending. She began picking fights with him about little things; his clothes, his habits, and his daily routines, hoping to evoke a passion in him that complemented her own highly emotional state. Jackie was an expert at using language to evoke responses. When she wanted to hurt Steve with her words, she succeeded.

Steve was slow to anger, but eventually he started fighting back. Jackie was almost relieved when he did. They began having terrible arguments, goading each other with hurtful jibes. They accused each other of being uncaring, insensitive, and unwilling to compromise or consider the other's views in choosing what was best for Katie.

Jackie recognized that her behavior was often irrational and hurtful. Nevertheless, she considered Steve's studied rationality in the face of Katie's illness equally perverse.

She found it easier to talk to Allan, who spent almost every night working in his office and welcomed her company. Jackie spent hours sitting cross-legged on the couch working on her laptop while Allan worked at his desk. She listened as he discussed the ongoing research with his students, technicians, fellows, and colleagues, and as he reflected on his personal and professional ambitions, competitions with his colleagues, and intimate details about the women he dated.

Jackie complained to Allan about Steve's insensitivity and intransigence as well as the terrible arguments that were crushing their relationship. She talked about how she missed his emotional support and intimacy and discussed her all-consuming fear that Katie would hit her head, bleed, or die from the disease before a cure could be found.

The hours Jackie and Allan spent together buoyed each other's confidence. Allan made Jackie believe that there was a cure. Jackie made Allan feel important and appealing.

Jackie also knew Allan wanted to sleep with her. It was apparent in the way he watched her when she was in the room, his compliments about her appearance and her clothes, and the frequency of his banter about sexual topics. While she did nothing to encourage Allan, she also did nothing to discourage him. She knew that his interest in her helped keep him focused on doing the work she wanted done. That was the only thing that mattered.

50

At the beginning of October, Allan's laboratory turned its attention to an experiment designed to cure ITP in the genetically engineered mice. Their first experiments had demonstrated that they could induce ITP in the mice having the mutant platB protein by infecting them with the cold virus. Allan hypothesized that, if the immune response against the mutant platB protein could cause the disease, then a drug that turned off the platB gene should provide a cure.

Allan designed such a drug. It was a small piece of DNA termed *antisense*, fashioned so that it would bind to RNA from the human platB gene in the mouse and interfere with its function. Allan expected that when mice with ITP were given the drug, production of the human platB protein would be turned off, and the mice would begin to produce platelets without this protein. If there were no platB on the platelets, antibodies would no longer attach to the platelets, and the platelets would not be destroyed. More importantly, if production of the platB protein could be turned off, even for a short time, there would be nothing stimulating the immune system to make more antibodies, and the immune response against platB should turn off naturally. The disease would be cured.

The experiment involved breeding large numbers of the genetically engineered mice with the mutant platB gene, and then infecting them with the cold virus to induce ITP, as they had done before. Half the animals would then be treated with the antisense drug. Half would be treated with an inactive molecule as a control.

It took several months for the antisense drug to be synthesized and for hundreds of mice with the mutant platB gene to be bred for the experiment. Jackie lived in a constant state of expectation, unable to concentrate on anything except the experiment that would provide a cure for Katie's disease.

* * *

One morning in early December, Jackie received a telephone call from the principal of Katie's elementary school.

"I'm sorry to bother you at work," the principal began, "but Katie isn't at school today, and it is school policy to call parents whenever their child is absent unless, of course, we have a note from you in advance."

"Katie should be there," Jackie answered casually, continuing to sort through papers on her desk.

"Her teacher reported her absent. I know Katie usually brings a note when she is going to be absent, so I hope everything is okay."

"There's nothing new." Jackie was not paying much attention.

"I wanted to talk to you anyway, Mrs. Brennan," he continued. "We all feel bad about Katie's illness and the fact that she is missing so much school."

"Excuse me?' Jackie looked up suddenly from her work.

"With all of her absences the last couple of weeks, her teacher is worried about her work. She really needs to make some effort to catch up on the classes she is missing and try to do some of the homework. Her teacher would be happy to spend some extra time with Katie—"

"I don't understand." Jackie turned her full attention to the telephone call. "Katie went to school this morning. I took Katie out of school one afternoon last week for a doctor's appointment. Other than that, she hasn't missed a day of school in weeks."

"I'm sorry, Mrs. Brennan." The principal sounded flustered. "The report I have from her teacher shows that she was absent two days last week, in addition to the afternoon you picked her up. She missed two days the week before and three days the week before that."

"There must be some mistake." Jackie reached for her Palm Pilot and looked at her calendar. "Katie was in school every day last week. I don't think she was absent at all the week before." She paged through her calendar. "She shouldn't have missed any days the previous week."

"Let me look in her file. I'll put you on hold for a minute." The phone went silent, while the principal retrieved Katie's files from his secretary. "Okay, I have her file now. There are notes here saying that Katie is going to be absent because her platelet counts are low. Here is one from last Wednesday saying that she would be out Thursday and Friday. Here is one from Tuesday the week before saying she would miss the rest of the week."

"I didn't write those letters."

"They are in our file."

"Katie's not there!" The realization suddenly exploded in Jackie's mind. "Where is she?"

"She brought the letters to the office—" the principal continued, still focused on his records. Then he stopped, suddenly realizing that none of the letters in the file were signed. "We assumed that if Katie brought the letters—"

"I don't care about the damn letters," Jackie exploded. "Where's Katie?"

"I guess no one thought to question the letters, because we all know about her illness."

"Where's Katie?" Jackie demanded again.

"I don't know. I can go talk to her teacher."

Jackie was no longer listening. Katie was not at school. She was missing. "I'll get back to you," Jackie concluded brusquely, and hung up the phone.

She immediately called Beatrice to confirm that Katie had left for school that morning, called Steve at work to tell him what had happened, and started for home. It was not until she had driven halfway home that she became calm enough to think. If Katie had been skipping school for weeks, she was probably hiding somewhere and was not in danger. She would probably return at the end of the day, as if she had been in school, thinking no one knew about her deception.

The rationalization was not reassuring. What if she did not come back? Where was she? What was going on? Jackie's mind raced through dozens of horrible scenarios.

Beatrice was waiting for Jackie when she arrived at the house thirty minutes later. Together, they tried to reconstruct Katie's activities. Katie had packed her lunch and her knapsack and started for school that morning, ahead of the twins, as she did every day. Somehow, she had never arrived at school.

Beatrice had an idea how to find Katie. It was Beatrice's habit to keep the dog in the house until the kids had left for school, and then put her out behind the house. Generally, the dog would stay out for twenty to thirty minutes, and then stand by the patio doors waiting to be let back in. For the past several weeks, she had noticed that when she put the dog out in the morning, it was running off into the woods and would return with Katie when she walked back from school at the end of the day. The dog often roamed freely in the woods behind the house, so her extended absences had not seemed significant, until now. Wherever the dog was during the day, Beatrice suggested, that was where they would find Katie.

Jackie went out on the back porch and shouted into the woods for the dog. Moments later, the big golden retriever came bounding up the hill and onto the porch, her tail wagging energetically at the unexpected attention.

"Good dog. Good dog." Jackie petted the dog nervously.

"Where's Katie?" Jackie commanded. The dog looked at her quizzically and sat down.

"Where's Katie? Go get her! Go get Katie!"

Suddenly, the dog recognized the game and raced back toward the woods. Jackie and Beatrice followed.

"Go get her! Go get Katie!" Jackie prompted her anxiously every time the dog stopped to look back.

They followed the dog several hundred yards down the hill into the woods and found Katie. She was playing happily under a crude lean-to constructed from downed branches, rope, and leaves. Her hideout was equipped with a battery-powered DVD player and a collection of Disney DVDs, books, and electronic games. She also had a cooler with sodas, peanut butter–and-jelly sandwiches, potato chips, candy, cookies, and treats for the dog.

Jackie was relieved that Katie was safe, but also furious. She wanted to scream at Katie, but for once in her life, she could not think of anything to say. Instead, she roughly grabbed Katie's wrist and dragged her back toward the house. "You are in big trouble, young lady!"

Steve arrived home several minutes later as Katie, Jackie, and Beatrice were walking back toward the house. Beatrice started putting Katie's things away while Steve and Jackie sat her down in the kitchen to talk.

"I don't care what you're going to tell me," Katie announced defiantly as soon as they were alone. "I'm not going to school anymore."

"You're not going to school?" Jackie echoed in disbelief.

"It's a waste of time. I'm going to die before I graduate. So what's the point? I can't do anything. I can't play soccer. My old friends won't talk to me anymore. You don't like my new friends." Steve and Jackie looked at each other in disbelief. "I guess I should have told you."

"You guess you should have told us?" Jackie was incredulous at Katie's audacity.

"I guess I'm sorry," Katie continued sheepishly. "I probably should not have written all those letters, but it was the only way I could think of not going to school without getting in trouble. I knew if I told you, you would make me go to school. I thought that if I wrote an absence note, the principal wouldn't call you or anything, and you never had to find out."

"So you thought it was better to lie?"

"I didn't fake your signatures or anything. I just said I wasn't going to be in school."

Steve and Jackie sat in stunned silence as Katie told them the details of her plan; how she had copied Steve and Jackie's letterhead on her computer, written letters saying she would be absent, and brought them to the principal's office. Everyone in the office had told her how sorry they were that she was sick, and no one had bothered to notice that the letters were not signed. She described stocking her hideout with food and toys when Beatrice wasn't looking, and how she started out toward school in the morning before doubling back through the woods to her hideout once she was out of sight. She spent her days reading, listening to music, playing electronic games, and throwing things for the dog to chase, before leaving the woods and pretending to return from school in the afternoon.

Steve finally interrupted Katie's soliloquy. "Katie," he said firmly, "stop this nonsense right now! This is completely unacceptable. You will go to school tomorrow. You will go to school every day, and you will make up every bit of work you have missed—every bit."

"I'm not going to school!" Katie interrupted defiantly. "I don't care about school. It doesn't matter! It doesn't matter if I learn geography, or history, or arithmetic, or anything—I am going to die!"

"Katie, we are *not* going to discuss whether or not you go to school," Steve said, setting a boundary on their discussion. "Do you understand?"

"But, Daddy!" Katie pleaded.

"We are *not* going to talk about it!" Steve repeated emphatically. "We *will* talk about why you think you are going to die."

"Everyone knows I am going to die!"

"Katie! How could you say such a thing?" Jackie exclaimed in anguish. "You're not going to die!"

"You tell everyone that I'm going to die!"

"I do not!" Jackie was aghast. "We're going to get through this. We're going to figure something out. We're going to find a drug. You're not going to die!"

"What are you going to do? Turn me into one of those cute little mice you play with in the laboratory and give me some little mouse medicine? Disney cartoons aren't true, you know! Mice don't turn into men! Frogs don't turn into princes! People die when they get blown up!"

"You're not going to die," Jackie repeated again, wanting to believe it was true, wishing she could say it with enough feeling and enough force to make it true.

"You think I'm going to die."

"You're going to be okay!" Jackie pleaded, unable to think of anything else to say.

"You think I am going to die," Katie goaded her again.

"I do not!" Jackie retorted.

"Yes, you do!"

"No, I don't!"

"Yes, you do!"

Recognizing they would not be able to have a sensible conversation at that moment, Steve sent Katie to her room with instructions to write a letter to the principal apologizing for her behavior. She could come down for dinner only when the letter was completed to his satisfaction.

Katie spent several hours sulking in her room before she appeared with a hastily scrawled letter of apology. She sat sullenly through dinner without eating anything. At the first opportunity, she asked to be excused and returned to her room and went to bed.

Jackie was apprehensive about talking to Steve that night. She knew they needed to talk, but it had been a long time since they had had any coherent discussion about Katie's care or had been able to make reasoned decisions together. Everything had become a fight. Every decision became a test of strength.

After Steve went up to the bedroom, Jackie sat for a long while in the kitchen with a cup of coffee. Eventually the coffee grew cold. She poured the residue slowly into the sink, washed the grains down the drain, and followed Steve upstairs.

"I didn't see this coming," Jackie said sadly, as she began undressing.

"Neither did I," Steve answered. "But I'm not surprised something like this happened."

"What do you mean? Where did she get the idea that she's going to die, that there's no reason to go to school?" Jackie was immediately on edge.

"She said she heard it from us."

"She didn't hear it from me!" Jackie answered indignantly. "I'm sure we're going to find a cure! Allan is getting close."

"I didn't say she heard it from you," Steve responded cautiously, trying to stay clear of another argument. "Look, Jackie, I know she isn't getting better as fast as we wanted, but the fact is that she has not had any serious bleeding since she was first diagnosed. We must be doing something right."

"How can you think this is all right?" She started a familiar line of attack. "How can you act like there's nothing wrong?"

"I didn't say that." Steve tried to hold the line without losing his temper. "We have a kid with a chronic disease, a child who is very sick."

"We have a kid who thinks she's dying, Steve! Dying! A kid who's so broken that she doesn't see any reason to live. Everyone else knows what's going on. Everyone else can see it. She's dying. Our kid is dying! Why can't you see it? What's wrong with you?" she finished angrily.

"I really am tired of this, Jackie," Steve started, trying unsuccessfully to control his temper. "You say you don't know where she got the idea that she's dying? Just listen to yourself."

"That's not what I meant." Jackie caught herself, realizing what she had just said.

"You tell the whole world that you think she's going to die. You have it on posters. You have it in the newspaper. You have it on television. You shout it at the top of your lungs."

"I tell *you* I'm afraid she might die. You're my husband. I'm supposed to be able to talk to you," Jackie protested. "I don't say that to anyone else."

"You are so damn certain she's going to die that it's the only thing you ever talk about! Don't you think Katie listens?"

She winced, knowing that Steve could be right.

"Okay!" Jackie responded with agitation. "I'm scared. I admit it! I'm scared that my daughter *is* going to die. Is that wrong? At least I'm trying to do something about it!"

"I don't know what you're doing!" Steve countered. "You're never home. You haven't spent an evening with Katie in weeks, let alone any time with the twins. You haven't been to church with us in months. When you are here, you act like you're in a trance. You spend more time sitting at your computer than you do with your family. You didn't even know your daughter was skipping school."

"Neither did you!" she retorted angrily.

"Neither did I," Steve admitted, defeated.

"What do you want me to do, Steve, sit at home and make believe everything is all right? Should I just sit at home and watch her die?"

"No, I want you to be here to watch her live!"

"For how long? Another month? Another year? What are we going to do a year from now if she isn't better? What are we going to do five years from now? What are we going to do when she learns how to drive—make her wear a crash helmet? Are we going to warn her boyfriends that she could bleed to death when she has sex for the first time? She can't live like this, Steve!"

"You're wrong. She is living. She can live! She will live. You're so damn sure she's going to die that you've forgotten she is alive."

"I haven't forgotten anything!"

"You've forgotten that you need to take care of her."

"I care for her!"

"Katie needs you to care for her. She needs you to give her the reasons to live—to make her think about living."

"She needs to be *cured,* Steve," Jackie said emphatically. "That's what she needs. Her problem has to be fixed."

"No. She needs you to believe she's going to live, not that it will take some miracle drug to keep her from dying!"

"And what difference is that going to make? This isn't a hurt that will go away when her mommy kisses it. Believe me, I've tried. It doesn't make any difference. She's going to die unless we can find a cure. She's dying, Steve! She's dying."

"Listen to me, Jackie!" Steve felt a momentary urge to grab her around the neck and shake her. "Katie is not going to die. She's sick, but that does not mean she's going to die. She doesn't need a miracle drug. She doesn't need scientists studying her and writing papers about her in some journal. You could spend a hundred million dollars sequencing her genome if you wanted, but it's not going to help her."

"You're wrong, Steve!"

"There is not going to be a magic bullet!"

"Stop it! You're wrong!"

"There is no quick fix. Why don't you get that?"

"Shut up, damn you!" Jackie was seething. Steve had attacked her only hope—the idea that science would save Katie, that research would find a cure. Jackie could take Steve's frustration and his anger, but she could not take him denying her faith. All that was left was irrational fury.

"I get it, Steve. I really do. You're the one who can't admit that your holy art of medicine is no better than crap thrown against the walls."

"The only crap on the walls is the posters you have hanging all over the place," Steve answered in equal anger. "Do you ever look at them, Jackie? Do you ever look at the face you put there? That's not Katie! Katie is upstairs in her bed—her eyes red from crying, convinced that you think she's going to die. That's not Katie's face you put on the posters, smiling at the world, telling them there is hope."

Steve stopped and looked at the frenzied woman in front of him. Her eyes were swollen and red. Her face was contorted and her fists clenched. Her shoulders and arms were coiled forward, and her hair was in disarray.

"Go to hell!" she hissed. "You're not going to do one damn thing to save your daughter!"

"I'm doing what I can."

"And what is that, Steve?" she taunted him. "Practice your art? Pray for a miracle? Had any discussions with God about a little miracle for Katie? What are you doing, Steve? There isn't going to be a miracle!"

Steve turned toward Jackie. The color drained from his face. His voice turned cold and commanding. "I don't have to take this. Katie doesn't have to take this. I think you should leave."

Jackie recoiled in shock. "You want me to leave?"

"If you can't be rational, if you can't stop shouting at the top of your lungs that your daughter is about to die or take the time to care for her, maybe you should just leave."

"You want me to leave?" Jackie's emotions suddenly deflated into bewilderment.

"Leave!" Steve answered dismissively.

"You want a divorce?"

Steve was suddenly aware he had crossed a line from which there might be no return. "I don't know. I just know this isn't working right now."

"Fine, then. I'll leave," Jackie said, struggling to regain her composure. "I'll leave right now." She awkwardly started pulling a sweatshirt and jeans over her pajamas.

"Jackie, stop. It's late," Steve protested. "You don't have to go. Don't go. We should go to bed and talk tomorrow when we're not so angry."

"No. If you want me gone, I'll leave now."

Steve watched in pain as Jackie finished dressing, threw some clothes and toiletries into an overnight bag, took her laptop computer from the study, and drove away into the night.

51

Jackie drove toward the refuge of Allan's laboratory, but it was already past midnight and there were no lights in his office. Seeing that the building was dark, she continued past the campus and checked into a hotel on the Charles River several blocks away. She immediately fell into a deep sleep, too tired to cry or even dream.

The next morning, Jackie did not go to work. She spent the entire day in her room, restlessly changing channels on the television, ordering meals from room service, and occasionally surfing the Internet or reading her e-mail.

It was mid-morning when she received a long e-mail from Steve. He apologized for the things he had said the night before and wanted to talk with her. Jackie deleted his message without reply.

She received several e-mail messages from her secretary throughout the day, reminding her about meetings that were on her calendar and asking for instructions when Jackie did not appear. Later, her secretary sent her an e-mail saying that Steve had come to the office looking for her. An hour later, Allan e-mailed, saying that Steve had been there too. Jackie did not respond to anyone.

That afternoon, she received e-mails from Stevie and Stephanie asking her to come home. Rachel and Danny also e-mailed her, saying that Steve had called them, hoping she was there. Erin sent an e-mail saying that she had also talked to Steve, and offering to set up a meeting with a grief counselor or marriage counselor to help them through the crisis.

It was nine o'clock that evening before Jackie finally dressed and walked over to the laboratory. "Jackie, you're alive!" Allan exclaimed as soon as he saw her. "Everyone in the world seems to be looking for you. Are you on the run from the law or something?"

As Jackie came closer, Allan saw the pained expression on her face. "Are you okay?" he asked, instantly concerned.

"No, I'm not okay," she said blankly.

"What's wrong?"

"I don't want to talk about it."

"What's going on? Why is everyone looking for you?"

"I said I didn't want to talk about it," she snapped. Then she paused, knowing she needed to tell him something. "I moved out of the house."

"Why?"

"None of your business."

"Do you need someplace to stay?"

"I want to be alone. Please don't tell anyone I'm here. I don't want to talk to anybody."

"Is there anything I can do?"

"What you can do is finish the damn experiment and make it work! That's the only thing anyone can do."

Jackie sat on the couch in Allan's office, as she did almost every night, but this time she silently stared into space. Allan tried unsuccessfully to get her to talk about her personal problems. Eventually, he gave up and gave her the daily status report on the experiments.

The laboratory was making final preparations for testing the antisense drug. The drug had been synthesized and purified so that it could be safely injected into animals. A hundred genetically engineered mice had been bred and were old enough to be treated. The experiment would begin the next day.

The first step was to infect the mice with the virus. If everything went according to plan, it would take several days for the mice to begin an immune response against the virus and produce the antibodies that would attack their platelets. Once the platelet counts began to drop, half the animals would be given daily injections of the antisense drug to stop expression of platB. The others would be given daily injections of the inert compound. If the drug worked as expected, the platelet levels in the treated mice should begin to rise within two to three days.

Jackie listened without emotion. Nothing else in her life mattered. She was almost relieved that she did not have to go home or talk to anyone.

The next day, Jackie received e-mails from Steve and from the twins. She responded to Stevie and Stephanie with a short note saying that she loved them very much and that they should do everything Beatrice and their daddy told them to do while she was gone. She didn't say when she would be home. She sent Steve a short e-mail saying that she was okay but that she needed some time alone. She asked him to stop trying to contact her. Then she e-mailed her secretary, telling her that she would be away for several weeks for personal reasons and asked her to cancel all of her appointments through the end of the year.

That evening, Allan told Jackie the experiment had started. The animals had been infected with the virus. It would take several days before the mice would develop symptoms and they could begin testing the drug. Jackie did not stay to hear any more. She did not care about anything else. She immediately went back to her hotel.

The next morning, Jackie checked out of the hotel and rented a small, furnished apartment across the river in downtown Boston. That afternoon, when she knew no one would be home, she drove to the house in Concord and retrieved several duffel bags of clothes and personal items. She spent the next several days anxiously pacing between the rooms of her rented apartment and aimlessly surfing the Internet. The twins e-mailed her every day, and Jackie responded with her love and a noncommittal answer about when she would be home. Steve sent her a daily e-mail describing the children's routines and things at home. Danny and Rachel also e-mailed daily, offering to come to her assistance if she needed help. She did not respond.

It was several days before Jackie received an e-mail from Katie. Her long e-mail said that she knew it was her fault that Mommy and Daddy had been fighting, that she was sorry, and that she wanted Mommy to come home. She wrote that she was sorry that she had gotten sick, that she was not getting better, that she had misbehaved, and that she had skipped school. She promised she would get better, go to school and get good grades, be nice to the people who Mommy introduced her to, and that she would not make Mommy and Daddy fight with each other. She also promised that she would keep her room clean and would not do any dangerous things that might get her hurt. She wrote that she knew Mommy and Daddy wanted her to get better, that Daddy had told her she was not going to die, and she believed him. At the end, she filled up twenty lines with Xs and Os.

Jackie answered Katie with a short e-mail telling her she loved her, that it was not her fault she got sick, and that everyone was working hard to find a way to make her better. She did not say when she would be home.

* * *

Five days after the mice were infected with the viruses, their platelet counts began to drop. As in the previous experiments, the immune response against the virus was also causing platelets to be destroyed. The mice had ITP. Allan decided to let the disease progress for one more day before they began testing the drug.

Jackie did not sleep that night, and was back at the laboratory at seven o'clock the next morning. She watched as the antisense drug was filtered one last time to ensure its sterility, drawn into syringes, and then injected into half the mice. The same procedure was used to inject the inactive compound into the other mice. She prayed mightily as the drugs were administered, unconscious and unconcerned as to whom or what she was praying.

Most of the mice tolerated the injections well. Some did not. By that evening, some of the mice had died. Many had bruises or blood on their fur from the unremitting course of the disease and the injection procedure.

Jackie did not sleep again that night and was at the laboratory before dawn.

Overnight, more of the mice had died of the disease. Most of the mice looked ill. There was no apparent effect of the antisense drug.

All the mice were treated for a second time, and blood was taken to count the platelets. Looking closely at the numbers, Allan thought there might be slightly higher numbers of platelets in the mice that had received the antisense drug compared to those that had received the inert compound, but it was too soon to tell.

By the third morning, the results of the experiment began to be clear. More of the mice that had been treated with the inert compound had died overnight, but none of the mice that had been treated with the antisense drug. Again, the mice were injected with the drugs and blood was taken to count the platelets. The platelet counts showed that all the mice treated with the inert compound had lower platelet counts than the day before. In contrast, the platelet counts in the mice treated with the antisense drug had remained steady. In several mice, the platelet counts were actually higher. Allan advised Jackie to be cautious in her expectations, but the results were encouraging.

When Allan checked the mice late that evening, all the mice that had received the inert compound looked near death and unlikely to survive until morning. In contrast, all the mice that had received the antisense drug were alive and recovering; only a few appeared to be acutely ill. He decided to end the experiment immediately.

When Jackie arrived at the laboratory that evening, Allan was hard at work with his research fellows sacrificing the mice, collecting samples for analysis, and counting the platelets in the blood. They did not finish until after midnight.

Jackie tried to act calm as Allan and his research fellow spent hours methodically labeling samples and entering data in their computers. Her heart was beating so hard she thought her entire body must be visibly shaking.

The drug had worked! The disease had been cured!

If was two thirty in the morning when the research fellow finally said good night and disappeared down the hallway. Jackie immediately abandoned any pretense of self-control.

"It worked!" she shrieked, grabbing Allan's hands and spinning him around in a frenzied dance. "It worked! It really worked! The drug worked! You did it! It's cured!" Then she grabbed him in a desperate embrace and again began to dance him around and around. "It's cured!"

After several minutes, Allan broke away from Jackie's animated celebration to retrieve a bottle of champagne, hidden in a laboratory refrigerator for just such occasions. He poured two drinks into paper cups and suggested the first of many toasts in celebration. They toasted to their success, to Katie's health, and to long life. They toasted to the Human Genome Project, to the Foundation, to science and medicine, and to hope. They toasted to small steps and giant leaps.

Soon they were both feeling the effects of the hour and the alcohol and sat together on the couch. Jackie's head was spinning. Her joyful excitement eased into a tranquil reflection. Allan became talkative.

He talked about what the experiment meant to science and his career. He talked about writing a paper to report the discovery of the gene that caused ITP, and another paper describing how the disease had been cured. He speculated about sending his work to prestigious journals, how he could get the papers published before his competitors heard about his discovery, where he should announce his breakthrough, what newspapers would report his success, and what reporters might want to do interviews. He speculated about whether he should start a company to commercialize the drug he had discovered, and how much money he might make once the drug was on the market. He talked about studying other diseases in which the immune system attacked normal tissues, such as diabetes and arthritis, to see if he could discover cures for them as well.

Jackie watched Allan as he talked about his accomplishments and his plans, not hearing the words he was saying. She watched the movements of his mouth, the intense darting motions of his eyes, and the expansive gestures of his hands. This was the man who had found the cure. This man had confirmed her faith and given her deliverance.

As she watched him, she was aware of his physical presence next to her on the couch. Her skin tingled from the contact of their legs, the accidental touching of their hands from his expansive gestures, and the tension on her hair when it caught in the folds of his shirt.

"I need to thank you," Jackie interrupted quietly, drawing Allan's attention away from his self-absorbed soliloquy.

"No, you don't," Allan replied, turning toward her.

"Yes, I do," Jackie insisted. "Do you know what this means to me?"

"I'm not sure." Allan was perplexed by the question.

"It means it was the right thing to do. It was the right idea."

"The idea?"

"Ever since I can remember, I have had this idea, this faith, that if men could land on the Moon, then anything was possible—that there were no limits, that there was always something that could be done."

"That's nice," Allan agreed, indifferent to the depth of Jackie's feelings.

"It's been so hard not to be afraid that Katie was going to die—so hard not to lose faith and believe that everything was going to be okay. The whole world was giving up on everything I believe in. I needed to know it was right—that it was possible—even though it seemed impossible. I needed to know that Katie was going to live. I needed to know I had the right idea."

"I'm glad," Allan murmured, uninterested in Jackie's epistemology.

"I do need to thank you," Jackie repeated, turning to give Allan an impulsive kiss on the cheek. Instead, Allan caught her lips with his. They froze for an instant, then he pressed his lips forward.

Jackie withdrew slightly. Their eyes met. Allan leaned forward to kiss her again.

This time, she leaned forward so that his lips brushed her eyes and fell on her forehead. Gently, he kissed her face, her eyelids, and her lips. His hands moved through her hair, then around the back of her head, pulling her mouth onto his.

Sensing her consent, Allan began kissing her with increasing intensity. His hands gently moved over her shoulders, her back, and her breasts. She allowed him to open the buttons on her blouse and the clasp on her bra. Then she lay back on the arm of the couch, feeling him reach beneath her skirt and feeling the coolness of the leather against her skin. Jackie had never felt so ecstatic and aroused.

Allan stood up and unbuttoned his pants. Jackie watched, as he fumbled with the buttons. She reached out and pulled him down with both arms.

Suddenly, she felt wetness on her leg. She brushed at it unconsciously with her hand, and then recoiled from the stickiness and the smell of semen that spread through the air.

Allan pushed himself away awkwardly, a mortified pallor blanching his tanned skin, a blank expression overwhelming his groomed features. His eyes were vacant as he struggled to raise his pants.

Jackie's skin still tingled. She was still flushed. She did not want it to end this way.

She rose from the couch and took Allan tightly in her arms, kissing him forcefully and rubbing her body against his, trying to help him regain his desire. Allan shrugged her off and stepped back.

"I'm sorry," Jackie murmured.

"It's not your fault," Allan answered quickly, his voice hardly audible.

"Can I do anything?"

"No, it isn't you."

"Maybe we were going too fast." Jackie fumbled for words.

"It happens sometimes." He stopped short in embarrassment.

"Maybe there's a gene that I need to turn on," she offered playfully, trying unsuccessfully to lighten the mood. Small talk failed.

Standing half-naked in Allan's office, she suddenly felt exposed and turned to restore her clothes. As she did, Allan retreated behind his desk. Neither could think of anything to say.

"Are you okay?" she asked tentatively when she was fully dressed.

"You're probably right. We probably went too fast," Allan answered without conviction.

"It's been quite a night." She looked at him, hoping he would say something. "Maybe I should go," she offered hesitantly.

"That's probably a good idea."

"Will I see you tomorrow?"

"Sure."

Allan watched her as she put on her coat and turned toward the door. "Jackie," he called to her so softly that she almost did not hear him. "Jackie, stop." She looked back at him. "I didn't—I mean, I don't know what to say. I didn't mean to take advantage of you. I'm—I'm sorry," Allan stammered uncomfortably.

"I'm not sorry." Jackie walked around the desk to where Allan was standing and gave him a purposeful kiss. "You did what you promised." She kissed him again. "Thank you."

"We're not done."

"I know. Good night, Allan. Thank you for everything."

52

At five o'clock the next morning, Jackie called Steve, knowing he was usually waking up at that time. "It's good to hear your voice," Steve said thankfully. "I miss you, Jackie. I'm so sorry for the things I said. We need to talk."

Jackie did not respond to his apologies or entreaties. She was all business. "Steve, it worked. The experiment worked. The disease can be cured. I need you to meet with me and Allan this afternoon to help us decide what to do next."

She quickly described how the mice had been cured with the experimental drug. Steve listened attentively, knowing how important it was to Jackie, and agreed to meet her at Allan's office that afternoon to hear about the work firsthand. He proposed bringing some of the fellows from his clinical research group who would be involved in testing the drug in humans, if that was what they decided to do.

"Steve," Jackie said, after they finished agreed on the time and place for the meeting, "I knew it would work. I knew there had to be something we could do. I knew we would find a cure."

Steve chose his words carefully. From Jackie's description of the experiments and the result, he recognized that Allan had made an important scientific advance, but he was not convinced that curing the disease in genetically engineered mice proved there was a cure for Katie. More than anything, however, Steve wanted to repair his marriage, so he kept his reservations to himself. "I'm looking forward to hearing about it. I'm also looking forward to seeing you. I really want to talk."

Jackie did not respond. She spent the day in a state of euphoria, calling everyone she knew to tell them about the triumph. She talked to her father, Danny, Rachel, William, and Tim. She called the Foundation's major donors to tell them that the goal had been achieved, and she spent hours drafting a press release to announce the accomplishment.

For a year, she had thought about nothing but the possibility of a cure. Now it was time to celebrate.

Jackie arrived at Allan's laboratory just before five o'clock that evening. Steve arrived punctually with his team several minutes later. She greeted him in a businesslike manner, without any physical contact or emotion. When everyone had taken a seat around the conference table, Jackie sat against the wall behind Steve.

Allan let his students and fellows describe the experiments they had performed over the previous year. Steve's team was intrigued, and there was a vigorous scientific discussion about immunology and genomics. Steve sat quietly through most of the meeting, occasionally prompting members of his group with a question or bits of information. Jackie sat silently, savoring her accomplishment, but also anxious for the group to talk less about science and more about curing Katie.

It was not until seven o'clock that one of Allan's fellows raised the question of whether the antisense drug could be tested in humans.

Steve immediately interrupted. "I think we need a break."

"Don't stop now. Let's keep going," Jackie responded with anger in her eyes.

Steve turned toward her. "We should talk, and everyone is probably hungry. How about if we take a break, let people get something to eat, and continue another time?"

"I can go out and get food for everyone so you can keep working tonight," Jackie countered. "There's no reason to stop. Let's keep working."

"Jackie," Steve pleaded, but she ignored him.

"I could use a short break." Allan agreed, "And I'm willing to keep working tonight."

"Okay. Okay." Jackie struggled to keep the meeting from dissolving before they could discuss what really mattered. "A short break. How about if I go out and bring back some pizza, and we can continue in like, say twenty minutes?"

"Agreed."

Jackie quickly left to pick up the food. Allan went to his office to check his e-mail. Steve followed him into his office and closed the door behind him.

When Jackie returned twenty minutes later, Steve was sitting at the keyboard of Allan's computer. Allan was standing behind him, gravely watching as columns of numbers flashed across the screen. Their postures were closed, their eyes focused resolutely on the computer screen. Neither said a word. The thought flashed through Jackie's mind that it probably had not been wise to leave her husband and frustrated lover in a room together.

Neither Allan nor Steve acknowledged her presence as she opened the door and entered the room. She stood silently for several moments, watching them work.

Allan was the first to turn toward her. His face had the same drained and lifeless expression she had seen the night before. Her heart began to race uncomfortably.

She looked toward Steve and saw darkness in his usually light eyes.

"Jackie," Steve started in a pained voice that made her fear what he was about to say. "We have to talk."

"About what?"

"There are some things you need to hear. It would be better if the three of us talked alone." Jackie was frozen. "You should sit down."

She sat hesitantly on the front edge of the couch. "What is it?" she asked.

"I'm afraid that a cure is not as close as you thought," Steve began.

Jackie was immediately incensed and rose aggressively. "Damn you! Obviously, you weren't listening to anything that's been said for the past three hours! Allan, tell him! Tell him that the disease was cured! Tell him you found a cure!" she demanded.

"Jackie," Allan cautioned gravely, "sit down. You need to listen to Steve." His voice was as cold and lifeless as his eyes.

She reluctantly sat back down on the couch. As she did, she became aware of the smell of spilled semen and of her own arousal moldering in the fabric.

Steve started talking in his measured manner. "Allan made some impressive discoveries. He clearly found a gene—a mutation—that can cause the disease. It's very impressive," he repeated before resuming with greater caution. "What you need to know, however, is that Katie does not have the disease that Allan has discovered."

"What?" Jackie was surprised.

"Not all the patients with ITP have the same mutation."

"I know that."

"Katie does *not* have the mutation Allan found," Steve said, carefully measuring his tone.

Jackie skipped a breath.

"Allan doesn't know—" Steve paused to make his statement less argumentative "—*we* don't know yet what is causing Katie's disease."

"Is that true?" Jackie turned to Allan, hoping he would tell her differently. Surely he had found Katie's mutation. Surely he had found the cure. "I thought that—"

"Since most patients with ITP had this mutation, I just assumed that Katie would have the same thing." Allan apologized awkwardly.

"You *assumed*? Why? You have Katie's samples. I brought them over here myself! Why didn't you just look at them?"

"We couldn't use the samples you brought over. We aren't allowed to."

"You aren't *allowed* to?" Jackie was incredulous.

"We can only use samples that come through the regular channels—you know, with the approval of the ethics committee. We need to have informed consent and the samples have to be anonymous, you know, de-identified to protect privacy and all that—"

"I signed the damn consent forms! I'll sign any damn consent form. I don't give a damn about privacy," Jackie protested. "I just want to know what is wrong with Katie."

"There are rules," Allan said again, "particularly since Katie is a child."

"You couldn't use Katie's samples?" Jackie repeated in disbelief.

"There's nothing I can do about it, Jackie." He stopped, aware that she was glaring angrily at him. "I could lose my funding, my grants."

"You could lose your grants? I could lose my child!" Jackie responded with disgust, but her thoughts were already moving frantically ahead. "But if there were no names on the samples, and you don't know where any of the samples came from, then maybe you did study Katie's DNA. Maybe she does have the mutation. You don't know if you didn't look at her samples," she finished hopefully.

"We know," Allan interrupted her. "Steve just broke the code. That's what we were doing when you came in. It's against the rules, but given the circumstances—"

"Jackie," Steve interrupted gently, "I sent Katie's samples to Allan when he first began his studies. I broke the rules a little—more than a little—and made sure Katie's samples were in the first batch that we sent over for his studies. I knew that's what you wanted."

"That's good," Jackie said expectantly, aware of the significant risk Steve had taken in circumventing the ethical rules that governed his work.

"Allan didn't know," Steve continued. "Katie's samples were coded like everyone else's and—"

"When Steve broke the code just now," Allan interrupted, "we found that Katie didn't have the mutation we discovered."

"We just looked at the data," Steve repeated. "I'm sorry."

"We know Katie's disease is not typical. It is possible that Katie could have a mutation somewhere else in the platB gene, or she might have a mutation in some other gene." Allan tried to sound hopeful. "I'm sure she has a mutation somewhere."

"She *could* have a mutation *somewhere*," Jackie mocked him, her anger rapidly rising. "She could have a mutation somewhere! I can't believe you didn't tell me you hadn't found Katie's mutation. That was the whole idea. Why the hell do you think I was raising millions of dollars for your laboratory and spending half my life in your office?"

"That's not fair," Allan started defensively. "I told you from the beginning, Jackie, that this is a science laboratory. We do scientific research."

"Don't give me that crap!"

Allan's tone became more forceful. "I told you, Jackie. This isn't a hospital. We don't take care of people. We don't diagnose or treat people. We do basic science. We never tell *anyone* what we find when we study their DNA."

"You never tell anyone?" Jackie repeated in disbelief. "So what about all the people who *do* have the mutation? You're not going to tell them? You're not going to tell them that you found the cause of their disease?"

"We're not allowed to. We will publish our results in medical journals. We will describe the results we obtained in aggregate through a statistical analysis of all the data and send it for peer review—" Allan said, slipping into scientific jargon to cover his discomfort with the conversation.

"I'm sure a lot of people will take comfort in that!" Jackie snapped.

"Those are the rules. Patients have to be anonymous."

"Tombstones aren't anonymous. When Katie dies, there will be a tombstone with her name on it. Everyone will know which body is hers—or maybe you only study people who agree to be buried in unmarked graves, so the world won't know you're impotent!"

Allan winced silently, giving Steve a sideways glance to assure himself that Jackie's slight had been missed.

"Jackie, calm down!" Steve said.

"I won't calm down." Jackie took a deep breath and looked up at the ceiling. "This is unbelievable."

"I'm sorry, Jackie." Steve tried to offer comfort.

Jackie's thoughts were racing ahead to the next step. "So you have to sequence Katie's DNA to find out what mutation she has. You said she must have a mutation somewhere. At least we know how to treat her once you find the mutation."

Steve and Allan looked at each other silently.

"You can always make an antisense drug that will match her sequence and do the same thing, right?" She stopped and looked at Steve and then at Allan. "Right?" she repeated, her heart sinking. Steve gestured to Allan to respond.

"Maybe. Maybe not."

"Why the hell not?" Jackie exploded.

"Well, it could work—" Allan began hesitantly.

"What Allan means," Steve interrupted with condescension in his voice, "is that while antisense drugs are often effective in mice, they have never worked well in humans."

"Why?"

"We don't know," Steve continued without breaking his cadence. "Maybe the diseases are different in mice. Maybe the drugs work differently in humans. Nobody knows."

"Is that right? I've worked on business plans for a dozen companies that plan to develop antisense drugs." Jackie turned to Allan, hoping he would contradict Steve's pessimism. "Antisense is only for mice?"

"Many people think antisense drugs are promising," Allan mumbled automatically.

"I'm not sure I trust your promises right now," Jackie answered scornfully.

"It could work," Allan repeated.

Steve was becoming exasperated at Allan's hesitation. "It doesn't work that way, Jackie. You can't just synthesize some chemical in a laboratory and expect it to work like a drug in people. I know every biotech company hires you to make it sound easy, but it isn't. Lots of drugs work in animals that never work in people. No one knows why."

"Is that right?" Jackie asked again, searching Allan's face for hope.

"I don't know much about drugs. That isn't my field," Allan apologized.

"It isn't your field?" Jackie snapped. "What *is* your field? Anonymous tombstones?"

"I am a scientist," Allan said, finally losing his temper. "I'm not a doctor. I'm not a pharmacologist. I don't discover or develop drugs. That's not what I do."

The stench from the couch was suddenly overwhelming. Jackie stood up to escape the smell.

"I thought medical research was about curing people," Jackie responded with biting sarcasm. "I thought you cared about curing people, curing my child!"

"Don't tell me I failed you!" Allan returned her anger. "I told you from the beginning that we do science. We study how genes work, how biology works, and how humans work. We've done more to understand ITP than anyone else has ever done. We found genes that can cause the disease! We know it can be cured. We'll publish our results so other people can figure out how to develop drugs and diagnose and treat people. That's just not what I do."

"Don't give me that crap!" Jackie scolded, and then paused to compose herself. "So how long is it going to take you to find Katie's mutation?"

Allan did not respond.

"You are going to find Katie's mutation, aren't you?" she demanded.

"I guess I owe you that much."

"You owe me? My daughter is dying and you're going to do it for me? She's dying! Doesn't anyone care? Isn't there anything anyone can do?"

The world around Jackie blurred as the tears began to flow. Allan, Steve, and Katie all floated away before her eyes into the distance of space. She struggled for breath. She felt an explosion of emotion and pain.

Suddenly, she turned and ran from the room and into the nearest stairwell so no one in the laboratory would see her cry. She continued down five flights of stairs to the ground floor, pushed through the door marked "Emergency Exit Only," and then ran out into the parking lot, oblivious to the wailing tone of the alarm sounding as she fled. This time, there was nowhere to duck or hide.

She continued running until she reached the banks of the Charles River and the bridge that led across the water toward downtown Boston. Only when she was hit by the freezing mist and frigid winter winds that coursed the river at night did she realize she was not wearing a coat.

Jackie had always known that Allan had no particular interest in Katie or her disease. She knew he had agreed to work on ITP partly because of the money she brought to his research, partly because of the public acclaim she orchestrated for him, and partly because he wanted to sleep with her. She had taken advantage of these interests to get Allan to do what she wanted.

She also realized that she should not have been surprised at the outcome. Allan had dutifully read the scripts Jackie wrote for him, telling the world that his work would lead to cures for disease; a cure for Katie's disease. He had told everyone else that his studies were simply basic science. Like Jefferson commissioning Lewis and Clark and the Corps of Discovery to explore the American West and Kennedy setting humankind's sights on the Moon, there had been different stories for different purposes.

Allan had made the first foray into the unknown, had seen things no one had seen before, and explored places where no one had ever been. He had planted a flag on the map of the human genome. He would publish his results in a prestigious scientific journal, receive the accolades of the scientific community, and accept the rewards that come with scientific achievement. He would not go any further.

* * *

By the end of 2000, the Human Genome Project, too, had accomplished all its stated goals. The three billion chemical base pairs that make up human DNA had been sequenced. All the genes that comprise the human genome had been discovered. Databases and tools for data analysis had been established. Technologies had been transferred to the private sector to develop new drugs and diagnostics. Ethical, legal, and social issues of genomics had been considered. Now the Human Genome Project would move on to study the genomes of other organisms, including bacteria, fruit flies, mice, rats, zebra fish, cows, and hundreds of other animals, plants, and microorganisms of scientific interest.

Jackie had long ago noticed that the Human Genome Project's original stated goals did not mention improving human health or curing disease; the public simply assumed it would. Who could doubt that the enormous amount of information and elemental understanding of human biology that would come from sequencing the human genome would inevitably bear fruit in new medical advances? Who could doubt that knowing how autoimmune diseases occurred would lead to a cure? Who could doubt that knowing what caused cancer would enable this scourge to be controlled? Who could doubt that understanding mechanisms of death would lead to ways to save lives?

Lewis and Clark and their Corps of Discovery achieved their goal of establishing America's claim to the West, but it was a generation until the telegraph and transcontinental railroad led to effective commercialization of its vast resources and brought the wealth the American people had been promised. The space program achieved its primary goal of reaching the Moon to establish America's preeminence, but it would be another generation before men would venture again beyond the gravitational pull of the Earth or look for profits in space. Like the other great endeavors that came before, the Human Genome Project provided new insights and mapped new territories. Great accomplishments would certainly come; but it would take time.

It took Jackie an hour to walk the several cold and wet miles to her rented apartment in downtown Boston. She was shivering uncontrollably when she arrived at the front door.

Steve was sitting on the doorstep waiting for her.

"What are you doing here?" she asked in surprise. "How did you know where I was living?" She was at once reluctant to confront him and thankful that he was there.

"You must have called Allan's office. Your number was on the machine. We hit redial and talked to your concierge."

"You're freezing," Steve continued, noticing her shivering. He took off his overcoat and placed it over her shoulders. "Jackie, I'm sorry for what happened back there. We really need to talk."

"I know," she answered miserably, before collapsing into his arms in tears. Steve held her close for the first time in many months. After a moment, he led her inside to the warmth of her apartment. Jackie changed into dry clothes, and then sat on the sofa while Steve fumbled around the kitchen making two cups of hot tea.

"I'm so sorry. I only wanted to do what was best for Katie," Jackie said, as he emerged from the kitchen and sat next to her.

"I know."

"It was the only thing I knew how to do. It was my only idea. I thought we had done it. I thought we had discovered what caused the disease. I thought we had found a way to cure it. It was all a waste of time."

"It was premature," Steve corrected. "Allan is a good scientist. The things he discovered are a big step forward."

"Don't defend him."

"I'm not defending him. I was thinking about contacting some of the companies I've worked with over the years to see if they would be interested in taking Allan's discoveries to the next level—you know, trying to find a real drug to treat the disease. They might find his results interesting." Steve realized that Jackie was not listening.

"It always sounded so easy—find a gene, find a mutation, find a cure," Jackie continued sadly. "I've heard the story a hundred times. I've written the story a thousand times. I always thought it was true." She put her head on Steve's shoulder and began to cry again. "It made sense. I had no idea what else to believe."

"Where are the kids?" Jackie finally asked, lifting her head from Steve's shoulder.

"Home with Beatrice and my mother. I called just before you got here. They're okay." Steve contemplated his next words carefully. "They need you, Jackie. I need you."

"I'm so sorry for everything, Steve. I'm sorry for all the horrible things I said to you. I'm sorry for making such a mess of everything."

"I'm sorry too." Steve pulled her head down onto his chest and began to stroke the windblown knots out of her hair. It had been days since she had slept, and she quickly fell into a fitful sleep, comforted by the steady sound of Steve's heartbeat.

Steve held her as she slept through the night. He tightened his arms around her when her nightmares made her twitch and moan, tucked his coat around her when she shivered, pulled it back when she started to sweat, and brushed her hair from her face when it strayed into her mouth or eyes. He watched as the morning Sun appeared in the window and the winter light moved across her face until it shone into her eyes and made her stir.

"Hi," she said sheepishly, holding her hand over her eyes to block the Sun and looking up at Steve.

"Hi," he said, gently brushing her hair behind her shoulders.

"You look terrible," Jackie said, weakly reaching up to touch his disheveled hair and unshaven cheek. Then she turned to glance at the clock on the wall. It was almost eight o'clock. "Aren't you supposed to be at work?" she asked, turning back to look at him.

"I need to be here."

"Thank you." Jackie pushed her face into his chest and felt his arms tighten around her. She fell asleep again almost immediately.

An hour later, Jackie opened her eyes again and sat up. They sat silently beside each other for almost an hour. Both were content to sit together, legs pressed against each other and hands clasped. Both were afraid to talk about anything.

It was late morning when Steve finally rose to go to work. "Monday is Christmas, you know," Steve said, as he put on his coat. "Everyone is expecting you to be there. We need you, Jackie."

"I know. Maybe tomorrow. It will take some time to get over everything that's happened, but I'll be there for Christmas. It's going to be hard."

"We'll get through this."

"I have no idea how," she replied miserably.

53

Jackie returned home the following day. Stevie and Stephanie were overjoyed to see her. Each grabbed one of her legs and refused to let go. Even Katie had a smile on her face, which Jackie had not seen in months.

Ever since Elaine had come to live with Steve and Jackie and closed the house in Pittsfield, the Brennan family had celebrated Christmas in Concord. Elaine was the matriarch who presided over the preparation of the traditional foods and told the traditional stories, but it was Jackie, Erin, and Beatrice who did more and more of the work each year.

Jackie had hoped that this Christmas would be a celebration of her success in finding a cure for Katie, and she had invited both extended families to stay with them over the holidays. Erin would be there. Bert Jr., who was now a vice-president with Compaq Computer Corporation in Houston, would come with his wife and four children. Corey would come from California with his partner. Allison would be there, and Bert and Mary would bring Cathy and Cathy's two children, who still lived with them. Rachel and Danny were also planning to come for the weekend before Christmas Eve.

By the time Jackie returned home, Erin and Beatrice had already spent weeks shopping, cleaning, and cooking for Christmas. Jackie tried to help cook, but kept fouling the recipes through inattention to the details. She tried cleaning out the dining room for Christmas dinner, but found herself sorting unhappily through the stacks of the Foundation's papers. Finally, she tried to wrap presents, only to discover that Beatrice was secretly rewrapping each one more neatly as soon as she was done.

Jackie spent most of the week alone in her room, restlessly flipping between satellite news channels, watching world events that seemed to reflect her own discontent. During the last months of 2000, the technology bubble burst. Hundreds of billions of dollars were lost as technology stock prices crumbled and the major stock exchanges crashed. Many feared that the economy could slide into depression. Much of her own portfolio of stocks was suddenly worthless.

Dissatisfaction with technology was apparent in many news stories that week. Opposition to genetically modified crops mounted in response to a report that pest-resistant corn could kill the elegant monarch butterflies. Reports appeared about the dangers of pharmaceutical products, the high frequency of medical errors, and the lack of privacy in Internet communications. There were stories about a dangerous new computer virus, the spread of mad cow disease, and the continuing epidemic of AIDS. One night, there was a heart-rending story about the fate of polar bears, whose habitat on the polar ice sheet was threatened by global warming.

There was also ominous news of resurgent chaos around the world. Ten years of stepwise negotiations between Israel and its Arab neighbors came to an abrupt end as Palestinians rejected the offer of an independent state and turned, once again, to violence. Bombings in Indonesia, India, Pakistan, and the Philippines were linked to Islamic militants, and the bombing of an American warship in Yemen was linked to a new terrorist organization called al Qaeda. A U.S. government report was released that cited the emergence of failed nations controlled by terrorists and the growing availability of weapons of mass destruction, including nuclear and biological weapons, as a major national security threat to the United States.

Jackie had nightmares every night. It was the recurring nightmare that had come intermittently since childhood, though it was now more vivid and more terrifying. She was at the controls of the space shuttle, as it disintegrated around her in front of her father's store. She was on the streets of Belfast, Jerusalem, or Manhattan as bombs exploded and the buildings around her crashed down. She struggled to survive on the killing fields of Boyne or Babi Yar. She felt the premonition of explosions and watched the people she loved plunging into the atmosphere in a ball of blood and fire and fading away into the abyss of space.

She tried to prevent the seemingly inevitable explosions, to shout a warning, to fly to safety, to change course, to duck and cover, to pull her mother, Katie, and Christa McAuliffe into the safety of the lunar module or a bomb shelter. She took control of the crippled spaceship and struggled to avoid the fields strewn with rock, until all the fuel was expended and she crashed. She woke repeatedly, shaking with fear, until she no longer dared to close her eyes, and she began to pace the darkened halls.

Jackie left the house only twice during the week before Christmas. The first was with Steve and the children to buy a Christmas tree. She watched distantly as the children excitedly picked an enormous tree that was too tall for even the ten-foot ceiling of their living room. When they returned home, Steve had to cut more than a foot off the base to make room for the crystal angel on top. Only then could the children begin hanging their assortment of artful clay and cardboard constructions on the tree, and could Jackie begin to hang the ornaments she had inherited from her mother in their accustomed places.

The second time Jackie left the house was to go to a camera store. On Christmas Day, there would be a solar eclipse over New England. She wanted to see it.

Jackie bought dark solar filters for the family's binoculars and cameras that would allow them to look safely at the Sun. She downloaded maps, charts, and photographs from the Internet, showing how the Moon would pass in front of the Sun and where the shadow of the Moon would bring darkness to the Earth. Looking toward the heavens would be a welcome diversion from her misery.

Steve and Jackie spent many hours that week talking through the frayed threads of their marriage. They both needed each other desperately, but they were also very cautious.

They talked comfortably about the mundane business of life; the weather, the condition of the house and the yard, the children's school activities and grades. They talked about who was coming for Christmas, where they would sleep, what food would be served, what presents had been bought, and what presents still needed to be found. They avoided talking about Katie's health or the dramatic decline of their fortunes due to their investment in technology.

Danny and Rachel arrived in Concord with their children on Friday before Christmas. It was the first night of Chanukah. Ruby and her brother lit candles in the menorah they had brought with them. Danny told stories about the miracles of Chanukah, how a small force of freedom fighters consumed with the idea of one God defeated the military might of ancient Greece, and how a single vial of sacred oil sustained the light in the holy temple for eight days. Danny had not changed, Jackie thought, as she watched him celebrate the idea of freedom with his children.

By Saturday, the house was filled with family. The tone of the weekend, however, was subdued. Concern about Katie's health and the tension between Steve and Jackie cast an omnipresent pall over the holiday. To the questions "How is Katie? How are you two?" Jackie and Steve answered only, "It has been a difficult time."

Their evasion did nothing to quench the desire of their family and friends to know more about what had happened. Throughout the weekend, Jackie felt every pair of eyes measuring her every emotion. Each time she made eye contact, she felt her soul being searched. Each time she talked, her words were examined for unspoken meaning. For most of the weekend, Jackie sat with her eyes lowered to the floor, to avoid eye contact, and answered in monosyllables that conveyed nothing of her inner turmoil.

The children spent Saturday playing in Katie's bedroom or watching DVDs on the large-screen television in the playroom. The adults spent the day in endlessly morphing groups of two or three by the fireplace in the living room, the kitchen, or on the porch, talking mostly about family and friends. Danny and Rachel talked about moving out of Manhattan to the suburbs of Westchester County and showed pictures of a house they hoped to buy. Bert and Mary talked about keeping up the house and their health. Cathy talked about her persistent marital and financial woes. Bert, Jr., talked about his children and their accomplishments in school, and tried unsuccessfully to engage Jackie in a discussion about Corey's lifestyle, Cathy's continued dependence on their parents for support, and Allison's lack of direction in life.

Jackie had trouble paying attention to any of the conversations. Instead, she wandered from one group to another, standing on the outside of each circle, close enough so she did not feel alone, but not so close that she would be expected to contribute.

"Do your parents still live in Spring?" Bert asked Danny, as they congregated in front of the fireplace that afternoon. "I haven't seen them recently."

"No. They moved to Florida when my dad retired several years ago," Danny answered.

"You should retire too," Mary chided Bert. "You work too hard."

"I wouldn't work any less if I retired. We can't afford to move to Florida, and it's a full-time job just fixing the house."

"What's wrong with the house?" Bert, Jr., asked with concern.

"It's falling apart. It seems that the glue that holds plywood together only lasts about forty years."

"Is it serious?"

"We can live with it. If we tried to sell the house, some builder would probably tear it down and build something new. That's what's happening all over. Everything built in the sixties is being torn down. They're even planning to tear down Spring Elementary School."

"Why are they going to tear down the school?" Danny asked.

"It's collapsing," Bert answered. "Last winter, part of the roof collapsed during an ice storm."

"Was anyone hurt?"

"One of the janitors was in the building when it happened, but he wasn't hurt. The school was closed for several weeks because the air was fouled with dust."

"I'm not surprised that the roof collapsed," Bert, Jr., offered. "It had a flat roof, didn't it? The ice and snow must have just accumulated. I never understood why the school had a flat roof. It never made any sense."

"Flat roofs were popular in the 1960s, particularly for schools," Danny responded. "It was one of the characteristic features of modern architecture. Architects thought that peaked roofs looked like the crowns of old monarchies, something that they thought had no place in the modern world."

"Who cares what shape the roof is?" Bert, Jr., interrupted.

"It was an important idea at the time," Danny replied, shrugging his shoulders.

"But the idea of a roof is for protection," Jackie offered tentatively.

"It is and it isn't," Danny answered casually. "Castles were built with towers and turrets for centuries, long after they were unnecessary for defense. Churches have steeples that don't do anything. Palaces have all kinds of ornaments that do nothing useful."

"But a roof is supposed to keep you dry," Jackie repeated so softly that no one heard.

"There were also new building techniques in the fifties and sixties that made it easier to span large spaces with straight beams," Steve interjected.

"That, too," Danny agreed.

"But the idea of a roof is to keep out water. It's supposed to keep you dry," Jackie repeated more loudly. "It's supposed to keep you safe. It's supposed to keep things from falling on your head." The pitch of her voice rose. Her eyes widened. She began to breathe in rapid, shallow breaths.

"Architects have their own ideas," Danny responded casually.

"But a flat roof is a bad idea," Jackie answered.

"It's an idea."

"It's a bad idea," Jackie insisted anxiously.

"It's a bad idea," Danny conceded, becoming aware of Jackie's mounting agitation.

"A flat roof is a bad idea. It can't keep you from getting wet! It can't keep things from falling on your head!" Jackie was nearly hysterical. She stopped abruptly, aware that everyone was staring at her.

"It's a bad idea," Jackie continued meekly before falling silent. "Why would you let someone die because of a bad idea?"

Rachel walked over to sit beside Jackie and took her hand to comfort her. "It's okay, Jackie."

"No, it's not okay." She jerked her hand out of Rachel's grasp and stepped away. Her face was contorted with pain and anger. Her pressed voice burned with the fever of her thoughts. "It's not okay! How can it be okay to build schools with roofs that collapse just because of some stupid idea that roofs should be flat? How can it be okay that everything explodes and all we can do is duck and cover? Why does it always end up this way? Why?"

"Jackie, calm down." Steve tried to interrupt her tirade.

"Ruben tried to tell me once," she continued hysterically. "He tried to tell me that it is all just a bad trip—that everything ends this way—that everything ends in a bad trip. He told me that every time there's a light at the end of the tunnel—every time we think we have wings—every time we start up some stairway to heaven or follow a path that seems to go somewhere, it always ends in a bad trip. There's always an explosion and everything burns and melts away until there's nothing except clouds and wind and rain and puddles and mud and no way to keep from getting wet."

"Jackie! Don't go there," Danny warned ominously.

"He tried to warn me that the only thing that matters is not getting wet!"

"Jackie!" Danny shouted anxiously.

"Maybe Ruben was right. It's always a bad trip. Everything always explodes. I didn't listen. He always smelled so bad," she began to sob.

"Jackie, stop it!" Danny demanded. "Ruben had no idea what he was saying."

"How do you know?" Jackie turned angrily to Danny. "Maybe he was right all along. Maybe Ruben was the one who had the right idea all along."

"Stop it now, Jackie!" Danny shouted with agitation in his voice.

"Maybe we should have listened to Ruben instead of sending him out into the rain."

"Jackie, Ruben is dead!"

"I know," Jackie responded.

"Jackie, he killed himself."

Jackie's anger instantly collapsed. She gasped. "He killed himself?"

"He jumped head first off a cliff overlooking the Pacific Ocean and landed on the rocks." Danny's voice was cracking in pain.

"Was it an accident?"

"No. He thought he could fly."

"You never told me. I didn't know." Her voice was barely audible.

"I care about you, Jackie. I don't want you to go there too!"

"I'm so sorry," Jackie answered sadly, reaching out to touch Danny's arm, but he pulled it away abruptly.

"Look, Jackie, you have your ideas, your foundations, and they've taken you a long way. Ruben wasn't like you. He was always looking for a nirvana—a way out—a way to escape. You can't go through life running away because it might rain. You know as well as anyone that sometimes you just have to go out into the rain on purpose and plant a tree."

"What the hell does that mean?" she challenged him derisively, her voice again harsh and irritable.

When they were children, Danny had been unable to explain to Jackie the meaning of planting trees to reclaim a promised land from the desert and idolaters. Now, he again found himself searching for words to explain the idea to her.

"I tried to explain to you once—there is a tradition," he started hesitantly, "a tradition which teaches that God's creation is not complete—that it is still imperfect—that it is broken, that it is our responsibility to help it grow, to help it heal, to make it whole."

"And if an all-powerful God couldn't get creation right, then what on Earth makes you believe we can?" Jackie snapped.

"You do, Jackie," Danny answered simply, looking deeply into her eyes. "You've believed that as long as I've known you."

"What?" Jackie was incredulous.

"You've always believed everything could be fixed, and you've never believed in a God who could do it."

Jackie stopped, transfixed by Danny's penetrating stare. "Was I wrong?" she asked meekly, staring unblinkingly into Danny's eyes, searching for the answer to a question she had first asked as a child. *How do we know if an idea is right? How do we know if something is true?* Ideas and images exploded in her mind. The voices of friends and family, saints and scientists, philosophers and priests all started shouting answers to her question in a cacophony of competing voices that drowned out the beating of her heart and the whirring of the planets and stars spinning through space.

"Was I wrong, Danny? Tell me. Was I wrong?"

Danny held her gaze for an instant, and then turned his eyes to the ground without a word. Jackie shivered and struggled for breath. No one else in the room even dared to breathe. A siren sounded on a distant highway. Unconsciously, Jackie listened to the tones to be sure it was not a warning that she should duck and cover.

"We should find out what the kids are doing," Steve interrupted emphatically, cutting through the tension and drawing everyone's attention away from Jackie. "They've been very quiet. I never know whether I should worry more when they're making a ruckus or when I can't hear what they're doing."

Jackie was grateful for the interruption, which enabled her to escape alone to her bedroom while the others went in search of the children.

* * *

From the pulpit that night, the priest conveyed the annual Christmas message from Pope John Paul II. The Pope spoke of the growing tide of discontent in the world: "Children subjected to violence, humiliated and abandoned; women raped and exploited; young people, adults, and the elderly marginalized; endless streams of exiles and refugees; violence and conflict in so many parts of the world—the Holy Land where violence continues to stain with blood the difficult path to peace." He acknowledged the pain of the recent waves of bombings against Christians around the world. He spoke of hope, of the "'triumph of the Light which appeared on this Holy Night at Bethlehem—the good that is being done, silently, by men and women who daily live their faith, their work, their dedication to their families and to the good of society.'" Finally, he prayed "'for an end to all forms of violence! To wars, oppression, and all attacks on life! O Christ, whom we look on today in the arms of Mary, you are the reason for our hope!'"

Ever since childhood, Jackie had sat in church with assurance in her faith. She recalled the Christmas Eve broadcast from the Moon and the vision of the Earth from the heavens. She had found her own dogma, her own doctrine, her own direction in the idea that anything could be accomplished.

She had not been alone. An entire generation born with *Sputnik* had been caught up by the promise of technology. Men had landed on the Moon and sent probes exploring beyond the solar system. Smallpox had been eradicated from the Earth. The space shuttle carried astronauts to a permanent station in space and home again. The human genome had been sequenced. The public was eating genetically engineered foods. There were treatments for heart disease, cancer, and even dementia. Satellites, computers, and the Internet had captivated even the most reasoned imaginations with their boundless promise. The world had successfully progressed through the social storms of the 1960s, the doldrums of the 1970s, and the extravagance of the 1980s, to experience a decade of unprecedented peace and prosperity. Many had believed that the world had entered a new, post-historical age. Now everything seemed to be exploding.

* * *

Later that evening, Jackie and Steve talked about Katie's health for the first time. "So what do we do now?" Jackie asked pensively, when the children were finally quiet and the food and dishes from the holiday dinner were put away.

"I don't know," Steve answered carefully. "We just have to take care of her and hope she gets better. There's really nothing else to do."

"Do you believe she's going to get better?" Jackie asked gently.

"I do, Jackie. I really do. I don't think she's going to wake up one morning suddenly cured. I'm sure we will have some bad times, but I think she will be okay."

"How can you believe that?" Jackie's tone was searching. "How do you know?"

"How do you want me to explain? Do you want me to tell you about pluripotential stem cells in the immune system or—?"

"That's okay." Jackie forced a laugh. "No science right now, please."

"The real answer is that, despite all the research that has been done, we don't know why diseases begin, and we don't know why people get better. We don't know what keeps people alive, and we don't know what makes them die." Jackie looked at him hopelessly. "I don't have a better answer," he continued apologetically.

"I don't know," Jackie sighed. She was skeptical but willing to give credence to Steve's views for the first time in many months. "I just don't know anymore."

"The work your Foundation is doing—" he corrected himself quickly, "things *the* Foundation is doing will make a difference. You know, I met with Allan the other day to go over his data again."

"You met with Allan? Why?" Jackie looked up in surprise.

"He did some remarkable work. I told you I would call around to some drug companies to see if they would be interested in following. He has some interesting results—there should be interest."

"I'm done with the Foundation," Jackie interrupted. "I've decided to resign."

"You can't give up," Steve answered quickly.

"I thought you would want me to quit."

"But you can't quit. It isn't just about Katie; it's about believing there are solutions. You can't give that up."

"But you don't believe it," she challenged him gently.

"I do believe it," he answered without apology. "But I believe there's also something more."

Jackie was in no mood to talk about philosophy or religion. "We have to get the Foundation out of our house. I want my dining room back. I want to put my mother's china back on the shelves."

"That would be nice," Steve agreed.

"I'm also going to need to do some real work," Jackie continued. "William is going to lay off more of the staff after New Year's. Technology is crashing. The market is a mess. I'm afraid to find out how much we've lost."

"We've invested in other things, too," Steve offered reassuringly.

"Do you really think Katie is going to be okay?" Jackie returned to the only subject she really cared about.

"I do. I really do."

"I have never understood how you can believe that," she said with pain in her voice. "How can you have faith that anyone will get better when you deal with death every day? How can you deal with everything that has happened to Katie and still believe something good is going to happen?"

"You have to believe in something," Steve answered quickly.

"Do you pray for Katie?" Jackie asked him abruptly.

Steve was surprised at the question. "I do."

"Do you think it helps?"

"Yes." He did not elaborate.

"It's strange the numbers of people who tell me that they are praying for Katie—people who I know don't believe in God and who would never step foot in a church. Now they say they will pray like they think it will help."

"They don't mean it literally."

"I know, but it makes you wonder who they are praying to."

Jackie was silent again for several moments, but her mind was racing. "I don't know what I believe anymore, Steve. I thought I knew. I thought there was this inevitable progression, this power, this promise that things would always get better, that these kinds of problems could always be solved, that there would always be a discovery, something. But now—" she closed her eyes, trying to stem the tears that were beginning to flow. "I don't think I believe in anything. I have no idea what to believe."

She stopped, her tears overwhelming her thoughts. For too long she had been consumed with her mission. She just wanted Steve to hold her while her tears rained from her eyes.

* * *

Christmas began in earnest the next morning, with the children taking turns opening presents from their parents, grandparents, aunts, uncles, cousins, and friends. There were electronic games and puzzles, dolls and robots, books and projects. The most popular toys of the year were Barbie dolls and retro-styled scooters with colored wheels and large handlebars. The children each received a scooter with wheels in their favorite color, along with matching helmets, kneepads, and a lecture on safety.

By late morning, all the presents had been opened and the children were happily riding their new scooters around the circular driveway at the front of the house. Just before noon, the adults came outside to watch the eclipse, and the scooters were parked on the porch. Jackie connected her laptop computer to a telescope and set it to project the image of the Sun onto a screen where everyone could see.

In every age, people have watched eclipses and searched for ideas to explain why the Sun would be stricken from the sky in the middle of the day. Some supposed that monsters or dragons were devouring the Sun. Some assumed that they were witnessing a titanic struggle between competing deities. Some sensed that the eclipse was a sign from God, an omen of victory or defeat in battle, or a portent of terrible events to come. Others, concluding that the world was coming to an end, turned to prayer, incantations, even sacrifices, to bring it back.

Jackie sat with Katie and the other children, teaching them about the orbits of the Earth around the Sun and the Moon around the Earth. She showed them how the Moon passed directly between the Earth and the Sun, creating a shadow and darkness on the Earth. As she did, she felt an intense flush of déjà vu. She saw the eye of God in the sky and heard Mrs. Leslie telling her not to look at it directly, warning her that she could become blind. She heard herself telling her classmates that she was going to be an astronaut and go to the Moon.

It had seemed so close. It had seemed so real. *Saturn V* rockets had stood proudly on the launch pad like church steeples pointing the way to heaven. Now it all seemed so very far away. It had been more than a quarter-century since men had last set foot on the Moon. There were rumors that the plans for the *Saturn V* rocket had been discarded or lost. Some believed the entire space program had been an elaborate hoax. Jackie wondered whether the footprints of the *Apollo* astronauts were still preserved in the lunar dust, whether the flags the astronauts had planted were still standing, and whether the words that promised peace were still there.

A generation had passed. Katie was now the age Jackie had been when *Apollo 11* landed on the Sea of Tranquility. Jackie wondered whether Katie, or any of her generation, believed they would fly to the Moon or to Mars.

Jackie shuddered as the shadow of the Moon darkened the world. The temperature dropped, and the wind blew her hair across her face. She felt a sense of awe at the place in the heavens that could blot out the light of the Sun, a place that had been claimed by men and bore their footprints, a place from which humans had looked back at their own planet and seen it as God might. She felt a familiar sense of peace and tranquility, as she turned her attention away from her turmoil and fear and toward the Sun and the stars and the Moon.

The End

About the Author

Fred Ledley is an accomplished physician, scientist, entrepreneur, and member of the baby boom generation. He has written extensively on topics ranging from biology and medicine to philosophy, ethics, education, and the sense of wonder. In his first novel, Sputnik's Child, he provides a human perspective on the ideas that influenced his generation and the faith that will inform the future. Ledley is a professor and the Chair of the Department of Natural and Applied Sciences at Bentley University in Waltham, Massachusetts where he teaches biology, management, and futurism.

Follow Sputniks Child on Facebook or at www.sputnikschild.com.

Notes

Idiopathic Thrombocytopenia Purpura (ITP)

Idiopathic thrombocytopenia purpura, also called *immune thrombocytopenia purpura* (ITP), is a real disease without a known cause or cure. The research described in the story is, sadly, fictional. The disease affects two hundred thousand people in the United States with twenty thousand new cases each year. Information about ITP is available from the National Institute of Health at http://www.ncbi.nlm.nih.gov/pubmedhealth/PMH0001562/ or through the Platelet Disorder Support Association at www.itppeople.org.

Source and Reference Materials

A uniquely valuable source of information for this book was the remarkable Television News Archive collection at Vanderbilt University. This collection holds videotape of more than thirty thousand individual network evening news broadcasts from the major U.S. national broadcast networks from 1967 to the present. The TV-NewsSearch capabilities available through the Television News Archive Web site (http://tvnews.vanderbilt.edu/) contains searchable listings, summaries, and descriptions for each of the broadcasts in the collection, which can be searched for keywords or viewed in chronological order.

Many outstanding scholars have chronicled the impact of *Sputnik* on society. I was inspired by Paul Dickson's *Sputnik, Shock of the Century* (New York: Walker & Company, 2001), the Pulitzer Prize–winning work of Walter A. Mcdougal in *The Heavens and the Earth: A Political History of the Space Age* (New York: Basic Books, 1985), and *Reconsidering Sputnik: Forty Years Since the Soviet Satellite* edited by Roger Lanius, John Logsdon, and Robert Smith

(New York: Routledge, 2000). The term "Me Decade" was coined by Tom Wolfe in his essay, *The 'Me' Decade and the Third Great Awakening*, New York, 23 Aug 1976: 26-40.

A vast amount of primary source material and scholarship on the space race and the American space program is available. A useful resource is the history by Courtney G. Brook, James M. Grimwood, and Loyd S. Swenson, Jr., entitled *Chariots for Apollo: A History of Manned Lunar Spacecraft, The NASA History Series—NASA SP-4205* (National Aeronautics and Space Administration, Scientific and Technical Information Office, Washington, DC, 1979), as well as Web sites on the Apollo program at the Smithsonian National Air and Space Museum (www.nasm.si.edu/apollo) and NASA (http://nssdc.gsfc.nasa.gov/planetary/lunar/apollo.html).

The Human Genome Project is described in many outstanding books. The early years of the Human Genome Project are described in Daniel J. Kevles and Leroy Hood (eds.), *The Code of Codes: Scientific and Social Issues in the Human Genome Project* (Cambridge: Harvard University Press, 1992) and Robert Cook-Deegan, *The Gene Wars: Science, Politics, and the Human Genome* (New York: W.W. Norton & Co., 1994). The early goals of the Human Genome Project were described in *A New Five-Year Plan for the U.S. Human Genome Project* by Francis Collins and David Galas in *Science*, Vol. 262, No. 5130, 1993, pp 43-44. The completion of the Human Genome Project is described in *Cracking the Genome: Inside the Race to Unlock Human DNA* (New York: Free Press, 2001), by Kevin Davies. Other information is available from the National Human Genome Research Institute at www.genome.gov/10001772.

Books referred to in the story include George Orwell, *1984* (New York: Harcourt Brace, 1949); *The Limits to Growth; a Report for the Club of Rome's Project on the Predicament of Mankind.* (New York: Universe Books, 1972); and Francis Fukuyama, *The End of History and the Last Man* (New York: Free Press, 1992). The text of the Helsinki Final Act can be accessed at www.osce.org. The text of the Convention on the Rights of the Child can be accessed at www.unicef.org/crc/crc.htm.

The Space Foundation

The foremost advocate for all sectors of the global space industry, the Space Foundation is developing the next generation of space professionals - and building the overall technological strength of the nation - through programs that stimulate students' interest and skills in science, technology, engineering and mathematics (STEM). A non-profit organization founded in 1983, the Space Foundation supports its mission "to advance space-related endeavors to inspire, enable and propel humanity," through space awareness programs, including Space Certification and the Space Technology Hall of Fame®; industry events, including the National Space Symposium; research and analysis products, including *The Space Report: The Authoritative Guide to Global Space Activities*; government affairs activities; and programs for teachers and students. Education programs include intensive graduate-level Space Across the Curriculum courses for PreK-12 educators; NEW HORIZONS community-centered science enrichment programs; STARS hands-on science enrichment programs for students; a cadre of Teacher Liaisons comprising advocates for space-related education; lesson banks and resources; and the Alan Shepard Technology in Education Award, given annually by the Astronauts Memorial Foundation, NASA and the Space Foundation to recognize outstanding contributions to technology education by K-12 educators or district-level personnel. Headquartered in Colorado Springs, the Space Foundation has offices in Washington, D.C., Houston, Texas, and Cape Canaveral, Fla. (www.SpaceFoundation.org)